Danton

A Study

by
Hilaire Belloc

Danton
A Study
by Hilaire Belloc

Copyright © 2023

All Rights reserved.

No part of this publication may be reproduced, stored in a retrieval system, or transmitted in any form or by any means, electronic, mechanical, photocopying or Otherwise, without the written permission of the publisher.
The author/editor asserts the moral right to be identified as the author/editor of this work.

ISBN: 978-93-60467-78-4

Published by

DOUBLE 9 BOOKS

2/13-B, Ansari Road
Daryaganj, New Delhi – 110002
info@double9books.com
www.double9books.com
Tel. 011-40042856

This book is under public domain

ABOUT THE AUTHOR

HILAIRE BELLOC was a writer and historian who was born in France on July 27, 1870, and died on July 16, 1953. Belloc also spoke in public, wrote poetry, sailed, satirized, wrote letters, served in the army, and worked for political change. His work was strongly affected by his Catholic faith. In 1902, Belloc became a naturalized British person, but he kept his French citizenship. He was President of the Oxford Union while he was at Oxford University. As a member of the British Parliament from 1906 to 1910, he was one of the few who was proudly Catholic. Belloc was known for getting into arguments, and he had a number of running feuds. He was also good friends with G. K. Chesterton and worked with him. "Chesterbelloc" was a nickname given to Belloc and Chesterton by their friend and regular debate opponent, George Bernard Shaw. Belloc wrote much more than just religious poems. He also wrote funny verse for kids. "Jim, who ran away from his nurse and was eaten by a lion," and "Matilda, who told lies and was burned to death" were two of his best-known and most-sold stories for kids. He wrote a lot of trip books and biographies of famous people, like The Path to Rome (1902).

CONTENTS

PREFACE 7

THE LIFE OF DANTON

CHAPTER I
 THE REVOLUTION 12

CHAPTER II
 THE YOUTH OF DANTON 38

CHAPTER III
 DANTON AT THE CORDELIERS 49

CHAPTER IV
 THE FALL OF THE MONARCHY 85

CHAPTER V
 THE REPUBLIC August 10, 1792 — April 5, 1793 122

CHAPTER VI
 THE TERROR 148

CHAPTER VII
 THE DEATH OF DANTON 174

CHAPTER VIII
 ROBESPIERRE 195

APPENDIX 220

FOOTNOTES 317

INDEX 328

PREFACE

An historian of just pre-eminence in his university and college, in a little work which should be more widely known, has summed up the two principal characters of the Revolution in the following phrases: "the cold and ferocious Robespierre, the blatant Danton."[1] The judgment is precipitate and is tinged with a certain bias.

An authority of still greater position prefaces his notebook on the Revolution by telling us that he is going to describe the beast.[2] The learned sectarian does not conceal from his readers the fact that a profound analysis had led to a very pronounced conviction. So certain is he of his ground, that he treats with equal consideration the evidence of printed documents, of autograph letters, and of a chance stranger speaking in a country inn of a thing that had happened forty years before.

The greatest of French novelists and a principal poet has given us in "Quatre-vingt-treize" a picture moving and living. Yet even in that work much is admitted, for the sake of contrast and colour, which no contemporary saw. The dialogue between Danton and Marat, with its picturesque untruths, is an example.[3]

If facts so conflicting be stated as true by men of such various calibre, it would seem a very difficult task to write history at all. Yet there is a method which neither excludes personal conviction, nor necessitates the art of deceit, nor presupposes a primitive ignorance.

It is to ascertain what is positively known and can be proved, and with the facts so gathered—only with these—to paint a picture as vivid as may be; on a series of truths—with research it grows to respectable proportions—to base a conviction, general, wide, and capable of constant application, as to the character of a period or of a man.

Such was the method of Fustel de Coulanges, and on his model there has arisen from the minute, the sometimes pedantic accuracy of French scholars, a school which is the strongest in Europe.

The method I have been describing has also this advantage, that the least learned may enter upon such a path without confusion and may progress, and that a book of no pretensions can yet, by following these rules, at least avoid untruth. With inferior tools, and on an over-rough plan, I shall yet attempt in this life of Danton to follow the example.

The motto which is printed at the head of this book, and which is borrowed from the most just of biographers, must give a note to the whole of my description. What was the movement which founded our modern society? what were its motives, its causes of action, its material surroundings? And what was the man who, above all others, represented that spirit at its most critical moment?

To find a right answer to such questions it is necessary to do two things.

First, we must make the sequence of cause and effect reasonable. In giving an explanation or in supposing a motive, we must present that which rational men, unbiassed, will admit. To put in the same character irreconcilable extremes is to leave no picture. To state a number of facts so that no thread connects them, so that they surprise by contrast but leave only confusion in the mind, is a kind of falsehood. It is the method most adopted by partisans; they frame a theory upon the lines of which such and such facts will lie, but they omit, or only mention as anomalies, facts which are equally true, but which would vitiate their conclusions. We must (to use a mathematical metaphor) *integrate* the differentials of history; make a complete and harmonious whole of a hundred aspects; strike a curve which shall unite in a regular fashion what has appeared as a number of scattered points. Till we can say, "This man—seeing all his character and innumerable known acts—*could not* have acted as such and such a report would have us believe;" or again, till we can say, "This epoch, with its convictions, its environment, its literature, *could not* have felt the emotions which such and such an historian lends it,"—till we can say this, we do not understand a personality or a period.

In the second place, we must recognise in all repeated and common expressions of conviction, and in all the motives of a time of action, some really existing ideal. There was a conviction common to many thousands of Parliamentarians in the earlier stages of the English Civil War. There was a genuine creed in the breasts of the well-paid Ironsides of its later period. There was a real loyalty and an explicable theory of kingship in the camp of Charles the First.

So in the period of which we deal there was a clear doctrine of political right, held by probably the strongest intellects, and defended by certainly the most sustained and enthusiastic courage that ever adorned a European nation. We must recognise the soul of a time. For were there not a real necessity for sympathy with a period which we study, were it possible for us to see entirely from without, with no attempt to apprehend from within, then of many stupendous passages in history we should have to assert that all those who led were scoundrels, that all their lives were (every moment of them) a continuous piece of consummate acting; that our enemies, in fine, were something greater and more wicked than men. We should have to premise that all the vigour belonged to the bad, and all the ineptitude to the good, and separate humanity into two groups, one of righteous imbeciles, and the other of genius sold to hell. No one would wish, or would be sincerely able to place *himself* in either category.

We must postulate, then, of the Revolution that which Taine ridiculed, that for which Michelet lived, and that which Carlyle never grasped—the Revolutionary idea. And we must read into the lives of all the actors in that drama, and especially of the subject of this book, some general motive which is connected with the creed of the time. We must make his actions show as a consonant whole—as a man's—and then, if possible, determine his place in what was not an anarchic explosion, but a regular, though a vigorous and exceedingly rapid development.

A hundred difficulties are at once apparent in undertaking a work of this nature. It is not possible to give a detailed history of the Revolution, and yet many facts of secondary importance must be alluded to. It is necessary to tell the story of a man whose action and interest, nay, whose whole life, so far as we know it, lies in less than five years.

Danton's earlier life is but a fragmentary record, collected by several historians with extreme care, and only collected that it may supplement our knowledge of his mature career. The most laborious efforts of his biographers have found but a meagre handful of the facts for which they searched; nor does any personal inquiry at his birthplace, from what is left of his family or in his papers, augment the materials: the research has been thoroughly and finally made before this date, and its results, such as they are, I have put together in the second chapter of this book.

He does not even, as do Robespierre, Mirabeau, and others, occupy the stage of the Revolution from the first.

Till the nation is attacked, his rôle is of secondary importance. We have glimpses more numerous indeed, and more important, of his action after than before 1789. But it is only in the saving of France, when the men of action were needed, that he leaps to the front. Then, suddenly, the whole nation and its story becomes filled with his name. For thirteen months, from that 10th of August 1792, which he made, to the early autumn of the following year, Danton, his spirit, his energy, his practical grasp of things as they were, formed the strength of France. While the theorists, from whom he so profoundly differed, were wasting themselves in a kind of political introspection, he raised the armies. When the orators could only find great phrases to lead the rage against Dumouriez' treason, he formed the Committee to be a dictator for a falling nation. All that was useful in the Terror was his work; and if we trace to their very roots the actions that swept the field and left it ready for rapid organisation and defence, then at the roots we nearly always find his masterful and sure guidance.

There are in the Revolution two features, one of which is almost peculiar to itself, the other of which is in common with all other great crises in history.

The first of these is that it used new men and young men, and comparatively unknown men, to do its best work. If ever a nation called out men as they were, apart from family, from tradition, from wealth, and from known environment, it was France in the Revolution. The national need appears at that time like a captain in front of his men in a conscript army. He knows them each by their powers, character, and conduct. But they are in uniform; he cares nothing for their family or their youth; he makes them do that for which each is best fitted. This feature makes the period unique, and it is due to this feature that so many of the Revolutionary men have no history for us before the Revolution. It is this feature which makes their biographies a vividly concentrated account of action in months rather than in years. They come out of obscurity, they pass through the intense zone of a search-light; they are suddenly eclipsed upon its further side.

The second of these features is common to all moments of crisis. Months in the Revolution count as years, and this furnishes our excuse for giving as a biography so short a space in a man's life. But it is just so to do. In every history a group of years at the most, sometimes a year alone, is the time to be studied day by day. In comparison with the intense purpose of a moment whole centuries are sometimes colourless.

Thus in the political history of the English thirteenth century, the little space from the Provisions of Oxford to the battle of Evesham is everything; in the study of England's breach with the Continental tradition, the period between the Ridolphi plot and the Armada; in the formation of the English oligarchy, the crisis of April to December 1688.

This second feature, the necessity for concentration, would excuse a special insistence on the two years of Danton's prominence, even if his youth were better known. The two conditions combined make imperative such a treatment as I have attempted to follow.

As to authorities, three men claim my especial gratitude, for the work in this book is merely a rearrangement of the materials they have collected. They are Dr. Bougeart, who is dead (and his clear Republicanism brought upon him exile and persecution); M. Aulard, the greatest of our living writers on the Revolutionary period; and Dr. Robinet, to whose personal kindness, interest, and fruitful suggestion I largely owe this book. The keeper of the Carnavalet has been throughout his long and laborious life the patient biographer of Danton, and little can now be added to the research which has been the constant occupation of a just and eminent career.

We must hope, in spite of his great age, to have from his hands some further work; for he is one of those many men who have given to the modern historical school of France, amid all our modern verbiage and compromise, the strength of a voice that speaks the simple truth.

THE LIFE OF DANTON

CHAPTER I
THE REVOLUTION

Before writing a life of Danton in English it is necessary to do three things. First, to take a definite point of view with regard to the whole revolutionary movement; secondly, to explain, so far as is possible, the form which it took in France; thirdly, to show where Danton stood in the scheme of events, the nature of his personality, the effects of his brief action. This triple task is necessary to a book which, but for it, would be only a string of events, always confused, often without meaning.

What was the Revolution? It was essentially a reversion to the normal—a sudden and violent return to those conditions which are the necessary bases of health in any political community, which are clearly apparent in every primitive society, and from which Europe had been estranged by an increasing complexity and a spirit of routine.

It has never been denied that the process of gradual remoulding is a part of living, and all admit that the State (which lives like any other thing) must suffer such a process as a condition of health. There is in every branch of social effort a necessity for constant reform and check: it is apparent to the administrator of every kind: it is the business of a politician continually to direct and apply such correction:—the whole body of the law of England is a collection of the past results of this guiding force.

But what are the laws that govern it? What is the nature of the condition that makes reform imperative? What distinguishes the good from the bad in the matter of voluntary change, and separates the conservative from the destructive effort?

It is in the examination of this problem that we may discover how great a debt the last century owed to nature—a debt which demanded an immediate liquidation, and was often only paid at the expense of violence.

It would seem that the necessity of reform arises from this, that our ideas, which are eternal, find themselves expressed in phrases and resulting in actions which belong to material environment—an environment, therefore, that perpetually changes in form. It is not to be admitted that the innermost standards of the soul can change; if they could, the word "reform" would lose all moral meaning, and a thing not being good would cease to be desired. But the meaning of words, the effect on the senses of certain acts, the causes of pleasure and pain in a society, the definition of nationality—all these things of their nature change without ceasing, and must as ceaselessly be brought into accordance with the unchanging mind.

What test can be applied by which we may know whether a reform is working towards this rectification or not? None, except the general conviction of a whole generation that this or that survival obstructs the way of right living, the mere instinct of justice expressed in concrete terms on a particular point. It is by this that the just man of any period feels himself bound. This is not a formula: it seems a direction of the loosest and of the most useless kind; and yet to observe it is to keep the State sane, to neglect it is to bring about revolution. This much is sure, that where there exists in a State a body of men who are determined to be guided by this vague sense of justice, and who are in sufficient power to let it frame their reforms, then these men save a State and keep it whole. When, on the contrary, those who make or administer the laws are determined to abide by a phrase or a form, then the necessities accumulate, the burden and the strain become intolerable, and the gravitation towards the normal standard of living, which should act as a slight but permanent force, acts suddenly at a high potential and with destructive violence.

As an example of the time when the former and the better conditions prevailed, I would cite the period between the eleventh and the fourteenth centuries, when a change of the most fundamental kind passed over the society of Europe, indeed a change from barbarism to civilisation, and yet the whole went well. Reform, being continual, was easy. New institutions, the Parliaments, the Universities, the personal tax, rose as they were demanded, and the great transition was crowned with the security and content that surrounded St. Louis. Simplicity, that main condition of happiness, was the governing virtue of the time. The king ruled, the knight fought, the peasant dug in his own ground, and the priest believed.

It is the lack of simplicity that makes of the three centuries following the fifteenth (with vices due perhaps to the wickedness of the fifteenth) an opposite example. Every kind of phrase, emblem, or cloak is kept; every kind of living thing is sacrificed. Conditions cease to be flexible, and the body of Europe, which after all still breathes, is shut in with the bonds of the lawyers, and all but stifled.

In the sixteenth century one would say that the political quarrels of the princes were a mere insult to nature, but the people, though they are declining, show that they still exist; the passions of their religions enliven the dead game of the Tudors and the Valois. In the seventeenth the pedants give their orders, the upper classes fight the princes, the people are all but silent. Where were they in the Fronde, or in that less heroic struggle the Parliamentary Wars? As the eighteenth century falls further and further into decay all is gone; those who move in comfort above the souls which they have beneath them for a pavement, the rich and the privileged, have even ceased to enjoy their political and theological amusements; they are concerned only with maintaining their ease, and to do this they conjure with the name of the people's memories.

They build ramparts of sacred tombs, and defend themselves with the bones of the Middle Ages, with the relics of the saint and the knight.

It is this which necessitates and moulds the Revolution. The privileged men, the lawyers especially, held to the phrase. They excused themselves in a time most artificial by quoting the formulæ of a time when life was most natural and when the soul was nearest the surface. They used the name of the Middle Ages precisely because they thought the Middle Ages were dead, when suddenly the spirit of the Middle Ages, the spirit of enthusiasm and of faith, the Crusade, came out of the tomb and routed them.

I say, then, that the great disease of the time preceding the Revolution came from the fact that it had kept the letter and forgotten the spirit. It continued to do the same things as Europe at its best—it had entirely neglected to nourish similar motives. Let me give an extreme example. There are conditions under which to burn a man to death seems admissible and just. When offences often occur which society finds heinous beyond words, then no punishment seems sufficient for the satisfaction of the emotion which the crime arouses. Thus during the Middle Ages (especially in the latter part of their decay), and sometimes in the United States to-day, a man is burned at the stake. But there are other conditions under which a society shrinks with the greatest horror from such a punishment. Security is so well established, conviction in this or that so much less firm, the danger from the criminal so much less menacing, that the idea of such an extreme agony revolts all men. Then to burn is wrong, because it is unnecessary and undesired. But let us suppose the lawyers to be bent on a formula, tenacious from habit and become angrily tenacious from opposition, saying that what has been shall be; and what happens? The Parliament of Strasbourg condemns a man to be burnt while the States General are actually in session in 1789!

Again, take the example of the land. There was a time when the relations of lord and serf satisfied the heart. The village was a co-operative community: it needed a protector and a head. Even when such a need was not felt, the presence of a political personage, at the cost of a regular and slight tax, the natural affection which long habit had towards a family and a name—these made the relation not tolerable, but good. But when change had conquered even the permanent manorial unit, and the serf owned severally, tilling his private field; when the political position of the lord had disappeared, and when the personal tie had been completely forgotten—then the tax was folly. It was no longer the symbol of tenure drawn in a convenient fashion, taken right out of the cornfield from a primitive group of families; it had become an arbitrary levy, drawn at the most inconvenient time, upsetting the market and the harvest, and falling on a small farmer who worked painfully at his own plot of ground.

It is difficult to explain to English readers how far this deadening conservatism had been pushed on the Continent. The constitution of England and the habits of her lawyers and politicians were still, for all their vices, the most flexible in Europe. Even Pitt could tinker at the representative system, and an abominable penal code could be softened without upsetting the whole scheme of English criminal law. To this day we notice in England the most fundamental changes introduced, so to speak, into an unresisting medium: witness those miniature revolutions, the Income Tax and Employers' Liability, which are so silent, and which yet produce results so immeasurable.

It has always been a difficulty in writing of the Revolution for English readers, that in England the tendency to reform, though strong, was not irresistible. It was a desire, but it was not a necessity, and that on account of the quality which has just been mentioned, the lack of form and definition in the English constitution and legal habit.

But if we go a little deeper we shall see a further cause. Nothing will so deaden the common sense of justice in a legislator or a lawyer, nothing will separate him so much from the general feeling of his time, as distinction of class from class. When a man cannot frequently meet and sympathise with every kind of man about him, then the State lacks homogeneity; the general sentiment is unexpressed, because it has no common organ of expression, and you obtain in laws and legal decisions not the living movement of the citizens, but the dead traditions of a few.

Now by a peculiar bent of history, the stratification of society which is so natural a result of an old civilisation, was less marked in England than elsewhere in Europe. The society of the Continent is not more homogeneous to-day, as contrasted with that of modern England, than was the society of England a hundred years ago, as contrasted with that of the Continent then; and any English traveller who is wise enough to note in our time the universal type of citizen in France, will experience something of the envy that Frenchmen felt when they noted the solid England of the eighteenth century. There great lawyers were occasionally drawn from the people; there a whole mass of small proprietors in land or capital—half the people perhaps—kept the balance of the State, and there a fluctuating political system could, for all its corruption, find a place for the young bourgeois Wolfe to defeat the great gentleman Montcalm.

But while in England reform was possible (though perhaps it has been fatally inadequate), in the rest of Europe it was past all hope. Everywhere there must be organs of government, and these on the Continent could no longer be changed, whether for better or worse: they had become stiff with age, and had to be supplanted. Now to supplant the fundamental organs of government, to make absolutely new laws and to provide an absolutely new machinery—all this is to produce a violent revolution.

You could not reform such a body as the Châtelet, nor replace by a series of statutes or of decisions such a mass as the local coûtumes. Not even a radical change in the system of taxation would have made the noblesse tolerable; no amount of personal energy nor any excellence of advisers could save a king enveloped with the mass of etiquette at Versailles. These numerous symptoms of the lethargy that had overtaken European society, even the disease itself, might have been swept away by a sharp series of vigorous reforms. Indeed, some of these reforms were talked of, and a few actually begun in the garrulous courts of Berlin and of St. Petersburg. Such reforms would have merited, and would have obtained, the name of Revolution, but they might have passed without that character of accompanying excess which has delayed upon every side the liberties of Europe. We should be talking of the old regime and of the Revolution as we do now, but the words would have called up a struggle between old Parliaments and young legists, between worn-out customs and new codes, between the kings of etiquette and the kings of originality, between sleep and the new science; the eighteenth and the nineteenth centuries would have been united by some curious bridge—not separated by an abyss.

As it is, the word Revolution recalls scenes almost as violent as those which marked the transition of Rome from the Republic to the Empire. We remember the name not of Condorcet but of Marat: in place of the divided Europe and complicated struggle which (on the analogy of the Reformation) should have attended a movement upon which sympathy was so evenly divided, in place of a series of long, desultory campaigns, you have a violent shock of battle between the French and every government in Europe; you have the world outlawing a people; you have, as a direct consequence of such a pressure, the creation of a focus from whose extreme heat proceeds the conquering energy of Napoleon. Blows terrible and unexpected are struck in the first four years of the war, and there appears in 1796 a portent—the sword that was not broken until it had cut down and killed the old society of the West.

To all these accidents which flow from the form the Revolution took, one more must be added, and that the most important. The shock was of such violence that all the old bonds broke. I mean the permanent things which hold society together, not the dead relics, which would in any case have disappeared.

Many great changes have passed over Europe and have left the fundamentals untouched; the Revolution, which might so easily have remoulded the shape of society, did more and possibly worse: it rebuilt from the foundations. How many unquestioned dogmas were suddenly brought out into broad daylight! All our modern indecision, our confused philosophies, our innumerable doubts, spring from that stirring of the depths. Is property a right? May men own land? Is marriage sacred? Have we duties to the State, to the family? All these questions begin to be raised. A German Pole has denied the sequence of cause and effect. Occasionally a man suddenly rises and asks, "Is there a God?" There is nothing left in reserve for the amusement of posterity.

Well, this unexampled violence, which, like the wind on the Red Sea, has bared for a moment things that had lain hidden for centuries—this war of twenty years and its results were due to the fact that the Revolution, which might have started in a different form from almost any European centre, started as fact from France.

That France was the agent of the reform is the leading condition of the whole story, for it was her centralisation that made the change so rapid and so effectual, her temperament that framed the abstract formulæ which could spread like a religion, her political position in Europe that led to the crusade against her; and this war in its turn (acting on a Paris that led and governed the nation) produced all the further consequences of the Revolution from the Terror to Waterloo.

Let us examine the conditions of the Revolution as a purely French thing, see what it was that made it break out when it did, what guided its course, what gave Paris its position, what led to the wars and the Terror.

In the first place, the causes of the Revolutionary movement in France. They were two: First, the immediate material necessity for reform which coincided with the Revolutionary period; secondly, the philosophy which had permeated society for a generation, and which, when once a change was undertaken, guided and controlled the development of that change.

As for the material circumstances that led to so urgent a necessity for reform, they may be stated as follows:—The governmental machinery, which had been growing more and more inefficient, had finally broken down; and this failure had been accelerated by a series of natural accidents, the most prominent among them being two successive years of scarcity.

Now why was France alone in such a deplorable condition? Why was she all but bankrupt, her navy in rapid decay, her armies ill-clothed, ill-fed, in arrears of pay? Why could Arthur Young, observant, honest, and inept, make his tour through France (in which the mass of accurate detail is balanced by so astounding a misconception of French society[4]), and in that book describe the land going out of cultivation, the peasant living on grass, the houses falling down, the roads impassable? The answer is discovered in the very causes that led to the past greatness of the country. Because France alone in Europe was a vast centralised body—a quality which had made the reign of Louis XIV.; because centralisation could not continue to work under the old regime—a condition which led to the abrupt wreck of 1788 and 1789.

The government of France, in the century preceding the Revolution, might be compared to a great machine made with admirable skill out of the disjointed parts of smaller engines; a machine whose designer had kept but a single end in view—the control of all the works by one lever in the hand of one man. But (to continue the metaphor) the materials to which his effort had been confined forbade simplicity; the parts would be repaired with difficulty, or sometimes not at all; the cleaning and oiling of the bearings was neglected, of necessity, on account of their position; and after two generations of work the machine had ceased its functions. It was clogged upon every side and rusty—still dependent upon one lever, but incapable of movement.

France had become a despotism, but a despotism which lacked organisation; all centred in the king, with the result that none could act but he, and yet, when he strove to act, the organs of action were useless. All had been made dependent upon one fountain-head, yet every channel was stopped up.

It is of the utmost importance in studying the Revolution to appreciate this fact: that nearly every part of the national life was sound, with the exception of the one supreme function of government. I do not mean that France and the world needed no new ideas, nor that a material change in the form of the executive would have sufficed for society. But I mean that, more than is usually the case in a time of crisis, a *political* act was the supreme need of the moment.

Capital was not well distributed, but at least it was not centralised as it is in our modern industrial societies. All men owned; the peasant was miserable beyond words, but his misery was not the result of an "Economic Law;" it was due to that much more tangible thing, misgovernment. The citizen was apathetic, but potentially he was vigorous and alert. If he knew nothing of the jury or of public discussion, it was the system oppressing the man, not the man creating, or even permitting, the system. In a word, the vices or the misfortunes of France were not to be traced to the character of the social system or of the national temper. They were to be found in an artificial centre, the Government.

Now of all governments a pure despotism can most quickly establish reforms. In Russia the serfs were freed, the Jews expelled, by a stroke of the pen; in India you may see great financial experiments, great military groups, come into being almost simultaneously with the decision that creates them. Why could not the central government have saved France? Because on every side its action was deadened by dead things, which it pretended were alive; because throughout the provinces and towns there lay thick the corpses of what had once been local institutions, and because so far from the Crown removing these, it had left to them the privileges which at one time were the salaries of their activity, but which had now become a kind of bribe to continue inactive.

How had this come about? How had a government been developed whose note was centralisation and despotism, and which yet carefully preserved the fossils of local administration?

To answer that question it is necessary to consider the original matter of which French society was composed and the influences that modified without destroying this matter in the course of the Middle Ages. The French, like every other national group in Western Europe, may be said to have differentiated from the mere ruins of the Empire in that dark period which follows the death of Charlemagne; until that epoch some shadow of unity remained, and certainly the forces working against unity had not yet begun to be national. The order of Rome, which had remained as an accepted ideal for five hundred years, takes under Charlemagne a certain substance and reality, as mystical and as strange, as full of approaching doom and yet as actual as a momentary resurrection from the dead. It ceases with the close of his reign, and what Dr. Stubbs has well called "the darkness of the ninth century" comes down.

The northern pirates fall on the north and west, and cut off the islands from the mainland, giving us in England the barrier of the Danish invasions, beyond which Anglo-Saxon history grows dim; they crush out the customs, and even the religion, of the coasts of the Continent. The Hungarian certainly, the heathen Slavs of the Baltic presumably, cut in streams through the Germanic tribes. The Saracens held the Mediterranean. Society fell back upon its ultimate units; in all that mechanical disintegration the molecules of which it is composed remained. The village community, self-sufficing, self-contained, alone preserved an organisation and a life.

For more than a century it hung upon a thread whether the Roman tradition should survive, or whether our civilisation should fall into the savagery which has apparently been elsewhere the fate of systems almost as strong. A new thing arose in Europe, destined more than any other factor to deflect the current of its Latin tradition. There was found, when the light began to grow upon this darkness, in nearly every village a little king. Whichever men had in the old times been possessed of power, local officials, large owners of land, leaders in the great armies, emerge from the cataclysm welded into one new class—the nobles; and with the appearance of this caste, with the personal emotions and the strong local feeling that their system developed, Europe becomes a feudal society. But that society contained another element, which was destined to control and at last to destroy the feudality. For strangely enough, this period, which had thrown Europe into such anarchy, had produced an idea the very opposite of such a character. The nationalities begin to arise. The kings—weak shadows—nobles, often of small power, but no longer the mere leaders of armies, become symbols of a local unit, separated from the Empire. They stood for the nation round which the patriotism that you will discover in the old epics was to gather.

France, more perhaps than any of the new divisions, illustrates all this. A small weak king, one Capet, was elected from among the nobles at the end of the tenth century, and the family which ultimately toppled over from the immensity of its burden, descended from him in direct line from father to son through more than eight hundred years.

In the early years of that crusading century which is the vigorous opening of the life that was to produce our Europe, a discovery was made which was destined to help this new kingship to take a very different shape. In the loot of Amalfi, in a petty war, the Roman Code of Law was rediscovered.

It had the effect which might be imagined in a barbarous society which the Normans and Hildebrand had at last aroused. It suddenly gave a text and an accurate guide to those splendid but vague memories of Imperial order and civilisation.

Everywhere the Universities arise; from Bologna come out the corporation of the lawyers, the students of the code, the men whose decisions were final, who led mediæval society as the scientists lead ours to-day; and everywhere they tended to the two bases of the Roman idea—absolute sovereignty in the case of the State, absolute ownership in the case of the Individual.

The logical end of such a movement should have been the Empire—citizens all equal before the law, the feudal system destroyed, the Church dominated by the State, the will of the prince supreme. But Europe contained a hundred elements beside the lawyers, though these were the most permanent and active force of her civilisation. The Manorial unit was strong; there are places where it survives to-day.[5] The aristocracy was strong. In Poland and England it ended by conquering the Crown and the Roman law. The Church, affected as it was by the new ideas, still had a host of anomalous habits and institutions, grown up since the fall of the Empire.

In the anarchy of the dark ages the framework of intense local differences had been constructed; the village, the guild, the chapter, each had their special customs born of isolation. Finally, the spirit of secondary nationalities was powerful in many places; notably among the Germans it conquered every other tendency.

Now France was especially favourable to the growth of the influences of this law; she was very Roman by tradition, and by tradition Imperial. Charlemagne had left his clothes to Germany, but his spirit to Gaul. The sub-nationalities, Provence, Normandy, the Gascons, had, in spite of their local patriotism, epics in which they harped on "Doulce France Terre Majeure." But though the national forces on the whole inclined towards the lawyers and the Crown, the path by which absolute centralisation could be reached was tortuous and had to be well chosen. The nobles are slowly bereft of political power, but their privilege remains; the peasant gradually acquires the land, but many feudal dues lie on a tenure which has lost all its feudal meaning. The Church becomes the king's, but it remains in administration of its vast possessions: to the last the Crown works through (or attempts to work through) the local organisation that was once supreme and is fast dying.

You may compare the progress of the Capetians towards absolute power to the action of a gentleman who obtains an estate at the cost of perpetual bribery, and finds himself crippled when he has at last succeeded.

Finally, the lawyers themselves become sterilised in the general decay which their policy has created. Even the Crown is half-allied to the privileged bodies in practice, and altogether allied in sentiment; the government which had for centuries created and sustained the people now found itself remote from them and the source of its power cut off.

I will give but a couple of examples to illustrate the centralisation and the hopeless confusion that accompanied it. The first is from De Tocqueville. A village near Paris wished to raise a small local rate to mend the steeple of the church. They could not do so without appealing to Versailles. The leave was granted after two years, but the steeple had broken down. The second is from the records of the election of '89. In a bailiwick of Champagne it was discovered that no one accurately knew the boundaries of the district, that the next bailiwick was similarly ignorant, and finally an arbitrary line was drawn. This is one out of dozens of cases. The population of Paris was not known; the number of electors in every division was uncertain.

Such was the France in which reform was necessary. The land, by a continual and misdirected interference with exchange, was going out of cultivation—or rather (for even in the worst cases of depression this symptom is rare) it was yielding less and less as time went on.

The classes into which society was divided had become separated by an etiquette as rigorous as a religion, and though the thing has gone, the phrases that described it are vigorous to this day, and lead continually to the gravest misconception. A France where one Frenchman has grown so like another still lets its literature run upon some of the old lines.

Five great divisions should especially be noticed in connection with the Revolution—the peasants, the artisans, the middle class, the professionals, the noblesse; and side by side with these, a separate thing, the Church, sharply divided into the higher and lower clergy. Let me, at the risk of some digression, enter into the details of these various groups.

The peasants were the majority of the nation, as they are to-day. At a rough guess, out of some five million heads of families, three and a half at least were of this class. What were they? They were more ignorant, more fearful, and more unhappy than ever the inhabitants of French soil had been before. I believe it is no exaggeration to say that the worst of the barbarian invasions had not produced among them such special and intense misery as had the running down of the governmental machine in the eighteenth century. Their songs had ceased. Search the folk-lore of France, and you will find a kind of gap after the centralisation was complete, and after the lords had left them—after the seventeenth century. It is as though that oldest sign of communal life, the traditions and the stories of the little circle of the village, had died just before the death of the village itself. As to religion, with which all this natural and fertile love of legend is so closely knit, it lingered, but it lingered hardly. The priest still survived, but his action was cut off by penury; in places the extreme physical needs of the peasantry, whose lot he shared, entered into his life to an intolerable degree, and a half-paganism resulted. Twenty, thirty pounds a year is not enough for the celibate who holds the sacramental power in the village. I will show you in the rural communes of France church after church part of whose buildings are very old, part very new: and what is the reason? That in all these places the church fell into ruins till the new State came to rebuild it. You may discover many cases of restoration in the eighteenth century where a great cathedral or a famous church or abbey is renewed: it is the work of the upper clergy, and the dole out of their vast fortunes. In the villages such cases are rare and eccentric. The Revolution, for all its antagonism, gave to the Faith a new life. There are to-day more monasteries and convents, more of the clergy, both regular and secular, by far more missionaries, than there were in 1789, but there are fewer bishops.

The peasant owned land, his roof and a few acres beside; he had been buying for generations, and the drift of the law when it turned feudal tenant-right into ownership was in his favour. But this ownership of the land, the foundation of his future citizenship, was for the moment his curse. It made him an independent man, while he still had to pay the dues of his feudal dependence. And independence works both ways. He stood, ignorant and extremely poor, face to face with the all-powerful State. His natural support and guide had left the village for the court; the lord was nothing more than a name for endless annoyance and local exaction. The symptom that comes just before death showed itself in the ploughman and the labourer in the vineyard. He lost heart; he was too tired and too beaten to work; the great burden of the State, its taxes, its follies, had accumulated on his shoulders, and had bent them so low that he could no longer stir the earth with vigour into harvests.

Such men did not make the Revolution; they were the inert mass upon which it worked. They did not sing the war-songs; they did not understand the meaning of the invasions. No peasant marked the assemblies with the sense or cunning of the fields, the sound of patois was lacking in the great chorus, and as you read the Revolution you feel continually the lack of something closely in touch with Nature, because the most French of all Frenchmen had forgotten how to speak.

The Revolution has made them; and to this day the heirs of the Republic wonder at the peasant in his resurrection. From him come the humour, the gaiety, the manhood; it is his presence in the suffrage that criticises and tones down the crudities of political formulæ. He has re-created a host of songs, he has turned all France into a kind of walled garden; underneath the politicians, and in spite of them, he is working out the necessary thing which shall put flesh on to the dry bones of the Revolution,—I mean the reconciliation of the Republic and the Church.

As to the artisans, they play in the story of the movement a subsidiary but an interesting part. The artisans (in the sense in which I use the term) were found only in the great towns. At least the artisans outside these centres must be reckoned as part of the peasantry, for their spirit was that of the village. These craftsmen of the towns did not form a large percentage of the nation. Perhaps half-a-million families—perhaps a trifle more. But their concentration, the fact that they could come in hundreds and hear the orators, the fact that they alone, by the accidents of their position, could form *mobs*, these were the causes of their peculiar effect upon the Revolutionary movement.

Like the peasant, the ouvrier gives hardly any type to politics. If we except Hébert, on the strength of his being a vagabond ticket-collector, there is hardly any one of prominence who comes from the labourers in the towns. But the combined effort of the class was great and was as follows:— It furnished for the party of revolt an angry and ready army of the streets; it was capable of follies and of violence almost unlimited; it was capable also of concentration and common action. It filled the tribunes of the clubs, and more than once terrorised the Parliament. It was patriotic, but wofully suspicious; and in all it did the main fault was a lack, or rather a dislike, of delay, of self-criticism, and of self-control: the ruling passion anger, and the motive of this anger the partial information, the extreme false idea, of the political movement, which it was willing to read into every speech delivered.

I will attempt to say why this character, the worst and the most dangerous of the period, was developed in the labour of the towns. In the first place, the industrial system is of itself fatal to the French character. It is not in the traditions of the nation; it is opposed to the tendencies which the most superficial observer can discover in them. The Frenchman saves and invests in small parcels, loves to work with his own tools, is impatient of a superior unless it be in some domestic relation, is attached to the home life, and above all is no good specialist: "Il veut rester homme." You will find too many artists, too few machines in a crowd of them.

It may be that a cheap distribution of power, or that some other economic change, will reinstate the small capitalist; till then, for all his industry, the French workman will be at a disadvantage. In the great towns, in the manufactory, under a central control which has no political basis of right, cut off from the fields for which the peasant in him always yearns, he is like good wine turned sour.

In the second place, the system of the old regime had produced an aristocracy of labour such as many reformers demand in England to-day. Mediæval restrictions, which had once applied to all workers, and had been designed to limit competition between men all of whom were employed, survived in 1789 as guilds and companies strictly protected by law, with fixed hours of labour, fixed wages—every kind of barrier to exclude the less fortunate artisans. A system that under St. Louis had made life more secure for all, had, under his descendants, separated the workmen into two classes of the over- and the under-paid, and these last increased.

In the third place, the recent treaty of commerce with England had worked most disadvantageously for French manufacture, and in all the great towns, especially in Paris, thousands of men were out of work.

In the fourth place, the general scarcity of agricultural produce struck the ouvrier, even if he were employed at good wages, in the heaviest fashion.

Between the cornfield and the city came the taxes, the feudal dues, the provincial frontier duties, and finally the octroi paid at the city gates. So inept a method of continually harassing exchange could not but react upon production, and even when the harvest was plentiful bread was dear in the great cities. Even when these internal taxes did not diminish the output, they raised the price in the towns.

Finally, the Church, which, as we have seen, had none too firm a hold on the villagers, had lost all power over the townsmen. To what was this due? Presumably to the apathy which had overtaken the rich higher clergy, a class which naturally congregated in the towns, especially in Paris, and whose example influenced all the surrounding priests. Add to this the destruction of the old unit of the *parish* in the city. The industrial system had broken up the neighbourliness of the capital. Men rarely lived in their own houses, often changed their lodgings to follow their work. There is no worse enemy to the parochial and domestic character of our religion than the economic change from which we suffer. Now with the Church was associated all the morality of their traditions; without it they were lost. They had not read the philosophers; Rousseau had not permeated so deep. For the matter of that, they would have cared little for him or for Seneca; and, deprived of any code, they were at the mercy of every passion and of all unreason. Only this much remained: that they honestly hated injustice; that egotism had very little to do with their anger; that they were capable of admirable enthusiasms. They had not the little qualities of the rich, and they also escaped their vices. One great virtue attached to them: they did nothing at the expense of the country's honour; no reactionary or foreigner bought them; they were patriotic through all their errors.

To these characters, which they brought into the Revolution, a further accident must be added. They became disfranchised. As we shall see later, the constitution of 1790, based upon the very sound principle of representing those only who supported the State, gave no provision (as it should have done) for making that support fall upon the shoulders of all. It enfranchised the great bulk of Frenchmen—over four million entered the ranks of the "Active Citizens"—but it disfranchised the very class which sat in the galleries of the Parliament or ran to the Place de Grève. The workman, living in lodgings or flats sublet, often changing his residence, rarely paid any direct tax; he alone, therefore, lost the vote to which practically every peasant was entitled. This accident (it was not planned) worked in two ways. It added to the discontent of the Parisian workman, but it also forbade his movements to take political shape. To the very last the initiative was in the hands of others.

These others were the three remaining divisions—the middle class, the professionals, and the nobles.

It would be an error to make too hard and fast the barriers between these classes. In the cart that took the Dantonists to the guillotine all three were to be found. Nevertheless it aids a history of the Revolutionary period to distinguish each from each.

The bourgeoisie meant almost anything from a small shopkeeper to a successful lawyer. It was not so much the man's occupation as his breeding and domestic surroundings that made him of this rank. Let me explain what I mean. Suppose the family of a linendraper (such as was Priestley's family or Johnson's in England) possessed of several thousand pounds. Let them put a son to the bar, and let the son succeed at the profession; well, the man and his son, so different in their pursuits, would yet remain in the class I desire to define, unless by some accident they got "in with" one of the literary coteries with which the noblesse mingled. And this separation would be something much more definite than in the parallel case in England. This class of the bourgeoisie stood like a great phalanx in the Revolution. Not one in ten of the class I am attempting to describe had entered the salons; there was not (as there is in an aristocratic state) any great desire to know the noblesse. An accident of surroundings, of eminence, or of friendship might lift a man from this class, but he would leave it with regret.

Of this class were Robespierre, Marat (in spite of his aristocratic milieu), Bonaparte,[6] Danton himself, Santerre, Legendre, Carnot, Couthon, Barrère—dozens of all the best-known names in the second period of the Revolution.

Brewers, builders, large shopkeepers, a host of provincial lawyers—these all over France, to the number of at least a million voters, formed a true middle class such as we lack in England. Note also that they might rise to a very considerable position without leaving this rank. A man might be physician to the first houses, a king's counsel, a judge, anything almost except the colonel of a regiment, and yet be a bourgeois, and his son after him. In the memoirs of the last century you will find continually a kind of disgust expressed by the upper class against a set just below them; it is the class feeling against the bourgeoisie, their choice of words, their restrictions of fortune, their unfashionable virtues. These men were often learned; among the lawyers they were the pick of France; they had a high culture, good manners, in the case of individuals wit, and sometimes genius, but they were not gentlefolk, and had no desire to be thought so.

Of those, however, who were technically bourgeois, possessing no coat of arms nor receiving feudal dues, some had practically passed by an accident of association into the upper class of all. They met constantly in some salon, library, or scientific body members of the privileged order; their dress, manners, and conceptions were those of the liberal noblesse. To such men, very small in number and very influential, I would give the name of Professionals. The class is complete if you add to it the many noble names who stood prominent in the sciences or the arts. It was recruited from legal families of long standing, from financiers. It was polite, wealthy, often singularly narrow. Of such a type were the Marquis de Condorcet, Bailly, Sieyès; even Roland might be counted, though he hardly stood so high. These were the theorisers of the Revolution, with no practical grievance, ignorant of the mob, despising and misunderstanding the bourgeoisie (save in their political speeches); they were the orators of the new regime, and died with the Girondins.

As to the noblesse (who partly overlapped these last, and yet as a class were so distinct), they formed a body with which this book will hardly deal, and upon which I will touch but lightly. In very great numbers, the bulk of them by no means rich (though some, of course, were the greatest millionaires of their day), they were defined by a legal status rather than an especial manner.

He was noble whom the king had ennobled or who could prove an ancestry from the feudal lords of the manors.[7] The family name was never heard, only the territorial name preceded by the "de." They had also this in common, that the whole great swarm of families, thousands and thousands, had a cousinship with that higher stratum which made the court. This cousinship was acknowledged; it put them in the army; it gave them the right to be spitted in a duel, and, above all, it exempted them from taxes. It made them, wherever they went, a particular class, to be revered by fools, and able to irritate their enemies merely by existing—a privilege of some value. They held together in the heat of the reform, and it was only from the higher part of the noblesse that the deserters came—Mirabeau, Lafayette, and De Séchelles. The great bulk of them were poor, and consequently determined in the matter of privilege and feudal right that gave them their pittance. The class was richer than the bourgeoisie, but numerous families in it had not the capital of a bourgeois household, and many a poor lady boasts to-day of family estates lost in the Revolution, whose ancestry had no estates at all, but only a few tithes and a chance in the spoil to be had at court.

Now to all these, without exception, reform seemed necessary; it was only when the Revolution was in full swing that the opposition of particular bodies appeared. The peasant was in misery; the artisan was angry; the middle class, possessed of that feeling which Sieyès expressed in a phrase: "Qu'est-ce que le Tiers État?—Rien;" and they were determined to work upon the sequel: "Que doit-il être?—Tout." To this general chorus of demand the professionals added a strong conviction (in the abstract) of the good of self-government and of the necessity for removing State interference. The noblesse, as a class, expected nothing in particular to happen, but they were not unwilling for a Parliament to meet; they also suffered from the extreme complexity, or rather anarchy, into which things had fallen. Talent saw itself wrecked by court intrigue; piety was offended by the sight of a starving priest side by side with a careless, wealthy, often irreligious member of the higher clergy. Moreover, there ran through the nobility this curious feeling—an error which you will always find in the more generous of a privileged class—namely, that in some mysterious way their special rights might be abolished and they not suffer for it—as though there were some vast sum in reserve, into which the State had but to put its hand and relieve the poor without taxing the rich. On the moral as on the material side this error obtained, and Lafayette, a man created by privilege, thought that when privilege was abolished his native virtues would lift him into the first rank.

To all this attitude of expectancy, and to this instant demand for reform, was added the insurmountable thing that made the Parliament necessary. The great symptom of decay had shown itself—the revenue could no longer be raised. Luckily for France, there existed in the last century no such international finance as exists at present, and the fatal temptation of external debt was not offered. With a population not quite two-thirds what it is to-day, the country failed to raise one-twentieth of what it now pays with ease. The debt was increasing with a terrifying rapidity, and since all the methods of centralised routine had failed, it was necessary to turn to the last resource, and the nation was asked to vote a tax. With promises of redress, with an understanding that the Assembly was to reform upon all sides, with a special demand for a statement of grievances, but especially for the necessities of revenue, the States General were summoned for the first time in a hundred and seventy-five years.

Such was the condition that preceded the Revolution. We have seen the attitude of the various social classes and the material necessity that prepared the reform. Now what were the ideas that were about to guide it? What theory was moving the men who met at Versailles? What form would the national character give to the changes which were in preparation?

It will be necessary here to propose a paradox. The French character, which has been blamed so frequently since the Revolution (and so justly) for an excess of idealism, possesses at the same time a passion for the positive, the objective, and the certain. In the same man you will continually find some idea which pushes him to extremes, and in the ordinary affairs of life a most exact sense of reality, even sometimes an exasperating accuracy of detail. They are not alone in discovering an antithesis in the national character; in England, Germany, or Northern Italy it would be equally possible to show two apparently opposite characteristics united in the same civic type. But perhaps the nearest parallel we have at home to the contrasts of the French is to be seen in the Scotch people; like the French, a nation of independents, thrifty, investing continually in small sums, zealous of pence; like the French, on the other hand, they delight in the abstract problem; they will attach themselves to some idea, and hold it to the point of martyrdom.

What was the result of these two tendencies? In some characters they balanced each other. Condorcet comes to the mind as an example. But, as with other nations, the two aspects of France appeared (in much the greater number of her citizens) exalted to a violent degree that corresponded with the extreme danger and the extreme hopes of a moment of crisis.

I do not mean that you would have found in France two factions, the one of visionaries, the other of practical men; I mean that throughout the Revolution the goal and the method of attaining it reflected this double nature. Consider the decrees and their effects. At the sight of what the Assemblies from 1789 to 1795 are trying to do you would say, "A set of men attempting to build a city of dreams;" there is hardly anything so unnatural but that they will attempt it; they are ready to reconstruct from the foundation. The most violent period, that of 1794, is nothing but an effort to make all men conform to civic virtue and believe the necessary things; the most sane, that of 1791, is yet an attempt to realise in the State an equality and a justice that can only exist in the soul.

But if you turn to their methods and to the measure of their success, then you have a very different idea. They succeeded beyond all hope. They struck in a few months the blows that remoulded all France. The centralisation which the practical side of the character had created was used to transform France as rapidly as though the nation had been a household; and not only do they find means to do this, but, when the necessity arises, they suddenly raise armies of three hundred thousand, of a million; they find the commissariat somewhere in a starving people, and they succeed.

While, then, the nation was fitted for action to such a degree, what was the theory which its idealism was about to embrace? There had permeated throughout the noblesse and the bourgeoisie something more than a philosophy. It was not only a set of eighteenth-century phrases, of Reason, and Nature, and Right, but all these things turned into a religion. The apostolic quality of Rousseau had touched the mind of France.

It is the fashion to belittle this man. Something in him angers our successful and eager century, and yet but for him our century would not have taken the shape it has. It is needless to recall the movement which had preceded and which surrounded him. He did but complete the theory of the social contract; he hardly did more than repeat the conclusions of the rationalists; in the matter of economics he was entirely ignorant; he fell continually into the error of superficiality where history or where the details of institutions were concerned. A resident in England, he imagined that her people were represented; writing his famous work at Nuneham Courtenay, he could not see that the squire was everything in the little village. He had all the faults of weakness; he invited a persecution which he had not the wit to attack nor the stamina to sustain. What, then, made him such a prophet? In the first place, the power of words. All his critics in this country (with the exception of Mr. Morley perhaps) have failed to appreciate how great this power was. See what the Jacobean translation of the Bible has done in England; note what the pure rhetoric of Burke, proceeding solely from passion and untouched by any movement of reason, effected in England within a year of the fall of the Bastille: it was this that Rousseau did in France. But not this alone. If he possessed the power of words, he also had to an extraordinary degree that other quality which does not reside in style but in the texture of the mind. He could write in the pure abstract, and produce a piece of clear exposition deduced in an unbreakable chain from some fundamental dogma. He never commits the error of supposing his first principles to rely upon reason; he postulates a Faith. He allows that Faith to illumine his every sentence. He is certain that the things common to all men are the things of immeasurable importance; he is certain that the accidents of living are secondary. He is certain that our being part of all nature is the condition of happiness and of good; he is certain that the complexity of living which separates us from Nature is an evil, and to a France tortured with age he proposes this simple water of youth: that it should return to the first conditions of a small hamlet; where the families met together dictate the law; where each sees himself to be a part of the whole, and where the harmony that all men sought comes easily to an ideal democracy hidden in happy valleys. It is idle to argue that complexity was there; that France could not have at once the patriotism of twenty million, and the institutions of a hundred, hearths. Every one saw that difficulty, and in the midst of '94 the most fervent apostles of Rousseau compromised on the chief point, for the principle of election, which he hated, remained of necessity the chief method in their scheme of democracy.

It is not the obstacles, but the motive force that you must examine if you would comprehend the fervour of the Republic. And the motive force was that passion for the conditions under which the race has passed how many æons of its tutelage, the harking back to the prehistoric things, the village and the tribe, all of whose spirit ran through the books that preached simplicity with such admirable eloquence.

There remains one feature to be discussed before we turn to a brief outline of Danton's place in the movement—a feature which will be of capital importance throughout this book. That feature is the hegemony of Paris. It was the rule of Paris that made the whole course of the Revolution. In that focus of discussion and of passion the great advances and the great blunders of the Revolution took place. Paris alone made the 14th of July, almost alone the 10th of August, alone and against France the 2nd of June. Many an historian has seen in her position an error that should have been and could have been avoided. It is an opinion which from the time of Mirabeau to our own day has lain in the mind of French statesmen, that Paris must be jealously watched, played, forbidden control.

Why does Paris hold this position? Here is a city-state, eager, concentrated, the centre in many things of our European civilisation; that it should continually exert a moral influence over the State is easily to be understood, but Paris did more—it conquered and dominated the State, and France continually permitted that leadership.

There is, I believe, a point of view from which this historical fact becomes no longer an accident but a reasonable thing; and if we take that point of view it will be possible to understand why from the beginning she preserved the initiative, and became and remained till Thermidor the mistress of France.

The people of that country are, for much the greater part, the peasants whom I have described. They have for centuries been owners of the soil, and for at least two thousand years (perhaps far longer) they have found all their social, all their physical, and most of their intellectual interests in the intense but narrow life of a village community. In any great expanse of view you see the white houses, all huddled together without gardens, and between each group bare vast brown fields empty of farmsteads. These peasants have in them an admirable cousinship with the soil; their phrases and their proverbs are drawn directly from the fields and rivers; they are as healthy as Nature herself. Such is the general mass of France; but these innumerable villages, these vigorous swarms of men who work in the sunlight, need a bond. Some concrete object must be present to give true unity to many vague national impressions. Something must be the *persona* of these millions, and through the mouth of that something they must hear action formulated, patriotism expressed, the law defined. From it must come the executive, and of it are expected the direct orders and the government by which, in times of crisis, a nation is saved.

This brain, which is necessary to a complex organism, might have been found in a high priest or a despot; but we in England unconsciously look for it in an oligarchy. Seeing the squires wanting, we think there is nothing, and we draw doleful conclusions when we note the absence in the French villages of the forces that invigorate our own. We complain of the centralisation that atrophies, forgetting the oligarchy that cows and debases the inferior class; and while we despise the political apathy of French country life, we ignore the negation of society in our great cities.

The truth is that no definite system can escape attendant evils, and that if one nation does not adopt the methods that have succeeded in another it is because those methods are connected with instinct, and instinct can neither be taught nor adopted.

It was instinct that forbade the growth in France of oligarchic institutions. Everything was ready for it; the feudal system would seem its proper parent; the lords of the manors were so many seeds of what should have been a territorial aristocracy. They were destined to fail, and to say *why* is impossible, because it is impossible to explain Nature; we can only feel. Something in the genius of the nation makes for equality with the depth and silence of a strong tide at night. It is not the Roman law—all the nations had that. It is not even the Church—there is a something in the Church which neglects if it does not despise civic ideals. It is not the distribution of capital—that can be distinctly proved to be an historical result and not a cause. No, it is not an exterior force, but something from within which has produced this passion, the soul (as it were) forming the body. "La France a fait la France."

If aristocracy were impossible, what remained? The walled towns. They are like pins on which the lace of France is stretched; the roads unite them and make a web which supports the rural communes. Never far apart, always living a life intensely their own, the walled towns stood guardian over surrounding villages. Here was the cathedral or the abbey, the judges, the college. It would give the name to a district, it would form with its dependent communes a kind of little state. News from the outside was concentrated here, and if a religious or political enthusiasm ran from the Rousillion to the Artois, it was not the villages that caught fire in the mass, but the towns, that passed the message on like beacons.

Now as the roots of this municipal system were to be found in Rome, these needed a little Rome to cap it. These towns being all of a kind, they of necessity fell grouped under the largest of their class. The tendency was well marked even before Gaul was re-united; the same force that made the great archbishoprics makes the metropolitan civil influence. Thus Rheims, Lyons,[8] and Toulouse stand out hierarchically the heads of provinces — a very different kind of town from Canterbury (let us say) or Lichfield, where once they talked of an archbishopric for Mercia.

Well, as the power of the Crown increases (which is another way of saying, "as the nation realises its memories of unity"), there increase with it the means of communication, and especially the strong centralised system which, as we have seen in another part of this chapter, had become a fatal necessity to France. Remember also that till the very end of the seventeenth century Paris had been uniquely the king's town, and had so been (with one short interval) for more than a thousand years. Here was every single organ which the executive of a centralised government may need, and (what is more important) here was the place where each organ had grown; they were in the fibre of the place. Even if we go back no farther than the Capetians, we have a full seven hundred years of development in one spot from the familiar domestic origins, the little barbarous court in the palace on the island to the great city of nearly a million souls, whose terms and professions and classes, and whose every institution had developed round the throne.

When one remembers that the king had abandoned Paris but a hundred years; that he had left in the capital by far the greater part of the central machinery, especially the lawyers; that even from what he had taken many relics remained, and that professional men of all classes had the family tradition of the court in the capital — then we can understand what Paris was, is, and must be to a France where no class is permitted to govern. Add to this the increasing specialisation of function as the organism develops — the concentration of the brain — and Paris of the eighteenth century, abandoned as it is, hurt in its dignity, and a little uncertain of its action, still fulfils the geography-books, and is the capital of France.

She herself hardly knew how certainly power would fall into her hands, yet from the first mention of the States General it was fated.

This, then, is the position as the States General meet. A nation in absolute material need of reform, that must have new institutions, especially new financial institutions, or die; classes separate from each other, mutually ignorant of each other, yet all in some degree feeling the position into which France had fallen: in the case of the bulk of the people, misgovernment appearing in the form of starvation; in the case of the upper classes and of the government itself, a conviction that the existing system was contrary to all reason and opposed to every sound interest.

In this society, at least in that part of it that will be called upon to govern, is a conviction—a religion, if you will—whose basis was the faith of Rousseau. Conditions will moderate this for a time; the necessary compromise with what exists, the desire for peace that was uppermost in the first two years, will make men slow to uproot and destroy what may touch the interests of friends and of large classes. They will always attempt a legal though a rapid reform. But, in spite of them, on account of that passionate conviction which underlay their most moderate actions, the Revolution will move up towards the region of unattainable things. The reformer will give way to the Republican idealist when once the serious opposition of the court is felt; he in his turn will give way to the man of passion and of action when the country is in danger; and even the man of passion and of action—the man of realities—will give way to the mere visionary before reaction can come to sweep the floor clean in 1794.

Such will be the phases through which the form of the Revolution will pass. As for the soul of it, France will be steadily transformed, and, in spite of visionaries, reactions, and every political accident, a new and a strong society will be created. So the salt water comes in through old dykes; on its surface you will note the phases of a flood, innumerable little streams, a torrent, a spreading lake, and ultimately calm, but only one thing all the while is happening—where there has been land there will be the sea.

What place did Danton take in this transformation? Of his opinions in detail, his habit of body and mind, his convictions, the accidents of his life, it is the purport of this biography to treat. I will attempt only a very brief description of his position, to make clear the drift of his Revolutionary career, and with this close a chapter whose only object has been to describe the surroundings of a character with which the rest of this book is concerned.

Danton belonged to the bourgeoisie in rank, to the less visionary in the bent of his mind. A young and successful lawyer of thirty, the Revolution found him unknown to politics and not desiring election. It was the accident of oratory that gave him his first position. He discovered himself to be a leader, and there grouped round him a knot of the most ardent, some of them the most brilliant, younger reformers. The electoral district to which he happened to belong became through him the most democratic, and, in some ways, the most violent of Paris.

That part of him which led to such a position was his sympathy. His tenderness (and he had a great share of this quality) was hidden under the energy of his rough voice, great frame, and violent gesture. His pity he was slow to express. But the great crowd of men who were unrepresented, the smaller but more influential class of those who felt and knew but could not speak—these were attracted to him because he had the instinct of the people. He was a demagogue at moments and for a purpose, but never by profession nor for any period of time. What he was, however, all his life and by nature, was a Tribune.

The secret workings of the soil, the power that makes all the qualities of a nation from its wine to its heroes, these had produced him as they produce the tree or the harvest. He is the most French, the most national, the nearest to the mother of all the Revolutionary group. He summed up France; and, the son of a small lawyer in Champagne, he was a peasant, a bourgeois, almost a soldier as well. When we study him it is like looking at a landscape of Rousseau's or a figure of Millet's. We feel France.

His voice was a good symbol of his mind, for there was heard in it not only the deep tone of a multitude, but that quality which comes from the mingling of many parts—the noise of waters or of leaves. In his political attitude he attained this collective quality, not by a varying point of view which is confusion, but by an integration. His opinions erred on the side of bluntness and of directness. They were expressed in plain sentences of a dozen words; he abhorred the classical allusion, he was chary of metaphor. He spoke as a crowd would speak, or an army, or a tribe, if it had a voice.

This was Danton, the public orator and the Tribune, who for two years was heard at the Cordeliers, who spoke always for the purely democratic reform, who opposed the moderates, and who helped to destroy the compromise. Never identified with Paris, he yet saw clearly the necessity of Paris. He admitted her claim, fenced with her arrogance, but never worshipped her idols; once or twice he even dared to blame her worst follies. Elected to the administration of the city, he played but a slight rôle, and until the spring of 1792 there is in him no other quality.

The spring of 1792 produced the war with Europe, and from that date Danton appears in another light. Had he died then, we should have known him only by chance references, a centre of strong reforming speeches, an obscure man in opposition. But with the outbreak of a war which he had done nothing to bring on, and which his party thought unwise, Danton shows that his character, in summing up his fellows, caught especially their patriotism. France was the first thought, and if we could hear not the debaters only, but all the voices of France when the invasion began, it would be this immediate necessity of saving the country that would drown all other opinions. Thence, and for a full year after, Danton becomes the leading man of France. The ability which has led to his legal success (now that his office is abolished and its reimbursement invested in land) seems turned upon the political situation, and such ability combined with such a representative quality pushes him to the front. Two qualities appeared in him which he himself perhaps had not guessed—the power of rapid organisation, and the power of so judging character as to bring diplomacy to bear upon every accident as it arrived.

It was not strictly he who made the 10th of August, but he was the leader. He saw that with the king in power the Prussians would reach Paris, and more than any man he organised the insurrection. That was the one act of violence in his life.

The rest of the nineteen months that fate allowed were spent in the attempt to reconcile and harmonise all the forces he could gather for the salvation of the nation, Perhaps it was his chief fault that in this matter he held to no pure idea.

A Republican and an ardent reformer, he yet seems to have thought France of so much the first importance that he compromised and trafficked with all possible allies. He attempted to stave off the war with England; he attempted to keep Dumouriez; he tried to prevent vengeance from following the Girondins; when the extremists captured the great Committee, he acquiesced, and still wrestled with the forces of disunion. He would have hidden, if possible, those wounds which weakened France in the eyes of the world, and he waged a futile war with the pure idealists—the men of one dogma, who in so many separate camps were destroying each other for their civic faith, and preparing all the evils of a persecution.

On another side of political action he appeared more resolute than any man. It was he who saw the necessity of a strong government, he who created the revolutionary tribunal, and he who is chiefly responsible for the first Committee of Public Safety. He made the dictatorship, caring nothing for the principle, caring only to throw back the foreigner. "He stamped with his foot, and armies came out of the earth." The violent metaphor is just. There is a succession, a stream of great armies (they say four millions of men!) pouring out from France for twenty years. If you will glance at the head of that stream, and wonder when you read of Napoleon what first called up the regiments, you may see on the Champ de Mars in '92, and later demanding the great levy of '93, the presence of Danton, the orator with the voice of command, the attitude of a charge, the right arm thrown forward in the gesture of the sword.

Possessed of astounding vigour, but lacking ambition, a lover of immediate but not of permanent fame, his superb energy after a year of effort spent itself in a demand for repose. In September 1793 he thought his work done and his position secure. He went back into his country home, walked in the fields he loved (and of which he talked before his death), revelled in Arcis, filling himself with the convivial pleasure that he had always desired. He came back in November secure and happy—ready, almost from without and as a spectator, to continue the task of welding the nation together. It was too late. He had created a machine too strong for his control. He had seen the Terror swallow up the Girondins, and had cried because he could not save them.

With the winter he began his protests, his persistent demands for reason and for common-sense; in the religious and in the political persecution he called for a truce; always his effort turned to the old idea—a united Republican France, strong against Europe, with exceptional powers against treason in a time of danger, but with a margin on the side of mercy.

He failed. The extreme theorists whom he despised had captured his dictatorship, and in April 1794 they killed him.

CHAPTER II
THE YOUTH OF DANTON

I shall attempt in the following chapter to tell all that is known of the first thirty years of Danton's life. Our knowledge of this period in his career is extremely slight. It is based upon a minute research, but a research undertaken only in the latter half of this century; and it is to be feared that the scanty materials will never be seriously augmented. Every year makes the task more difficult, and a century has rendered impassable the gulf which Michelet, Bougeart, and even Dr. Robinet, have been able to bridge with living voices.

He was born at Arcis-sur-Aube,[9] a lesser town of the Champagne Pouilleuse, that great flat which stretches out from the mountain of Rheims beyond the twin peaks, till it loses itself in the uplands of the river-partings. Here, though it is cold in winter, there are still vineyards making their last bastion on the covered slopes of the hills that form the northern boundary of the plain.

The day of his birth was the 26th of October 1759;[10] the date gives us his relation to the drama in which he was to be a chief actor. Five months older than Desmoulins, born some months before De Séchelles, eight years older than St. Just, he was the junior of Robespierre by one and a half, of Mirabeau by ten years; Louis XVI. and Marie Antoinette were respectively five and four years his seniors. He was sixteen years old when their predecessor died in ignominy and in dirt. Born six weeks after the fall of Quebec, he received the lasting impressions of early youth during the rapid decline of the French monarchy—the end of a slow decay which threatened to be that of the nation itself. But just then Rousseau was writing the *Contrat Social*, to be published in two years; Voltaire was still in the full vigour of his attack, with nineteen years of life before him; it was the year of Candide; Diderot was founding the Encyclopædia.

The time of his birth coincided with the rising of a certain sun which has not yet set upon Europe, but the boy's eyes turned to more immediate things, and saw in a little provincial place the break-up of a wretched, experimental reign.

This point must be insisted upon, that a country town was the best possible place for noting the collapse of misgovernment. The country manors were more wretched, the provincial capitals more loud and able in their expressions of opinion; but few places could show the fatal process of disintegration more clearly than these little provincial centres, the sub-prefectures of to-day. The confusion of power, the excess and the ill-working of privilege, the complexity and weakness of government, were there apparent upon every occasion. The wealth of the nation was diminished most especially by the interference with exchange. This (though ultimately a source of their penury) was less directly evident to the villagers, while the large town with its varied production could (in another form) disguise the evil; but to the small borough the experience was direct and terrible.

Again, the practical equality of educated men was there more apparent and more sinned against than in the wider societies of the large towns. In a place like Arcis-sur-Aube, isolated specimens of classes technically distinct were continually in contact. The less the number of their caste and order (and the less their importance), the more do the noblesse, to this day, put on their pride; and yet the more necessary is it, in the life of a small town, that they should associate with those whose conversation and abilities are precisely their own. In Paris or in Lyons, where large cliques were occupied in general interests, such differences were often neglected; in the forgotten towns of the provinces never.

On the other hand, the blind and dumb anger of the peasantry would hardly reach Arcis. All over France the town misunderstood the countryside, and in the early Revolution actually fought against it. This will appear strange to an English reader, who sees scarcely any contrast between a country market and an overgrown village. In England the distinction hardly exists, but in France the borough is very separate from the peasant society outside, and, though often smaller than some large neighbouring village, it keeps to this day the Roman traditions of a city.

We see, then, that Danton's birthplace in great part accounts for the peculiar bent of his future politics: practical, of legal effect, inspired by no hatred, though strongly influenced by a personal experience of misgovernment. But his parentage will show us still more clearly how the conditions of his origin affected his career.

He was of the lawyers. His father was *procureur* in the bailiwick of Arcis. It is difficult to explain the functions of his office at this date and to an English reader, for it belongs to that "Administration" which is so essentially Latin, and which we are but just beginning to experience in England. Let it suffice to describe him as the *official* whose duty it was to supply that which in England the *institution* of the grand jury still in theory provides, as it did once in reality. It was his business to "present" the cases and the accused to the local criminal court—local, because in France the circuit of assize is unknown. Added to this were many duties and privileges of registration, of stamping and so forth; and the position required an accurate, and even a minute knowledge of the royal law and provincial usage, the complicated customary system of the old regime.

It is perhaps of still more importance to appreciate the social position of Jacques Danton. Belonging to the lower branches of the legal profession, and placed in a lesser borough of Champagne, the father of Danton held something of the same rank as would a small country solicitor in one of our market-towns, with whatever additions of dignity might follow from a permanent office in the municipality of the place.

As to fortune, we do not accurately know the amount of the family income during Danton's boyhood, but we know that the office which was afterwards purchased for him was worth some three to four thousand pounds; that the money was found largely upon the credit of his father's legacy,[11] and that the house in which the family lived was their own—a useful rule existing throughout provincial France. It is a substantial building, among the best of the little town, standing in the market-place, with the principal rooms giving upon the public square. What with the probable capital and the known emoluments of his position, we may regard Jacques Danton as a man disposing of an income of about four to five hundred pounds a year.

His mother was of a somewhat lower rank. She was the daughter of a builder from the Champagne, and her brother was a master-carpenter of the town. Of her two sisters, one had married a postmaster and the other a shopkeeper, both in Troyes; her brother was the priest of Barberey, near Arcis.

The father died when the boy was two and a half years old, leaving four children. We must presume, though we are not certain, that Danton had one brother: and we know he had two sisters, one of whom married in Troyes; the other died a nun at the same place in the middle of this century.[12]

On both sides of his family, through the connections and marriages of his relations, their employment, their dwellings, their descendants, we see the origin of Danton absolutely separate from the lower and from the higher ranks of the old regime. Only by an effort of imagination could he later understand the workman or the peasant; only by daily conversation could he appreciate the strange nobles of 1790, with their absence of national pride.

In fine, Danton came out of that middle class which has made the modern world, and which still insecurely sustains it. "Respectability and its gig" is an epigram that would exactly suit the dull and provincial surroundings of his first home; but the converse of such provincialism is sanity, order, and strength, and out of fuel so solid and so cold the bourgeoisie has time and again built a consuming fire.

From his father's death, before he was three years old, till his ninth year, the child was with his mother in the house at Arcis, for she had from the little fortune just enough revenue to keep the family together and to educate the children. The little boy was taught his Latin elements in the town, and then sent to the "Lower Seminary" at Troyes.[13]

It was the intention of his uncle at Barberey to make him a priest, and in that case he would have passed through the regular stages, taking the higher forms in the Upper Seminary, and finally being admitted to orders a year or two after finishing his "Philosophie." However, this programme was never completed, and the Church lost in him the material for a vigorous, charitable, and obscure country vicar.

The decision was probably the result of one of those family meetings, such as were habitually held in France to decide the career of an orphan child, and which the Revolution raised to the dignity of an institution with legal form. Some biographers have read the politics of a man of thirty into the action of a little child, and have made this step a precocious protest against clericalism. These biographers have no children.

The uncle consented to the change, and, with Madame Danton's two married sisters, agreed upon the bar as his future profession. He was sent to Troyes and placed with the Oratorians, a religious order which has had the honour of training so many of the great reformers. In their College he went through that training which no amount of social change or new theories in pedagogy has been able to uproot from the secondary education of France. Little Greek, much Latin, two years all employed in the literature of the late Roman republic and early empire—a groundwork in the elements which gives the educated French an almost mediæval familiarity with Roman thought; such was the course which the bourgeois did and does go through in the French schools. A system founded upon the humanities of the sixteenth, but developed in the classicism of the seventeenth century, it has lost the Hellenism, the subtlety, and the breadth of the former, while it has preserved the rigidity, the strength, and the clearness which the latter owes to the influence of the Jesuits. It fails to develop that initiative coupled with originality to which we in England attach so much importance; it achieves, upon the other hand, a strength in the convictions, and above all a soundness in the judgment, which our public schools often fail to produce.

From just such a curriculum came the exaggerated classicism of Robespierre, the more brilliant but equally Latin style of Desmoulins, though it must be admitted that the first is a reminiscence of Cornelius Nepos, while the second is at times well modelled upon Tacitus himself. The error of such imitation, however, never marred the speech of Danton in his later life; he owed this singular freedom from the spirit of his age to travel, to his vivid interest in surrounding things and men, and to his intimacy with English and Italian.[14]

Yet in a famous speech upon public education he makes a just reference to the influence of this schooling upon the mind of his contemporaries, and notes truly its tendency to turn men republican.[15]

Unfortunately he did not remain at such a school long enough to receive its last and most beneficial impressions. The head form at a French school is called "Philosophie," and the last year is spent largely in reading the sociology and the metaphysics of the old world. Danton left at the age of sixteen, when he had just completed "Rhétorique," but what he lost in polishing he gained in being left to his own development for one more year of his life than were his fellows.

Active, often rebellious, full of laughter, he showed his intelligence in the final examinations, his vigour in an escapade that endeared him to at least one of his school-fellows,[16] who has given us, with Rousselin, the only notes we possess as to this period of his life. He ran off in his last year to Rheims, seventy odd miles away, that he might see the crowning of Louis XVI. Going and returning on foot, he satisfied the desire which he had expressed to his school-fellows of "seeing how they made a king." So as a boy he went to look at the making of a king, and afterwards, when he grew older, Danton himself unmade him.

In 1780—his twenty-first year[17]—he entered the office of a solicitor at Paris named Vinot. Apprenticed as a clerk in order to read law, and above all to watch the procedure of the courts, he spent the next four years in preparing for the bar. If we are to depend on a chance phrase dropped just before his death, he was at that time entirely dependent on his master and his pen.[18] We know, at any rate, that he received no salary, but lodged and boarded with his employer; nor is it probable that he received any money from home, for his mother had married again, and a short time after this second husband (a certain Recordain) was so deeply involved that Danton was begged to hand over the most part of his inheritance to save the family. He did so, and remained with some five or six hundred pounds only as his share of the family fortune. It was invested in land near Arcis, and he kept it for his ultimate purpose of buying a barrister's practice in one of the higher courts.

He was called to the bar (a process in the same form as taking a degree) in 1785,[19] choosing, with provincial patriotism, Rheims as the place in which formally to join the profession; but he intended to practise in the capital, and returned thither at once.

It is not easy to render to an English public the meaning of the various courts before 1789. Even in France (so completely has the new order supplanted the old anarchy) their forms have been forgotten, and research purely antiquarian cannot give us more than disjointed particulars as to their procedure.[20] There was a division corresponding to the English between Common Law and Equity. This was to be discovered in every country of the West, and had arisen of necessity from the imposition of the king's power and the Canon Law over those local customs, mixed with reminiscences of Rome, which had once been the whole life of the early Middle Ages.

To the body of lawyers who in Paris (or in any of the great centres) formed the courts for all ordinary pleas, the name of "Parliament" was given. But that it comprised more persons, that it never went upon circuit, and that it included many barristers as well as judges, the Parliament of Paris corresponded more or less to what the English Bench would be were our judges to form a kind of permanent council for advising the Crown and registering its decrees, as well as for trying the cases brought before them. To plead at their bar was no difficult matter. It required but the taking of one's degree in law, and the fees of entrance were slight. Danton determined to adopt this branch of the profession, and to use it as a stepping-stone towards the higher court, which he soon reached.

This higher court, "Court of Appeal," as we should call it, or "Cour de Cassation," as it is named in the modern French system, bore a title significant of the intense conservatism of old France. It was called the "Court of the King's Councils"—very much what we should have to-day in England had we preserved in fact the theory that the king in his council is the final authority. But though it bore a name drawn from the Curia Regis of the thirteenth century, it had of course lost all its old simplicity. It was a Bench like any other, but there pleaded at its bar an order of lawyers strictly limited in number and highly privileged.[21] It dealt, as did its parallel in the English system, mainly with disputed inheritances, especially in matters of land, and, as we shall see, it showed the true mark of a court of Chancery, in that it took more than a hundred and thirty years to make up its mind. To plead before this court, with its monopoly of valuable causes, was to have at once an assured income and prestige; therefore its vacancies were prizes to be bought and sold. Danton determined to plead so long at the common law courts as might assure him, with economy, a substantial addition to the few hundred pounds that formed his whole capital, and then to seek a loan that might eke out these savings and place him at the Chancery bar.

Young, eloquent, eminently capable of seeing a real issue, he was well fitted for the lower practice, and he succeeded. Within two years he had a sum to offer as part payment, which was at once a proof of his business habits and of his talents. His family, therefore, especially those members of it who had urged him to go to the bar, were willing to advance the necessary sums in addition to his own savings and his little patrimony. The purchase-money was delivered, and a bond to the amount of £3000 (a sum which he could not then have furnished) was signed by his aunts and uncles at Troyes. It was in March 1787[22] that this step was taken, and this date was in some sense his entry into public life, for it brought him into direct contact with the wealthy—that is, with the ruling class.

We have on this date a vivid anecdote surviving. A Latin oration had to be delivered off-hand to the assembled college on the reception of a candidate to the order. The subject set for Danton when he entered the hall was "The Moral and Political Situation of the Country in their relations with the Administration of Justice." A fine theme for 1787! Such a quaint scene the old regime delighted in, and its older members delighted also in catching here and there a phrase of quotation which they could understand. The genius and the memory of their candidate seem on this occasion to have furnished something new, to have given them less platitude than was expected. He mentioned reform; he spoke of the struggle in which the Parliament was engaged against the ministers—a struggle of which he wisely said, "They are fighting for the sacred centres of civic liberty, but present no positive reform by which that liberty may be brought into existence." "Sacred centres" was, of course, *aris et focis*. The speech was necessarily in a large measure a series of *clichés*, a stringing together of the well-worn Latin mottoes. It even contained *salus populi suprema lex*, but its argument was Danton's own. There is to be marked also this phrase, for it is the note of all his future work: "Let the government feel the gravity of the situation sufficiently to remedy it in the simple and in the natural way downwards from its own authority."

The young men understood and applauded; the old men were assured that, if they had not quite followed an unconventional harangue, it was due to the originality of the speaker. Presumably their souls were softened by *aris et focis*, and *salus populi suprema lex*.

For the next two years his forensic reputation is continually rising. No longer the Common Law pleader, with pathetic and oratorical appeals for a shepherd against his lord, he had shown how large a part intellect had to do with his power of commanding attention. On the intricacies of his Chancery practice and the clearness and ability of his analysis we have an excellent witness in one of the most learned of the modern Parisian bar,[23] and three of his opinions, on the Amelinau, Dubonis, and De Montbarey cases, have come down to us, and have received the favourable criticism of an opponent.

The last case (that of De Montbarey) shows us Danton defending the claims of an old house and at work in the rustiest of all the legal grooves. It had been on the stocks since 1657, and Danton, in attempting to give the quietus to this intolerable longevity, uses a phrase which shows us the feeling that spared one grave at least when the mob sacked St. Denis: "Jeanne d'Albret[24] is a name dear to all Frenchmen, for it recalls the memory of that other Jeanne d'Albret who was the mother of Henri IV."

There came to be his clients, among others De Barentin, the minister of justice, and De Brienne,[25] comptroller-general; it is on his intimacy with the former that his first recorded opinions on public affairs turn. They will be dealt with in the next chapter.

It is, of course, difficult to give an exact proof of a man's private income at any moment, but we are certain that Danton's cannot have fallen far short at this date of a thousand pounds a year. His immediate success at the bar, the monopoly and privilege of the body to which he now belonged (the work certain to come to the most inept was worth a lump sum of 60,000 francs, to which talent would add indefinitely), his eloquence and proved ability, the name of his clients, their importance and their wealth—everything leads to this as a certain conclusion. Immense fortunes were not then made in the profession; his position was not an obscure one.

He married, on attaining this status, the daughter of a man who kept one of the students' restaurants, Charpentier by name. It was a café (Café des Écoles) very much frequented by the University and the younger men at the bar, and still one of the few remaining cafés of the last century. Danton himself was a regular customer, and there is an interesting picture, drawn by a friend, of the avocats in their special costumes at this place. It occupied the site of what is now the south-western corner of the Place de l'École,[26] nor has any change been made in it save the raising of the road level. Looking on the river, and just over the river from the Palais, it was the natural rendezvous for the young barristers in the mid-day adjournment and after the court rose.

Charpentier, the "limonadier" of Mdme. Roland, was a man worth from five to six thousand pounds, part only invested in his business;[27] he had, moreover, a little post under the Taxes, requiring a slight amount of work and bringing in only a hundred pounds a year. When he married his daughter to Danton, she was given 20,000 francs.[28]

As will be seen later, it is of the first moment in proving Danton's position to know accurately the capital amount of which he disposed when the Revolution broke out; for in the case of generous men in a democracy, the accusation of venality is the most common and the hardest to rebut.

Passionately fond of his wife, and successful in his profession, on the threshold of a great career, I would apply to him a phrase which one of his worst enemies has given us to describe a far lesser man, "Actif et sain, robuste et glorieux, il aima sa femme et la parure."

We leave him, then, at the summit of a laborious and perhaps of an arduous youth. He is twenty-eight years old, in the best of his vigour and of his intelligence—the age at which Jefferson ten years before had drafted his immortal paragraph; the age at which Napoleon, with his moving island of men, was ten years later to break five armies of the Austrians from Lodi to Campo Formio.

What picture shall we make of him to carry with us in the scenes in which he is to be the principal actor?

He was tall and stout, with the forward bearing of the orator, full of gesture and of animation. He carried a round French head upon the thick neck of energy. His face was generous, ugly, and determined. With wide eyes and calm brows, he yet had the quick glance which betrays the habit of appealing to an audience. His upper lip was injured, and so was his nose,[29] and he had further been disfigured by the small-pox, with which disease that forerunner of his, Mirabeau, had also been disfigured. His lip had been torn by a bull when he was a child, and his nose crushed in a second adventure, they say, with the same animal. In this the Romans would perhaps have seen a portent; but he, the idol of our Positivists, found only a chance to repeat Mirabeau's expression that his "boar's head frightened men."

In his dress he had something of the negligence which goes with extreme vivacity and with a constant interest in things outside oneself; but it was invariably that of his rank. Indeed, to the minor conventions Danton always bowed, because he was a man, and because he was eminently sane. More than did the run of men at that time, he understood that you cut down no tree by lopping at the leaves, nor break up a society by throwing away a wig.[30] The decent self-respect which goes with conscious power was never absent from his costume, though it often left his language in moments of crisis, or even of irritation.

I will not insist too much upon his great character of energy, because it has been so over-emphasised as to give a false impression of him. He was admirably sustained in his action, and his political arguments were as direct as his physical efforts were continuous, but the banal picture of fury which is given you by so many writers is false. For fury is empty, whereas Danton was full, and his energy was at first the force at work upon a great mass of mind, and later its momentum.

Save when he had the direct purpose of convincing a crowd, his speech had no violence, and even no metaphor; in the courts he was a close reasoner, and one who put his points with ability and with eloquence rather than with thunder. But in whatever he undertook, vigour appeared as the taste of salt in a dish. He could not quite hide this vigour: his convictions, his determination, his vision all concentrate upon whatsoever thing he has in hand.

He possessed a singularly wide view of the Europe in which France stood. In this he was like Mirabeau, and peculiarly unlike the men with whom revolutionary government threw him into contact. He read and spoke English, he was acquainted with Italian. He knew that the kings were dilettanti, that the theory of the aristocracies was liberal. He had no little sympathy with the philosophy which a leisurely oligarchy had framed in England; it is one of the tragedies of the Revolution that he desired to the last an alliance, or at least peace, with this country. Where Robespierre was a maniac in foreign policy, Danton was more than a sane—he was a just, and even a diplomatic man.

He was fond of wide reading, and his reading was of the philosophers; it ranged from Rabelais to the physiocrats in his own tongue, from Adam Smith to the "Essay on Civil Government" in that of strangers; and of the Encyclopædia he possessed all the numbers steadily accumulated. When we consider the time, his fortune, and the obvious personal interest in so small and individual a collection, few shelves will be found more interesting than those which Danton delighted to fill.[31]

In his politics he desired above all actual, practical, and apparent reforms; changes for the better expressed in material results. He differed from many of his countrymen at that time, and from most of his political countrymen now, in thus adopting the tangible. It was a part of something in his character which was nearly allied to the stock of the race, something which made him save and invest in land as does the French peasant,[32] and love, as the French peasant loves, good government, order, security, and well-being.

There is to be discovered in all the fragments which remain to us of his conversations before the bursting of the storm, and still more clearly in his demand for a *centre* when the invasion and the rebellion threatened the Republic, a certain conviction that the revolutionary thing rather than the revolutionary idea should be produced: not an inspiring creed, but a goal to be reached, sustained him. Like all active minds, his mission was rather to realise than to plan, and his energies were determined upon seeing the result of theories which he unconsciously admitted, but which he was too impatient to analyse.

His voice was loud even when his expressions were subdued. He talked no man down, but he made many opponents sound weak and piping after his utterance. It was of the kind that fills great halls, and whose deep note suggests hard phrases. There was with all this a carelessness as to what his words might be made to mean when partially repeated by others, and such carelessness has caused historians still more careless to lend a false aspect of Bohemianism to his character. A Bohemian he was not; he was a successful and an orderly man; but energy he had, and if there are writers who cannot conceive of energy without chaos, it is probably because in the studious leisure of vast endowments they have never felt the former in themselves, nor have been compelled to control the latter in their surroundings.

As to his private life, affection dominated him. Upon the faith of some who did not know him he acquired the character of a debauchee. For the support of this view there is not a tittle of direct evidence. He certainly loved those pleasures of the senses which Robespierre refused, and which Roland was unable to enjoy; but that his good dinners were orgies or of any illegitimate loves (once he had married the woman to whom he was so devotedly attached) there is no shadow of proof. His friends also he loved, and above all, from the bottom of his soul, he loved France. His faults—and they were many—his vices (and a severe critic would have discovered these also) flowed from two sources: first, he was too little of an idealist, too much absorbed in the immediate thing; secondly, he suffered from all the evil effects that abundant energy may produce—the habit of oaths, the rhetoric of sudden diatribes, violent and overstrained action, with its subsequent demand for repose.

Weighted with these conditions he enters the arena, supported by not quite thirty fruitful years, by a happy marriage, by an intense conviction, and by the talents of a man who has not yet tasted defeat. I repeat the sentence applied to another: "Active and sane, robust and ready for glory, the things he loved were his wife and the circumstance of power."

CHAPTER III
DANTON AT THE CORDELIERS

A man who is destined to represent at any moment the chief energies of a nation, especially a man who will not only represent but lead, must, by his nature, follow the national methods on his road to power.

His career must be nearly parallel (so to speak) with the direction of the national energies, and must merge with their main current at an imperceptible angle. It is the chief error of those who deliberately plan success that they will not leave themselves amenable to such influences, and it is the most frequent cause of their failure. Thus such men as arrive at great heights of power are most often observed to succeed by a kind of fatality, which is nothing more than the course of natures vigorous and original, but, at the same time, yielding unconsciously to an environment with which they sympathise, or to which they were born.

It is not difficult to determine the accidents of action, temperament, and locality which predispose to success in one's own society. It is less easy to appreciate what corresponds to them under foreign conditions.

It was seen in the first chapter that Paris sums up in herself those conditions in the case of the French nation; and it was seen also (a point of peculiar importance) that Paris at the close of the eighteenth century was ill at ease—out of herself, demanding her place and yet anxious as to the means by which it might be attained.

It might be imagined that this was a kind of usurpation. Such a belief is entertained by most foreigners, and certainly it has not been lacking among the more idealist of the French Republicans. Nevertheless, such a view is erroneous, and the Girondists, for all their virtues, went (as we shall discover) against the nature of things when they would have made of Paris but one of the cities, or rather but "an aliquot voting part" of the nation. The demand of Paris was essentially reasonable, and had to be satisfied. Why? Because without her leadership not this thing or that thing would have been done, but nothing would have been done. The crowds who waited round the coaching inns in the country towns for news of the city in the great early days of '89, by their very attitude asked and expected Paris to move.

Paris, then, is Danton's gate. It is up the flood of the Parisian tide that he floats. That tide rises much higher than even he had thought possible, and it throws him at last on the high inaccessible place of the 10th of August. Once there, from a pinnacle he sees all France. Just as Cromwell was the Puritan soldier till he reached power, and then became, or desired to become, the representative of England, so Danton is the Parisian Frondeur till from a place of responsibility and direction he aims partly at the realisation of French ideas, but mainly at the integrity and salvation of France itself.

Here he is, then, in the two years of active discussion that precede the elections, by an accident of ambition, Parisian; one of a group of young provincial lawyers, but the most successful of them all. Some months after his marriage, in the course of 1788[33] (we are not certain of the exact date), he moved into the house in which he lived to his death, six angry years. It was the corner house of the Cour du Commerce and the Rue des Cordeliers. [34] The house was better than that which he had inhabited in the Rue des Mauvaises Paroles, when he bought his practice; on the other hand, it was in a somewhat less expensive neighbourhood. We may justly infer, however, from the greater size of his new apartments, and from the fact that he kept his office still in the old house in the Rue de la Tixanderie, just behind the Hotel de Ville, that he had prospered in his profession, and the inference is sustained by our knowledge of the importance of his cases and his clients. As to the exact situation which he chose, it was doubtless determined by its proximity to the apartments of his friends. Here lived Desmoulins, his chief friend, a year younger than himself, coming (after his marriage in 1790) to live in the same house; for then, as now, in Paris it was not the habit to take a whole house but a flat, and Danton was on the first, Desmoulins on the second floor. Just across the river, over the Pont Neuf, was the café on the Quai de l'École which his father-in-law had kept, and above all, he was here in the midst of the youth of the schools. It was the slope of the famous hill of the University. Close by he would find the Café Procope, of which Desmoulins had written with such enthusiasm, which had once been illuminated with the little smile of Voltaire, which had heard the assertion of Diderot, and which in 1788 was noisy every night with discussion and speech and applause. All that atmosphere of debate which comes unconsciously to young men learning rose on the sides of the Mont Parnasse and centred in the room; and here in the winter of the year, in a society so entirely of his own rank that the high bourgeoisie and the noblesse knew nothing of its power, his great voice and generous face filled the circle with their energy. But there was yet no dream of revolution, still less of violence. France was waiting for great things, but they were to come of themselves, or on the wave of universal enthusiasm. The fire, however, was lit, and the group which afterwards passed from the Montagne to the scaffold of Germinal was already formed.

To all this, however, which was but the relaxation of an abundant spirit, must be added days of continual and serious work on the other side of the river. If his nights were in the Latin Quarter, his days were in the office of the Rue de la Tixanderie. A minister of the crown[35] does not intrust his family affairs to such a wastrel as the chance memoirs of opponents would make of Danton at this period, nor a lawyer who is never in his chambers, but gadding about politicising, get the conduct of one of the most important Chancery cases of his day.

There is one matter in these pre-revolutionary months which is of no very great importance, but which is well worth noticing, though the confusion apparent in our one account of it has lessened its value. There can be no doubt that Barentin, apart from his business relations, was personally intimate with Danton; and when that careful and moderate man had succeeded Lamoignon in September 1788, there was some kind of informal offer made to Danton of what we should call an official secretaryship to the minister[36]—or rather we have no name for it, for the ministry in France was not associated with legislation, but only with executive power, and therefore positions in its gifts had not the political importance they have with us.

As to the precise date of the offer, how far it was pressed, or how seriously it was made, we can have no exact knowledge. But it seems to me unwise to reject so characteristic an anecdote, and one which fits in so well with Danton's known position, merely on the somewhat strained theory that documentary evidence alone should be admitted in history, and documentary evidence sifted by the rules of a rigid cross-examination.[37]

At any rate, Danton refused it. And not only did he refuse it, but there is no trace of an attempt to use his friend's influence or to make a political success at a time when nearly every man's head was turned by the chances of a great social change. He felt no need of politics, and it was not till much later, after quite twelve months of action and speech, that his oratory found foothold, and he felt the imperious appetites of a new power. Success in his profession was without question the one ambition which occupied him in the close of 1788, it was an ambition closely bound up with that business sense which was a strong element in the sane and practical mind of the Champenois lawyer.

It was upon him and his group of friends, in a Paris that every day grew keener in its discussion and attention, that the long-expected decree of the 27th of December fell. There were to be elections. Paris, all pamphleteered to death, but inclining as a whole to the moderate criticism of the more practical men, was at last called upon to act.

Many conditions must be made clear before we can understand the effect of these elections upon the history of the next three years. In the first place, France was suffering from a great material evil: she was going bankrupt, her agriculture was hopelessly depressed, her industries ruined, and thousands and thousands of men out of work were wandering about the streets of the cities. In the second place, the class which was going to vote for the Commons was the tax-paying class. And in the third place, the voting was by two degrees. I name these three conditions as qualifying a broad and often erroneous impression. I do not mean that the ideals were not abroad; all the world knows how bright the eyes of the young men were getting, and we are all familiar with Desmoulins, eager, passionate, stuttering but voluble, and passing from group to group as they discussed or dreamed. But it is too common to read the spirit of '93 into those elections of '89, and the error is a grievous one. As well might you interpret the spirit of an eloquent man who is about to defend a just and practical cause by hearing what he said later in the day, should his opponents have taken to fists and fought him heavily for several hours.

The immediate need was fiscal; the class called upon to meet it were the middle class; the men they were about to elect were of professional rank.

The electoral units and all corporations were asked to state their grievances before the gathering of the Parliament, and it is in these "cahiers" that the spirit of the time is best discovered. The abstractions, the phrases, the great general conceptions are found (as we might have expected, though it comes as a new thing) mainly in the complaints of the clergy and nobility; the peasant, the bourgeois, and the artisan have a more material grievance.

Thus the nobility of Caen in their cahier talk of the "National Contract," and the clergy of Forez (after some remarks on the care and cleansing of ponds) end up with an admirable little essay on individual liberty, its limits and proper extension.[38] The nobility of Nantes and of Meulan talk roundly of the "rights of man,"[39] and generally this order calls for a Constitution—of which word they had in a very short time supped and dined. With lesser men the demands are rather for sublunary things, but the complaints that made Beugnot laugh give a good picture. "To have one's dogs killed if necessary but not hamstrung, to be allowed to keep a cat, to be allowed to light a fire without paying dues, to sell one's wine when one liked;" and from the bourgeoisie, regular trial, abolition of lettres de cachet, the old European policy that the growth of rich corporations should be checked and much of their property confiscated, the equalisation of taxation—such are the points upon which (a mere redress) the great bulk of Frenchmen were determined. One might sum up and say, "They demanded the freedom and common justice obtainable in the modern State." But the privileged orders, for all their phrases, resisted when the time for reform was come, and their friction lit the flame of the ideal, disastrously for themselves and happily for the world.

As for the cahier sent from the electoral district of Paris in which Danton lived, it was destroyed by the Commune when they burnt the Hotel de Ville in 1871. We know, however,[40] that it demanded "the destruction of the Bastille," a symbolic act ever present to the minds of Parisians, and, for the matter of that, by several cahiers of the provincial noblesse and clergy. There is no direct documentary evidence that Danton helped to draw up this cahier, but I cannot believe that a man of such influence in so small a space and among (comparatively) so few voters[41] had nothing to do with the framing of this document, especially when we consider the cry he gave as a boy, swimming in the river just beneath the walls of the prison.[42] There is, however, nothing to prove it, and he certainly took no memorable part in an action where all was tranquil and even tedious.

The mention, however, of the districts of Paris, and especially of that which could claim Danton, makes very necessary a view of that focus of revolutionary energy. It was called the district of the Cordeliers. It was small, one of the smallest of the sixty into which Paris was divided, yet it contained the very strongest of the brains and eloquence of its time, very few nobles, and, for the matter of that, very few of the artisans and har any of the proletariat. Later, when Danton threatened the reactionaries with the populace, it was not to the district of the Cordeliers, but to the Faubourg St. Marceau that he appealed; for the workmen were rare in its ancient, narrow streets, with their tall houses and little dark courts framing each some relic of the Middle Ages. Here were found many of the clergy, but above all a swarm of the young lawyers and students, the class that think high and hard and breed thoughts in others, a kind of little united clan of what was strongest in the youth of the University and the professions; and the whole homogeneous group centred round Danton.

If you stood in the Cour du Commerce in Danton's time, and looked north to where his house made the corner of the narrow entry, you would have seen a main street only a trifle broader than the court, and running at right angles. Standing in the mouth of the narrow passage, you would have seen on the other side of the main street, and a hundred yards up it, a little fifteenth-century turret, capped with a pointed slate roof and jutting outward on round supports.[43] This was the extreme angle of an old convent called the Cordeliers.[44] Here the Franciscans had settled in St. Louis's time, five hundred years before, but the walls you would have seen were not of the thirteenth, but rather of the early fourteenth century, while the church which flanked the street was of the sixteenth, and additions had been made of all periods. As you came out of the Cour du Commerce and went up the street, you would have the convent running all along the opposite side, from the little turret on the corner to the church of St. Come in the Rue de la Harpe, save where it was interrupted by private houses, and where it was broken in one place by a little lane leading to the hall of the University College, which the convent supported. Like so many great foundations, this rich place was in full decay, and the vaulted hall, with its dim light and resonant echoes, was given over to the meeting of the district, and later to the thunder of the voice that threw back the armies of Europe. Alone of all the mediæval buildings of the Cordeliers this hall remains to-day as the Musée Dupuytren.

There is yet one further point to be mentioned before we can make a complete picture of Danton's position before these elections of 1789. There can be no doubt that the Masonic lodges had proved a powerful instrument in the preparation of opinion, and though our information on their formation in Paris is scanty, we can safely affirm that Danton belonged to the lodge of the "Nine Sisters," which included such members as Sieyès or Bailly on the one hand and Collot D'Herbois on the other.[45] It would be foolish to overestimate the influence of these societies. The subsequent history of their members proves quite clearly that the bond between them was slight (who can, for instance, reproach Desmoulins with a secret support of Bailly?), and (what is much more important) the very character of their composition disproves effectually any secret or prearranged action. The foolish Bailly, the learned Sieyès, the admirable, unpractical, high-minded Condorcet, the weak Garat, Collot D'Herbois the potential Red, all members of one lodge! They can have been little more than associations whose character of mutual help and whose opportunities of club-life (that comfort so lacking in Paris) attracted men. They were authorised, and were one of the very few kinds of refuge from a society where political discussion had decayed and where combined action was almost unknown.

This is all the importance, I think, which should be attached to them. Where men are free, and where the suffrage is open and common, secret societies may very justly be dreaded; their action will be at all times separate from that of society in general, and may be in a hidden antagonism to the will of the nation. But in a society where reunion, discussion, and all that is the blood of civic political life has been exhausted, then, like a special drug which cures, they have an excellent use. They may, in such societies, just keep alive the habit of political conversation and expectancy, and they may develop in some at least that organising spirit without which a political movement degenerates into anarchy.

This, then (to recapitulate), is Danton's position just before the Parisian elections. He is in the midst of what are to be his group of young Revolutionary friends on the outskirts of the Latin quarter; his daily occupation is the conducting in his office on the north bank and at the Palace in the Cité of those important pleas in the highest court, which bring him into contact with the ministers, with the great corporations, and especially with the various organs of government of the old regime—for it was in cases for and against these that the Conseil du Roi came into play. His income is sufficient for his needs and for a slow but methodical payment of the price of his practice. It amounted (we may presume) to something in the neighbourhood of 25,000 francs, possibly a little less, but not much, for it was drawn from one of the most important Chancery cases of his day, and his clientele, to judge by the names which alone have reached us, was wealthy and of influence. He was thoroughly well read; he was not expecting nor planning a political career, as were so many of his friends (for instance, Desmoulins), but certain characters which he was rapidly developing, or rather discovering, in himself were preparing that career of necessity. He was learning in discussion and laughter, first that he was an orator, and secondly that his energy sufficed for a whole group of men, and that he could avoid leadership only at the expense of entire seclusion. In a time of innumerable pamphlets, he never put pen to paper outside his profession; and in days that were producing the ardent similes of Camille, and that were just beginning to feel the ravings of Marat, he wrote nothing but three grave, learned, concise, and dull opinions, which were admirable in argument, clear in exposition, and tolerable only to elderly lawyers.

As for his politics, he was centred wholly on the outward thing. He seems to have lacked almost entirely the metaphysic. Here was France all ruined and every day approaching more nearly to disaster; let her be turned into a place where men should be happy, should have enough to eat and drink, should be good citizens to the extent of making the nation homogeneous and strong. Reform should be practical: in part it would require discussion, not too much of it. In part, however, its lines were laid down for it. Economics taught certain truths; let them be applied. He had read in Adam Smith certain indubitable principles of this science; let them be used. Science had in such and such matters definite remedies to offer; let them be applied. Such were his over-simple aims. He was of the Encyclopædists. Had he no beliefs, then, in his politics? Undoubtedly he had; no man could desire "the good" without feeling it. But, like all minds of his type, he refused to analyse. His dogmas were all the more dogmas because he took them so entirely for granted that he refused even to define them. At a time when all men had their first principles ready-made in words, his was rather that confused instinct which is, after all, nearest to the truth. Patriotism, good-fellowship, freedom for his activities, the satisfaction of the thirst for knowledge—all these he desired in himself and for the State. And that is why you will find his great body at the head of mobs and daring criminal things when it is a question of saving the nation, or later of breaking an inquisitorial idea. It is this simplicity which makes him daring, and this concentration on a few obvious points which makes him judicious, unscrupulous, and successful in the choice of means and of phrases.

On the 24th of January 1789, the Primaries were convened. It was the opportunity for movement, in Paris especially, since it was the first definite action after so much discussion, attention, and fever. The district of the Cordeliers met in the hall of which so much mention has been made above. But there does not seem to have been anything of importance transacted, unless we call this important; I mean the beginnings of the habit of reunion and of open discussion. For three months the place seems to have had its doors open to the first comer of the quarter. The cahier was drawn up here, and the rough foundations of what was to be the famous permanent survival of the "République des Cordeliers" were laid. But of Danton's part in all this we have, as I have said above, no trace. We can only conjecture and infer.

It was on April 21 that the elections were finally held. The voters all met together in the central halls of their districts (churches for the most part) and elected the electors, who in their turn were to nominate the deputies for Paris. Of Danton's rôle in this important action, again we know nothing. M. Bougeart[46] has taken it for granted that he was at least "president of the district," chairman (as we should say) of the electoral meeting; but he is either in error, or else he is relying on some verbal evidence which he has not given us. We have no document to prove it, and we know that three months later Timbergue and Achimbault, two barristers of the district, were successively presidents, not Danton.[47] What we do know of importance is that the Cordeliers were among those districts which did not disperse after the elections, but maintained themselves as a permanent club. This action by the districts was of the very first importance in the history of the Revolution. It created the municipal movement in July, it made Paris an organisation, gave the town a method and a voice, and more than any other accident it placed the ladder for Danton's feet.

The elections of Paris once completed, the gates of the Revolution are passed, and the States-General, whose Commons formulated its first principles, are definitely formed; for Paris completed its voting much later than the provinces. The Parliament meets at Versailles, and that town presents for the next six months the centre of official interest. But since Paris is going to be, by its destiny, the heart of the reform, and since Danton is the tribune of Paris, we must, for the purposes of this biography, mention the assembly only in its relation to what passed in the capital.

The tone of Paris during the first two months of the Parliament was, as has been expressed earlier in this chapter, essentially one of ill-ease and watching. But this anxiety of the town took long to find a formula and to recognise its own nature. What Paris needed was the leadership; but to hear the confused murmur of the thousand voices, you would have thought that all her demands were for a number of more or less conflicting ideals. And yet there was no appearance of Party. One may say, by a just paradox, that her very cliques made for solidarity. The higher bourgeoisie could afford at first to ignore the group of the Latin Quarter, thinking the young lawyers and students to be merely foolish demagogues, not even dangerous. The ears of these last were closed to the confused demands of the populace, and the orators could honestly believe that ideas rather than hunger were to be the goad of change. By great good fortune their position was never wholly abandoned, and the Revolution from first to last mastered Materialism and its attendant Anarchy. Finally, the poor—the out-of-work, the starving labourers of the economic crisis—standing apart from both these leading classes, could convince themselves that the great phrases meant bread, and that a constitution was allied in some vague way to a lowering of prices. They were right in that instinct, but, with the picturesque inexactitude of mobs, they fearfully under-estimated the length of the connecting links.

The place where the average of these different views could best be found was the Palais Royal. Here a great popular forum gathered in the gardens which the Duke of Orleans had thrown open to the people. It was not a bad thing that the debts of this debauchee and adventurer had led him to let out the ground-floor of the wide quadrangle, for the cafés and shops that surrounded it made it a more permanent resort than the squares or gardens could have been, and there could be a perpetual mob-parliament held from day to day. Its orators were the Dantonist group; its instigators, I fear, the unprincipled men who surrounded D'Orleans, its committee-room and centre (as it were) the Café Foy. Still, by the action of the main virtue of revolutions, the general sense of the meeting was stronger than any demagogue; for in such times society is not only turbulent but fluid, and while it will support a leader who can swim, no mortal force can give it any direction other than that which it desires.

In this great daily crowd Danton was a prominent but not a principal figure; undoubtedly (though we cannot prove it by any record) he had begun to speak in his district, and we may presume that his voice had been heard in the Palais Royal before July; for just after the fall of the Bastille his name is mentioned familiarly. But even had he desired to identify himself with the place, which is doubtful, his profession would not have permitted it. He was not briefless, unmarried, and free, like Desmoulins, but a man of three years' standing in the highest branch of his profession; doubtless, however, he was present daily when the crowd was thickest—I mean on the holidays and during the summer evenings.

All this pamphleteering, discussion, violence, salonising, oratory, and anxious criticism, even the mob violence which hunger and bad laws had inflamed, found a head in the three famous days that followed July 12, 1789. All the world knows the story, and even were it unfamiliar it would be impossible to treat of it at any length in this book, for Danton's name hardly touches it, and our only interest here, in connection with his life, is to discover if he took part in the street fighting; for the event itself, one of the most decisive in history, a few words must suffice.

Paris, and especially the Palais Royal, had been watching the struggle at Versailles with gathering anger. There, twelve miles off, every purpose for which the Parliament had met, and every good thing which the elections had seemed to ensure, lay in jeopardy. Step after step the Commons had in fact, though not in their phrases, been beaten, and the promises of six months before seemed in danger, not through any known or calculable enemy, but from the sudden appearance of an opposition which the nation, and especially Paris, had ignored. The King had retreated from his position of the last December, and the privileged orders were sympathising with a growing reaction. How far all this was due to the unconstitutional and unprecedented action of the Commons in insisting on a General Assembly cannot be discussed here. Suffice it to say that, in the opinion of the nation, the new departure of the Commons was in thorough accordance with the spirit, if not with the letter, of the recent decrees; the King was held to have broken his word, and the privileged orders to have abandoned their declarations in the face of facts. The symbol, though a poor one, of the constitutional position was the personality of Necker. Conceited, foreign, and common-place, the father of an authoress whom neither Napoleon nor posterity could tolerate, Genevese and bourgeois to the backbone, this mass of impotence yet stood, by one of the ironies of history, in the place of an idol. He, the banker, was the imagined champion for the moment of that other man from Geneva, who had died of persecution ten years before, the tender-eyed, wandering, unfortunate Rousseau, between whom and him was the distance between a financier and an apostle.

While the king was changing his advisers, and even while the foreign troops—fatal error—were being massed in wretched insufficiency on the Champ de Mars (not three miles from the Palais Royal) Necker still stood like a wooden idol, a kind of fetish safeguard against force. He just prevented the growing belief in the dissolution from becoming a certitude, and on account of his attitude Paris waited. These things being so, the king began his great programme of working out the good of his people alone. Relying on the three thousand foreigners, a regiment of home troops, and practically no guns wherewith to hold in check a tortuous city of close on a million souls, the king on Saturday, July 11, dismissed Necker.

Desmoulins first brought the news, running. It was the morrow, Sunday, and the Palais Royal was crowded. He forgot his stammer and hesitancy, and shouted to the great holiday crowd in the gardens to strip the trees for emblems, led them as they marched to the Place Louis Quinze, saw the French troops defend their fellow-citizens against the mounted mercenaries, and heard during a night of terror and of civil war the first shots of Revolution.

All the next day, Monday, July 13, 1789, Paris organised and prepared. Thanks to the permanence of the assemblies in certain districts, a rough machinery was ready, and on the 14th, a Tuesday, two great mobs determined upon arms. The time is not untainted, for St. Huruge was there promising and leading, but if D'Orleans was trying to make the most of the adventure, he no more created the uprising than a miller makes the tide. One stream of men seized the arsenal at the Invalides on the west side of the town, the other going east in a smaller band demanded arms of the governor of the Bastille, a place impossible to take by assault. The demand was refused.

A body of men, however, were permitted to enter the courtyard, for which purpose the drawbridge had been lowered: once in that trap, De Launay fired upon them and shot them down. There is no evidence, nor ever will be, as to the motives of that extraordinary act; but to the general people who were gathering and gathering all about in the narrow streets, it was an act of deliberate treason, part of that spirit with which our own time is not unfamiliar, and which has ruined a hundred reforms,—I mean the sentiment that there is no honour to be kept between government and insurrection. The misfortune or crime of De Launay struck a clear note in the crowd; if after that they failed, the blow that was being struck for the Parliament would fail also. Thus it was that, under a dull grey sky, the whole of Paris, as it were, ran up together to the siege of the fortress. Curés were there gathering up their soutanes and joining the multitude, notably the man who had once been Danton's parish priest, the vicar of St. Germains, with his flock at his heels, like the good Curé of Bazeilles in later times, or the humorous Bishop of Beauvais six centuries before. Lawyers, students, shopkeepers, merchants, the big brewer of the quarter, the pedants, the clerks in the offices, soldiers and their officers, the young nobles even—there was nothing in Paris that did not catch the fever. The castle fell at last, because its garrison sympathised with the mob (of itself it was impregnable); the old governor made a futile attempt to blow up his stronghold and his command; some few who still obeyed him (probably the twenty Swiss) fired on the mob just after the white flag had been hoisted on the Bazinière tower, and a great tide of men mad with a double treason swirled up the fortress. Second on the wall was a man with whom this book will have to deal again—Hérault de Séchelles, young, beautiful, and of great family, beloved at the court and even pampered with special privilege, the friend and companion of Danton, and destined five years later to stand in the cart with him when they all went up to the scaffold together on a clear April evening in the best time of their youth.

The Cordeliers were in the attack, and presumably Danton also, since all the world was there. But his only allusion to the scene is a phrase of his circular to the courts when he took the Ministry of Justice in 1792, and he mentions his district only without including his own name. One anecdote, and only one, connects him with the days of July. It seems that in the night of the morrow, the early morning of the 16th, he was at the head of a patrol in that sudden levy of which mention will be made in this chapter. He thought it his duty to pass into the court of the Bastille, probably in order to gather some detached portion of his command; but he was met by Soulès, whom the informal meeting at the Hotel de Ville had named governor. Full of new-fangled importance, Soulès pompously forbad him to enter, and showed his commission. Danton did a characteristic thing, part and parcel of that intense sectionalism upon which he based all his action until Paris was at last in possession of herself: for him power was from below, and the armed district had a right of passage: he called the informal commission a rag, arrested Soulès, and shut him up in the guardroom at the Cordeliers; then, with a rather larger force, he marched him back through the streets and gave him into the custody of the Hotel de Ville, whose authority for judgment he admitted. The matter would be of no importance were it not for the fact that, in the very natural and on the whole just censure which the informal municipality passed on Danton's action, Lafayette showed an especial bitterness.[48] It was the first clash between two men one of whom was to conquer and drive out the other; and it was a typical quarrel, for Danton stood in the matter for the independence of the electoral unit and for the power of Paris over itself: Lafayette represented the principle of a strong municipality based on moderate ideas and on a limited suffrage; in other words, the compromise which was planned for the very purpose of muzzling the capital.

I have spoken of an armed force and a patrol: it is in this connection that the meaning of the days of July—for Danton and for the Revolution—must be considered. They form above all a municipal reform. Those towns of which I have spoken as being the bond of France harked back suddenly to their primitive institutions, and were organising communal government. Paris of course was the leader. Even before the taking of the Bastille, the districts had in some cases maintained their electoral colleges as a permanent committee, and these electoral colleges met at the Hotel de Ville, forming a rough government for the two nights of the revolt, and finally directing the whole movement. Such a body was of necessity too large to work. But its plans were rapidly formed. They named a committee, which was formed of electors with one citizen (not an elector) added. They invited and obtained the aid of the permanent officers of what had once been the old dying and corrupt corporation, and they thus had formed an irregular but sufficient organ of government for the city. It was not confirmed from above, nor had it, for days, any authority from the King, but it reposed on a force which was admitted in the theory of those times to be the source of power, for it was composed of men elected by the new suffrage. They had been elected for another purpose, but they were the only popular representatives present at all in Paris.

Their weakness, however, lay in this quality of theirs. Reposing merely upon power from the districts, they could not act with central authority, nor had they an armed force of their own. They could, indeed, prevent the success of the rough anarchy which threatened the Hotel de Ville itself in the early morning of July 14, before the attack on the Bastille, but they could not prevent the lynching of those against whom the popular rage had arisen—De Launey, De Méray, De Persan. As for force, they organised a huge levy of 1200 men from each of the sixty districts, a force which, with certain additions, rose to 78,000. It was in this suddenly armed militia that Danton was elected a captain (for the moment), and in connection with its duties of police on the nights following the taking of the Bastille that his quarrel with Soulès had occurred. They named Bailly their first mayor. They gave the command of the new national guard to Lafayette; on the 16th they ordered, with a pomp of trumpets in the Place de Grève, the destruction of the Bastille, in which their new governor was installed. But through all this vigorous action there is one cardinal fact to be remembered: the whole of their power was from below, not only in theory but in fact. We may construct a metaphor to express the future effect of this, and say that, at the very origin of the Revolution, the body of government in Paris was tainted by an organic weakness which no structural changes could remove, and to whose character all subsequent events for three years can be traced. It was essentially *federal*; feeble at the centre, continually asking leave, morally a servant and not a master; lacking above all things the supreme force of conviction, it acted without power because it did not believe in itself.

The history, then, of its struggle with the extremists is the history of a body attempting by compromise and ruse to attain a position whose theory it openly denies, whose moral right it will not affirm, and whose very existence is made dependent upon those whom it would coerce against their will. The municipality tried to be a strong government while it openly approved of voluntaryism, to be powerful in its acts and weak in its structure. Ultimately the centre of compromise is captured by ardent revolutionaries whom it has attempted to check, and *then* we get a true despotism in Paris—the terrible commune of the second period of the Republic and of the Terror.

But if the character of the new municipal government (a character which became specially prominent after the legislation of the whole system later in the year) is the special feature of the movement, its general motive is of course more important. We have called it the Reform; what occurred in the next few days was without any question the origin of the active Revolution, and a little examination of facts will show that the taking of the Bastille was not merely a dramatic incident, still less the exaggerated *bagarre* that certain modern special pleaders would make it, but, on the contrary, the foundation of everything. The contemporaries are proved to have been right in their view of this matter, as of so many others.

Why was this? Because, first, in taking the Bastille, after having sacked the Invalides, the people of Paris (for it was not a particular mob, but a gathering of every possible class) held all the cannon in the city, and were thoroughly provided with small arms. They were suddenly become the masters of that insufficient camp in the Champ de Mars on which the King had relied. In open country and without artillery these seventy thousand civilians would, of course, have been so many sheep, but in the town and with a number of old artillerymen (officers and men) to work their guns, it was another matter. On and after July 14, 1789, Paris had found that possession of herself which we postulated as her first great appetite in the Revolution.

Secondly, by this sudden stroke Paris forced the Court to capitulate. At Versailles the King went bareheaded to the Assembly, gave permission for the reunion of the three orders, for a discussion of grievances before supply, for the title of National Assembly, for the formation of a constitution before the voting of fiscal measures—in a word, for all that the Commons had demanded, and for the fulfilment of all the promises from which he had attempted to recede.

Thirdly, the victory, or rather the act of Paris, changed and weakened the opposition. From openly gathering troops, and boasting an approaching attack on the Parliament, they are reduced to intrigue and to the difficult business of arming in the dark. Many of the heads of the reaction (notably the Comte d'Artois) leave France in the "first emigration," and the whole action of the uncompromising party is made weaker, and clearly unnational.

Fourthly (and perhaps this is the most important point), that municipal movement, of which mention has been made above, took its rise directly from the 14th of July. The towns hear of Necker's dismissal and of the Parisian rising by the same courier, and in a week or ten days the story is repeated all over France. Rouen, Lyons, Valence, Montpellier, Nîmes, Tours, Amiens (to cite but a few of the more prominent examples), organise a new town government. Sometimes the old hereditary or appointed body is deposed, more often it is enlarged by the addition of the electoral college of the city; occasionally it takes upon itself the task of adding to itself representatives of the three orders. Again, the towns arm themselves as Paris did; and finally, by what a contemporary called "spontaneous anarchy," the whole network of cities has received the pulse and vibration of Paris; the National Guards are being drilled in thousands; the rusty, confused, and broken machinery of the *ancien régime* is replaced by a simple if rough system of local government. Moreover, since all this has been done by the people themselves, and without a command or a centralised effort, since it is natural and not artificial, it has entered into the body of the Revolution and cannot be undone.

You see, then, that the days of July gave Paris the first word, and made the spirit of sectionalism and local autonomy based upon a highly democratic theory. All these things are the conditions of Danton's rise; they make possible, and even necessary, the society of which he is to be the guide. After the 14th of July the Cordeliers meet daily; the bell was rung above the church at nine in the morning, and an assembly of the district was held. [49] It was not yet in name the famous "club"; but when we consider the action of the popular societies in Paris, we must always remember that this, even before it regularly assumed its final name and functions, was a society organised for debate and action, and that it was the first to be established.

From its origin, this famous meeting is sharply marked in its spirit—the spirit that will later divide it not only from the moderate clubs, such as the Feuillants, but from the Jacobins themselves. In the first place, it is Parisian; it attempts no provincial propaganda; it confines itself to action in Paris, and even to its own immediate neighbourhood. In the second place, it is purely popular. But (it may be asked) were not the Jacobins in their later stage a purely popular club? No, not in the same sense. The Jacobins, as will be seen later in this book, were an organised body; the public was admitted to their galleries; but, even in the most feverish time of the Revolution, they are distinguished by a close bond from the general people. Their membership is almost exclusively confined to the politicians, and their business is inquisitorial. They preach certain political dogmas, and make it their affair to canalise the Revolutionary current; they desire to establish in France a Republican religion, as it were, and we shall see later in Robespierre their high priest and dictator.

The Cordeliers had nothing of all this. If the Royalist writers begin calling them from the outset the "République des Cordeliers," it is because they show the general spirit which Danton surely gave to, rather than received from, his district. Freedom of opinion, the value of varied discussion, open doors, and even an intermingling with the street—such were their methods. The men who sat on the benches would vary from one hundred to three,[50] according to the interest of the debate or the value of the occasion. The number inscribed on the registers of the society were simply the whole voting strength of the district; under the limited suffrage of the time it would fluctuate round the figure six hundred; and hence we may observe that those who were so strongly touched by the contemporary movement as to add meeting and debating to their mere votes numbered a good half of the electorate. Standing grouped, or moving in and out of the far end of the hall, would be the chance-comers, the disfranchised multitude of the district—those even who had no residence in the quarter, but whom anger, interest, or curiosity might attract. It was composed of every kind of man—the pedantic but accurate Sieyès; the fastidious radical and poet D'Eglantine; the coarse, brutal, and atheistic Hébert; Desmoulins, ardent and admirably polished, linked by his style to the classics of his own country and of Rome; Legendre, the master-butcher, no great politician, but an honest friend; and, added to all these, the lawyers. There was a preponderance of the young men, the students and barristers in their thirtieth year; but take it all in all, it was the most representative, the most general of the meetings.

The society, then, from which Danton rises is marked by these characters: it tends always to defend the presence in politics of the whole people; it is unitarian, designing above all things a common ground where Frenchmen may found the new order in harmony; and finally, it possesses nothing of the metaphysical spirit abroad at the time. It is all for action along the lines of common sentiments—the defence of the new individual liberty, the destruction as soon as may be of whatever relics of the old machinery might be spared by the fear or inertia of certain reformers.

I cannot leave what has already grown to an over-lengthy description of their political attitude without touching upon a quality of theirs, which was not indeed a principle, but which was a method of action necessarily flowing from the ideas they held. The Cordeliers are essentially "Frondeurs." They are rebellious and in opposition so long as the Revolution remains incomplete. They do things deliberately illegal, but which they justly consider to be in the spirit of the reform and calculated to aid its rapid development. Why was this? Because the day after Paris had captured the position, in the very moment when the city had forced reaction into subterranean channels, her power was bridled. The King came to Paris on the 17th of July and confirmed the revolutionary appointments. Bailly is mayor, and Lafayette is commissioned head of the National Guard. In those two names you have the forces, or rather the resistances, against which Danton and the Cordeliers made it their business to fight. Both of them were amiable, both weak, and both sincere; but they belonged, the one to the high bourgeoisie, the other to the noblesse; they were both full of an intense class-prejudice; both thought rather of the restraints to be imposed than of the great change in the midst of which they lived. The little movements that Bailly might have mistaken for an enthusiasm would arise at the sight of his telescope; the undoubted excitability of Lafayette was aroused by the public mention of his own name. Under these weaknesses their external sign was pomposity, their political action an attempt to confine the Revolution to the middle class. Thus, later, the sixty districts are replaced by the forty-eight sections in order to jerrymander the Parisian radicals; thus Bailly tries to oppose Parisian appeals to the Parliament; and thus Lafayette not only attempts to convert the National Guard into a political army, but makes it impossible for the poor to join it.

Against all this the Cordeliers set their face. Such a partial conception of the State was the enemy of that ideal by which they lived and which has formed the Republic in France and the Jeffersonian democracy in America. Only four days after the King had worn his tricolour cockade, smiling on the balcony of the Hotel de Ville, they issue and print a resolution to use the armed force of their district at its own discretion; they do not (of course) claim to act further, but they determine to be themselves the police which shall conduct prisoners to the tribunals.[51] At the close of 1789, and especially in the succeeding year, we shall find them in the affair of Marat, of Danton's election, of the *Mandat Imperatif*, and of the Châtelet continually acting in the spirit of local autonomy, and refusing to admit any central authority save that of the whole people—bowing after every revolt to the Assembly, but refusing to admit the bourgeois power.

The end of July was the destruction of the feudality in France. When the towns had fallen with a shock into the new conditions, the great dust of villages rose of itself into a storm, and there passed over all the countrysides that strange panic, "The Great Fear," whose legend alone of Revolutionary memories remains among the peasantry to-day.

The woods were full of terrors; ploughmen started out at night by bands to meet invisible armies; an unsubstantial enemy threatened the thousands of little lonely villages that lie undefended on the skirts of forests or lost on the leagues and leagues of plains. In that mysterious panic the Jacquerie arose; the cowed and the oppressed, who had forgotten the generous anger which makes men brave, rose under the lash of fear. They had heard of the promises of reform, they had seen the cahiers drawn up that they might become free men, and yet the town close by had risen and armed because something had gone wrong; the King, whom they loved, was not allowed to help his people; some one was delaying or destroying their hopes, and the brigands were coming down the road. Not with committees, organisation, and battalions, as the intelligence of the towns had just done, but instinctively and with the anarchy of the torch they destroyed the skeleton idol of the old regime. Like their fathers of four hundred years before, they were out to destroy the records of their servitude, and where the records were defended the country-houses burned. But this time no vengeance followed: the wild beast was dead. When in the noisy night of the 4th of August the privileged men scattered away their rights, then that last largesse of the nobles, the "Orgy," as Mirabeau called it, was but a gift of things already taken. After Paris, after the cities, the peasantry had suddenly stiffened the phrases by an act; perhaps it was their formless and vague energy that laid the heaviest of the foundation-stones, for we are told that in twenty years an exile returning thought that France had been re-peopled with a new kind of men.

It is not wonderful that, with such a fire just smouldering down, and with the spirit of renunciation abroad as well, a regular stream of emigration should set out. But it did not leave the opposition powerless though it deprived it of chiefs. If we consider the Court, the capital, and the Assembly in the months of August and September, the next great step (and the first in connection with which the name of Danton is directly connected) becomes clear.

At Versailles all the first part of August is taken up in voting the famous decree which consecrated the debate of the 4th. The Parliament abolished feudal dues, declaring all rights in service at an end, and establishing a period for the national purchase and subsequent abolition of the rest of the feudal dues. All the second part of August and the whole of September were occupied in drawing up the declaration of the rights of man and in decreeing the fundamental articles of the new Constitution. The National Assembly, then, as a whole, is thoroughly the organ of France. It is not yet so divided as to arouse definite party feeling in the capital, nor to prevent on important occasions a practically unanimous vote. But there is another factor. The Court (especially the Queen) has a definite party formed; it has its correspondence with the emigrés, and they with the personalities, if not with the official organs of foreign governments. It was without any question the object of this very small and very powerful group to arrest the Revolution, and if possible to wipe out the last six months. Between and above these stands the King. Louis (we are too apt to forget it in our knowledge of what follows) still possessed far more power even than the National Assembly; not only by the political decrees of the time, but by that immeasurable force of custom, by the affection which he personally had inspired in the great bulk of men, he was a powerful king. What was his attitude? He was patriotic; he greatly sympathised with the ideas at the root of the reform; he was sensible, and saw the practical value of casting away what is broken and worn out. On the other hand, he was not brave (especially in the face of the unknown); new developments irritated him; he was (by the inevitable result of his training) determined to preserve in his own hands the bulk of power, and sometimes he was panic-stricken at a phrase or a debate which seemed to put it in jeopardy. Finally—a matter of the utmost importance with a character of such well-balanced mediocrity— the people with whom he hunted, dined, and conversed were almost all of them members of a powerful, bitter, and skilful faction, headed by the most determined and able of all—his wife, for whom he had latterly developed a marked tenderness and even respect.

This ring of courtiers, who were Louis's evil fates, had a certain quality that gave them great power in spite of their small numbers. It must be remembered that they were of the high cosmopolitan type, those who, a generation earlier, delighted in the wit of Voltaire, who, a generation later, smiled at merely hearing the name of Talleyrand. Perhaps there was never a body better fitted to influence an isolated man by phrases, continual conversation, and intrigue.

What is the effect? That the King, always honestly intending the reform, always hesitates a little too long, with doubts that are often intellectual in origin and sometimes wise in their nature, but foolish at the moment. He hesitates to sign the decree of the 4th of August;[52] he hesitates about this and that expression in the Declaration of rights. He has a very strong reluctance to forego the absolute veto; all through September you can hear the machinery creaking, and it gets worse as the autumn advances.

Meanwhile in Paris two forces are at work to aid this crisis at Versailles. First, the popular societies, notably that meeting in the Palais Royal, which now is almost a Parliament, where every prominent Parisian name is heard, and whence those curious documents, parodies of the old-fashioned decrees, emanate,[53] not unfrequently with the power to cause insurrection. Secondly, the price of food, especially of flour, is rising rapidly. We have explained in the first chapter how largely the lack of food in the towns was due to vicious interference with exchange: when such is the prime cause of economic trouble, the least disturbance aggravates it to a high degree; thus it was that while the harvest was being gathered in the north, and in the south had been already stored, the supply of cereals in the capital was all but exhausted.

Thus curiously side by side (and partly overlapping) the intense political interest of the voting class and the growing misery of the populace ran fatally towards the days of October. At the Cordeliers, innocent of pedants, practical, alert, debating with open doors, there met the two revolutionary interests, those of the politicians and of the poor; and this is why they are heard so loudly in September, and why Danton and his district become famous just before the march on Versailles.

It will be remembered that the assembly of electors at the Hotel de Ville had guided Paris through the great storm of July 13-17; their powers were vague and unconstitutional, for they had been elected at first merely to choose Deputies for Paris, nevertheless it was they who had made Bailly mayor, who had nominated Lafayette, who had formed the National Guard, and who had been confirmed by the King in their functions of a provisional municipality. It was acting on this decree which gave them a right to take political initiative, that on Thursday, July 23, they had sent a circular to the sixty districts asking each to name two members. The hundred and twenty so elected were to draw up a plan for a new municipality; they met, did so, and the result of their labours was the issue on August 30th of a scheme for a new municipal system, upon which the primaries in every districts were asked to debate. Somewhat illogically, however, the complicated document was accompanied by a writ demanding the immediate election in each district of five members to form the new corporation. In other words, the primaries were asked to form a new municipality, to give it full powers, and then to debate academically upon what they had done.

It may have been only a blunder, but the Cordeliers took alarm at what certainly seemed to be a plot on the part of the Moderates. The project and the writ had reached them on *Sunday* August 30th; by Thursday, September 3rd, they had arrived at a decision to refuse the writ. They argued that it was absurd to ask the districts to debate on a project *after* its most essential part had been realised, namely, the election of deputies. On that election, its methods, the powers of the members, and so forth, the greater part of the discussions would turn, and by the time the districts had arrived at such and such conclusions, or had modified the powers of their deputies in such and such a fashion, those deputies would already have been sitting for some time as a municipal council, would be helping to frame or to modify

the new municipal system on their own account. It would have been not only confusion but an encroachment on the principle by which (nominally) the districts had been consulted, viz., that the electors themselves in their districts should thrash out the new system. The Cordeliers named commissioners who examined the whole matter, and, on Saturday, the 12th, definitely rejected the writ. Nevertheless, as the other districts had all obeyed and had elected their five members each, the Cordeliers elected their five under protest[54] on the following Monday, the 14th, and sent them, bound by a strict oath, to the Hotel de Ville.

This little incident merits a very considerable degree of attention, although it has been somewhat neglected by the historians, and even by Danton's biographers. It was the first skirmish in that decisive struggle between the democratic idea, headed by the Cordeliers, and the limited suffrage of the first municipality—a struggle which is at the root of all the action of Paris. It is the first act of Danton in an official position; in much that the Cordeliers had done he was evidently the leader, but in this document we learn that he is elected president of the district, and see his name signed. [55] And finally, there appears here, for the first time in the Revolution, the *Mandat Imperatif*, the brutal and decisive weapon of the democrats, the binding by an oath of all delegates, the mechanical responsibility against which Burke had pleaded at Bristol, which the American constitution vainly attempted to exclude in its principal election, and which must in the near future be the method of our final reforms. It had been raised, and Danton had raised it; for these five deputies, before being permitted to attend at the Hotel de Ville, swore to a definite plan of action whose terms were dictated at the general meeting of the district.

The struggle as it continues becomes of greater importance, until, within four months, it faces Danton himself in the Hotel de Ville; but we cannot describe its further steps until we have mentioned the next action with which the Cordeliers are associated, and in which their decisive rôle is largely determined by the Revolutionary championship which this brush with authority had given them.

We have described above the various forces that were fatally converging to form the whirlpool of October—the hesitancy of the King, the desperate intrigues of the Court, the intense political excitement of the Palais Royal and of the electors in Paris, the growing misery of the populace. We have pointed out how the Cordeliers, with their popular audience and popular sympathies, were at once the only great debating place in Paris and the only spot where the forces of voters and non-voters could join hands. Add to this the effect of the protest described above and of the position such a struggle gave them in the democratic movement, and their importance in the days of October becomes evident.

It was at the close of September that all these tendencies came together. Again, after three months of silence, the reaction found its voice, and the King's uncertainty, the Court faction's plotting, culminated in the arrival at Versailles of military reinforcements. The body-guards were doubled, and there marched in the Regiment of Flanders—a body (by the way) to whose name clings something of comedy, and whose raggedness has passed into a marching legend. This book is not the place to describe at any length what followed, save in its connection with Danton and the Club. On Thursday, October the 1st, a famous dinner was given by the body-guard to the newly arrived regiment. The Court dealt with excellent material, and with the wine and the night the admirable feelings of loyalty arose: the poor King assumed the halo of a leader to these men whose regimental traditions were knit up with the monarchy; soldiers, they appreciated his defeat, and, being comrades, they were angry at his loneliness. They greeted him with a passionate song, destroyed the three-coloured cockades, and pinned on the white ribbons; for the first time in a year enthusiasm was with the beleaguered, though it lasted but a few hours and stretched to but a few hundred of men. To Paris, hearing of it on the next day, Friday, it was a challenge, discussed, oddly enough, with some contradictions and confusions. Men talked of Bouillé, the courtier, and his frontier command at Metz; people were afraid that he would protect the King in some flight to the provinces; there ran a vague uneasiness and a fear of anarchy with the King's disappearance; above all, in the minds of the politicians a fear of armed reaction, and in the minds of the starving a terror that the reforms which were so material to them were in jeopardy. Still, all Saturday the waters only moved at the surface, and you might have thought that Paris was incapable of any combined action.

But if the reaction contained a powerful integrating force in the Court party, Paris also possessed it in a small meeting and in one supremely energetic man. On the morning of Sunday, a day when there was leisure to read, the walls were placarded with the manifesto of the Cordeliers. It demanded an insurrection, and was signed with Danton's name. On Monday morning they rang the tocsin at the belfry of the convent, and the battalion of the district was drawn up and armed. De Crèvecœur, their commander, prevented them marching in a body, but a number of the district determined to merge with the crowd. Meanwhile, the mob gathered from every quarter, especially the Place de Grève—a true mob this time, and accompanied, as all the world knows, by a crowd of women, poured up the Versailles road. They made a hideous night in the great space before the palace. Lafayette followed tardily with his organised volunteers, the National Guard; but on the Tuesday the palace was forced, and some of its defenders killed. The royal family came in their heavy coach down the twelve miles of falling road into Paris, and, not without some state, they entered the Tuilleries. The National Assembly followed the King into the capital.

Thus the second milestone of the Revolution was passed. Of all the revolutionary days, these were the most purely anarchic. The action was that of men hardly possessing ideas, but fixed upon a practical thing—the presence of the King in Paris. It had for its main object good, and for its method mad anger. Nevertheless, the instinct of the mob had hit the mark. Like all sudden actions, it had made issues definite which had till then been confused. It put an end once and for all to the idea of crushing the reform at its outset by force; it gave Paris a mastery over every subsequent action; of the many ways the Court party might have tried it reduced them to one only, namely, an organised secret diplomacy with the object of raising Europe against France.

As for Louis, we may honestly believe that his capture was not entirely distasteful to him: as he was less acute, so he had certainly more common-sense than his wife. If he was jealous of his dignity, which had been grievously offended, yet he was very French, patriotic, and not unwilling to see himself the object of a violent demand. Everybody saw—the King must have seen it too—that the whole uprising was monarchic. There was not any class more monarchic in France than the poor. The King as their father was an idea bred in them for centuries, and he knew that they made of him a kind of providence who could give them food; that they rose not to make him less powerful, but to make a faction impotent. And there was nothing distasteful to him in being a King of the French, seated in the midst of his great capital, and on the summit, as it were, of a new order. October did not threaten to make him less, but more of a King. It was later, in questions that affected the heart, especially in matters of religion, that the gulf opened between Louis and his people.

With the King, then, at the Tuilleries, with the Assembly some three hundreds yards off down the gardens in the riding-school of the palace,[56] we enter the long avenue by which Paris obtains the initiative in every subsequent reform. Let us turn, then, to follow once more the action of the society and the man who, between them, determine the direction of Paris for the next three years.

The quarrel which was sketched earlier in this chapter, the assault of the district upon the Moderates, continued throughout the autumn and winter. Four times running Danton is elected President,[57] and it is under his guidance that the affair proceeds. While the Assembly are making a new France at the Manège, organising the departments,[58] fixing the restricted suffrage,[59] creating the communes over all France,[60] the Cordeliers are making the spirit of a new Paris on the hill over the river; this spirit will conquer and transform the debaters in the Parliament.

On the 22nd of October they follow up their previous action. Already before the revolt they had come into collision with the municipality: in this new resolution they protest against a demand of Lafayette for regular courts-martial in the National Guard. The protest had a meaning, for Lafayette was raising an armed bourgeois power, but the motive of the Cordeliers was mainly the desire to harass the Moderates. A week later the Municipal Council gave its reply to these various encroachments on the part of the Cordeliers in a decree of the 29th of October: it condemned the action of the district in three definite points: first, its habit of passing resolutions like a small municipal body; secondly, its habit of asking the fifty-nine other districts to pass spontaneous resolutions on important matters; thirdly (and most important), its revolutionary action in demanding an oath from its delegates. In this last point the purely democratic idea on the one hand, and the senatorial theories of the Moderates on the other, came face to face, and on that point the issue turned. On the 2nd of November the district replied by a resolution denying the right of the elected to control the electors, and especially condemning the interference of the Hotel de Ville with debates in the districts. On the 12th, ten days later, they came out into the open with a resolution that was like a declaration of war against Bailly and Lafayette; they drew up a form of oath which their five deputies were to swear, and this oath bound the members of the district not only to obey the district in all its resolutions, but also to admit that they could be dismissed after being called upon three times to resign by a majority of the district. It was the full doctrine of delegacy and of the corporate will.

Only two of the five members took the oath, the rest resigned and were promptly replaced by others, and these presented themselves at the Hotel de Ville on November 16th. Condorcet was President of the municipal body, and practically everybody there was furious against the Cordeliers. They demanded a recital of the causes which had led to the dismissal of the three members, and then they insisted on hearing the terms of the famous oath that bound the five deputies. Of the two who had consented to take the oath in the first instance, one (Peyrilhe) muttered excuses, but the other (Croharé), who seems to have been more of a true Cordelier, was very proud of the position he held, and would have explained the true doctrine at great length, had not the meeting cut him short by a vigorous vote, declaring all such oaths inadmissible, sending away the three new members, and recalling those who had resigned. On the next day the municipality broke the law. It turned Croharé out, but by a very small vote, in which many abstained.[61] Of course such an action was not to be tolerated, for it would have made the majority of the municipality able to end all opposition or debate, and the mistake of Condorcet was Danton's opportunity.

Every character he possesses is apparent in the struggle that follows. He carries it on with something of the diplomacy that later was matched against all Europe: he secures his allies and isolates his enemies: he pleads to convince and to obtain official support, not (as do so many of his contemporaries) in order to follow a line of thought. In a word, he is *habile*, and practically he succeeds.

Observe the quality of this action. When the district meets on the 17th (while the Commune was dismissing Croharé), Danton sees the importance of keeping its debate in bounds. That gathering, which is so enamoured of abstract rights, is suddenly bound down by the superior ability of its chairman: the discussion is made to follow points of legal technicality, and Danton imposes upon the Cordeliers so strict a discipline for one day, that two points alone emerge from the speeches, and they are precisely the two which could be used as arguments. (1.) That the Commune was *provisional*, and its *raison d'être* was the formation of a new municipal system: in such cases (say the Cordeliers) the subjects of the experiment must remain masters, and it would be absurd to take away the power of control, that later would have to be readmitted when the new municipal constitution should be sent to the districts for acceptance or rejection: in a word, they argued on the *vice de raisonnement*—the want of logic—in the Commune's action. (2.) They appealed to the Assembly—that is, they recognised and submitted to the centre of national power.[62] The Assembly was in a dilemma. It was in full sympathy with the Moderates with Bailly and with Lafayette; on the other hand, it could not, without a great loss of prestige, deny the very principles upon which its own power rested. Their committee on the subject desired a complete admission of the Cordeliers' claim; the Assembly rejected this, and tried to compromise by saying that both parties should go back to "the state of things of November 10th"—that is, to the state of things before the oath and before the whole trouble. The compromise would not hold. The deputies thus legally reinstated all resigned (except Croharé) on account of the feeling in their district, and the Cordeliers then, with full legality, re-elected their popular champions of the *Mandat Imperatif*.

The Commune took its defeat ill. They tried to prove that the old members had not really resigned. They sent a committee to interview them, but the committee came back with proof that the resignation was voluntary, and finally, on November 28, the little company of democrats were sworn in to a very ungracious and unwilling Assembly, and Danton had won.

My readers must excuse so detailed an account of an event which is empty of picturesque detail and which is so small a part of that fertile winter. From the point of view of general history it is the first appearance of the *Mandat Imperatif* in action; and from the point of view of Danton's rôle in the Revolution it is of the utmost importance, though it is so insignificant a catalogue of quarrels. It was Danton's first victory, and it was decisive. It put a wedge, as it were, into the gate that he was forcing open by persistent effort; and though his final position in the administration of Paris is won after many further failures, it is a direct consequence of this success in 1789. At the same time it showed that a young, loud-voiced lawyer of the middle class could have that one necessary quality of skill lying under the coarse exterior; he could play the game with the subtlety of appreciation which was so necessary in the terrible year of invasion, the keen aptitude of the mind which the visionaries were too unpractised, the demagogues too brutal to attain. That aptitude had appeared in Danton's pleading, and was to make him during the war a man necessary to France.

It was a month or six weeks after these events, on some date in January which we can only fix by indirect evidence, that Danton was himself elected to represent the district. The restless society had caused a further resignation, and five new members came to the Hotel de Ville.[63] He came unimportant, effaced, known merely as a demagogue, into that municipal assembly which contained the most dignified, the most learned, and the most representative of the noblesse and higher bourgeoisie, to sit under the frowns and endure the silence, and at first the contempt, of Condorcet, of D'Espagnac, of the academicians Laharpe and Suard, the astronomer De Cassini, Lavoisier, De Moreton-Chabrillant captain of the guard, Bailly and Lafayette themselves. And in the very first hours of his presence, before he had taken the oath, an incident occurred which clinched, as it were, the disfavour in which he was regarded, and which for a year put him in the background of a council which he was destined ultimately to master. I refer to what is known as the incident of Marat.

Marat was more of a gentleman than Danton; it is also fair to say that he was nearly mad. No two men could have been more different than the learned, irritable, visionary physician and the young, healthy country lawyer who was for a moment his champion. The one has met continually the ruling class, and has suffered from its insolence and privilege; the other has known professional friends indeed of the first rank, but has passed his life with the trading middle class, and has entered perhaps during all his career in Paris not one salon, nor met perhaps one of the brilliant women of his time.

Marat presented from the outset the first problem to be faced by a people who are testing liberty. He was a journalist and pamphleteer of unbridled license, one of those who cannot find in themselves that control which, when it is absent in public writers, can only be supplanted by the cumbersome, dangerous, and necessary machinery of the Censor. Not for money, of course, nor for any unworthy motive, but for the excellent end of attaining freedom, this morbid mind poured out the wildest, the most sensational, and the most dangerous appeals.

Now the courts were in process of transition; rapidly as the reform had marched since the summer, much of the old judicial procedure necessarily remained, and among the rest a body known as the Châtelet, whose removal was already planned, but which had to be maintained until the new system could be put in working order. It was very typical of the old regime. A body of privileged lawyers, many of them young and ignorant, holding their places by inheritance or purchase, and charged with what we may call the police of the capital. They had formerly possessed (and it had not yet been abolished in detail) the power of arbitrary arrest. They drew their name from the heavy fortress which had once defended the Pont au Change when Paris was confined to the island of the Cité; some of its walls dated at latest from the Norman siege of the tenth century, and beneath it were cellars which had for centuries been the prisons of those arrested in Paris by the city guard. It stood gloomy and strong on the site of the modern place that bears its name, dominating the close streets of the Boucherie, and possessing in its associations and its waning power all the qualities that had made the Bastille odious to the people. It may be imagined how the jurisdiction which it contained was bound to attract the chief efforts of the reformers; it could not, however, cease to exercise its functions until there was some more liberal institution to supply its place, and it came of necessity into violent collision with that spirit which was determined to break down by force what the resolutions of the Assembly had abolished in theory, but had not yet supplanted in fact.

The principal object of Marat's tirades was the moderate town council, and especially Bailly. Moreover, the worthy astronomer was an admirable butt. He assumed a livery, and put a fine coat-of-arms on his carriage, and, while he weakly opposed the rising democracy of Paris, he was very strong in the matter of pomposity. Marat was called to the bar of the Commune to answer for these attacks upon the mayor on the 28th of September. A warrant for his arrest was made out by the Châtelet on the 6th of October, but the day was too critical for an action of police against an individual. On the 8th another warrant was sent out, and Marat fled to a hiding-place up on Montmartre, from which, like a mad prophet on a hill-top, he pamphleteered the city at his feet. His quarrels, therefore (though very different in kind) were contemporaneous with the important struggle between the Cordeliers and the Municipality which are detailed above. The two attacks began to merge in December.

Marat, on the 12th of that month, was hunted out of his retreat, and brought before a lower court, but so confused were the powers of the Châtelet in this period of its reform and extinction that the prosecution was dropped. Emboldened by this failure on the part of his opponents, he came to live and print his sheet openly in the Rue des Fossés St. Germains—that is, in the midst of the district of the Cordeliers. What followed is well known. At a moment when the struggle between the district and the Hotel de Ville is at its height, just after the scene in which Danton's deputation had protested against the mayor's commission to the militia officers, while the insulting irony of the term "my lord" was still ringing in Bailly's ears, and when Danton himself had been actually elected for the district, and was present in the Municipality on the point of taking the oath—when all these causes of quarrel were, so to speak, met in one date, the Moderates determined to strike. Marat was pouring out his impossible diatribes from the territory of the rebellious district, and no opportunity could be more favourable. The Châtelet issued once more the warrant for his arrest, and this time it was supported by Lafayette, who promised to lend four thousand of the National Guard.

Now note the importance of what follows. Neither side in the struggle of the autumn had definitely won. The National Assembly had temporised, the advantage of the Cordeliers in the matter of the disputed elections had been achieved by a trick, and in the dead-lock between two principles, the central power of the Municipality and the local autonomy of the district, neither of the two theories was based upon tradition, neither even (in the confusion of rapid reforms) could justify itself by a definite pronouncement of the law. On the one side was the theory of a highly restricted suffrage, government by a class socially refined and lying with the nobility rather than with the people; this side was determined to form an army to support their politics, and it was they who, when they did act at last, achieved—but much too late—the sharp and sanguinary reaction of July 1791. On the other side was the desire for a wide, later for a universal, suffrage; a determination to emphasise in the development of the Revolutionary theory, equality and the general will, rather than order and the practical working of new laws; a political attitude which was to lead the Revolution into the intense idealism of 1792, and to end by declaring the Republic. And all this was represented in the demand which, of its nature, is the expression of extreme democracy—I mean the demand for local autonomy, the idea that an act of government is most just when it emanates not even from representatives, but from the lips of the governed themselves.

Such were the two forces opposed to one another in the affair of Marat—forces which, if not in all France, were in Paris at least the two great camps of the Revolution. Already the district had declared its intention to protect the liberty of the press within its boundaries,[64] and had been wise enough to specially condemn Marat's violence; already had it named a committee of five to see that no arbitrary arrest should take place in its territory,[65] when Lafayette sent his militia, cavalry and infantry, on the 22nd of January to help the arrest of Marat. Not content with the 3000 men thus employed, he clinched the matter with cannon, placing a couple of pieces at the end of the Rue des Fossés St. Germains.[66] He was determined to settle things by force, and beat the extremists with their own weapons. His effort did not find force opposed to it, as he had hoped; it broke itself in the most unexpected manner upon the legal ability of Danton.

The district might have raised, all told, 1500 men, and it possessed two pieces of artillery; but Danton was far too wise to use them in such a cause as that of defending Marat. A street fight, and one in which the Cordeliers would have been infallibly beaten, would have ruined the future chances of their politics. He armed no one, and did not add a single man to the small guard which each district kept permanently drilled, but he assigned them as their guard-room for the week the ground-floor of Marat's house. Then he went there himself with his four companions on the newly elected committee, and awaited developments.

The great body of the National Guard were massed in their blue and white at the end of the street, their two pieces sweeping it, and there was opposed to them nothing but a small crowd and few arguments. Through their ranks, and accompanied by a small detachment, came the two officers or policemen of the Châtelet.[67] They presented their writ, and Plainville, the commander of the little detachment that accompanied them, asked to be allowed to place sentries at the door. The commissioners gave them leave with the greatest pleasure in the world, but when the officers presented their warrant, the opportunity which Danton had been waiting for with some anxiety presented itself. With a slovenliness that was part and parcel of the old regime, the Châtelet had not made out a new warrant, but had issued the old one which had done duty on the 8th of October.

Now, since that date the Assembly had passed several important changes in the criminal law, notably one in the same month October which declared that "no warrant for arrest can be issued against a householder save in case of those charges which, if proved, would lead to imprisonment."[68] A very obvious principle; but in France of the old regime to seize a man, hold him, and even to let him go without trial, merely for some purpose of the police, was permitted, and the Châtelet may have acted upon this tradition. Add to this the fact that the Assembly had created elective councils in each district to watch the interest of every inhabitant arrested in criminal cases,[69] and it is easily apparent that the Châtelet had committed a great blunder, the value of which a man trained in the courts and quick to seize an error in procedure immediately recognised.

Danton affirmed that the writ was illegal, offered to prove it, and led the officers of the Châtelet to the hall of the district. There he had the new procedure read to them, compared it with the date of their warrant, and so confused the minds of those simple men that they signed a *procès-verbal* which declared that, after hearing such reasons, they doubted how they should act. They came back escorted by Fabre d'Eglantine through an angry crowd, and were received by the officers of the National Guard with some heat. They stood firm, however, and refused to pursue the arrest until they could consult with those who sent them, and finally the difficulty was removed by Danton's promising to appeal to the National Assembly and to abide by its decision. The terms were accepted, the sentries left Marat's door, and the troops withdrew.

All this debate and turmoil had taken up the morning and the luncheon-hour, the Rue des Fossés St. Germains was evacuated in the early afternoon, and by four o'clock of that day, 22nd of January 1790, Danton and his companions were pleading their cause at the bar of the House. It was the old policy of resorting to the National Assembly as the last place of appeal, and of using this principal result of the Revolutionary movement as a weapon against the Parisian Moderates. The Assembly found itself in the old dilemma, and adopted the old compromise. By its theory it was democratic; all its phrases and many of its decrees were based on the "Contrat Social," but by its personnel and its connections it was naturally allied to the high professional class, to the Baillys and the Lafayettes. It instructed Target (the President of the fortnight) to write to the district; he condemned the attitude of the Cordeliers, but Parliament "relied upon their patriotism to execute the will of the Assembly." The district, true to its policy, at once submitted. They sent Legendre and Testulat to tell the commander of the forces (who had re-entered the Rue des Fossés) that they had no longer the right to prevent the arrest; whereupon he sent in the police and awaited Marat in the street below. The house was empty, and Marat was on his way to England, a country with which he was not unfamiliar, and the vices of whose constitution had already furnished a theme for his too facile pen.

Such are the details of the story of the famous Friday in the district of the Cordeliers, events which put Danton's name into some prominence, but which also showed him to the most educated of his time, and therefore to posterity, in something of a false light. He appears as the friend of Marat, a man for whom he felt no sympathy, to whom he was immeasurably superior, and whom he had supported only because Marat's quarrel was a tactical opportunity against the Moderates. To have been from the outset admitted by the cultured would have been difficult to him—it would have needed tact, self-effacement, and silence. For he showed by nature just those rough gestures and loud, ill-chosen phrases which should be the sign of a foolish and dangerous man; of what underlay it, of his learning, his patriotism, and his common-sense he was to give plenty of proof; but so violent were the prejudices he had raised that only great length of time has effaced the false impression of his first appearance on the scene of politics. *We* can see the statesman clearly, but his contemporaries never quite pierced the medium that had gathered round him; here and there a just and noble man, as was Condorcet, would admit his own misconception, but to the bulk of the gentlemen in power he was and remained the demagogue.

Two years of careful action fail to clear him, because, being already one of those whose superficial qualities repel the close attention necessary to a just opinion, he had also the misfortune to enter the arena from the wrong door. Those who were most with him adored him, the great bulk of his district-voters signed a fervent declaration in his favour, and later his immediate friends are willing to die with him. But the class with which at heart he had most in common held aloof; he had succeeded twice in a pitched battle with them; they apologise for his acquaintance, vilify him in their letters, and if his name has emerged from all this error, if he has been given his statue in a time of social order and reconstruction, it is because this man, who never wrote, who left only a confused legend of his personality, saved his country when it was at war with the whole world, and such actions compel history to inquiry and restitution.

On the 23rd, the day after the trouble, he was sworn in to the reluctant Commune, and there follow two long years[70] of patient attempt to gain the place for which he feels himself fitted, but years (on the whole) of disappointment, and in which his real position in Paris (I mean the prominence he held in the thoughts of men) contrasts curiously with the little part he played.

1790 contains so great a portion of the Revolution, and sows the seed of so much future division and civil war, that it seems ridiculous to confine oneself to the description of the restricted action of one man who had not yet even attained power. It will be necessary, however, to make a survey of this restricted action in order that we may comprehend the greater rôle of Danton in the two years that follow.

Danton came, then, with Legendre and the three others into a city Council very much opposed to him and to the district whose spirit he had formed. He was not often heard, and there is no doubt that he deliberately tried to purchase by silence the more just and equable judgment of such men as he respected, but who knew him only by unfavourable report. For the bulk of the Assembly he cannot but have felt contempt; they had no instinct of the revolutionary tide; even when they were attempting to check the movement that Danton represented, they were inefficient and unworthy opponents, from whom his eye must have wandered inwards to the great battles that were preparing.

In the eight months during which he was a member of the Provisional Commune, that is, from January to September 1790, his name appears in the debates but a dozen times.[71] More than half of these are mention of committees upon which his common-sense and legal training were of service; in one only, that of February 4, does he speak on a motion, and that is in support of Barré to admit the public when the oath was taken: one other (that on the 19th of March concerning the formation of a "grand jury") would be interesting were it not that the whole gist of the debate was but a repetition of the much more significant discussion at the Cordeliers. Finally, there is one little notice which is half-pathetic and half-grotesque: he is one of the committee of twenty-four charged with the duty of "presenting their humble thanks, with the mayor at their head," to the King for giving the municipality a marble bust of himself. But every entry is petty and unimportant: Danton at the Provisional Municipality of 1790 is deliberately silent—he can do nothing.

If we turn, however, to a field in which he was more at home, we find him during that year more than ever the leader of the Cordeliers, which itself becomes more than ever the leader of Paris.

There are two important features in the part he plays at the assemblies of the district during the spring and summer in which he was a silent member of the Commune. First, the affair of his arrest; secondly, his campaign against what may be called "the municipal reaction."

As to the first, it is a very minor point in the general history of the Revolution, but it is of considerable influence upon the career of Danton himself. When the affair of Marat was (or should have been) forgotten, the Châtelet, with that negligence which we have seen them display in the business of the warrant for Marat's arrest, saw fit to launch another warrant, this time for the arrest of Danton himself. Once more that unpopular and moribund tribunal put itself on the wrong side of the law, and once more it chose the most inopportune moment for its action. It was on the 17th of

March,[72] nearly two months after the affair—two months during which Danton had been hard at work effacing its effects upon his reputation—that the warrant was issued, and the motive of arrest given in the parchment was of the least justifiable kind. In the district meeting of the day, when the police officers had been taken to the hall of the Cordeliers, and had had the changes in the law read out to them, Danton had made use of a violent phrase: its actual words were not known; some said that he had threatened to "call out the Faubourg St. Antoine, and make the jaws of the guard grow white." Other witnesses refused to attribute those words to him, but accused him of saying, "If every one thought as I do, we should have twenty thousand men at our back;" his friends admitted that some angry and injudicious speech, such as he was often guilty of, had escaped him, but they affirmed that he had added, "God forbid that such a thing should happen; the cause is too good to be so jeopardised."

Whatever he said (and probably he himself could not accurately have remembered), the place and the time were privileged. It was a test case, but the logic of such a privilege was evident. Here you have deliberative assemblies to which are intrusted ultimately the formation of a government for Paris: what is said in such a constituent meeting, however ill-advised, must in the nature of things be allowed to pass; if not, you limit the discussion of the primary, and if you limit that discussion you vitiate the whole theory upon which the new constitution was being framed. It must be carefully remembered that we are not dealing with deliberative bodies long established, possessed of the central power, and holding privilege by tradition and by their importance in the State; we are dealing with the elementary deliberative assemblies in a period which, rightly or wrongly, was transforming the whole State upon one perfectly definite political theory—namely, that these primary assemblies were the only root and just source of power. When, therefore, Parisian opinion rose violently in favour of the president of a district so attacked, when three hundred voters out of five signed a petition in Danton's favour, when he was re-elected president of the district twelve days after the issue of the warrant, it was because the whole body of the electors felt a great and justifiable fear of what was left of the old regime. The Châtelet had acted so, not from a careful appreciation of public danger—to fend off which temporary powers had been given it— but because it was blind with old age; because it dated from a time and was composed of a set of men who hated all deliberative assemblies, and it was justly thought that if such actions were justified, the whole system of revolutionary Paris was in danger.

As though in proof of the false view that the Châtelet took of their man, on the 19th of March, two days after the warrant was issued, Danton was urging the replacement of the Châtelet by a Grand Jury; he had an admiration and a knowledge of the old English system, and it was against a man attempting so wise a reform that the last relic of the old jurisprudence was making an attack.

An appeal was lodged with the National Assembly, and Anthoine read a long report to the Assembly upon May 18. This report was strongly in favour of Danton. It was drawn up by a special committee—not partisan in any way—and after examining all the evidence it came to this conclusion against the Châtelet. Nevertheless the House, a great body of nearly a thousand men, to most of whom the name of Danton meant only a loud Radical voice, hesitated. To adopt the report might have irretrievably weakened the Châtelet, and the National Assembly was extremely nervous on the subject of order in Paris. It ended by an adjournment. The report remained in Danton's favour; he was not arrested, but the affair was unfortunate for him, and threw him back later at a very important occasion, when he might have entered into power peaceably himself and at a peaceable time.

But while this business was drawing to its close, during the very months of April and May which saw his partial vindication, another and a far more momentous business was occupying the Cordeliers—a matter in which they directed all their energy towards a legal solution, but in which, unfortunately for the city, they failed.

Ever since the days of October—earlier if you will—there had been arising a strong sentiment, to which I have alluded more than once, and which, for lack of a better name, may be called the Moderate reaction in Paris. It is difficult to characterise this complex body of thought in one adjective, and I cannot lengthen a chapter already too prolonged by a detailed examination of its origin and development. Suffice it to say that from the higher bourgeoisie (generally speaking), from those who were in theory almost Republican, but whose lives were passed in the artificial surroundings of wealth, and finally from the important group of the financiers, who of all men most desired practical reform, and who of all men most hated ideals; from these three, supported by many a small shopkeeper or bureaucrat, came a demand, growing in vigour, for a conservative municipal establishment—one that should be limited in its basis, almost aristocratic in quality, and concerned very much with the maintenance of law and order and very little with the idea of municipal self-government.

It is a character to be noted in the French people, this timidity of the small proprietor and his reliance upon constituted authority. It is a matter rarely observed, and yet explaining all Parisian history, that this sentiment does not mark off a particular body of men, but, curiously enough, is found in the mind of nearly every Frenchman, existing side by side with another set of feelings which, on occasion, can make them the most arrant idealists in the world.

For the moment this intense desire for order was uppermost in the minds of those few who were permitted to vote. In the Cordeliers it was the other character of the Parisian that was emphasised and developed. They were determined on democracy, like everybody else; but, unlike the rest, they were not afraid of the dangerous road. They were inspired and led by a man whose one great fault was a passionate contempt of danger. On this account, though they are taxpayers and bourgeois, lawyers, physicians, men of letters and the like, they do all they can to prevent the new municipal system from coming into play, but they fail.

Now, consider the Assembly. That great body was justly afraid of Paris; indeed, the man who was head and shoulders above them all—Mirabeau—was for leaving Paris altogether. The Assembly, again, had the whole task of re-making France in its hands, and it could not but will that Paris, in the midst of which it sat, should be muzzled. Through all the debates of the Provisional Commune it could easily be seen that Bailly and Lafayette were winning, and that the Parliament would be even more Moderate than they. Three points were the centres of the battle: first, the restricted suffrage which was to be established;[73] secondly, the power which was to be exercised over the new Commune by the authorities of the Department; thirdly, the suppression of those sixty democratic clubs, the districts, and their replacement by forty-eight sections, so framed as specially to break up the ties of neighbourhood and association, which the first of the Revolution had developed. It was aimed especially at the Cordeliers.

Against the first point the Cordeliers had little to say. Oddly enough, the idea of universal suffrage, which is so intimate a part of our ideas on the Revolution, was hardly thought of in early 1790. Against the second they debated, but did not decree; it was upon the third that they took most vigorous action. The law which authorised the new municipal scheme was passed on May the 27th, and, faithful to their policy, the Cordeliers did not attempt to quarrel with the National Assembly, but they fought bitterly against the application of the law by Bailly and his party. The law was signed by the King on June the 27th, and on the same day the mayor placarded the walls, ordering an immediate installation of the new system. The 27th was a Saturday. Within a week the new sections were to be organised, and on the Monday, July 5, the voting was to begin. The very next day, the 28th, the Cordeliers protested in a vigorous decree, in which they called on the fifty-nine other districts to petition the National Assembly to make a special exception of the town of Paris, to consider the great federation of July 14, which should be allowed to pass before the elections, and finally to give the city time to discuss so important a change. All through the week, on the 1st, 2nd, and 3rd of July, they published vigorous appeals. They were partially successful, but in their main object—the reconstruction of the aristocratic scheme and the arousing of public spirit against it—they entirely failed. Bailly is elected mayor on August 2 by an enormous majority—practically 90 per cent. The old districts disappear, and, like every other, the famous Cordeliers are merged in the larger section of the Théâtre Français. It may not sit in permanence; it may not (save on a special demand of fifty citizens) meet at all; it is merely an electoral unit, and in future some 14,000 men out of a city of nearly a million are to govern all. The local club, directing its armed force and appealing to its fellows, is abolished. Danton then has failed.

But, as we shall see later, the exception became the rule. No mechanical device could check the Revolution. The demand for permanent sections is continuous and successful. From these divisions, intended to be mere marks upon a map, come the cannon of the 10th of August, and it is the section of the Théâtre Français, wherein the traditions and the very name of the Cordeliers were to have been forgotten, that first in Europe declared and exercised the right of the whole people to govern.

If I may repeat a common-place that I have used continually in this book, the tide of the Revolution in Paris was dammed up with a high barrier; its rise could not be checked, and it was certain to escape at last with the force and destructive energy of a flood.

CHAPTER IV
THE FALL OF THE MONARCHY

I have taken as a turning-point in the career of Danton the municipal change which marks the summer of 1790, concluding with that event the first chapter of his political action, and making it the beginning of a new phase. Let me explain the reasons that have led me to make such a division at a moment that is marked by no striking passage of arms, of policy, or of debate.

In the first place, a recital of Danton's life must of necessity follow the fortunes of the capital. The spirit of the people whose tribune he was (their growing enthusiasms and later their angers)—that spirit is the chief thing to guide us in the interpretation of his politics, but the mechanical transformations of the city government form the framework, as it were, upon which the stuff of Parisian feeling is woven. The detail is dry and often neglected; the mere passing of a particular law giving Paris a particular constitution, a system not unexpected, and apparently well suited to the first year of the Revolution, may seem an event of but little moment in the development of the reform; but certain aspects of the period lend that detail a very considerable importance. In the rapid transformation which was remoulding French society, the law, however new, possessed a strength which, at this hour, we can appreciate only with difficulty. In a settled and traditional society custom is of such overwhelming weight that a law can act only in accordance with it; a sudden change in the machinery of government would break down of itself—nay, in such a society laws can hardly be passed save those that the development of tradition demands. But in a time of revolution this postulate of social history fails. When a whole people starts out to make fresh conditions for itself, every decree becomes an origin; the forces that in more regular periods mould and control legislative action are, in a time of feverish reconstruction, increased in power and give an impetus to new institutions; the energy of society, which in years of content and order controls by an unseen pressure, is used in years of revolution to launch, openly and mechanically, the fabric that a new theory has designed. Thus you may observe how in the framing of the American constitution every point in a particular debate became of vast moment to the United

States; thus in our time the German Empire has found its strength in a set of arbitrary decrees, all the creation of a decade; thus in the Middle Ages the Hildebrandine reform framed in the life of one man institutions which are vigorous after the lapse of eight hundred years; and thus in the French Revolution a municipal organisation, new, theoretic, and mechanical, was strong enough, not indeed to survive so terrible a storm, but to give to the whole movement a permanent change of direction.

This, then, is the transitional character of the summer of 1790, as regards the particular life of Danton and the particular city of Paris. What the Cordeliers had fought so hard to obtain as a constitutional reform had failed. The direct action of the districts upon the municipality was apparently lost for ever, and the centre of the new system was in future to be controlled in the expression of ideas and paralysed in its action. What the Cordeliers had represented in spirit, though they had not formulated it in decrees—government by the whole people—was apparently equally lost. The law of December (that which established the "active and passive citizens") was working for Paris as for all France; and though a suffrage which admitted two-thirds of the male population to the polls could not be called restrictive, yet the exception of men working for wages under their master's roof, the necessity of a year's residence, and the qualification of tax-paying did produce a very narrow oligarchy in a town like Paris: the artisans were excluded, and thousands of those governed fell just beyond the limits which defined the municipal voter. Danton may receive the provincial delegates, may make his speeches at the feast in the Bois de Boulogne; but once the organ of government has been closed to his ideas, the road towards the democracy lies through illegality and revolt.

Now there is another and a wider importance in this anniversary of the fall of the Bastille. It is the point at which we can best halt and survey the beginning of the heat which turned the Revolution from a domestic reform of the French nation to a fire capable of changing the nature of all our civilisation. I do not mean that you will find those quarrels in the moment; in 1790 there is nothing of the spirit that overturned the monarchy nor of the visions that inspired the Gironde; you cannot even fairly say that there are general threats or mutterings of war, although the Assembly saw fit to disclaim them: it is a year before the fear of such dangers arises. But there is in this summer something to be discovered, namely, an explanation of why two periods differing so profoundly in character meet so suddenly and with such sharp contrast at one point in the history of the movement; it is from the summer of 1790 and onwards that the laws are passed, the divisions initiated, which finally alienate the King, from that lead to his treason, from that rouse Europe, and from the consequent invasion produce the Terror, the armies, and the Empire. The mind needs a link between two such different things as reform and violence, and because that link is not supplied in the mere declaration of war or in the mere flight to Varennes, men commit the error of reading the spirit of the Republic into the days of Mirabeau, or even of seeing temperate politics in the apostolic frenzy of '93. Some, more ignorant or less gifted than the general reader, explain it by postulating in the character of the French nation quaint aberrations which may be proper to the individual, but which never have nor can exist in any community of human beings.

Let me recapitulate and define the problem which, as it seems to me, can be solved by making a pivot of the anniversary of the States-General.

There are, then, in the story of the Revolution these two phases, so distinct that their recognition is the foundation of all just views upon the period. In the first, the leaders of the nation are bent upon practical reforms; the monarchy is a machine to hand for their accomplishment; the sketch of a new France is drawn, the outlines even begin to be filled by trained and masterly hands. Phrases will be found abundantly in those thirty months, because phrases are the christening of ideas, and no nation of Roman training could attempt any work without clear definitions to guide it. But these phrases, though often abstract in the extreme, are never violent, and the oratory itself of the National Assembly is rarely found to pass the limits which separate the art of persuasion from the mere practice of defiance.

In the second phase, for which the name of the Convention often stands, those subterranean fires which the crust of tradition and the stratified rock of society had formerly repressed break out in irresistible eruption. The creative work of the revolutionary idea realises itself in a casting of molten metal rather than in a forging, and the mould it uses is designed upon a conception of statuary rather than of architecture. The majestic idol of the Republic, in whose worship the nation has since discovered all its glories and all its misfortunes, is set up by those artists of the ideal; but they forget, or perhaps ignore, the terrible penalties that attach to superhuman attempts, the reactions of an exclusive idealism.

What made the second out of the first? What made a France which had discussed Sieyès listen to St. Just or even to Hébert? The answer to this question is to be discovered in noting the fatal seeds that were sown in this summer of 1790, and which in two years bore the fruit of civil war and invasion.

In the first place, that summer creates, as we have seen, a discontented Paris—a capital whose vast majority it refuses to train in the art of self-government, and whose general voice it refuses to hear.

In the second place, it is the moment when the discontent in the army comes to a head. The open threat of military reaction on the side of a number of the officers, their intense animosity against the decrees abolishing titles, their growing disgust at the privileges accorded to the private soldiers—all these come face to face with non-commissioned officers and privates who are full of the new liberties. These lower ranks contained the ambitious men whose ability, the honest and loyal men whose earnestness, were to carry French arms to the successes of the Revolutionary wars.

In the third place, it is the consummation of the blunder that attempted to create an established National Church in France. Before this last misfortune a hundred other details of these months that were so many mothers of discord become insignificant. Civil war first muttering in the South, counter-revolution drilling in Savoy, the clerical petition of Nîmes, the question of the Alsatian estates, the Parisian journals postulating extreme democracy, the Jacobins appearing as an organised and propagandist body, the prophetic cry of Lameth—all these things were but incidents that would have been forgotten but for the major cause of tumult, which is to be discovered in the civil constitution of the clergy.

Of course, the kings would have attacked, but they were divided, and had not even a common motive. Of course, also, freedom, in whatever form it came, would have worked in the moribund body of Europe like a drug, and till its effect was produced would have been thought a poison. But against the hatred of every oppressor would have been opposed a disciplined and a united people, sober by instinct, traditionally slow in the formation of judgments, traditionally tenacious of an opinion when once it had been acquired. It would have been sufficient glory for the French people to have broken the insolence of the aggressors, to have had upon their lists the names of Marceau and of Hoche.

But with the false step that produced civil war, that made of the ardent and liberal West a sudden opponent, that in its final effect raised Lyons and alienated half the southern towns, that lost Toulon, that put the extreme of fanaticism in the wisest and most loyal minds—such a generous and easy war was doomed, and the Revolution was destined to a more tragic and to a nobler history. God, who permitted this proud folly to proceed from a pedantic aristocracy, foresaw things necessary to mankind. In the despair of the philosophers there will arise on either side of a great battle the enthusiasms which, from whencever they blow, are the fresh winds of the soul. Here are coming the heroes and the epic songs for which humanity was sick, and the scenes of one generation of men shall give us in Europe our creeds for centuries. You shall hear the "Chant du Départ" like a great hymn in the army of the Sambre et Meuse, and the cheers of men going down on the *Vengeur*; the voice of a young man calling the grenadiers at Lodi and Arcola; the noise of the guard swinging up the frozen hill at Austerlitz. Already the forests below the Pyrenees are full of the Spanish guerillas, and after how many hundred years the love of the tribe has reappeared again above the conventions that covered it. There are the three colours standing against the trees in the North and the South; and the delicate womanly face of Nelson is looking over the bulwarks of the *Victory*, with the slow white clouds and the light wind of an October day above him, and before him the enemy's sails in the sunlight and the black rocks of the coast.

It may be well, at the expense of some digression, to say why the laws affecting the clergy should be treated as being of paramount historical importance. They ruined the position of the King; they put before a very large portion of the nation not one, but two ideals; and what regular formation can grow round two dissimilar nuclei? Finally—a thing that we can now see clearly, though then the wisest failed to grasp it—they went against the grain of the nation.

It is a common accusation that the Revolution committed the capital sin of being unhistorical. Taine's work is a long anathema pronounced against men who dared to deny the dogmas of evolution before those dogmas were formulated. Such a criticism is erroneous and vain; in the mouths of many it is hypocritical. The great bulk of what the Revolution did was set directly with the current of time. For example: The re-unison of Gaul had been coming of itself for a thousand years—the Revolution achieved it; the peasant was virtually master of his land—it made him so in law and fact; Europe had been trained for centuries in the Roman law—it was precisely the Roman law that triumphed in the great reform, and most of its results, all of its phraseology, is drawn from the civil code. But in this one feature of the constitution of the clergy it sinned against the nature of France. Of necessity the Parliament was formed of educated men, steeped in the philosophy of the time, and of necessity it worked under the eyes of a great city population. In other words, the statesmen who bungled in this matter and the artisans who formed their immediate surroundings were drawn from the two classes which had most suffered from the faults of the hierarchy in France.

Mirabeau, for example, has passed his life in the rank where rich abbés made excellent blasphemy; the artisan of Paris has passed his life unprotected and unsolicited by the priests, whose chief duty is the maintenance of human dignity in the poor. Add to this the Jansenist legend of which Camus was so forcible a relic, and the Anglo-mania which drew the best intellects into the worst experiments, and the curious project is inevitable.

In these first essays of European democracy there was, as all the world knows, a passion for election. In vain had Rousseau pointed out the fundamental fallacy of representation in any scheme of self-government. The example of America was before them; the vicious temptation of the obvious misled them; and until the hard lessons of the war had taught them the truth, representation for its own sake, like a kind of game, seems to have been an obsession of the upper class in France. They admitted it into the organisation of the Church.

Now let us look in its detail at this attempt to make of the Catholic Church in the eighteenth century a mixture of the administration of Constantine, of the presbyteries of first centuries, and of the "branch of the civil service" which has suited so well a civilisation so different from that of France.

The great feature of this reform was the attempt to subject the whole clerical organisation to the State. I do not mean, of course, the establishment of dogmas by civil discussion, nor the interference with internal discipline; but the hierarchy was to be elected, from the parish priest to the bishop; the new dioceses were to correspond to the new Departments, and, most important of all, their confirmation was not to be demanded from the Pope, but "letters of communion" were to be sent to the Head of the Church, giving him notice of the election.

This scheme passed the House on July 12, 1790, two days before the great feast of the federation. A time whose intellect was alien to the Church, a class whose habits were un-Catholic, had attempted a reformation. Why was the attempt a blunder? Simply because it was unnecessary. There were certain ideas upon which the reconstruction of France was proceeding; they have been constantly alluded to in this book; they are what the French call "the principles of '89." Did they necessarily affect the Church? Yes; but logically carried out they would have affected the Church in a purely negative way. It was an obvious part of the new era to deny the *imperium in imperio*. The Revolution would have stultified itself had it left untouched the disabilities of Protestants and of Jews, had it continued to support the internal discipline of the Church by the civil power. It was logical when it said to the religious orders: "You are private societies; we will not compel your members to remain, neither will we compel them to leave their convents." (In the decree of February 13, 1790.) It would have been logical had it said to the Church: "It may be that you are the life of society; it may be that your effect is evil; we leave you free to prove your quality, for freedom of action and competition is our cardinal principle." But instead of leaving the Church free they amused themselves by building up a fantastic and mechanical structure, and then found that they were compelling religion to enter a prison. Nothing could be conceived more useless or more dangerous.

On the other hand, if this scheme as a whole was futile, there were some details that were necessary results of what the clergy themselves had done, and some which, if not strictly necessary, have at least survived the Revolution, and are vigorous institutions to-day. It might have been possible for Rome to seize on these as a basis of compromise, and it is conceivable, though hardly probable, that the final scheme might have left the Church a neutral in the coming wars. But if the councils of the Holy See were ill-advised, the Parliament was still less judicious; its extreme sensitiveness to interference from abroad was coupled with the extreme pedantry of a Lanjuinais, and the scheme in its entirety was forced upon Louis. He, almost the only pious man in a court which had so neglected religion as to hate the people, wrote in despair to the Pope; but before the answer came he had signed the law, and in that moment signed the warrant for his own death and that of thousands of other loyal and patriotic men.

While these future divisions were preparing, during the rest of the year 1790 Danton's position becomes more marked. We find a little less about him in the official records, for the simple reason that he has ceased to be a member of an official body, or rather (since the first Commune was not actually dissolved till September) he remains the less noticeable from the fact that the policy which he represented has been defeated; but his personality is making more impression upon Paris and upon his enemies. We shall find him using for the first time moderation, and for the first time meeting with systematic calumny. He acquires, though he is not yet of any especial prominence, the mark of future success, for he is beginning to be singled out as a special object of attack; and throughout the summer and autumn he practises more and more that habit of steering his course which up to the day of his death so marks him from the extremists.

The failure of his policy, the check which had been given to the Cordeliers, and the uselessness of their protests on the 1st, 2nd, and 3rd of July, had a marked effect upon the position of Danton even in his own district. He had been president when they were issued, and his friend D'Eglantine had been secretary. One may say that the policy of resistance was Danton's, and that but for his leadership it would have been unheard. Hence, when it has notoriously failed, that great mass of men who (when there is no party system) follow the event, lost their faith in him.

Bailly is not only elected by an enormous majority in all Paris[74] on the 2nd of August, but even Danton's own district, now become the Section of the Théâtre Français, abandoned his policy for the moment. In a poll of 580, 478 votes were given for Bailly.

In this moment of reverse he might with great ease have thrown himself upon all the forces that were for the moment irregular. The Federation of July had brought to Paris a crowd of deputies from the Departments, and to these provincials the good-humour and the comradeship of this Champenois had something attractive about it. In a Paris which bewildered them they found in him something that they could understand. In a meeting held by a section of them in the Bois de Boulogne it is Danton who is the leading figure. When the deputies of Marseilles ask for Chenier's "Charles IX.," it is Danton who gets it played for them at the Théâtre Français in spite of the opposition of the Court; and again it is Danton who is singled out during an *entr'acte* for personal attack by the loyalists, who had come to hiss the play.[75]

The unrepresented still followed him, and he still inspired a vague fear in the minds of men like Lafayette. Innocent of any violence, he stood (to those who saw him from a great distance) for insurrection. He was remembered as the defender of Marat, and Marat in turn annoyed him by repeated mention and praise in his ridiculous journal. Note also that the time was one in which the two camps were separating, though slowly, and the rôle of a demagogue would have been as tempting to a foolish man on the Radical, as the rôle of true knight was to so many foolish men on the Conservative side. Each part was easy to play, and each was futile.

Danton refused such a temptation. He, almost alone at that moment (with the exception, in a much higher sphere, of Mirabeau), was capable of being taught by defeat. He desired a solid foundation for action. Here were certain existing things: the club of the Cordeliers, which had for a while failed him; the Friends of the Constitution, which were a growing power; the limited suffrage of Paris, which he regretted, but which was the only legal force he could appeal to; the new municipal constitution, which he had bitterly opposed, but which was an accomplished fact. Now it is to all these realities that he turns his mind. He will re-capture his place in the Section, and make of the quarter of the Odéon a new République des Cordeliers. He will re-establish his position with Paris. He will attempt to enter, and perhaps later to control, this new municipality. It was for such an attitude that St. Just reproached him so bitterly in the act of accusation of April 1794, while at the moment he was adopting that attitude he was the mark of the most violent diatribe from the Conservatives. Nothing defines Danton at this moment so clearly as the fact that he alone of the popular party knew how to be practical and to make enemies.

The month of August may be taken as the time when Danton had to be most careful if he desired to preserve his place and to avoid a fall into violence and unreason. It was the 2nd of that month (as we have said) that saw Bailly's election, the 5th that gave Danton a personal shock, for on that date he received, for an office which he really coveted and for which he was a candidate, but 193 votes out of over 3000 present.

From that moment he devotes all his energy to reconstruction. The first evidence of his new attitude appears with the early days of September. Already the old meeting of the Cordeliers had been changed into the club, and already his influence was gaining ground again in the debates and in the local battalion of the National Guard, when the news of Nancy came to Paris.

A conflict between the National Guard and the people, an example of that with which Lafayette continually menaced Paris—the conflict of the armed bourgeoisie and the artisans, or rather of the militia used as a professional army against the people—this had happened at last. It was an occasion for raving. Marat raved loudly, and the royalists gave vent to not a little complacent raving on their side. In the great question whether the army was to be democratic or not, whether reaction was to possess its old disciplined arm, it would seem that reaction had won, and France had seen a little rehearsal of what in ten months was to produce the 17th of July.

In such conditions the attitude of the Cordeliers was of real importance. During all Lafayette's attempt to centralise the militia of Paris this battalion had remained independent; its attitude during the days of October, its defence of Marat in January, had proved this. The crisis appeared to demand from this revolutionary body a strong protest against the use of the militia as an army to be aimed against the people. Such a protest might have been the cause of an outbreak in Paris. Under these circumstances Danton—by what arguments we cannot tell (for the whole affair is only known to us by a few lines of Desmoulins)—obtained from his battalion a carefully-worded pronouncement. "For all the high opinion we have of the National Guards who took part in the affair of Nancy, we can express no other sentiment than regret for what has happened."[76] It was moderate to the degree of the common-place, but it saved Danton from the abyss and from the street.

There followed another check in which he showed once more his power of self-control. The "Notables"—corresponding something to the aldermen of our new municipal scheme in England—were to be elected for Paris a little after the elections for the mayor and for the governor of the Commune. Each Section was to elect three, and Danton had so far regained his influence at home as to be elected for the Théâtre Français.

Unfortunately the new constitution of Paris had been provided with one of those checks whose main object it is to interfere with direct representation. The choice of each Section was submitted to the censure or the approval of all the others. It is by the judgment which they pass that we can best judge the suspicion in which he was held by the great bulk of his equals. A regular campaign was led against him. The affair of Marat was dragged up, especially the warrant for Danton's arrest which the Châtelet had issued six months before. That very favourite device in electioneering, the doubt as to real candidature, was used. The voter, not over-well informed in a detail of law (especially at a time when all law was being re-modelled), was told that the warrant made Danton's candidature illegal. They said he was sold to Orleans, because he had haunted the Palais Royal and because he hated Lafayette. The character of demagogue—the one thing he desired to avoid—was pinned to his coat, and alone of all the Notables he was rejected by forty-three Sections (five only voting for him) in the week between the 9th and the 16th of September.[77]

In these five were the Postes, Invalides, Luxembourg. It was not the purely popular quarters that supported Danton, but rather the University and the lawyers.

He took his defeat as a signal for still greater reserve, letting his name take perspective, and refusing by any act or phrase to obscure his reputation with new issues. The tactics succeeded. When, in October, a public orator was needed, they remembered him, and he presents the deputation of the 10th of November. The circumstances were as follows:—

The ministry which surrounded the King was frankly reactionary. I do not mean that it was opposed to the constitution of the moment. Perhaps the majority (and the less important) of its members would have been loath to bring back anything approaching the old regime. But there were in the Revolution not only the facts but the tendencies, and in a period when every day brought its change, the tendencies were watched with an extreme care. France may have thought, seeing the federation on the Champ de Mars and the altar where Talleyrand had said mass, that the Revolution was at an end and the new state of affairs established in peace, but those in the capital knew better; and the men immediately surrounding the King, who saw the necessary consequences of his signing the civic constitution, and the growing breach between himself and the assembly—these men were on the King's side. The affair at Nancy, which had aroused so many passions, was the thing which finally roused Parisian opinion; and at the very moment when the King is secretly planning the flight to Montmédy—that flight which six months later failed—Paris is for the first time claiming to govern the councils of the kingdom.

It was the Sections that began the movement, those Sections whose action was to have been so restricted, and which, upon the contrary, were becoming the permanent organs of expression in the capital.

The Section Mauconseil on the 22nd of October sent in a petition for the dismissal of the cabinet and appealed to the National Assembly. The Section of the National Library followed suit three days later, and sent its petition not only to the Assembly but to the King. It must be remembered that the legend of a good king deceived by his advisers held at the time. Indeed, it survived the flight to Varennes; it partly survived the 10th of August, and only the research of recent times has proved clearly the continual intrigue of which the King was the head.

On the 27th Mauconseil came forward again with a petition to the mayor, Bailly, to call the general council of the Commune and consider the complaints. Fourteen other Sections backed this petition. Bailly hesitated, and while he temporised, all the forty-eight Sections named commissioners and sent them to an informal gathering at the Archbishopric.[78]

Danton was a member of this big committee and was made secretary. He drew up an address; the mayor was twice summoned to call the general council of the Commune. Hesitating and afraid, Bailly finally did so, and after a violent debate the resolution passed. Bailly was sent by the town to "present the Commune at the bar of the Assembly and demand the recall" of the Ministers of Justice, War, and the Interior—De Cicé, La Tour du Pin, and St. Priest.

Danton was taken out of the informal body to which he had acted as secretary, and asked to be the orator of the legal Commune. There followed on the 10th of November a very curious scene.

Bailly pitifully apologising with his eyes brought in the representative body of Paris. It was present for the first time in the National Parliament, and before three years were over Paris was to be the mistress of the Parliament. At present they were out of place; their demand frightened them. It needed Danton's voice to reassure them and to bring the opposing forces to a battle.

His voice, big, rough, and deep, perhaps with a slight provincial accent, helped to strengthen the false idea that the gentlemen of the Parliament had formed. This Danton, of whom they heard so much, had appeared suddenly out of his right place—for he had no official position—and the Right was furious.

Yet Danton's harangue was moderate and sensible. There is, indeed, one passage on the position of Paris in France which is interesting because it is original, but the bulk of the speech is a string of plain arguments. This passage is as follows:—

"That Commune, composed of citizens who belong in a fashion to the eighty-three Departments—(*The Right*, No! no!)—jealously desiring to fulfil in the name of all good citizens the duties of a sentinel to the constitution, is in haste to express a demand which is dear to all the enemies of tyranny—a demand which would be heard from all the Sections of the Empire, could they be united with the same promptitude as the Sections of Paris."[79]

For the rest, he is continually insisting upon the right of the Parliament to govern—the right, above all, of a representative body to dismiss a ministry. He had in this, as in certain other matters, a very English point of view, and certainly the arguments he used were able. But he was interrupted continually, and we get, even in the dry account of the *Moniteur*, a good picture of what the scene must have been like—

"A dismissal which the Assembly has the right to demand."

The Abbé Maury: "Who ever said that?" [Murmurs and discussion followed. The Abbé was called to order, when....]

M. Cazales remarked: "It is our duty to listen, even if they talk nonsense."

Danton began again with: "The Commune of Paris is better able to judge the conduct of ministers than...."

The Abbé Maury: "Why?" [He is again called to order.]

And so it went on. But in a duel of this kind lungs are the weapons, and Danton had the best lungs in the hall. He had also perhaps the soundest brain of any; but the Abbé Maury and his friends had chosen more rapid methods than those of arguments. The short address ended (it did not take a quarter of an hour to read), and the deputation left the Assembly. This last debated and refused the decree; yet the Commune had succeeded, for in a few days the Archbishop of Bordeaux left the Ministry of Justice, and La Tour du Pin, "who thought that parchment alone made nobility" (a phrase of Danton's which had upset the Right), left the Ministry of War.

The deputation had petitioned on Wednesday, the 10th of November. Four days later he was elected head of the militia battalion in which he had served for a year.[80] There is some doubt as to whether he remained long at this post. Some antagonists talk vaguely of his "leading his battalion" in '92, but never as eye-witnesses. On the other hand, there is a letter in existence talking of Danton's resignation; but it is unsigned and undated. Only some one has written in pencil, "Gouvion, 22nd November."[81]

At any rate, the interest of the little incident lies in the fact that it meant a meeting between Danton and Lafayette, and, as Freron remarks in his journal, "Cela serait curieux."[82] Perhaps they did not meet.

The campaign continually directed against Danton was as active in this matter as in all others. It gives one, for instance, an insight into the management and discipline of the guards to learn that "Coutra, a corporal, went about asking for signatures against Danton's nomination."[83] He had just risen above the successes of his enemies. November had put him on a sure footing again, and in January he reached the place he had had so long in view, the administration of Paris.

It will be remembered that the voting was by two degrees. The electors nominated an "electoral college," who elected the Commune and its officers. Already in October Danton had been put into the electoral college by twenty-six members chosen by his Section, but not without violent opposition. Finally, after eight ballots, on the 31st of January 1791, he became a member of the administration of the town—the twenty-second on a list of thirty-six elected. He failed, however, in his attempt to be chosen "Procureur," and through all the year 1791 he keeps his place in the administration of Paris merely as a stepping-stone. He does not speak much in the Council. He used his partial success only for the purpose of attaining a definite position from which he could exercise some measure of executive control; this position he finally attains (as we shall see) in the following December, and it is from it that he is able to direct the movement of 1792.

The year 1791 does not form a unit in the story of the Revolution. It is cut sharply in two by the flight of the King in June. Before that event things went with a certain quietude. The tendency to reaction and the tendency to extreme democracy are to be discovered, but there can be no doubt that a kind of lassitude has taken the public mind. After all, the benefits of the Revolution are there. The two years of discussion, the useless acrimony of the preceding autumn, began to weary the voters—there is a sentiment of joviality abroad.

After the flight of the King all is changed. To a period of development there succeeds a period of violent advance, and of retreat yet more violent; there appears in France the first mention of the word republic, and all the characters that hung round Lafayette come definitely into conflict with the mass of the people. The action of the troops on the Champ de Mars opens the first of those impassable gulfs between the parties, and from that moment onward there arise the hatreds that are only satisfied by the death of political opponents.

In that first period, then, which the death of Mirabeau was to disturb, the 18th of April to endanger, and the flight of the King to close, Danton's rôle, like that of all the democrats, is effaced. Why should it not be? The violent discussions that followed the affair of Nancy led, as it were, to a double satisfaction: the loyal party saw that after all the Radicals were not destroying the State; the Radicals, on the other hand, had learnt that the loyalists could do nothing distinctly injurious to the nation without being discovered. At least, they thought they had learnt this truth. They did not know how for months Mirabeau had been in the pay of the Court, and how the executive power had concerned itself with the King rather than with the nation.

A sign of this appeasement in the violence of the time (a movement, by the way, which was exactly what Danton desired) is his letter to La Rochefoucald, the president of the Department, when the successful election, which I have described above, was known. This letter, one of the very few which Danton has left, is a singularly able composition. He alludes to the mistrust which had been felt when his name was mentioned; he does not deny the insurrectionary character of the quarter of Paris which he inspired. But he replies: "I will let my actions, now that I hold public office, prove my attitude, and if I am in a position of responsibility, it will have a special value in showing that I was right to continually claim the public control of administrative functions." The whole of the long letter[84] is very well put; it is Danton himself that speaks, and it is hard to doubt that at this moment he also was one of those who thought they were touching the end of the reform, that goal which always fled from the men who most sincerely sought it.

He did not, however, come often to the Council—to less than a quarter of its sittings, at the most; moreover, the men who composed it still looked upon him with suspicion; and when, on the 4th of May, the committees were drawn up, his name was omitted. He asked on the next day to be inscribed on the committee that contained Sieyès, and his request was granted.

The activity of Danton during these few months was not even shown at the Cordeliers; though that club occasionally heard him, it was at the Jacobins that he principally spoke.

This famous club, on which the root of the Revolution so largely depends, was at this period by no means the extreme and Robespierrian thing with which we usually associate the name. It hardly even called itself "the Jacobins" yet, but clung rather to its original name of "Friends of the Constitution." Its origin dated from the little gathering of Breton deputies who were in the habit, while the Assembly was still at Versailles, of meeting together to discuss a common plan of action. When the Assembly came to Paris, this society, in which by that time a very large number of deputies had enrolled themselves, took up their place in the hall of the Dominicans or "Jacobins," just off the Rue St. Honoré. (Its site is just to the east of the square of Vendôme to-day.) It was a union of all those who desired reform, and in the first part of the year 1790 it had been remarkable for giving a common ground where the moderate and extremist, all who desired reform, could meet. The Duc de Broglie figures among its presidents. It was the Royalists, the extreme Court party, that dubbed these "Friends of the Constitution" "Jacobins," and it was not till somewhat later that they themselves adopted and gloried in the nickname. It was composed not only of deputies, but of all the best-born and best-bred of the Parisian reformers, drawn almost entirely from the noble or professional classes, and holding dignified sessions, to which the public were not admitted.

Almost at the same moment, namely, towards the autumn and winter of 1790, two features appeared in it. First, the Moderates begin to leave it, and the schism which finally produced the "Feuillants" is formed; secondly, there come in from all over France demands from the local popular societies to be affiliated to the great club in Paris. These demands were granted. There arises a kind of "Jacobin order," which penetrates even to the little country towns, everywhere preaches the same doctrine, everywhere makes it its business to keep a watch against reaction. These local clubs depended with a kind of superstition upon the decrees of what, without too violent a metaphor, we may call the "Mother House" in Paris; it was this organisation that aroused the apathy of provincial France and trained the new voters in political discussion, and it was this also that was later captured by Robespierre, who, like a kind of high priest, directed a disciplined body wherever the affiliated societies existed.

Danton first joined the society at the very moment when this double change was in progress, in September 1790. His energies, which were employed in the club to arrange the difficulty with the Moderates (if that were possible), were also used (to quote a well-known phrase) in "letting France hear Paris." The Cordeliers had been essentially Parisian; steeped in that feeling, Danton spoke from the Rue St. Honoré to the whole nation.

It is with the end of March that he begins to be heard, in a speech attacking Collot d'Herbois; for that unpleasant fellow was then a Moderate. It is apropos of that speech that the "Sabbots Jacobites" give us the satirical rhyme on Danton, which recalls his face when he spoke, looking all the uglier for the energy which he put into his words:—

"Monsieur Danton,

Quittez cet air farouche,

Monsieur Danton,

On vous prendrez pour un démon."[85]

On the 3rd of April it was known in Paris that Mirabeau was dead. He had been killed with the overwork of attempting to save the King from himself. A masterly intrigue, a double dealing which was hidden for a generation, had exhausted him, and in the terrible strain of balancing such opposite interests as those of France, which he adored, and Louis, whom he served, his two years of struggle suddenly fell upon him and crushed him. He smiled at the sun and called it God's cousin, boasted like a genius, gave a despairing phrase to the monarchy, demanded sleep, and died.

Danton had always, from a long way off, understood his brother in silk and with the sword. On this day he passionately deplored the loss. Like all Paris, the Jacobins forgot Mirabeau's treason, and remembered his services when the news of his sudden death fell upon them. From their tribune Danton spoke in terms in which he almost alone foretold the coming reaction, and he was right. The King, hardly restrained from folly by the compromise of the great statesman, plunged into it when his support was withdrawn. He had been half Mirabeau's man, now he was all Antoinette's.

It was the fatal question of religion that precipitated the crisis. Louis could not honestly receive the Easter communion from a constitutional priest. On the other hand, he might have received it quietly in his household. He chose to make it a public ceremony, and to go in state to St. Cloud for his Easter duties. It was upon April 18th, a day or two more than a fortnight after Mirabeau's death, that he would have set out. As one might have expected, the streets filled at once. The many battalions of the National Guard who were on the democratic side helped the people to stop the carriage; in their eyes, as in that of the populace, the King's journey to St. Cloud was only part of the scheme to leave Paris to raise an army against the Assembly.[86]

On the other hand, those of the National Guard who obeyed Lafayette[87] could not, by that very fact, move until Lafayette ordered them. Thus the carriage was held for hours, until at last, in despair, the King went back to the Tuilleries.

Meanwhile, what had occurred at the Hotel de Ville? The testimony is contradictory and the whole story confused, but the truth seems to have been something of this kind. Lafayette certainly called on the administration of the Department and asked for martial law. Bailly as certainly was willing to grant it. Danton was called from his rank and came to oppose it; but did he end the matter by his speech? Camille Desmoulins[88] says so, and draws a fine picture of Danton carrying the administration with him, as he carried the club or the street. But Desmoulins is often inaccurate, and here his account is improbable. Danton's own note of the circumstance (which he thought worthy of being pinned to his family papers) runs: "I was present at the Department when MM. the commandant and the mayor demanded martial law." Nothing more.

Desmoulins makes another mistake when he attributes to Danton the letter which was written to the King, and which was sent on the night of the 18th; it reproached him for his action, sharply criticised his rejection of constitutional priests. It was not Danton, it was Talleyrand (a member also of the Department) who wrote this letter.

It is probable that Danton and Talleyrand knew each other. Talleyrand was a good judge of men, and would have many strings to his bow—we know that he depended upon Danton's kindness at a critical moment in 1792—but the style of the letter is not Danton's, and the document as we find it in Schmidt is definitely ascribed to Talleyrand.

This is all we can gather as to his place in the popular uprising to prevent the King's leaving Paris. A placard of some violence issued from the Cordeliers, saying that he had "forbidden Lafayette to fire on the people;" but Danton disowned it in a meeting of the Department.

This much alone is certain, that the 18th of April had finally put Danton and Lafayette face to face, and that in the common knowledge of Paris they would be the heads of opposing forces in the next crisis. But their rôles turned out to be the very opposite of what men would have predicted. It was Lafayette who shot and blustered, and had his brief moment of power; it was Danton who made a flank movement and achieved a final victory. For the next crisis was the flight of the King.

It would be irrelevant to give the story of this flight in the life of Danton. Our business is to understand Danton by following the exact course of his actions during June and July, and by describing exactly the nature of the movement in which his attitude took the form which we are investigating.

Two things command the attention when we study the France of 1791. France was monarchic and France was afraid. History knows what was to follow; the men of the time did not. There lay in their minds the centuries of history that had been; their future was to them out of conception, and as unreal as our future is to us. You may notice from the very first moment of the true Revolution a passion for the King. For most he is a father, but for all a necessary man. They took him back to Paris; they forced him to declarations of loyalty, and then, with the folly of desire, accepted as real an emotion which they had actually dictated. Such was the movement of the 4th of February 1790; such the sentiment of the Federation in July of that year. And the people understood his reluctance in taking communion from a nonjuring priest, however much the upper class might be astonished. What no one understood was that only Mirabeau stood between the Crown and its vilest temptations; only his balance of genius, his great and admirable fault of compromise, prevented Louis from yielding to his least kingly part, and while he lived the king of the French preferred the nation to his own person. But Mirabeau was dead. They did well to mourn him, those who had smelt out his treason and guessed the weakness of the artist in him; they did well to forgive him; his head misunderstood France, but his broad French shoulders had supported her. The 18th of April was a direct consequence of his death; the 21st of June was a fall through a broken bridge: Louis had yielded to himself.

Well, France was also afraid. This democracy (as it had come to be), an experiment based upon a vision, knew how perilous was the path between the old and the new ideals. She feared the divine sunstroke that threatens the road to Damascus. In that passage, which was bounded on either side by an abyss, her feet went slowly, one before the other, and she looked backward continually. In the twisting tides at night her one anchor to the old time was the monarchy. Thus when Louis fled the feeling was of a prop broken. France only cried out for one thing—"Bring the King back." Tie up the beam—a makeshift—anything rather than a new foundation.

Here is the attitude of Danton in this crisis. France is not republican; his friends in Paris are. He inclines to France. It was Danton more than any other one man who finally prepared the Republic, yet the Republic was never with him an idea. The consequences of the Republic were his goal; as for the systems, systems were not part of his mind. At the close of this chapter we shall see him overthrowing the Crown; he did it because he thought it the one act that could save France; but the Crown as an idea he never hated: he lived in existing things.

These were the reasons that made him hesitate at this date. A man understanding Europe, he saw that the governments were not ready to move; a man understanding his own country, he saw that it would have the King in his place again; a man, on the other hand, who had met and appreciated the idealists, he saw that the Republic already existed in the mind; and a man who understood the character of his fellows better than did any contemporary, he saw that the men who were bound to lead were inclined to a declaration against the King. He suffered more than his action should have warranted, and he goes through a sharp few days of danger on account of association and of friends in spite of all his caution.

When Louis was known to have fled, and when Paris, vigilant beyond the provinces, and deceived by the declaration of April, had undergone its first wave of passion, the word Republic began to be spoken out loud. The theorists found themselves for once in accordance with public humour; and against the keenness, if not the numbers, of those who petitioned for the deposition of the King on his return, there stood two barriers—the

Assembly and the moderate fortunes of the capital. Danton lived with the former, thought with the latter, and was all but silent.

The bust of Louis XIV. before the Hotel de Ville was broken; men climbed on ladders to chisel off the lilies from the palaces, and there soon appears a new portent: some one cries out, "Only a Republic can defend itself at the last."

To this somewhat confused cry for a Republic came the very sharp announcement from no less a person than Condorcet. Condorcet, the moderate and illumined, was also half a visionary, and there had always floated in his mind the system of contract by which England had excused the movement of 1688, but which France took seriously. England had for him the attraction which it had for all the professionals of that date—an attraction which lasted till the disasters of 1870, and which you may yet discover here and there among those who are the heirs of Lamartine. England had given them Locke, and Condorcet's reasoning on the King's flight[89] reads like a passage from the Bill of Rights. Yet he was a good and sincere man, and died through simplicity of heart.

On the 4th of July, ten days or more after the King had been brought back to Paris,[90] it was Condorcet who made the demand for the Republic; in a speech at Fauchet's club he asked for a National Convention to settle the whole matter. He wrote so in the papers[91] all through July, and even after the affair of the Champ de Mars he continued his agitation.

Now how do we know Danton's attitude? The Cordeliers presented a petition of June 21st itself and demanded the Republic. It is largely from this document that the error has arisen. But Danton was not then with the Cordeliers; his name does not appear. It is at the Jacobins that he is heard, and the Jacobins took up a distinctly monarchical position. They all rose in a body on the 22nd and passed a unanimous vote in favour of the constitution and the King.[92] Danton was present when this vote was passed, and he had just heard the hissing of the Cordeliers' petition; he was silent. Thomas Payne is demanding the Republic in the *Moniteur*; Sieyès replies for the monarchy;[93], even Robespierre tardily speaks in favour of ideas and against change of etiquette; Marat shouts for a dictator;[94] Danton, almost alone, refuses to be certain. On June 23rd he spoke at the Jacobins in favour of a council to be elected by the Departments immediately, but he proposed nothing as to its actions; it was merely his permanent idea of a central, strong power.

Lafayette amused himself by arresting people who repeated this in the street, but Lafayette hated Danton blindly. Nothing republican can be made of a speech which his enemies said was "a loophole for Orleans."

Danton attacked Lafayette: he saw persons more clearly than ideas, and Lafayette was Danton's nightmare. He was that being which of all on earth Danton thought most dangerous, the epitome of all the faults which he attacked to the day of his death; in Louis, in Robespierre, "The weak man in power." He drove him out of the Jacobins on the 21st, and later in the day gave the cry against his enemy in the street, which the fears of the Assembly so much exaggerated.

For the events of the twenty-four hours had all added to his natural opposition to Lafayette, and as we relate them from Danton's standpoint, we shall see this much of truth in the idea that he led the movement, namely, that the three days of the King's flight and recapture, while they put Lafayette into a position of great power, made also Danton his antagonist, the leader of the protest against the general's methods. It is the more worthy of remark that in such conditions the word "Republic" never crossed his lips.

At eleven o'clock at night on the Monday of the King's flight, Danton and Desmoulins were coming home alone from the Jacobins. Each remarked to the other the emptiness of the streets and the lack of patrols, and at that moment, when the evasion was little suspected, each was in a vague doubt that Lafayette had some reason for concentrating the National Guard.[95] Desmoulins will even have it that he saw him enter the palace, as the two friends passed the Tuilleries.

The next morning at the Cordeliers Danton cried out against Lafayette for a moment, and then at the Jacobins he made the speech that has been mentioned above. Continually he attacks the man who was preparing a counter-revolution, but I do not believe he would have attached the least importance at that moment to a change in the etiquette of government. Thus, as the Department was sent for by the Assembly in the afternoon, Danton came later than his colleagues, provided himself with a guard, and as he crossed the Tuilleries gardens he harangued the people, but against Lafayette, not against the King.

Now, to make sure of this feature, the duel between Lafayette and Danton, and to see that it is the principal thing at the time, turn once more to the scene at the Jacobins, and compare it with Lafayette's Memoirs, and you will find that Danton was the terror of the saviour of two worlds, and that it was upon Lafayette that Danton had massed his artillery.

Here is Danton at the Jacobins, sitting by Desmoulin's side; he goes to the tribune and speaks upon the disgrace and danger that the Moderates have brought about. When Lafayette entered during the speech, he turned upon him suddenly, and launched one of those direct phrases which made him later the leader of the Convention: "I am going to talk as though I were at the bar of God's justice, and I will say before you, M. Lafayette, what I would say in the presence of Him who reads all hearts.... How was it that you, who pretend to know nothing of me, tried to corrupt me to your views of treason?... How was it that you arrested those who in last February demanded the destruction of Vincennes? You are present; try to give a clear reason.... How was it that the very same men were on guard when the King tried to go to St. Cloud on the 18th of April were on guard last night when the King fled?... I will not mention the 6000 men[96] whom you have picked as a garrison for the King; only answer clearly these three accusations. For in their light you, who answered with your head that the King should not fly, are either a traitor or a fool. For either you have permitted him to fly, or else you undertook a responsibility which you could not fulfil: in the best case, you are not capable of commanding the guard.... I will leave the tribune, for I have said enough."[97]

This is clear enough in all conscience to show what was Danton's main pre-occupation in the days of June 1791. And if, upon the other hand, you will turn to Lafayette's Memoirs, the third volume, the 83rd and following pages, you will find that Danton was Lafayette's pre-occupation, and that he makes this moment the occasion to deliver the most definite and (luckily) the most demonstrably false of his many accusations of venality. He tells us that he could not reply because it would have "cost Montmorin his life;" that Montmorin "had the receipt for the 100,000 francs;" that Danton had been "reimbursed to the extent of 100,000 francs for a place worth 10,000," and so forth. We know now exactly the amount of compensation paid to him and his colleagues at the court of appeal,[98] and we know that Lafayette, writing a generation later, animated by a bitter hatred, and remembering that somebody had paid Danton something, and with his head full of vague rumours of bribing, has fallen into one of those unpardonable errors common to vain and vacillating men. But at this juncture the main point that should be seized is that Danton was taking the opportunity of the King's evasion to attack Lafayette with all his might, and that a generation later the old man chiefly remembered Danton as leading the popular anger which the commander of the guard thought himself bound to repress. It is this that will explain why Danton, who so carefully avoided giving the word for the Republican "false start," was yet marked out, fled, and returned to lead the opposition.

The Cordeliers followed Danton's lead. They got up a petition,[99] signed by 30,000 in Paris, demanding that the affair should be laid before the country, but not demanding the abolition of the monarchy. Memdar, their president, declared himself a monarchist. But the petition, though read at the Assembly, was not adopted, and, on the 9th of July, the Cordeliers presented another. Charles de Lameth (who was president that fortnight) refused to read it. The Assembly, in other words, was dumb; it was determined (like its successor a year later) to do nothing—an attitude which (for all it knew) might be very wise, and those who were following Danton determined upon a definite policy. On Friday the 15th, at the Jacobins, it was determined to draw up a petition which begged that the Assembly should *first* recognise Louis as having abdicated by his flight, unless the nation voted his reinstatement, and *secondly* (in case the nation did not do so), take measures to have him constitutionally replaced. Now the constitution was monarchist.

The petition was to be taken to be read at the Champ de Mars on the altar, and there to obtain signatures. It was drawn up by Danton, Sergent, Lanthanas, Ducanel, and Brissot, who wrote it out and worded most of it. The events that follow must be noted with some care, because on their exact sequence depends our judgment of Lafayette's action and of Danton's politics.

On Saturday[100] the 16th, about mid-day, a deputation of four from the Jacobins came to the Champ de Mars. The petition was read by a little light-haired Englishman on one side, and by a red-haired Frenchman in a red coat on the other; picturesque but unimportant details. Danton leapt on to the corner of the altar, and read it again to the thick of the crowd. The signatures were written in great numbers, and when the completed document was about to start for the Assembly, when the deputation that was to take it was already formed, it was suddenly spread abroad that the Assembly had passed a vote exonerating Louis.

The Jacobins were appealed to, and replied that under the conditions the petition which they had drawn up could not be presented. The Cordeliers, however, lost their tempers, and Robert determined to draw up a new petition. Now in this second action Danton took no part. It was this new petition that (signed by Robert, Peyre, Vachard, and Demoy) was drawn up hastily in the Champ de Mars on Sunday the 17th, to this that the 6000 signatures were attached, and this which demanded a "Convention to judge the King." There followed the proclamation of martial law, the appearance of Lafayette and Bailly in the Champ de Mars with the red flag, the conflict between the National Guard and the crowd, and all that is called the "Massacre of the Champ de Mars."

That petition was not signed by Danton.[101] He was not even present,[102] as we know from his speech on his election to be "Substitut-Procureur," and especially from the fact that in the fortnight of terror, when the red flag stood over the Hotel de Ville, when the democrats were arrested or in hiding, when the door of the Cordeliers was shut and nailed, and when the Radical newspapers were suppressed, no warrant of arrest could be issued, because there existed nothing definite against him. Lafayette was determined, however, to act in a military fashion, and on the 4th of August the arrest of Danton was ordered, on some other plea which he alludes to in his speech of the next January, but the exact terms of which have not come down to us.

He had left Paris at once when he saw that Lafayette had practically absolute power for the moment. He first went to his father-in-law's, Charpentier, at Rosny-sur-Bois, and then escaped to Arcis. Before the warrant was actually made out, Lafayette had sent a man to watch him at Arcis. He was "giving a dinner. It would need a troop of cavalry to arrest him. Everybody was on his side."[103] Marseilles and Bar spoke up for him. But the attack only grew stronger. On the 31st of July he moved again to Troyes, to the house of Millaud, of his father's profession, and a friend, because he feared a new arrival from Paris who seemed a spy.[104] He was there when the warrant was sent down to the "procureur" for the arrest; the official in question was Beugnot, and Beugnot told Danton jocularly that he would not arrest him. He did not think this a sufficient guarantee, and as his stepfather, Recordain, was off to England to buy some machinery for a cotton-mill that he thought of starting, Danton went to England with him, and remained in this country for a month, staying in the house of his stepfather's sons, who were established in London. It was in the last days of July or the first days in August[105] that he arrived, and he did not return to Paris until the appointment of his friend Garran de Coulon as President of the Court of Appeal. He appears again at the Jacobins on the 12th of September; some say he was in Paris on the 10th.[106]

It would be of the utmost interest to know how he passed those thirty or forty days. Unfortunately there is no direct evidence as to whom he met or what negotiations he entered into. As to his English acquaintances, his letters from Priestley and Christie, the relations he had with Talleyrand, and their common diplomacy for the English alliance—all these properly belong to Danton in power, the minister directing France after August 1792, and it is in that place that they will be dealt with. Of historical events in his voyage we have none, and there is no more regrettable gap in the very disconnected series of ascertained facts concerning him.

On his return, he discovered that the Section of the Théâtre Français had named him a member of the electoral college which sat at the Archbishop's palace. Many members of this Assembly had been arrested, or had fled during Lafayette's violent efforts of reaction in August and September. The new Parliament which had just met did not decree an amnesty (as it was asked to do on the 5th of September), but it was of course far more democratic than the old Assembly, and it was understood to be tacitly in favour of the return of those whom Lafayette had driven out. Following Danton's example, they slowly came back; but a curious incident shows how much of the danger remained.

On the 13th of September the Parliament, at the desire of the King, voted the amnesty. While it was actually voting, a constable called Damien got into the gallery of the hall in which Danton and the electors were debating, and sent a note to the president asking him to allow the arrest. The president and the electoral college (who did not like Danton, by the way, and who would not give him more than forty votes when it came to electing members for Paris) yet ordered the arrest by Damien, and it was only when they learnt of the amnesty that, on Danton's own motion, he was released.

It has just been said that Danton failed to be elected: let us point out the conditions under which the Legislative met, that short Parliament of one year which made the war, and saw to its dismay the end of the monarchy.

The Legislative was not elected in one of those moments of decision which were the formative points of the Revolution. It came upon a very curious juncture, and showed in all its first acts a marked indecision.

The members were chosen under the action of a peculiar combination, or rather confusion of emotions. The King had fled, had been recaptured. France, of many possible evils, had chosen what she believed to be the least when she reinstated him. "The New Pact" was accepted even by those who had spoken of the Republic in July. Condorcet, who had led the civic theorists towards the Republic, leads them also now in this movement of reconciliation. Again, these were the first elections held since the middle class and the peasantry had been given the suffrage over the heads of the artisans: it was the most sober part of France that dictated the policy of the moment. The divisions that the King's flight had laid bare, the sharp reaction and terror of the Champ de Mars—all these were forgotten.

Thus the Parliament will not have Garran-Coulon for its first president, and yet on the next day passes the extreme democratic etiquette as to the reception of the King should he visit the Assembly. Next day it repeals this, and when the King does visit the Assembly, he is met by an outburst of loyalty and affection.

As to parties, the power lay, as it always does in a French Assembly, with the centre—some three hundred men, unimportant, of no fixed idea, unless indeed it were to keep the Legislative to the work for which it had been elected, that is, to keep it moving moderately on the lines laid down for it by the constitution of 1791.

The right, well organised, loyal and brave, was Feuillant; that is, it was monarchic and constitutional, but more monarchic than constitutional. It was the support of Lafayette, and on the whole the centre would vote with it on any important occasion.

But there sat on the left a group less compact, full of personal ambitions and personal creeds, containing almost all the orators whose names were to make famous the following year. It was but a group of 130 men, even if we include all those who signed the register of the Jacobins when the Assembly met; yet it was destined, ill-disciplined as it was, part wild and part untrue, to lead all France. Why? Because the King was to make impossible the action of the Moderates, because his intrigue made Frenchmen choose between him and France, and in the inevitable war the men who were determined to realise the Revolution could not but be made the leaders.

As has been said above, Danton was not elected. The electoral college, of which he was a member, chose Moderates for the most part, such as Pastoret and De Quincy, and the narrow suffrage represented the true drift of Parisian feeling only in the case of a few—De Séchelles, Brissot, Condorcet, and a handful of others. But though Danton did not sit in the Legislative he was free for action in two other directions, which (as it turned out) were the commanding positions in the great changes that came with the war. He was free to attain an administrative position in the municipality of Paris, and he was free to use his power of oratory at the Jacobins.

As to the first, it came with his moderate but important success in the municipal elections at the close of the year. Bailly, frightened out of place, half-regretting his action of the Champ de Mars, had resigned, and Pétion, on November 16th, was elected in his place. Only ten thousand voted, and he obtained 6700 votes. On the same day the Procureur of the new Commune was to be elected. A Procureur under the new system was a position of the greatest importance. He was, so to speak, the advocate of the town, its tribune in the governing body, and with his two substitutes (who aided and occasionally replaced him) was meant to form a kind of small committee whose business was to watch the interests and to define the attitude of the electorate whenever those interests were in jeopardy or that attitude was opposed to the policy of the elected body. These three positions were dangerous, but would lead to popularity, and perhaps to power, if they were directed by a certain kind of ability. It was precisely such a power, the quality of a tribune, that Danton knew himself to possess.

His candidature for the principal position was cordially supported by the Cordeliers, but the Jacobins were divided, and they hesitated. Manuel was elected, and Danton obtained only the third place. This vote, however, was not decisive, and there was a second ballot on December the 2nd. In this Manuel was definitely elected.

Cahier de Gerville (the second substitute) was made Minister of the Interior, and Danton, on December 6th,[107] was elected to his place by a majority of 500 over Collot d'Herbois. It was from this position that he prepared the 10th of August, and it was still as substitute that he remained side by side with the insurrectionary commune, and lending it something of legal sanction when the King was overthrown.

Let me, before leaving this point, define exactly the position in which his new dignity placed him. Three men were charged with the advocacy of public opinion, the Procureur and his two substitutes. Manuel, who was elected to the principal position, was energetic, kindly, and conscientious, but a man of no genius; he was good to Madame De Staël in the days of September, as is apparent from her rather contemptuous description of how she appealed to him for safety; he did his very best (with no power in his hands) to stop the massacres at that same time. He was fond of work, and a little pompous in his idea of office; he was, therefore, a man who would only leave his substitutes the less important work to do, and, from close by, would have been the dominating member of the three. On the other hand, his lack of decision and of initiative effaced him in moments of danger or of new departures, and it is thus his second substitute who seems to lead when seen from a distance, from the point of view of the people, who only look round when there is a noise.

The first substitute was Desmousseaux. He had not resigned, and had therefore not been re-elected. Forming part of the old Commune, and in office since the winter of 1790, he was a Moderate by preference and long tradition.

As for Danton himself, standing third in the group, it was for him a position of honour and of dignity. That part of him which was so capable of high office and so desirous of an opportunity to act was well served by the election. It seemed to put a term to the misconceptions which his person, his faults, and the course of the Revolution had created. But the great stream of events moved him at their will. This office wherein he desired to appear settled at last, to show himself an administrator rather than a leader of unreasoning men, was precisely suited in case of danger to call out those other qualities which had made him despised by many whom he himself respected, and had aroused against him hatred—a passion which he himself had never allowed to arise from anger.

If the spirit of 1791 had been kept, and if after so many false promises the Revolution had been really accomplished, then the official, or, if you will, the statesman, would have appeared in him. I can see him in the difficulties which even a settled kingdom would have had to meet, convincing his contemporaries as he has convinced posterity. He was the man to impress on others the true attitude of Europe—the only diplomat among the patriots. His disadvantages were of the kind that are forgotten in the constant proof of ability; and his learning, which was exactly of the kind to be used in the new regime (a knowledge of languages, of law, of surrounding nations, a combination of detail and of comprehension)—this learning would have made necessary a man so popular with the people to be ruled, and, in the matter of the heart, so honestly devoted to his country. Had France, I say, by some miracle been spared her Passion, and had she been permitted to be happier and to do less for the world, then as the new regime settled into the lower reaches of quiet and content, I believe Danton would have remained for us a name, perhaps less great, but certainly among the first. England has been permitted. She has been given good fortune, and no fate has asked her to save civilisation with her blood, and therefore in England we are accustomed to such careers; men whose origin, whose exterior, and whose faults might have exiled them, have yet been seen to rise from the municipal to the imperial office, because they were possessed of supreme abilities, and because they devoted those abilities to the service of England. They have died in honour.

I will not discuss what it was that made the war. There are no causes. Burke raved like a madman, but then so did Marat. The King was alienated by the clerical laws, but nothing is an excuse for treason. Pilnitz was an affront and even a menace, but it was not a declaration of war. There were peoples behind the kings, as Mayence tragically proved; and if France fought intolerable evils, she also seemed the iconoclast when she put out the altar-lamp, which she is lighting again with her own hand. There are no causes. Only, if you will look and see how Europe has lived, and how our great things have been done, you will find nothing but armies upon armies marching past, and our history is an epic whose beginning is lost, whose books are Roncesvalles and Cortenuova and Waterloo, and whose end is never reached. The war came, and with it a definite necessity to choose between France and the Crown. In that crisis Danton is thrown back upon insurrection. He, who desired men to forget the days of October, was compelled to the 10th of August because he was aroused. Even the massacres were attached to his name, and there still trails after him an easy flow of accusation, only a little less sordid or less terrible.

To follow his action during the first months of 1772, to hear his speeches on the war, and to note his policy, we must leave him at his post in the Commune (where we shall find him again when Paris rises in the summer), and see how he stands for the Mountain at the Jacobins.

This club was now definitely the organ of the left. It was after Danton had been elected, but before he was definitely installed in office,[108] on the 14th of December, a week after the former and five weeks before the latter event, that the debate on the war was begun at the Jacobins,—a debate of the first importance, because it opened the breach between the Girondins and the Mountain, between the orators who insisted on going to meet Europe, and even on a war of propaganda, and the reformers who wished Europe to take the first step, who dreaded war or who thought a war of aggression immoral. At the head of these last was Robespierre. But it is not too much to say that in the first months of the year Danton was more important at the Jacobins than Robespierre. What was his attitude? It was part of the general policy upon which he had determined: he compromised. In his first motion on the 14th of December, he attacked the idea of declaring war. On the 16th he still attacked it, but in other terms. "I know it must come. If any one were to ask me, 'Are we to have war?' I would reply (not in argument, but as a matter of fact), 'We shall hear the bugles,'" But the whole speech is taken up with an argument upon its dangers, and especially upon "those who desire war in the hope of reaction, who talk of giving us a constitution like that of England, in the hope of giving us, later, one like that of Turkey."

In March and April, the months when the war was preparing and was declared, he was silent. And we can understand his silence when we turn to his speech in the Commune when he was given office. He alludes to the false character given him; he speaks of the reputation which his past actions in Paris had given; he says things that indicate a determination to play the part of a Moderate, and to see whether in his case, as in that of so many others, there would not be permanence in the compromise of the last six months. But there rankled in his mind the insults of the men with whom he sat, Condorcet's disavowal in his paper of so much as knowing Danton, and he made a peroration which at the time offended, but which possesses for us a certain pathos. "Nature gave me a strong frame, and she put into my face the violence of liberty. I have not sprung from a family which was weakened by the protection of the old privileges; my existence has been all my own; I know that I have kept and shown my vigour, but in my profession and in my private life I have controlled it. If I was carried away by enthusiasm in the first days of our regeneration, have I not atoned for it? Have I not been ostracised?... I have given myself altogether to the people, and now that they are beyond attack, now that they are in arms and ready to break the league unless it consents to dissolve,[109] I will die in their cause if I must, ... for I love them only, and they deserve it. Their courage will make them eternal."

This outburst is the one occasion of his public life in which Danton spoke of himself, and it has the ring of genuine emotion; for in all his harangues he preserved, both before and after this, an objective attitude, if anything too much bent upon the outward circumstances.

Thus, when the notes came to go between the Austrian and the French governments, he was silent. He fears that France is unprepared; he fears that the King is betraying the nation. How much he was a traitor was not known till a far later period; but when at least it is proved that something is undermining the French people, that, apart from the defeats and the lack of preparation, there is treason, then he leaves his silence. The policy of the Moderate acting in a settled state is no longer possible to any one; the court and the nation stood one against the other, and one side or the other must be taken by every man. Then he put off the conventions which he respected, and which he regretted to the end; he went back into the street; he headed the insurrection, destroyed the monarchy; for twelve months he took upon himself all the responsibility of errors in his own policy, and of crime in that of his associates. He saved France, but at this expense, that he went out of the world with a reputation which he knew to be false, that he saw his great powers vulgarised, and that he could never possess, either in his own mind or before the world, not even in France, his true name. The whole of this tragedy is to be found in his trial, and here and there in the few phrases that escape him in the speeches or with his friends. If you sum it up, it comes to this paraphrase of a great sentence: *Son nom était flétri mais la France était libre.*

It was upon April the 18th that the new Girondin ministry received the note from Vienna rejecting the French proposals of a month before. The poor King, who had been protesting his loyalty to the nation in Paris, had been protesting in Vienna the necessity of sending an army to save him, and Austria gave this reply. On April 20th the Assembly declared war with practical unanimity[110] upon "the King of Hungary and of Bohemia." But the phrase was useless. You might as well put a match into gunpowder and say, "It is the sulphur I am after, not the charcoal." Prussia joined, and within a year we shall see all Europe at war with France, in a war that outlawed and destroyed.

Danton was right. France was hopelessly unready. She had not learnt the necessary truth that the soldier is a man with a trade. The orators had mistaken words for things; honest and great as they were, they had fallen in this matter into the faults common to small and dishonest verbiage. The rout and panic under De Dillon, his murder by the troops, the occupation of Quiévrain, came one upon the other. Paris was full of terror and anger in proportion to the greatness of the things she had done, which now seemed all destroyed. "We said and did things that should have convinced the world; we were to be a people unconquerable from our love of liberty, and we appear a beaten, panic-stricken lot—volunteers and babblers who cannot stand fire." The King dismissed the Girondin ministers, even sent Dumouriez away, heard Roland's remonstrance, knew that the Assembly was more and more against him; but he remained calm. There was a plan of the simplest. There was to be nothing but a few days of monotonous marching between the allies and Paris. Lafayette with his army of the centre was on his side. The Assembly decreed a great camp of 20,000 men under Paris, and the disbanding of the guard; the guard was disbanded, but the King vetoed the decree. Lafayette wrote his letter menacing the Parliament with his army; the reaction seemed in full success and the invaders secure, when Danton reappeared.

On the 18th of June he found the old phrases against Lafayette at the Jacobins. "It is a great day for France; Lafayette with only one face on is no longer dangerous." He did not make, but he permitted the 20th of June; and as Paris rose, and the immense mob, grotesque, many-coloured, armed with all manner of sharp things, passed before the Assembly and into the Tuilleries, it might have been a signal or a warning. The excited citizen makes a poor soldier, but if Paris moves the whole great body of France stirs. Such giants take long to be fully awake, and it is a matter of months to drill men; still it is better to let great enemies sleep. There was in that foolish, amiable crowd, with its pleasure at the sight of the King, its comic idea of warning him, something serious underlying. Danton will be using it in a very short time; for there are points of attack where mobs are like machine-guns—ridiculous in general warfare, but very useful indeed in special conditions, and in these conditions invincible. This something serious was that vague force (you may call it only an idea) which you will never find in an individual, and which you will always discover in a mass—the great common man which the French metaphysicians have called "Le Peuple;" that, drilled, is called by the least metaphysical an army.

A week later Lafayette appeared. He demanded the right to use the army, and July opened with the certainty of civil war.

July is the month of fevers; the heat has been moving northward, and all France is caught in it. The grapes fill out, and even in Picardy or in the Cotentin you feel as though the Midi were giving her spirit to the north. July made the Revolution and closed it. A month that saw the Bastille fall and that buried Robespierre is a very national time.

If you overlook France at this moment, you may see the towns stirring as they had stirred three years before; it is from them that the opposition rises—especially from Marseilles. A crowd of young men dragging cannon, the common-place sons of bourgeois, whom the time had turned into something as great as peasants or as soldiers, surged up the white deserts along the Rhone, passing the great sheet of vineyards that slopes up the watershed of Burgundy. As they came along they sang an excellent new marching song. When they at last saw Paris, especially the towers of Notre Dame from where they just show above the city as you come in from Fontainebleau, and as the roads came in together and the suburbs thickened they sang it with louder voices. On the evening of the 30th they came to the gates, and the workmen of the south-eastern quarter began to sing it and called it the "Marseillaise." No one can describe music; but if in a great space of time the actions of the French become meaningless and the Revolution ceases to be an origin, some one perhaps will recover this air, as we have recovered a few stray notes of Greek music, and it will carry men back to the Republic.

For ten days the insurrection grew. In a secret committee which the Sections formed, men violent like Fournier, or good soldiers like Westermann, or local leaders of quarters like Santerre—but all outside the official body—organised the fighting force, and at their head the one man who held the strings of the municipality—Danton. The Assembly had heard Vergniaud's angry speech, but it had also confirmed the constitution and the monarchy in the "baiser Lamourette." Paris had to work alone, and the King, seeing only Paris before him, filled the Tuilleries, and stood by with a small garrison to repress the mere movement of the city—"something that should have been done in '89."

It was on a Paris thus enfevered, doubtful, nursing a secret insurrectionary plan, but full of men who hesitated and doubted, having still many who were loyal, that there fell[111] the document which the King had asked of his friends—but which he must, on seeing it, have regretted—the manifesto of the commander of the allies. This extraordinary monument of folly is rarely presented in its entirety. It is only in such a form that its full monstrosity can be appreciated, and I have therefore been at pains to translate for my readers the rather halting French in which Charles William proposed to arrest the movements of Providence. It ran as follows[112]:—

"Their Majesties the Emperor and the King of Prussia having given me the command of the armies assembled on the French frontier, I have thought it well to tell the inhabitants of that kingdom the motives that have inspired the measures taken by the two sovereigns and the intentions that guide them.

"After having arbitrarily suppressed the rights and the possessions of the German princes in Alsace and Lorraine, troubled and overset public order and their legitimate government, exercised against the sacred person of the King and against his august family violence which is (moreover) repeated and renewed from day to day, those who have usurped the reins of the administration have at last filled up the measure by causing an unjust war to be declared against his Majesty the Emperor, and by attacking his provinces in the Netherlands.

"Several possessions of the German Empire have been drawn into this oppression, and several others have only escaped from a similar danger by yielding to the imperious threats of the dominant party and its emissaries.

"His Prussian Majesty with his Imperial Majesty, by the ties of a strict and defensive alliance, and himself a preponderant member of the Germanic body (*sic*), has therefore been unable to excuse himself from going to the aid of his ally and of his fellow State (*sic*). And it is under both these heads that he undertakes the defence of that monarch and of Germany.

"To these great interests another object of equal importance must be added, and one that is near to the heart of the two sovereigns: it is that of ending the domestic anarchy of France, of arresting the attacks which are directed against the altar and the throne, of re-establishing the legitimate power, of giving back to the King the freedom and safety of which he is deprived, and of giving him the means to exercise the lawful authority which is his due.

"Convinced as they are that the healthy part of the French people abhors the excesses of a party that enslaves them, and that the majority of the inhabitants are impatiently awaiting the advent of a relief that will permit them to declare themselves openly against the odious schemes of their oppressors, His Majesty the Emperor and His Majesty the King of Prussia call upon them to return at once to the call of reason and justice, of order, of peace. It is in view of these things that I, the undersigned, General Commander-in-Chief of the two armies, declare—

> "(1) That led into the present war by irresistible circumstances, the two allied courts propose no object to themselves but the happiness of France, and do not propose to enrich themselves by annexation.
>
> "(2) That they have no intention of meddling with the domestic government of France, but only wish to deliver the King, and the Queen, and the Royal Family from their captivity, and procure for his Most Christian Majesty that freedom which is necessary for him to call such a council as

he shall see fit, without danger and without obstacle, and to enable him to work for the good of his subjects according to his promises and as much as may be his concern.

"(3) That the combined armies will protect all towns, boroughs, and villages, and the persons and goods of all those that will submit to the King, and that they will help to re-establish immediately the order and police of France.

"(4) That the National Guard are ordered to see to the peace of the towns and country-sides provisionally, and to the security of the persons and goods of all Frenchmen provisionally, that is, until the arrival of the troops of their Royal and Imperial Majesties, or until further orders, under pain of being personally responsible; that on the contrary, the National Guards who may have fought against the troops of the allied courts, and who are captured in arms, shall be treated as enemies, and shall be punished as rebels and disturbers of the public peace.

"(5) That the generals, officers, non-commissioned officers, and privates of the French troops of the line are equally ordered to return to their old allegiance and to submit at once to the King, their legitimate sovereign.

"(6) That the members of departmental, district, and town councils are equally responsible with their heads and property for all crimes, arson, murders, thefts, and assaults, the occurrence of which they allow or do not openly, and to the common knowledge, try to prevent in their jurisdiction; that they shall equally be bound to keep their functions provisionally until his Most Christian Majesty, reinstated in full liberty, has further decreed; or until, in the interval, other orders shall have been given.

"(7) That the inhabitants of towns, boroughs, and villages who may dare to defend themselves against the troops of their Imperial and Royal Majesties by firing upon them, whether in the open or from the windows, doors, or apertures of their houses, shall be punished at once with all the rigour of the laws of war, their houses pulled down or burnt. All those inhabitants, on the contrary, of the towns, boroughs, and villages who shall hasten to submit to their King by opening their gates to the troops of their Majesties shall be placed under the immediate protection of their Majesties; their persons, their goods, their chattels shall be under the safeguard of the laws, and measures will be taken for the general safety of each and all of them.

"(8) The town of Paris and all its inhabitants without distinction shall be bound to submit on the spot, and without any delay, to the King, and to give that Prince full and entire liberty, and to assure him and all the Royal Family that inviolability and respect to which the laws of nature and of nations entitle sovereigns from their subjects. Their Imperial and Royal Majesties render personally responsible for anything that may happen, under peril of their heads, and of military execution without hope of pardon, all members of the National Assembly as of the Districts, the Municipality, the National Guards, the Justices of the Peace, and all others whom it may concern. Their aforesaid Majesties declare, moreover, on their word and honour as Emperor and King, that if the Palace of the Tuilleries be insulted or forced, that if the least violence, the least assault, be perpetrated against their Majesties, the King, the Queen, and the Royal Family, and if steps be not at once taken for their safety, preservation, and liberty, they, their Imperial and Royal Majesties, will take an exemplary and never-to-be-forgotten vengeance, by giving up the town of Paris to military execution and to total subversion, and the guilty rebels to the deaths they have deserved. Their Imperial and Royal Majesties promise, on the contrary, to the inhabitants of Paris to use their good offices with his Most Christian Majesty to obtain pardon for their faults and errors, and to take the most vigorous measures to ensure their persons and goods if they promptly and exactly obey the above command.

"Finally, since their Majesties can recognise no laws in France save those that proceed from the King in full liberty, they protest in advance against any declarations that may be made in the name of his Most Christian Majesty, so long as his sacred person, those of the Queen and of the Royal Family, are not really safe, for which end their Imperial and Royal Majesties invite and beg his Most Christian Majesty to point out to what town in the immediate neighbourhood of his frontiers he may judge it best to retire with the Queen and the Royal Family, under good and sure escort that will be sent him for that purpose, in order that his Most Christian Majesty may be in all safety to call to him such deputies and counsellors as he sees fit, call such councils as may please him, see to the re-establishment of order, and arrange the administration of his kingdom.

"Lastly, I engage myself, in my own private name and in my aforesaid capacity, to cause the troops under my command to observe everywhere a good and exact discipline, promising to treat with mildness and moderation all well-meaning subjects who may show themselves peaceful and submissive, and to use force with those only who may be guilty of resistance and of recalcitrance.

"It is for these reasons that I require and exhort, in the strongest and most instant fashion, all the inhabitants of this kingdom not to oppose themselves to the march and operations of the troops under my command, but rather to give them on all sides a free entry and all the good-will, aid, and assistance that circumstances may demand.

"Given at our headquarters of Coblentz, July 28.

(Signed) "Charles William Ferdinand, Duke of Brunswick-Lunebourg."

With that weapon the insurrection was certain of all Paris. Mandat, who had replaced Lafayette at the head of the armed force in the town, was still loyal to the King; he organised, as far as was possible, the forces that he could count upon. The other side also prepared, and the movements had all the appearance of troops entrenching themselves before battle.

Danton went to Arcis and settled an income on his mother in case of his death, came back to Paris, and on the night of August the 9th the Sections named commissioners to act. They met and formed the "insurrectionary commune." At eight the next morning they dissolved the legal commune, kept Danton, and directed the fighting of the morning.

Meanwhile the King had gathered in the Tuilleries about 6000 men, and depended very largely upon the thick mass of wooden buildings in the Carrousel for cover. The Swiss Guard, whom the decree had removed, were only as far off as Rueil, and were ordered into Paris, over 1500. They were the nucleus, and with them some 2000 of the National Guard, 1500 of the old "Constitutional Guards," and a group of "Gentilshommes." Mandat had ordered a battery of the National Guard's artillery to keep the Pont Neuf; they revolted and joined the people, and Mandat himself, the chief of the defence, was killed on the steps of the Hotel de Ville. Danton, who had not slept, but had lain down in Desmoulin's flat till midnight, had been to the Hotel de Ville since two in the morning, and he took before posterity—in his trial—the responsibility of Mandat's death. He did more. He acted during the short night (a night of calm and great beauty, dark and with stars) as the organiser and chief of the insurrection. Especially he appoints Santerre to lead the National Guard. On these rapid determinations the morning broke, and the first hours of the misty day passed in gathering the forces.

Meanwhile all morning the King had waited anxiously in the Tuilleries gardens, and asked Roederer, like a king in comic opera, "when the revolt would begin."

All night the tocsin had sounded, but the people were slow to gather— "le tocsin ne rend pas"—and it was not till the insurrectionary commune had done its work that a great mob, partly armed, and in no way disciplined, came into the Carrousel.

Westermann (riding, as was Santerre) came up to parley with the Swiss Guard; he asked them in German (which was his native tongue, for he was an Alsatian) to leave the Tuilleries, and promised that if the guard retired and left the palace un-garrisoned the people would also retire. The Swiss— the only real soldiers in Paris—replied that they were under orders, and when Westermann retired to the crowd they opened fire.

Antoinette had said, "Nail me to the Palace," and even Louis, timid and uncertain, thought that the chances were in his favour. Let only this day succeed, and the city could be kept quiet till the allies should arrive; that had been the boast in the Royalist journal of August 1st; it was Louis's hope now.

Had the Carrousel been a little more open, the battle might have ended in favour of the garrison, but the numerous buildings, on the whole, helped the attack, and the Swiss, unable to deploy, fought, almost singly, a very unequal fight. There were no volleys except the first. Rapid individual firing from the doors and windows of the palace, the crowd pressing up through the narrowest space (but at a loss of hundreds of lives), and finally, by the end which gave on the "Grande Galerie" the Tuilleries were forced, the garrison killed, and only a small detachment of the Swiss Guard retreated through the gardens, firing alternate volleys, and saving themselves by an admirable discipline.

But while the issue was still doubtful, Louis and his family had gone slowly through the same gardens to the Riding-school, and had taken refuge with the Assembly. The noise of the fusillade came sharply in at the windows, and the event was still uncertain when the Parliament received the King and promised him protection. The president opened for him a small door at the right of the chair, and the King and Queen and their children watched the meaningless resolutions through a grating as they sat in the little dark box that gave them refuge. The debate, I say, lacked meaning, but the battle grew full of meaning as they heard it. The shots were less frequent, the noise of the mob—the roar—was suddenly muffled in the walls of the palace. The crowd had entered it. Then came the few sharp volleys of the retreating guard right under the windows of the Manège, and finally the firing ceased, and the Assembly knew that their oath was of no value, and that the Tuilleries had fallen. Louis also knew it, eating his grotesque roast chicken in the silent and hidden place that was the first of his prisons. He saw in the bright light of the hall many of the faces that were to be the rulers of France, but for himself, in his silence, he felt all power to be gone. He had become a Capet—there was truth in the Republican formula. There had been played—though few have said it, it should be said—a very fine game. The stakes were high and the Court party dared them. They played to win all that the Kings had possessed, and for this great stake they risked a few foolish titles without power. The game was even; it was worth playing, and they had lost. But the man who had been their puppet and their figure-head hardly knew what had happened. Perhaps the Queen alone comprehended, and from that moment found the proud silence and the glance that has dignified her end. In her the legend of the lilies had found its last ally, but now the great shield was broken for ever.

So perished the French monarchy. Its dim origins stretched out and lost themselves in Rome; it had already learnt to speak and recognised its own nature when the vaults of the Thermae echoed heavily to the slow footsteps of the Merovingian kings. Look up that vast valley of dead men crowned, and you may see the gigantic figure of Charlemagne, his brows level and his long white beard tangled like an undergrowth, having in his left hand the globe and in his right the hilt of an unconquerable sword. There also are the short, strong horsemen of the Robertian house, half-hidden by their leather shields, and their sons before them growing in vestment and majesty, and taking on the pomp of the Middle Ages; Louis VII., all covered with iron; Philip the Conqueror; Louis IX., who alone is surrounded with light: they stand in a widening interminable procession, this great crowd of kings; they loose their armour, they take their ermine on, they are accompanied by their captains and their marshals; at last, in their attitude and in their magnificence they sum up in themselves the pride and the achievement of the French nation. But time has dissipated what it could not tarnish, and the process of a thousand years has turned these mighty figures into unsubstantial things. You may see them in the grey end of darkness, like a pageant all standing still. You look again, but with the growing light and with the wind that rises before morning they have disappeared.

CHAPTER V
THE REPUBLIC August 10, 1792—April 5, 1793

The 10th of August is not, in the history of the Revolution, a turning-point or a new departure merely; it is rather a cataclysm, the conditions before and after which are absolutely different. You may compare it to the rush of the Atlantic, which "in one dreadful day and night" swept away the old civilisation in the legend. It is like one of the geological "faults" which form the great inland escarpments, and to read or to write of it is like standing on the edge of Auvergne. You have just passed through a volcanic plateau, rising slowly, more and more desolate: you find yourself looking down thousands of feet on to the great plain of Limagne.

There is no better test of what the monarchy was than the comparison of that which came before with that which succeeded its overthrow. There is no continuity. On the far side of the insurrection, up to the 9th of August itself, you have armies (notably that of the centre) contented with monarchy; you have a strong garrison at the Tuilleries, the ministers, the departments, the mayor of Paris (even) consulting with the crown. The King and the Girondins are opposed, but they are balanced; Paris is angry and expectant, but it has expressed nothing—it is one of many powers. The moderate men, the Rolands and the rest, are the radical wing. It is a triumph for the Revolution that the Girondins should be again in nominal control. Pétion is an idol. The acute friction is between a government of idealists standing at the head of a group of professional bourgeois, and a crown supported by a resurrected nobility, expecting succour and strong enough to hazard a pitched battle.

Look around you on the 11th of August and see what has happened. Between the two opponents a third has been intervened—Paris and its insurrectionary Commune have suddenly arisen. The Girondins are almost a reactionary party. The Crown and all its scaffolding have suddenly disappeared. The Assembly seems something small, the ministry has fallen back, and there appears above it one man only—Danton, called Minister of Justice, but practically the executive itself. A crowd of names which had stood for discussion, for the Jacobins, for persistent ineffective opposition, appear as masters. In a word, France had for the moment a new and terrible pretender to the vacant throne, a pretender that usurped it at last—the Commune.

The nine months with which this chapter will deal formed the Republic; it is they that are the introduction to the Terror and to the great wars, and from the imprisonment of the King to the fall of the Girondins the rapid course of France is set in a narrowing channel directly for the Mountain. The Commune, the body that conquered in August, is destined to capture every position, and, as one guarantee after another breaks down, it will attain, with its extreme doctrines and their concomitant persecution, to absolute power.

What was Danton's attitude during this period? It may be summed up as follows: Now that the Revolution was finally established, to keep France safe in the inevitable danger. He put the nation first; he did not subordinate the theory of the Revolution; he dismissed it. The Revolution had conquered: it was there; but France, which had made it and which proposed to extend the principles of self-government to the whole world, was herself in the greatest peril. When discussion had been the method of the Revolution, Danton had been an extremist. He was Parisian and Frondeur in 1790 and 1791; it was precisely in that time that he failed. The tangible thing, the objective to which all his mind leaned, appeared with the national danger; then he had something to do, and his way of doing it, his work in the trade to which he was born, showed him to be of a totally different kind from the men above whom he showed. I do not believe one could point to a single act of his in these three-quarters of a year which was not aimed at the national defence.

It is a point of special moment in the appreciation of his politics that Danton was alone in this position. He was the only man who acted as one of the innumerable peasantry of France would have acted, could fate have endowed such a peasant with genius and with knowledge. The others to the left and right were soldiers, poets, or pedants every one. Heroic pedants and poets who were never afraid, but not one of them could forget his theories or his vision and take hold of the ropes. Such diplomacy as there is is Danton's; it is Danton who attempts compromise, and it is Danton who persistently recalls the debates from personalities to work. It is he who warns the Girondins, and it is he who, in the anarchy that followed defeat, produced the necessary dictatorship of the Committee. Finally, when the Committee is formed, you glance at the names, the actions, and the reports, and you see Danton moving as a man who can see moves among the blind. He had been once "in himself the Cordeliers"—it had no great effect, for there was nothing to do but propose rights; now, after the insurrection, he became "in himself the executive," and later "in himself the Committee." So much is he the first man in France during these few months of his activity, that only by following his actions can you find the unity of this confused and anarchic period.

It falls into four very distinct divisions, both from the point of view of general history and from that of Danton's own life. The first includes the six weeks intervening between the 10th of August and the meeting of the Convention; it is a time almost without authority; it moves round the terrible centre of the massacres. During this brief time the executive, barely existent, without courts or arms, had him in the Ministry of Justice as their one power—a power unfortunately checked by the anarchy in Paris.

The second division stretches from the meeting of the Convention to the death of the King. It covers exactly four months, from the 20th of September 1792 to the 21st of January 1793. It is the time in which the danger of invasion seems lifted, and in which Danton in the Convention is working publicly to reconcile the two parties, and secretly to prevent, if possible, the spread of the coalition against France.

The third opens with the universal war that follows the death of Louis, and continues to a date which you may fix at the rising of the 10th of March, or at the defeat of Neerwinden on the 19th. Danton is absent with the army during the greater part of these six weeks; he returns at their close, and when things were at their worst, to create the two great instruments which he destined to govern France—the Tribunal and the Committee.

Finally, for two months, from the establishment of these to the expulsion of the Girondins on the 2nd of June, he is being gradually driven from the attempt at conciliation to the necessities of the insurrection. He is organising and directing the new Government of the Public Safety, and in launching that new body, in imposing that necessary dictator, we shall see him sacrificing one by one every minor point in his policy, till at last his most persistent attempt—I mean his attempt to save the Girondins—fails in its turn. Having so secured an irresistible government, and having created the armies, the chief moment of his life was past. It remained to him to retire, to criticise the excesses of his own creation, and to be killed by it.

Immediately after the insurrection, a week after he had taken the oath and made the short vigorous speech to the Assembly,[113] Danton sent out his first and almost his only act as Minister of Justice, the circular of the 18th of August,[114] which was posted to all the tribunals in France. It is peculiar rather than important; it is the attempt to convince the magistracy and all the courts of the justice and necessity of the insurrection, and at the same time to leave upon record a declaration of his own intentions now that he had reached power. In the first attempt he necessarily fails. The old judicature, appointed by the Crown and by the moderate ministers, largely re-elected by the people, wealthy for the most part, conservative by origin and tradition, would in any case have rejected such leadership; but the matter is unimportant; this passive body, upon which the reaction had counted not a little, and which De Cicé had planned to use against the Revolution, was destined to disappear at the first demand of the new popular powers. France for weeks was practically without courts of law.

Those passages, on the other hand, in which Danton makes his own apology are full of interest. They contain in a few sentences the outline of all his domestic policy, and we find in them Danton's memories, his fears of what his past reputation might do to hurt him.

"I came in through the breach of the Tuilleries, and you can only find in me the same man who was president of the Cordeliers.... The only object of my thoughts has been political and individual liberty, ... the maintenance of the laws, ... the strict union of all the Departments, ... the splendour of the State, and the equality, not of fortune, for that is impossible, but of rights and of well-being."

If we except the puerilities of the new great seal, the Hercules with eighty-four stars (to represent the union of the Departments), replaced by the conventional Liberty and fasces, there is practically nothing more from Danton as Minister of Justice. But as the one active man in the Cabinet he is the pivot of the whole time. Those qualities in him which had so disgusted the men of letters were the exterior of a spirit imperatively demanded in Paris at the time. His heavy, rapid walk, the coarseness and harshness of his voice, his brutality in command, exercised a physical pressure upon the old man Roland, the mathematician Monge, and the virtuous journalists who accompanied them. I know of but one character in that set which could have prevented Danton's ascendancy, and have met his ugly strength by a force as determined and more refined. Roland's wife might have done it, but though she was the soul of the ministry, she was hardly a minister, and being a woman, she was confined to secondary and indirect methods. Her hatred of Danton increased to bitterness as she saw him succeed, but she could not intervene, and France was saved from the beauty and the ideals which might have been the syrens of her shipwreck.

The three weeks following the 10th of August were filled with the news of the invasion. The King of Prussia had hesitated to march. France, full of herself, never understood that such a thing was possible. The kings were on the march, the great and simple ideas, so long in opposition, had met in battle. All France thought that 1792 was already 1793. Perhaps there were only two men in the country who saw the immaturity, the complexity, and the chances of the situation—I mean Danton and Dumouriez: Dumouriez, because he was by nature a schemer who had seen and was to see the matter from close at hand; Danton, because, from the first moment of his entrance into the ministry, he had gathered up the threads of negotiation into his hand.

The King of Prussia had hesitated, so had Brunswick. It was the success of the insurrection that decided them. They made the error that the foreigner always makes, the error that led the most enlightened Frenchmen to exaggerate the liberal forces in England, the error of seeing ourselves in others. They imagined that "the sane body of the nation," the Frenchmen that thought like Prussians, would rise in defence of the monarchy and in aid of the invasion. They had no conception of how small in number, how hesitating, and how vile were the anti-national party.

On Sunday the 19th the frontier was crossed; on the Thursday Longwy capitulated, and a German garrison held the rocky plateau that overlooks the plain of Luxembourg. A week later, Thursday the 30th, Verdun was surrounded.

From the hills above the town, the same hills which make of Verdun the fifth great entrenched camp of modern France, the Prussian batteries bombarded with a plunging fire. There may have been food and ammunition for two or three more days, but fire had broken out in several quarters, and the town council was imploring Beaurepaire to surrender. Brunswick proposed a truce and terms of capitulation. On the Saturday, the 1st of September, after a violent discussion, the terms were rejected, but Beaurepaire knew that nothing could save the town, and in the night he shot himself. On the next day, Sunday the second, Verdun yielded and the road to Paris lay open.

Meanwhile, in the capital itself, a vortex was opening, and the poor remnants of public authority and of public order were being drawn down into it. The 10th of August had been a victory into which there entered three very dangerous elements. First, it was not final; it had been won against a small local garrison under the menace of an invasion, and this invasion was proving itself irresistible. Secondly, it had left behind it terrors accentuated by success; I mean whatever fears of vengeance or of the destruction of Paris existed before the insurrection were doubled when so much greater cause had been given for the "execution" that Brunswick had threatened. Finally, the success of the insurrection had of itself destroyed the last shadow of executive power, for all such power, weak and perishing though it was, had centred in the King.

But besides these clear conditions which the 10th of August had produced, there was something deeper and more dangerous—the fear which fed upon itself and became panic, and which ran supported by anger growing into madness. There was no news but made it worse, no sight in the streets and no rumour but increased the intolerable pressure. Trade almost ceased, and the whole course of exchange, which is the blood of a great city, seemed to have run to the heart. Over the front of the Hotel de Ville hung that enormous black flag with the letters "Danger" staring from it in white, and in the heavy winds another blew out straight and rattled from the towers of Notre Dame. Every action savoured of nightmare, and suffered from a spirit grotesque, exaggerated, and horrible. The very day after the fight a great net had been cast over Paris and drawn in full of royalists. The gates had been shut suddenly, and every suspect arrested by order of the Commune. The prisons were full of members of the great conspiracy, for in civil war the vanquished appear as traitors. Then there arose a violent demand for the trial and punishment of those who had called in the foreigner, and a demand as violent, touching on miracle, for innumerable volunteers. In every project there ran this spirit of madness mixed with inspiration.

If Paris lost its head, so did the Assembly and the Moderates, but in another fashion. Paris was pale with the intensity of anger, Roland from a sudden paralysis. The fear of Paris was an angry panic; with the Girondins it was the sudden sickness that takes some men at the sight of blood. Paris had clamoured for an excess when it demanded the trial of the Swiss, who had done nothing beyond their mercenary duty; but the executive met it by an excess of weakness when it produced its court of ridiculous and just pedants, afraid to condemn, afraid to decide. Already the people had learned the secret payments of the old civil list,[115] the salaries paid to the emigrants, the subsidised press. Golier's report had appeared but a day before the invasion.

The news of Longwy was already known. Verdun stood in peril, when the acquittal of Montmorin on Friday the 31st seemed to be the deciding weakness of the government that pushed the populace to their extreme of violence.

He had been governor of Fontainebleau, openly and patently a conspirator on the side of the Tuilleries; he was not acquitted of this. It was admitted that he had "planned civil war;" he was released by that heroic but fatal fault of the Girondins, the fault that later sent them to the guillotine, and that now inspired their tribunal—they would not bend an inch to compromise with necessity; rather than do so they would deliberately aggravate the worst conditions by inclining against the passions of the moment. They seemed to say, "You clamour for mere reprisals; we will show, on the contrary, that we are just, and we will even irritate you with mercy." Yet they knew that Montmorin deserved death.

After that decision, and when Osselin the judge took with great courage the prisoner's arm in his own and led him away, a voice in the court cried out, "You acquit him now, and in a fortnight his friends will march into Paris." The massacres were certain from that moment; the thing had been said which made the small band of murderers start out, which made Paris look on immovable, and which kept the National Guard silent, refusing to stop the carnage. "We will go to the frontier, but we will not leave enemies behind us. If the law will not execute them, the people will." The damnable spirit which runs in colonies and wild places had invaded civilised Europe, and the lynching was determined.

When the Assembly had yielded to the Commune, when it was certain that the insurrectionary Commune would have its own way, and when it was known that Longwy had fallen, that Verdun was surrounded, there took place one of those scenes that stand out like pictures in the mind, and that interpret the characters of history for us better than any accumulation of detail.

In the garden of the Ministry of Foreign Affairs, at its end, and away from the house, and under the low foliage, the six ministers were met in an informal gathering—rapid, half-silent, a council not predetermined, suited to the time; a few hurried words, whose description has come down to us by no minute, but by the accident of Fabre's presence. Fabre d'Eglantine, the uncertain poet, Danton's protégé, and dangerous, ill-balanced friend,[116] stood watching at a little distance.

Roland spoke for all his friends. He was very pale and broken-down; he leaned his head against a tree—"We must leave Paris." Danton spoke louder, "Where do you mean to go?" "We must go to Blois. We must take with us the King and the treasure." So said Servan; so said Clavière. Kersaint, whom Danton had known at the old Commune in 1791, and who was something of Danton's kind, added his word: "I have just come from Sedan, and I know there is nothing else to be done. Brunswick will be here in Paris within the fortnight as surely as the wedge enters when you strike." Danton stopped six waverers by a phrase, a phrase of just such a character, exaggerated, violent, as his good sense made use of so often in the tribune. "My mother is seventy years old, and I have brought her to Paris; I brought my children yesterday. If the Prussians are to come in, I hope it may be into a Paris burnt down with torches." Then he turned round to Roland in person and threw out a fatal sentence, necessary, perhaps, but one of many that dug the great gulf between him and the Girondins. "Take care, Roland, and do not talk too much about flight; the people might hear you."[117]

I know of no anecdote that tells more about Danton, or explains with greater clearness his attitude during the crisis that brought on the massacres. For these over-vigorous words, full of excess, were uttered by a man whose character was all for material results—results obtained, as a rule, by compromise. This same Danton, who talked of "torches" and "Paris en cendres," was the only man in France who had the self-control to negotiate for the retreat of the Prussians after Valmy. His "mother of seventy years" had indeed been brought to Paris, but from Arcis, which every one knew to be right in the track of the invasion. What we have to discover in this speech, as in every phrase he uttered, is the motive; for with any other of the great Revolutionaries words were the whole of the idea, and sometimes more than the idea, but with Danton alone words were the means to a tangible end.

He desired to prevent that fatal breach with Paris which he had foreseen to be a risk from the beginning, and which Mirabeau in his time had thought so near as to be necessary. He was determined to keep this shadow—the national executive—in reach of the one thing that was alive and vigorous and defending the nation. It is of the greatest importance in appreciating his attitude to know that he dreaded the Commune. Later, no one of the deputies of Paris in the Convention saw as he saw the necessity of amalgamation with the Departments. Marat he thoroughly despised. Most of the men of the Commune had sat in one room with him; Panis and Sergent had even desks under him. He knew them, and he contemned them all. He did not know to what crimes they were about to commit themselves, or perhaps he would have interfered, but he knew they were worthless.

Behind them, however, he saw Paris, and in Paris he ardently believed, in its position and in its necessity. He was entirely right. Once let the ministers leave the city, and civil war would begin—a civil war waged within ten days' march of the enemy, and between what forces? An imbecile, a man like one of our moderns, who thinks in maps and numbers, would have said, "Between eighty-three departments and one." But Danton knew better. He had that appreciation which is common to all the masters; he knew the meaning of potential and of the word 'quality.' It would have been a fight between the members and the brain, and the brain would have died fighting, leaving a body dead because the brain had died.

Thus while the Assembly and the Commune fight their sharp battle of the last days of August, while the Parliament commands new municipal elections, breaks the municipality, then flatters it, then yields and permits it to be practically reinforced under the form of a fresh vote from the Sections,[118] Danton acts as though both Parliament and Commune had dropped from the world. There are two speeches of his, one of the 28th of August, one of the 2nd of September, and between them they mark his attitude and form also the origins of that full year of action and rhetoric which define him in history.

In the first, he proposes and carries the measure which has been made an excuse for laying upon his shoulders the responsibility of the massacres. The speech was made for a very different purpose. He authorised the domiciliary visits, but his object was to obtain arms. One thought only occupied him: to counteract the intense individualism of the Moderates, to force despotic measures through a Parliament that hated them, and to force these measures because without them the situation was lost. He got his arms, and just afterwards his mass of volunteers, but the other measure which he had introduced to pacify the Commune, the domiciliary visits, have marked more deeply in the memories of the time, because in the troubled days that followed these visits seemed to be a beginning.

It was Sunday morning, the 2nd of September. Verdun (though no one knew it yet in Paris) had just fallen; Beaurepaire was dead. The "Comité de Surveillance" of the Commune had admitted Marat illegally,[119] and for a sinister reason. For three days the prisons had been marked, and those whom the Comité wished to save had been withdrawn; and though the movement was spontaneous, though the most of the Sections spoke before Marat,[120] yet there was an executive and a directory, and that madman was its chief. The moment that the massacres were beginning at the Carmes, Danton was making the last effort to turn the anger of the moment into an enthusiasm for the Champ de Mars and for the volunteers. If ever there was an attempt to influence by rhetoric a popular emotion which could not be checked, and to direct energy from a destructive to a fruitful object, it is to be found in this his most famous speech—the speech that even the children know to-day in France, the closing words of which are engraved upon his pedestal. For the only time in his life he turned and leant upon the mere power of words: there is something in their extraordinary force which savours of despair, and they rise at the close to an untranslatable phrase in which you hear rhythm for the first and last time in his appeals: "De l'audace, encore de l'audace, toujours de l'audace—et la France est sauvée."[121]

He did not wholly fail. When he had rung the great bell of the Hotel de Ville and had gone to the Champ de Mars, he looked over a great and growing crowd of young men running to the enlistment. But for four days— days in which he doggedly turned his back to the Commune which called him—the killing went on in the prisons. He and his volunteers, his silence, were most like this: a man in a mutiny on ship-board, in a storm at night, keeping the helm, saving what could be saved and careless whether the morning should make him seem a traitor on the one hand or a mutineer upon the other. For the tragedy of those five days—the days of Sedan— always seems to be passing in a thick night. We read records of action at this or that hour in the daylight, but we cannot believe the sun shone. Maillard, tall and pale in his close black serge and belt, is a figure for candles on the Abbaye table and for torches in the cloisters and the vaults. There never was a horror more germane to darkness.

But why did Danton not save the prisoners? I know that question is usually answered by saying that he was indifferent. So much (it seems to me) survives of a legend. For history no longer pretends that he organised or directed the crime. Indeed, history finds it daily more difficult, as the details accumulate, to fix it upon any one man. But the fact that he persistently defended the extremists in the following month, that he made himself (for the purposes of reunion) an advocate for many men who were blameworthy, and tried to reconcile the pure minds of the Girondins with such terrible memories—in a word, the fact that for months he sacrificed himself in the Convention, that he demanded union, has condemned him to every suspicion. *Que mon nom soit flétri et que la France soit libre.*

He might, indeed, have spoken. Popular, the one vigorous and healthy personality in the face of Paris, he might have bent his energy to the single aim of preventing an outbreak. I will not deny that in his mind, over which we have seen passionate anger falling suddenly in October 1789 and in June 1792, there may have arisen some such feeling as that which restrained the vast mass of the Parisians from interfering with the little band of murderers—a feeling of violent hatred, a memory of the manifesto and a disgust which made the partisans of Brunswick seem like vermin. There is something of that deplorable temper in the anecdote which Madame Roland gives of him, striding through the rooms on the second day and saying that the prisoners "could save themselves." But this anecdote is not history; it is an accusation, and one made by a partisan and an enemy.[122] There is another and better reason for his action, which must, I think, have made the greater part of his motive. To have spoken would have been to play a very heavy stake. If he spoke and failed to prevent the rising, he ceased to be Danton. His influence fell, he became a Moderate, and himself, the one man left to direct affairs, entered the confused ranks of opposition—un-Parisian, rejected of either party, while France beneath him fell into mere anarchy.

It would have been gambling with all that he most desired: the English neutrality, the union of the coming Parliament, the rapid organisation of the armies, all this staked to win something that was not precious to him at all—the lives of a mass of men the bulk of whom had demanded the success of the invasion.

Why did he not act? Because nobody could act. Remember the phrase which he delivered while Louis was being executed four months later: "Nulle puissance humaine."[123] We are so accustomed to an aristocratic and orderly society that a title of office implies power. The Home Secretary or some other man "does this," but the man who really does it—does it with his hands—is the policeman or the soldier. Now these did not exist at the moment in Paris. It explains a hundred things in the Revolution to remember that every successive step reduced society to powder, to a mere number of men. Rousseau had said that this compact, this thing based on voluntary union, was not made for the cities. Paris gave us in September an awful proof. Roland, a man whom Marat had put upon his list and whom Danton had saved, talked on the Monday of the "just anger of the people." Yet Roland was a just man, and brave in matters that affected himself alone, and the massacres chiefly concerned him. He was Minister of the Interior, that is, responsible for order, but there was nothing with which to work. On the Tuesday he sent to Santerre and said, "Call out the National Guard." Santerre answered that he could not gather them. He was right. Again, Pétion was an honest man, a Moderate, the mayor of Paris; all he could do was to sit at a useless committee of the Sections and talk of the "National Defence;" that utter disintegration which the theories of the Revolution had produced—that purely voluntary condition of the soldier, the official, the police (a mere anarchy)—was irresistible when there was spontaneity of action; it was useless where the conditions demanded organisation and initiative. It withstood the cannonade at Valmy, it stormed the height of Jemappes, but it fled in rout when the spring had melted enthusiasm. So here police, the function that most requires discipline, was lacking in the State. And the whole situation is summed up in the sharp picture we have of Manuel pushing his way though the crowd with "two policemen" who had "volunteered," and trying in vain to stop the lynching at the Carmes. It was to this anarchy that Danton, after six months of struggle, succeeded in giving government during 1793.

Danton himself, after four months of vain effort to reconcile his enemies, put the whole matter in the last phrase of his defence: "No human power" could have stopped the massacres;[124] all that could be done was to work, from that moment forward, against the extreme theories of a voluntary state, and towards the establishment of a strong government.[125]

When, on the Thursday, September 6, the wave receded, and when on the morrow Pétion was able to interfere, the people and the Assembly looked round them and saw that a thing had happened which was to hurt the future of the Revolution more than all the armies. It was like the breaking of day after that moral night, a daybreak in which the wind goes down and you see the wreckage.

Paris was very silent; the accusations had not yet begun; the Assembly was dying. The electoral council of Paris had met during the very days of the massacre, and had proceeded to choose the members who were to represent the capital in the Convention that was about to meet. It also voted in silence, and sat in the mingled panic and remorse that oppressed the whole city. The names came out in the balloting. On the 5th (the murderers were still growling in the streets) Robespierre was elected in a small meeting of 525; on the 6th Danton was elected second, but with a much larger attendance and with a much greater majority—638 votes out of an attendance of 700, a curious result. Danton's name forced itself upon them, was acclaimed beyond any other; yet his attitude of conciliation, his attempt to have all Paris represented, was set aside. The man and his reputation succeeded, his policy failed. They elected also Marat, Panis, Sergent—those who had directed the crime. Danton and Manuel alone of all the twenty-four had any touch of the Moderate about them. The long list ends with the name of Egalité, elected by a majority of one.[126]

There came, therefore, into the Convention an apparently united body of men from Paris—the Mountain. Up on the benches of the extreme left, in the grey, dark theatre of the Tuilleries, there were to sit, in a compact group, these extremists; and across the floor the Departments, the pure Republicans of the south, who despised the city and them, who feared them terribly, and who hated with the force of a religion, were to single them out as tyrants. And in this Mountain, this body of Reds, Danton was to find himself imbedded, bound up, falsified. He had determined to prevent such parties. He had tried hard to make Paris elect not only Robespierre but Pétion also as a mark of unity: he had failed.

When the country members came up to the capital, September had grown to be an awful legend. The number of those killed was multiplied ten times,[127] twenty times—number lost meaning. Paris seemed a city of blood. Guides volunteered story after story. "Here, in the Abbaye, the blood had risen so high"—they made a mark in the wall; "there, under that tree, the massacres were planned by such and such a one"—any name suited, sometimes it was Robespierre, sometimes Danton. The deputies came from their little towns and from the fields, over seven hundred—pilgrims from places where the pure enthusiasms of 1790 still lingered, where even 1792 had brought no passion. They came, many of them for the first time, bewildered in the enormous city; its noise confused them, its crowds, its anger—"Yes; that was where the massacres were committed a fortnight ago—we can believe it." The Convention from its first day seemed a battlefield—Paris defiant in the Mountain, and the Departments silent with an angry fear in the plain and on the benches of the right. And when the newcomers asked to be shown the group of deputies for Paris, as men would ask to be shown lurking enemies or wild beasts, they would have their gaze directed to that high place on the left where sat the names that had terrified and fascinated them in the prints of their country-sides.

There were no windows; the skylight, high above that deep well of a room, sent an insufficient light downwards upon the foreheads, making the features sharp and yet lending them a false gloom. That man with the small squat body and the frog's face was Marat; you could just see his great vain mouth in the dim light. Those small, keen features, well barbered and set up, the high forehead, the pointed bones of the cheek and chin, stood for Robespierre. The light fell chiefly on the white of his careful wig; his thin smile was in shadow. And who was that huge figure, made larger by the darkness and carrying a head like Mirabeau? They saw it moving when the others were fixed. He would speak to his neighbours with heavy, sweeping gestures. They grew accustomed to the half-light, and they could distinguish his face—the strong jaw, the powerful movement of the lips, torn and misshapen though they were; the rough, pitted skin, the small, direct, and deep-set eyes. Who was he? He seemed to them the very incarnation of all the bloodshed and unreason which they hated in Paris, a master of anarchy. It was Danton.

Against that impression all policy and wisdom broke. He demanded unity; he checked the growing attack on the rich; he said things that were like France speaking. But the voice was harsh and loud; they heard it in their minds at the head of mobs; they fled from him to the Girondins; they forced him back upon the Mountain, and he had to do his work alone in spite of those orators whom he would have befriended and whose genius he loved—in spite of those madmen who surrounded him, and who later killed him and the Republic with one axe.

It was on the 25th of September, a Thursday, that the Convention met in the Tuilleries; on the Friday, in the same place, with doors shut and with the galleries empty, they declared the Republic, and moved off to the Manège, where their predecessors had sat. In those two days the violent quarrel between Paris and France was hushed for a moment. Danton, in the lull, said all he could to define his own position and to prevent that quarrel from ever reaching a head. He went out to meet the Moderates. He declared, with the common sense of the peasant, that property must first be declared inviolable; and it is curious that the Convention, the majority that misunderstood him and broke with him, was yet less moderate than he; it passed the resolution, but in the form, "property is under the safeguard of the nation." In order to calm opinion he resigned the Ministry of Justice on the spot;[128] he did everything to make his position clear and true, and to save the unity of the Parliament.

But the attack came from the others. Within a week Lasource had proposed a guard for the Convention, "drawn from the departments;" and in the face of this proposition, that was almost civil war, Danton found himself able to speak once more for unity. The Girondins had elected one of themselves for president, and had chosen from among their own members the secretaries of the Assembly; they had wittingly ostracised the left, and they desired to make it dumb. Danton still attempted union. "I myself come from the Departments, from a place to which I always turn my eyes. But Paris is made of the Departments, and we are not here as members of this place or that, but as members for France." He continually presented the idea of France united; the Girondins as continually rejected it. He knew that they thought him a shield for Marat; he rejected Marat openly from the tribune. But all this intense and personal action had but an effect upon individuals. Two especially it moved—Vergniaud, the young orator, sincere and brave beyond all his colleagues, and more far-seeing than any of the dreamers around him; Condorcet, to whom a year before Danton had seemed so repulsive, but whose calm and just mind had arrived at the truth; who had said, "Danton has that rare faculty of neither hating nor envying genius in others;" who had voted and spoken for his appointment as Minister of Justice, and who, up to the catastrophe of the following June, continued to understand and to support him.

But, for the mass of the Girondins, he remained an outcast. He used words that one could not use before Roland's wife, and the great group that surrounded her (men over-full of utopias, but heroic, men whom Danton himself regretted bitterly) made him an outcast. He replied often with passion, and once with insult, but as we shall see he did not abandon them entirely till the insurrection destroyed them in '93.

Meanwhile, while they voted the Republic in Paris, under Argonne a battle among the most curious in history was making a momentary security— that is, a momentary union of good feeling throughout France, and even in Paris itself. The Prussian army had been checked on the little rise of Valmy. As you stand upon the field in that same season of the year to-day, in the mist of the early morning, as the volunteers and the battered remnants of the line stood then; as you look from that standpoint at the open road, at the great plain of Champagne, so well suited to maintain an army; as you see to the east the long wall of the Argonne, and remember that Dumouriez had been outflanked in his Thermopylæ, a confusion seizes the mind. Why on earth was Valmy so important a victory? It is a common-place to say that Valmy was a cannonade, but what was a cannonade in 1792? If indeed to-day a line of guns were drawn up and served, as I have seen them served in the manœuvres within sight of these same hills, and if a force should be discovered capable of withstanding the shrapnel of twelve batteries of artillery, sure of their range, turning the mark into a ploughed field—then that force would merit peculiar names, for it would be immortal. But in the eighteenth century guns were not the arbiters of battles. Infantry could charge the batteries then. France, which was crushed yesterday and will succeed to-morrow solely through artillery, had not a hundred years ago to dread the random solid shot of smooth bores; what she had to dread was the bayonet charge of that superb infantry which the great Frederick had trained, and on which the monstrous scaffolding of Prussia still reposes. All we can say of Valmy is this, that men quite ignorant of warfare, badly held together, managed to stand firm under an ill-directed, at times a desultory and distant cannon fire.

Valmy was not a victory. The results of Valmy have changed the world, but no one could have seen it then. Goethe, in the course of a long life, discovered it, and put it beautifully into his own mouth over one of the bivouac fires: "We entered on a new world then;" but there were better prophets than Goethe, and not one perceived it. For days the Prussian army hesitated. Dumouriez did not dare to meet them. A pitched battle in the last days of September might have changed all history.

Why then did the King of Prussia retreat? No force compelled, but two arguments convinced him. The peasantry, and Danton, the man who through the whole year is, as it were, a peasant trained and illumined. The resistance of the peasantry had taught the King that to reach Paris it required not a war of the dynasties, such as had filled the eighteenth century—wars in which armies passed like visiting caravans; the invasion of France would need a crusade. He was no crusader. He had undertaken the war with only half a heart, and at this slight check he hesitated. The second argument came from Danton. He bargained like a peasant secretly for the purchasable and obvious good, while the Parliament was talking as might talk a conqueror who was something of a poet and well read in the classics. When there was a talk of negotiations just after the battle, it launched the great words, "That the Republic does not discuss till its territory is evacuated." That was on Tuesday; the Republic was young to discuss anything—it was four days old. On Wednesday night, Westermann, Danton's man of the 10th of August, and his companion at the scaffold, started off secretly to diplomatise. That foolish man D'Eglantine followed him, but his folly was swallowed up in the wisdom of Danton, who sent him, a secretary and a mouthpiece, to do that which, had he done it himself, would have produced some violent and ill-considered vote. Between them this clique settled the matter, and the invaders passed back through the Argonne heavily, in wet roads and through drenched woods, with Kellermann following, impatient, above the valleys, but bound by Danton's policy not to harass the retreat; till at last, more than a month after Valmy,[129] he fired the salute from Longwy, and the territory was free.

Did Danton know, as he was pursuing these plans, why Dumouriez helped him? Did he understand thoroughly that vain, talented, and unprincipled soldier? I think it certain. It is among those things which cannot be proved; one does not base such convictions upon documents, but rather on the general appreciation of character. Thus Danton undoubtedly helped and used Talleyrand at another time in England, and Talleyrand was patently false. But Talleyrand was, as patently, the cleverest diplomatist he could find. Dumouriez wished the King of Prussia to be left unmolested for a number of very mixed reasons, in which patriotism played a small part; Danton wished it for the sake of France, and for that only; but if Dumouriez at the head of an army was to hand, so much the better. Danton supported Dumouriez, his policy, even his retreats up to the disaster of March. To say "he sympathised with a traitor" is one of those follies which men can only make when they forget that contemporaries cannot have known what we know. With all his time-serving and his separate plans, no one dreamt that in six months the general would join the Austrians; it was a sudden blow even to those who sat in his tent.

October was a month of reconciliation. When the man broad awake succeeds, the dreamer is ready to build a new dream on that result. The Gironde was almost silent, the Mountain was afraid. In the short visit that Dumouriez paid, between a victory and a victory, to Paris, Danton appears for a moment a partner in the mental ease, the brilliant expression, and the Republican faith of the Girondins. He might perhaps have ended there, and with his great arms and shoulders have held apart the men whose mutual hatred killed the Republic. In his success—and every one bore him gratitude after Valmy—that which he most desired almost happened, and the alliance between the opposing Girondist and the Mountain was half realised.

Michelet gives us two pictures[130] which, like the revelation of lightning, show us that rapid drama standing still. In the first it is Madame Roland, in the second Marat, who makes the tragedy. In the first Dumouriez and Danton sat in the same box at the theatre, and Vergniaud was coming in with the soul of the Girondins. The door opened and promised this spectacle: Danton and the general and the orator of the pure Republicans, and the woman most identified with the Right. It would have been such a picture for all the people there as Danton would have prayed or paid for. The door was ajar, and, as she came near, Madame Roland saw Danton sitting in the box; she put out her hand from Vergniaud's arm and shut the door. There is in her memoirs a kind of apology,"des femmes de mauvaise tournure." Utter nonsense; it was Roland's box, and his wife was expected. Danton and Dumouriez were not of the gutter. No, it was the narrow feminine hatred, so closely allied to her intense devotion, that made Madame Roland thrust Danton at arm's length. The same spirit that made her vilify the Left like a fury made her the calm saint of the Girondins. For she lived entirely in the Idea.

The second scene is a reception. I will not repeat Michelet's description; its spirit is contained in an admirable phrase: "France civilised appealed therein against France political." Danton was surrounded with those whom he would have taught, as he taught all who ever knew him closely, to respect or to love him. Marat heard that he was there—Marat, whom he had repudiated in public a few days before. He heard that Danton was there, surrounded by the soldiers, and the women, and the orators. He called at the door, and shouted in the hall, "I want to see Danton," and at the sound of his voice everybody grew troubled, and Danton was left alone. On the 29th of October Danton attempted openly to break with Marat: "I declare to you and to France," he said in the Convention, "that I have tried Marat's temperament, and I am no friend of his." But the attempt came too late.

The discussions broke out again in November. On the 10th, the victory of Jemappes was heard in Paris. This book, dealing only with a man, cannot detail those famous charges; it was a victory won by men singing the new songs; it is the inspiration of "La victoire en chantant." But the security it gave only went further to destroy what was left of union. Danton found himself more and more alone. He who had been named on a committee with Thomas Paine, with Condorcet, with Pétion, on the very day after his election to the presidency of the Jacobins,[131] who had in his own temporary success seemed to realise his policy of union, found himself after a month once more pushed back towards the Mountain. The growing sense of security had destroyed the chances of union. He remained silent. One would say that the time passed him by untouched, because the one thing he cared for had failed, and because the inevitable civil dissensions of the next spring covered his mind with clouds. France was irretrievably divided. The arraignment of the King, the discovery of the secret papers, all the movement of November leaves him, as it were, stranded, waiting his mission to Belgium.

There belongs to this period only one considerable speech. It is the only thing in all his public acts in which you can discover beauty. You may find in this speech the pity and the tenderness which his intimates loved, the memory which they for sixty years defended, but which no document or letter remains to perpetuate.

Cambon, careless of anything but his exchequer, had thought the new era come. That cold and inflexible head determined, seeing the steep fall towards bankruptcy that France was making, to save a hundred millions, but to save it at an expense. He proposed to separate the State from what was left of the Church, to break the vow of 1790. In almost the last speech before he went off to the armies, Danton opposed him and gave this passage—a passage better fitted to the defence of an older and stronger thing than the wretched constitutional priesthood:—

"... It is treason against the nation to take away its dreams. For my part, I admit I have known but one God. The God of all the world and of justice. The man in the fields adds to this conception that of a man who works, whom he makes sacred because his youth, his manhood, and his old age owe to the priest then: little moments of happiness. When a man is poor and wretched, his soul grows tender, and he clings especially to whatever seems majestic: leave him his illusions—teach him if you will ... but do not let the poor fear that they may lose the one thing that binds them to earth, since wealth cannot bind them."

Before he left on the mission to the armies there occurred a scene which has always been, since Michelet described it, the most striking passage of his relations with the Girondins. He, the man who saw safety for France only in diplomacy, had, for the sake of unity, held his tongue when the Girondins passed the decree of the 19th November, which was to sustain a revolutionary crusade against Europe. I say that November is full of Danton's attempt to maintain the unity of the Parliament. After all these efforts he was worsted, because the Girondins were possessed by a dream which admitted of no compromise and of no realities.

The scene of his last attempt was this:—He made a rendezvous with their party. They were to meet secretly at night and away from Paris in a house in the woods of Sceaux at the very end of November. The whole life of this man was a tragedy, and we see in this sad journey that kind of dramatic presentiment of his death and of theirs, the "foreknowledge" with which the tragedies of the world are filled.

He went through the desolate bare woods of November, under the hurrying sky, that recalls to our minds in France to-day the charges of Jemappes. The night was as wild as the time, and as dark as his forebodings, when he came on to the little group of men in the candlelight, and argued with them, and against them, and alone. Michelet gives to Danton's mind a sentiment of coercion. He shows us Danton dragged by necessity. But I can see no necessity except the supreme desire to unite the parties and make the government real. They would not receive his alliance, and he went away from that meeting at midnight, pushed back upon Paris, thrown into the comradeship of violence. Guadet rejected him with an especial fervour. Danton as he left turned upon him with this phrase: "Guadet, Guadet, you cannot understand and you do not know how to forgive; you are headstrong, and it will be your doom." The next day he started on his mission to the army.

During the arraignment and during the trial of the King the opinions that divided the Left and the Right fought it out in his absence.[132] He was not there to attempt such a movement as his character demanded. No one in all the Assembly dared hold out a hand as he would have done and see whether after all Vergniaud might not perhaps be right on the one hand, and the Mountain perhaps be patriots on the other.

There was in this debate upon one man's life an element to which Danton's nature was well suited. There had to be kept in view for the French nation the effect upon Europe which would follow from the determination as to the death or life of the King, and Danton's great voice has so strongly and so rightly affected the historians of the period that he thrusts his personality forward into their narrative, and in at least one notable place Danton appears, in history, and in one of the greatest pages of history, by no right, and figures upon scenes which do not possess the advantage of his voice. He has been made to defend Louis's life, to plead for a respite, and then by a violent change to vote for his death.

Let me now explain how this error passed into the mind of Michelet and of other men. Danton returned from Belgium on the night of the 14th January. On that same day a certain Dannon, apparently an honest man,[133] rose late in the evening and demanded respite for Louis. When Gallois reprinted the *Moniteur*, he saw this obscure name coupled with a politic demand; he read it again, and said, "This Dannon must be a misprint for Danton." He corrected it so. On this chance venture there fell the eye of Michelet, the eye that from a glance or a word could bring back the colours and the movements of living men. In him also the tragedy of Danton powerfully worked; he moulded a figure from these few words in the *Moniteur*, and made of them an admirable anti-climax. Here was Danton (Dannon) hot from the armies, knowing in what peril France stood, having seen with his own eyes how momentary had been the effects of Jemappes. He comes from his travelling coach to the Assembly, and with the mud of the road yet upon him, gives his expression as an ally to the Girondins and to the Moderates. Then some rebuff, some unrecorded insult throws him back again as he had been so often thrown back into the arms of the Extremists. On the next day, the 15th of January, we are asked to watch him sitting by the side of his dying wife, sullen and despairing. On the 16th he comes back furious, and votes for the death of the King.

There are those for whom detail in history is pedantic, yet here upon three letters and their order hangs the interpretation not only of an individual character but of a policy whose effects we are still feeling. Michelet's great picture is false from beginning to end. Danton had returned on the 14th, and came jaded with his journey to the bedside of her who had been his young wife of five years, who was now near to childbirth and to death. He had his own drama as well as that of the historian's, and our own dramas are acted upon a stage where the results are real. All that night of the 14th and all the 15th he was watching in his flat of the Passage du Commerce a fate which was coming upon him, and certainly for whose thirty-six hours the Revolution was a little thing to him. He came back wearily to his position and to his duties on the 16th; he remembered there was such a thing as the Revolution—that Louis was after all on trial, and descended from his home into the hall of the Parliament to give the short angry sentence in which we seem to read less moderation and less of diplomacy than was his by nature. The scene in the home had made him not only bitter but weak, for there is surely weakness in saying, "I am not a statesman," in borrowing, that is, the vulgar acrimony of Marat, or in talking of "the tyrant," and in repeating the phrases of the Mountain.

But in the days that followed Michelet finds a good excuse. Certainly one would say, if one knew nothing about him except his action of January 1793, that Danton was the Mountain and nothing else. This error would be supported by the unreasoning vehemence, the almost brutal anger, into which he allows himself to fall.

They asked whether the King could be condemned to death by a mere majority, and whether that majority was decisive. Danton threw back at them: "You decided the Republic by a mere majority, you changed the whole history of the nation by a mere majority, and now you think the life of one man too great for a mere majority; you say such a vote could not be decisive enough to make blood flow. When I was on the frontier the blood flowed decisively enough."

So naturally was he at that moment the Danton of unreason, so much had his character yielded to its persistent temptation of violent words, that there could be heard a voice once calling out to him as he rushed to the tribune without leave from the Speaker, "You are not a king yet, Danton." And yet this was the man who had saved France from any folly of defiance after Valmy, who was determined upon saving her in the future by keeping upon the helm a quiet and unswerving hand. Vergniaud's great simile, "That France might become, if she did not take care, like the statues of Egypt; they astonish by their greatness, and yet are enigmas to all who see them, because the living spirit that made them has died," passed him by without effect. He was one of those who voted in the fatal majority, and he threw down as gage of battle the head of a king.[134]

The word had become reality, and Louis had stood at mid-day trying to be heard beyond the ring of soldiers, had cried out that he was innocent, and had died in the noon of that cold January day. This act was destined to produce the one thing that Danton had most ardently desired to avoid—it put an end once and for all to the neutrality of England.

Another people, then in their infancy, now old, whom Louis had been persuaded to help against his will, received the death of Louis like a kind of blow in the face. The people of the United States in their simplicity had imagined the French king to be their saviour; they did not know Louis's phrase, "I was dragged into that unhappy affair of America; advantage was taken of my youth." They regarded his crown with a certain superstition, as they still regard what is left of baubles in Europe; and when the axe fell upon him, France lost not only the calculating hypocrisy of Pitt, but the genuine sympathy of the American people.

In the days that followed (they were only ten) between the 21st of January and the end of the month, it is still plain that the shock which most affected Danton's vigorous and independent judgment was that return after seven weeks to the wife whom he had passionately loved, and whom this ugly Orpheus felt slipping from his arms back into the shades. After her death, as we shall see, he did not reel so heavily, but in that fortnight of January, which was of such supreme importance, he permitted misfortune to rouse mere passion in his mind; and he who might have led the Moderates, who might have played with the life of Louis like a card, chose to remember his rebuff in the winter and threw his trump away.

Many have tried to explain Vergniaud's vote. Is it not probable that he was drawn by the example of a man whom he did not understand, and whose opinion attracted an orator not unappreciative of energy? Vergniaud has always before history a doubting and a hesitating face, and it seems more than possible that the wrath of Danton carried him and many others into the vote for death.

Ever since the 10th of August had thrust him into unexpected power, Danton had held in one way or another the threads of a certain diplomacy. It was as follows:—To rely upon all the elements in Europe which admired or were indifferent to the Revolution, and to combine them in a kind of resistant body; to use, as it were, their inertia against those who were setting out as crusaders against France. On this account the foolish war of propaganda was most distasteful to him. On this account England's neutrality haunted his mind. He knew that in this country there existed a body strong in its influence though not in its numbers, a body which would have supported the French. Priestley had written to him before his exile. Talleyrand was working for him at the moment, and opposing as an informal Dantonist the Girondin acerbity of Chauvelin.[135] Danton was even willing to use Dumouriez, mainly because Dumouriez was about to compromise with England. To this policy of observation, a policy which took advantage of England as the lover of individual liberty and of England as the merchant, the death of the King put a sudden stop. It was Danton that killed his own intrigue.

Before he left on his second mission to the armies on the 31st January 1793, he shows that new face in which he attempts to retrieve, as far as possible, the errors of which he had been largely the author. In a speech which shows once again all his old power of party political action, he demands the annexation of Belgium. He has seen that general war is inevitable, and harking back again to that unique French conception of which he was the heir, the *raison d'état*, he determines to save the State, and to do it by an action which opposed every theory of the Revolution. He asked "everything of their reason, nothing of their enthusiasm," and he demanded the annexation of Belgium with France. It was pure opportunism—the determination to get hold of a revenue by force of arms; and the next day, after having painfully come back to his old policy of the real and objective, burdened by a past error, and having broken with all that he valued in French opinion, he went off again to the army. While his chaise was yet rolling on the flat roads of Flanders, Chauvelin returned with Pitt's scrawl in his hand, and France was at war with the whole world.

This next voyage to Belgium occupied but a very short time. He did not get there until the 3rd February, and he started to come back on the 15th. But the moment, which is necessarily a silent one in his biography, would be one of capital importance to us had he remained in Paris to speak, and to leave us by his speeches some clue as to the revolution through which his mind had passed.

Consider these contrasting pictures: Danton, up to the death of the King, seems uniquely occupied in pursuing the threads of a very careful diplomacy, and in welding as far as possible the opposing factions of the Parliament. Of course, his general theories in politics remain unaltered, but something has happened which makes him, on returning from Belgium for the second time, pursue this different policy: the immediate construction of a strong central government, and the providing of it with exceptional and terrible machinery. He works this as absolutely the unique policy. He seems to have forgotten all questions of diplomacy, nearly to have despaired of settling the quarrel between Paris and the Girondins. In fine, Danton, when first in power, had been a man so representative of France as to have many different objects, and to attempt their co-ordination. We see him the brief fortnight of Louis's execution violent, angry, unreasoning; we see him again in less than a month transformed into a man with a single object, pursued and succeeded in with the tenacity common to minds much narrower than his own.

I know that events will largely account for the change. The Girondins had repelled him; diplomacy had no further object when once the universal war was declared; the grave perils, and later the disasters of the French armies, which he had seen with his own eyes, called imperatively for a dictatorship. Nevertheless events will not of themselves account for the very great transformation in all that he says and does. I believe that we must look to another cause—one of those causes which historians neglect, but which in the lives of individuals are of far more importance than their political surroundings. By nature he had great tendencies to indolence as well as to violence. He was capable of temporising to a dangerous extent, and this, I think, was largely the cause of his action in the autumn. But such natures are also of the kind which disaster spurs to action. As we have seen, the return in January to his household, ruined by an impending fate, made him the violent and bitter speaker who spoiled his own plans by his own speeches. But returning from Belgium in February, not a menace but a definite disaster awoke in him a much more useful energy.

Coming from fields in which he had seen the whole force of the early battles breaking up in confusion and retreat, he had suddenly to meet the news of his wife's death. He bought a light carriage for himself in order to travel with greater speed, and arrived at the city in time, they say, to have her coffin taken out of the grave and opened, so that he might look once more upon her face. The home was entirely empty. The two little children, one of whom was in arms, the other of whom was just beginning to talk, had been taken away to their grandmother's. The seals were on the furniture and on the doors. One servant only remained. The house had been without a fire for a week when he entered. It was an opportunity and a command for another origin in his political life. Coming and going from these rooms, he found them intolerable; he took refuge in direct and determined action, calling to his aid all that vast reserve of energy which he was accustomed to expend at the cost of so much future exhaustion.

Here was the first thing to be done—to construct at once that strong and simple government which he had talked of so long. The report which he and the other commissioners had prepared on the state of the army[136] was one deliberately intended to make such a government voted. The Commune of Paris immediately after the preparation of the report made its vigorous appeal for a further levy, and on the 8th of March Danton made the first of those speeches which riveted the armour all round France.[137]

In the first phrase of this speech he strikes the note upon which depended so much of his power. He reads his own character into that of the nation. "We have often discovered before now that this is the temper of the French people—namely, that it needs dangers to discover all its energy." Then he strikes the other note, the appeal to Paris which had marked so much of his career. "Paris, which has been given so ill a fame" (a stroke at the Girondins), "I say is called once more to give France the impulse which last year produced all our triumphs. We promised the army in Belgium 30,000 men on the 1st of February. None have reached them. And I demand that commissioners be named to raise a force in the forty-eight Sections of Paris."

If there was some talk at that moment of making him Minister of War after Beurnonville's resignation, it was because no one but Danton himself understood how much his energy could do. He rejected the proposal, but he had the desire to replace the ministers themselves by a power more formidable and more direct.

In these days one disaster after another came to help his scheme. More than one of his enemies had suspected in a vague fashion that he was framing a new power,[138] but they could not imagine in Danton anything higher than ambition, and they lent him the ridiculous project of forcing a new ministry upon the Assembly. What he was really preparing, and what he produced on the 10th of March, was the weapon which history has called the Revolutionary Tribunal.

It was the moment when the mutterings against the Girondins seemed about to take the form of an insurrection, when their printing presses were broken, and when, in the vague panic that always followed any popular movement since September, men feared a renewal of the massacres. The proposal is put forward with ability of argument rather than with passion; but, in the teeth of the majority and a ministry to which such methods were detestable, in the teeth, that is, of the Girondin idealism which was ruining the country, he affirmed the necessity of his scheme, and he passed it.[139] He had given the Revolutionary Government its first great weapon, a weapon that was later to be turned against himself; his second move was to put it into vigorous hands.

This next proposition, which, combined with the establishment of the Revolutionary Tribunal, was to change the history of France, did not proceed from Danton alone, but it was based upon Danton's suggestion; it sprang largely from the vivid impression he had given of the peril in which France lay and of the necessity of forming something central and strong, of providing a hand which could use the dictatorship of the Terror. The Committee of Public Safety, in a word, could not have been declared but for the interpretation which Danton had given to the disasters of March.

The crowning defeat of Neerwinden, which at the time must almost have seemed the death of the Republic, gave the first impulse. The old Committee of General Defence was renewed. But though this committee was far too large and far too feeble, we owe it to Danton that it contained a vigorous minority from the Left. The final blow that replaced it by an institution round which the rest of this book will turn was the treason of Dumouriez.

Let us consider what the situation was at this moment. The Republic had lost every man upon whose ability she could rely in the leadership of armies. Of all the school of generals who had grown up under the old regime, Lafayette alone in his weak way had loved freedom, and Dumouriez alone had remained on the side of the French. Spain, England, the German Powers—nine allies—were threatening the territory of the Republic and the very existence of the new regime; the civil war, which was soon to take such gigantic proportions, had already made its successful beginning at Machecoul. Between the Convention and immediate disaster there lay only the personality of Dumouriez. When the news of his desertion, following on the news of his defeat, reached Paris, the Girondins were hopelessly discredited, and the line of their political retreat, the pursuit of their enemies, ran in a direction that Danton's speeches had prepared.

For several days he had himself been the object of the most violent attacks, especially for his friendship with Dumouriez and on the question of the Belgian accounts. For he had just returned from a third mission to the army, and had been close to the general. On the 1st of April practically the whole sitting was devoted to an attack upon him and to his defence. Had you been sitting in the house that night, you would have said that a violent demagogue, surrounded by a little group of yet more violent friends, was resisting with some difficulty the attacks of an honest and loyal majority. But this demagogue was so far-seeing, was so much the greatest of all those in the hall, that when three days afterwards the Parliament was brought face to face with the reality, Danton's method becomes the only solution. They hear of Dumouriez' treason, and on the night of the 4th of April, Isnard, himself a Girondin, proposed the creation of the Committee. Danton supported him at midnight with a definite speech such as no Girondin would have dared to make. He said practically, "This Committee is precisely what we want, a hand to grasp the weapon of the Revolutionary Tribunal."

It was Isnard that formulated the idea, but it was Danton that baptised it "A Dictator." It was at midnight that he spoke, and he closed his short speech just on the turn of the morning of the 5th of April. That very day a year later the Dictator seized him, and his own Tribunal put him to death.

On the 5th of April, the next day, in the evening, we begin to get those large measures and rapid which came with the new organ of power. And Danton speaks with a kind of joy, and demands at once such measures as only a dictatorship can produce—calling all the people to the defence, fixing a maximum upon the price of bread, even the first mention of a levée *en masse*. The air is full of such a spirit as you get in an army, the certitude that with discipline and unity and authority all things can be done. On the following day, the 6th, the Committee was chosen, and on the 7th the names were read out, which showed that the power had finally passed from the Girondins to those whom they had rejected at the moment when France was forgiving everything for the sake of Jemappes. The Convention, in need of men of action, had been forced to abandon its own leaders and to turn to Danton.

The names that they heard read out were Barrère, Delmas, Bréard, Debry, Morvaux, Cambon, Treilhard, Lacroix, and Danton.

CHAPTER VI
THE TERROR

From the 6th April 1793, from the act which was described at the end of the last chapter, we have something new in the course of the Revolution. We have at last an Institution.

It is in the nature of the French people (for reasons which might to some extent be determined, but whose discussion has no place in this book) that their history should present itself in a peculiarly dramatic fashion. Their adventures, their illusions, their violence, their despair, their achievements, seem upon a hundred occasions to centre round particular men or certain conspicuous actions, in such a fashion that those men and these actions fit themselves into a story, the plot and interest of which absorb the reader. But if we attempt to connect the whole into a series, even if we attempt to give the causes or the meaning of a few years' events, the dramatic aspect fails. This quality, which has fascinated so many, has also mistaught us and confused us, and, in the desire to "throw the limelight" upon the centre of action, one historian after another has left in obscurity that impersonal blind force which directs the whole.

This force in France is the Institution. Understand the character and methods of her central power, and you find yourself possessed of this great key to the understanding of her history, namely, that events follow each other in the order that the Institution requires, and the nation moves along the lines which the Institution determines. The Institution provides a standpoint from which all falls into perspective, even the details of personality no longer remain in confusion. You find, in a little while, that you are dealing with an organism more simple and of far greater vitality than any man, as truly a living, and much more truly a permanent, force than a monarch or a great minister can be.

The consideration of half-a-dozen examples will make this clear. What is all that marvellously dramatic action between Pepin le Bref and the coronation of Hugh but confusion? It ceases to be so when we follow with Fustel de Coulanges the transformation of the Imperial system. You can make nothing of the tenth and eleventh centuries, for all their personal interest, until you have grasped Feudalism, and it is a common-place that the six hundred years that follow are but the development of the Capetian method. It is not in Louis the XI., or in Mazarin, or in Louis XIV. that we find the Force—it is in the French monarchy. Look about you at the present day, ask yourself what has recreated the prosperity of modern France, and you will certainly not be able to find a special man. It is the System that has done the work.

Now it is the note of all the Revolution, as we have followed it up to this point, that the Institution was lacking. France without it was France without herself: she dissolved. The cause of this lack was as follows: The monarchy, round which everything had centred, was dying, and the social theories of the time—the great Philosophy on which France was fed—neglected and despised the Institution, relying as it did upon the vague force of general opinion. It was the chief—I had almost said the only—fault of the Jeffersonians in America and the idealist Republicans in France, that they could see neither the necessity of formulæ nor the just power of systems. Nevertheless it was the instinct which remained in the French mind, the "sub-conscious" sense of what the Institution was to France, that made half the violence of the time. I do not mean that the speeches recognised this character openly—on the contrary, the enmities and the divisions seem to turn entirely upon personal hatreds; but I mean that the underlying fear, unexpressed but real, was that such and such a proposition would create a permanent tendency, and that Girondin or Jacobin success meant the deflection of the torrent into one or the other of two divergent channels. Here in England, living under an order which is well established and old, we wonder at the intensity of passion which some abstract resolution could arouse in the Convention. We should wonder no longer were we to comprehend that in the extreme rapidity with which all France was being remoulded, a few words agreed upon, a mere principle, might add a quality to all the future history of the nation.

Two men in the Revolutionary period rose higher than the flood, Mirabeau and Danton. Each was able to perceive what the permanent character of the nation was, and each gave all his efforts to the uniting or welding round some stable centre the new order to which both were attached. In a word, each understood what the Institution was to France, and desired to lend it force and endurance. With Mirabeau it was the monarchy. Would he have saved, recreated, and restored that declining power which had once been the framework of the nation? We cannot tell. Had he lived, '92 would have shown us; only we know that if the monarchy had seemed to him at last beyond repair, he would have proposed at once some similar power to replace it. Now Danton had survived; doubtful in 1791, "more monarchist than you, M. de Lafayette," he was determined in 1792 that the crown and France were separate for ever. He overthrew the palace, but from that very moment all his policy was directed to the construction of a governing power. It is here that he and the Girondins, for all his personal attempts at unity, were hopelessly divided. The Girondins were bent upon that local autonomy and that extreme individual liberty in which the central power disappears. With the growing danger, with his own experience of Belgium, Danton, during the early part of 1793, becomes set upon the idea of government and of nothing else. He gave it a weapon before it existed, for he made the Revolutionary Tribunal, and though Isnard first proposed it, it is known that Danton led the movement which ended in the establishment of the Committee.

All government since that time in France has been its heir. It was the Committee that forged the centralised system, that showed how the administration might radiate from Paris, that gave precedent for the conscription and for all determined action. That dictatorship so plainly saved the country in its worst peril that under many different names the French people have often recalled it, and rarely without success.

All the remaining year with which this chapter must deal is the story of the Committee. The Committee explains and gives us the clue to every action. Its changes, the men who dominated it, the reasons it had for violence or for clemency, its main object of throwing back the invasions—these are the central part of 1793 and 1794.

Had we an accurate account of what passed in that secret council, almost every event could be referred to it. But such an account is lacking. Barrère, always inconsistent, wrote a rigmarole in his old age which has anecdotes of interest, but which is almost valueless for our purpose. Here and there we have a disconnected anecdote or a lame confession, but the doors of the room are as closed to us as they were to the contemporaries who stood in the outer hall and received the official nothings of Barrère, or later of St. Just. Nevertheless what we can reconstruct of its spirit and action, imperfect as our effort may be, does more to explain the time than any descriptions of the orators or of the crowd.

The action of this new executive, as it touches Danton, changes rapidly during the year. In the first Committee of nine Danton is everything. He made it and he directs it. Towards the close, however, of its short existence, he is beginning to feel the pressure of the Jacobins, and of Robespierre and of St. Just, the victory of the Mountain. This loss of power on his part ends with the dissolution of the old Committee, and when the new one is formed—with the 10th of July—another period begins. The members are increased to twelve; then enter the Robespierrians. Danton, for motives which we shall discuss later, resigns, and there are two doubtful summer months when he still maintains, from without, the power of the Committee, but first begins to check so far as is possible the tyranny upon which it has embarked. He retires in a kind of despair to Arcis, and with his return a new phase is entered. The Committee is striking furiously; the Terror has taken root; and by an action of generosity, or perhaps of wisdom, Danton sets himself against his own creation. These few months—the winter of 1793-1794—give us that side of Danton which at the time was least explicable, but which best defines him for posterity. He puts his whole weight as an orator, and, through the genius of his friends, he puts the journals also against the Terror. Knowing (as he must have known) how strong was the engine he had made, he yet withstands it, and attempts by a purely personal force, without an organisation and without executive power, to reduce the action of the Committee. So great was he that for some weeks his success hung in the balance. France, we must presume, was with him. Paris doubted, but might have been won. When the violent and unscrupulous Hébertists were executed he seemed to have succeeded, and the Terror appeared to be closed. But the Committee had a deeper policy; in the same week that saw the fall of Hébert, Danton was himself suddenly arrested with his friends. How far Robespierre permitted and how far directed the action will never be fully known. The Committee struck the one great force opposed to it, and the Dantonists were executed on the anniversary of its creation.

The first part of the story of the Committee in its relation to Danton is the period between April the 6th and July the 10th 1793. It is the period of the fall of the Girondins; and to make clear the importance of the new power I shall adopt this method:—

To give first in their order the events that led to the attack on the Parliament and the expulsion of the twenty-two; to show in what confusion the whole story lies, and how difficult (or impossible) it is to follow the motives of the deputies, or to say why they acted as they did. Then to give, as a parallel account, the position and action of the Committee, and to show how fully (in my opinion) its motive determines the history of the time; to look at the insurrection of June 2 from the room where the nine members debated in secret, and to point out how, from that standpoint (which was Danton's own), the confusion falls into order.

First, then, what was the exterior history of the movement that destroyed the Gironde? It will be remembered that when the Convention first met in September, the great majority of its numbers inclined to a certain spirit. That spirit was best represented by a small group of men, idealists and orators—and of these a number, the most powerful perhaps, had come from the vineyards of the peaceable southern river. The warmth, the calm, the fruitfulness of the Valley of the Gironde, appeared in Vergniaud's accents. To this devoted band of men, whose whole career was justice and virtue, no one has dared to be contemptuous, and history on every side has left them heroes. They were own brothers to the immortal group that framed the American Constitution, the true heirs of Rousseau, and worthy to defend and at last to give their lives for the Republican idea. They hated the shedding of blood; they tested every action by the purest standard of their creed; and from the first speeches in which they demanded the war, to the day when they sang the Marseillaise on the scaffold, they did not swerve an inch from the path which they had set before themselves.

What led such men into conflict with Paris, and perhaps with France? This fault: that the pure theory which they justly maintained to be the one right government could not meet Europe in arms. What a few millions lost on the littoral of the American continent could do, without frontiers and without memories, that France could not do with civil war raging, and with the world invading her frontiers. A modification was imperative, a compromise with necessary evil. The men who felt reality knew that well. Danton had forced on a dictatorship, and gave it the method of the Terror. But the Girondins, though they had been compelled to give up so much, yet refused to follow the necessary path. They refused the conscription; a volunteer army was the only one tolerable to free men. They refused diplomacy; it involved a secret method, and was of its nature based on compromise. They refused the requisitions to the armies, the forced taxes, the hegemony of Paris, the preponderance of talent or genius in the committees—in a word, they refused to sanction anything, however necessary, in that crisis, which they would not have sanctioned in a time of order and of a pure republic.

The result of this sublime obstinacy was the ruin of France and of themselves. The Royalists saw it, and called themselves "Girondins;" the great name became a label for every reaction, and in every new disaster Paris saw with increasing clearness the restraining hand of the Gironde. For it was Paris and its Commune that took the leadership in the attempt to depose or expel the men who led the Parliament. Already before the Committee had been formed, the Commune on April the 2nd had begun to correspond with the municipalities of France—the fatal step that had so often preceded insurrection. To Paris as a centre, to Paris radical, and especially to Paris violent and unreasoning, the Girondins had grown detestable. Paris for a thousand years had stood for unity—the Girondins were autonomist and federal. Paris was passionate—the Girondins as calm as light. To all this enmity the Gironde answered by no force, but only by an assertion of their inviolable right. All April and May is consumed in the tale of great disasters without, and of the acute battle between the Right and the deputation from Paris within.

It is when we turn to this struggle within the Convention that the confusion arises which can only be made clear by considering the Committee. Especially is this the case with regard to Danton's action. Thus, on the 10th of April, he opposes the prosecution of those who sent a petition from the Halle aux Blés for the resignation of Roland; on the 13th there is the famous speech in favour of diplomatic action as opposed to the violence of the Mountain. Yet the day before he also opposed in a formal and well-reasoned speech the arrest and trial of Marat. When that madman, with whom his name had been so often linked, came back in triumph from his acquittal, Danton took a yet more inexplicable attitude. While all the Mountain were shouting for joy, and while Paris welcomed the verdict as the first wound of the Gironde (which, indeed, it was), Danton merely said, "Paris, we see, so loves the Convention as to applaud the acquittal of one of its members"—a very transparent speech. On the 1st of May Danton is the only man to speak with sobriety and good sense against the petition of the Faubourg St. Antoine, which attacked the rights of property; yet on the 10th he turns against Isnard, that is, against the Gironde and the Moderates, and causes the proposal of what was practically a popular referendum on the constitution to be rejected. We see, therefore, even when we look at the action of Danton alone, the apparent confusion that was indicated above. Were we to turn to almost any other of the Committee the same would be apparent. Barrère, the chief spokesman, seems to take now one side, now the other. At one moment he attacks the Girondins purposely; at another the petitions from Paris; at every point, in the action of every prominent speaker outside the two opposing groups, there appears this inextricable tangle.

With the 10th of May the battle between Paris and the Gironde entered into its last phase. It was upon this date that the Convention began to sit permanently in the little theatre of the Tuilleries, where they had first met. The news that met them was the death of Dampierre and the taking of Thouars by the Vendeans. Every rumour of disaster (and the rumours were being confirmed with fatal rapidity) was like oil spilt from the lamp of the Gironde. Their own followers were shaken, the great mass of the Convention who put their trust in these pure doctrines grew afraid and doubtful. Within a week (on the 17th) the Commune took a further step; they made their own law, and put Boulanger at the head of the armed force of the town—a force that was not theirs to govern. Later they gave Henriot the place. The Convention answered by electing Isnard their president; and Guadet, the headstrong, proposed to break the Commune, and to call the "suppliants" to Bourges. By this proposal a kind of Parliament in reserve would have existed to take up the work if the Parliament in Paris should be mutilated. Had the motion passed, the civil war, which was muttering in Lyons and had broken into open flame in Vendée, would have embraced all France.

But at this juncture Danton's Committee comes in again with its curiously mixed action. By the mouth of Barrère it pleads against the motion, and proposes instead the appointment of twelve members, as Girondin as they pleased, to judge the Commune, to "inquire." The commission was named, and acted on thorough principle and with haste, and without judgment, as any one might have foretold; for such was the Girondin weakness. Against the army that the Commune was gathering, all it could propose was to double the sergeant's guard at the Tuilleries, while it exasperated its enemy by ordering the arrest of Hébert.

Hébert was the one man in the Revolution of whom the truth has certainly been told by enemies. There was something of the pickpocket in Hébert, but not of the pickpocket only. He was also a blasphemer, an atheist, a man delighting in the foulest words, and in the most cowardly or ferocious of actions. His prominence was due to two things. First, he was the pamphleteer of the time, the "Père Duchesne." France had not yet discovered the danger of a free press. Secondly, in the Parisian exasperation against "the Moderates," the most extreme and the least rational became of necessity a kind of symbol, an accentuated type, and was thrust forward as a defiance. It is not too much to say that the Girondins themselves, by their lack of all measure, pushed Hébert to the front.

Such measures as those which "the twelve" had decreed were but fuel for the insurrectionary flame. Once more Danton appears, this time against the Gironde. To the demand for a large guard drawn from the Departments he said, "You are decreeing that you are afraid!" Whereupon a voice from the right cried with some humour, "I am." Danton had his way, the guard was not formed, and on the following day (the 25th of May) Isnard's imprudence brought on the catastrophe.

It was in the matter of the petition for the release of Hébert. Isnard rose in the chair, lifted his hand, and pronounced in his hollow voice the words that have enriched history at the expense of his country: "If such a thing should happen as an attempt upon the representatives of the nation, I say to you, in the name of all France, that very soon men would search upon the banks of the Seine for proofs that Paris had once been there." Danton intervened, but he could do nothing. The glove had been thrown down. He asked for the withdrawal of those words; the Girondin majority reaffirmed them. Two days later he obtained the freedom of Hébert; but though for a moment he was promised the dissolution of the "Commission of the Twelve," his effort failed, for they were immediately reinstated. In the night between the 30th and the 31st of May the Sections named a new and insurrectionary Commune; for one day the danger was warded off, and you may see Danton, still so difficult to understand, urging the Committee, while Barrère is proposing the conciliatory message to France, a document which blamed neither the Girondins nor Paris, and the twelve were dissolved. But the final blow was not to be avoided. On the 2nd of June the news of the counter-revolution in Lyons reached Paris. The Convention was surrounded; Henriot, at the head of the city militia, guarded its approaches, lined the corridors. Even in that moment, when Isnard proposed to retire, and made his superb apology, the Gironde, as a whole, stood firm. The inflexible Jansenist, Lanjuinais, proposed, with heroic folly, "a decree dissolving the authorities of Paris," at a moment when these very authorities were holding the doors with fixed bayonets; but in spite of Barrère's demand for Henriot's condemnation, in spite of Danton's demand for "a signal punishment," the Convention yielded, voted the arrest not only of the twenty-two, whom the Commune had demanded, but of twenty-nine, and Vergniaud, Barbaroux, Guadet; Le Brun, and Clavière (who were nominally ministers); Roland (who had fled, and whose wife was imprisoned by the Commune)—in fine, the whole body of those great orators who had made the Republic—were thrust out of the Assembly, some to be held in the honourable confinement of their own houses, some to fly and raise civil war in the Departments. The Commune offered hostages in equal number, but they were refused; and before the day was over the Parliament was mutilated, and the obstacle to the dictatorship and to the Terror had been swept away.

Such is a rapid summary of the fall of the Girondins—a story of contradictions and of inextricable cross-purposes, in which for two months men seem (especially the men of the new Committee) to change sides, to hesitate, and to falter, in which the majority passes over to the Jacobins with a startling rapidity, and in which (apparently) the only two fixed points are the immovable figures of the Gironde and their opponents of the Commune.

I know that this confusion has commonly led writers to adopt an equal confusion in their explanation of the insurrection and of its motives. To disentangle such a skein it was apparently necessary to make Robespierre a prophet, Isnard for once a coward, Barrère a skilful diplomatist, Danton a vacillator. Such a method appears to me false. If, to explain a difficult passage in history, we make men behave in a way which contradicts all their lives, we must (it seems to me) be in error. These special theories are mechanical, and do not satisfy the mind.

The question is this: Somewhere a power existed; why was not that power in evidence either on one side or on the other? And why do we not see it acting? I believe the answer is as follows:—

The power was in the Committee. The Committee believed it necessary to be rid of the Girondins. But the Committee was part of the Convention – the existence and the authority of the Convention was necessary to it. It saw on the one hand a set of Parliamentary leaders who would not permit it to act with vigour, on the other it noted the angry spirit of Paris. The Committee permitted that spirit to act, but gave it its measure and its direction unknown to itself, desiring to eliminate the Moderates, but anxious to avoid their proscription, exile, or death. With this clue the maze seems to me resolved. It was the Committee that expelled the Gironde, using Paris for its arm.

Now to prove this certain steps are necessary. In the first place, why can we say that the Committee was the centre of power? Because it alone had access to a complete knowledge of France, it alone debated in secret and it alone existed for the express purpose of dictatorship. When once the generals, the deputies in mission, and the police became familiar with the new organ, they referred to the Committee as naturally as the corresponding men to-day would refer to a cabinet or to a monarch. If the reader will glance at any portion of the document which is printed as Appendix XI. of this book, and to which I shall continually refer in this passage, he will at once perceive that the men who drew it up had in their hands every lever of public machinery. I would not maintain that this power sprang at once into existence on the 6th of April, but the two months that produced such a report was ample time to have developed a corresponding grasp upon the armies, upon the diplomacy, and upon the internal resources of Revolutionary France. Where else will you find such a document in all the offices of the time? Compared with it the decisions of the ministry are vague abstractions, the reports of the Commune puerilities or ravings. Revolutionary France, until the formation of the Committee, may be compared to a marsh in which the water tends to flow to no one centre; the information, the revenue, the public forces stood incoherent and stagnant. The creation of this secret body may be compared to a pit dug in its centre, to which the waters would immediately flow. It may be objected that they had not the control of finance. No; but they had Cambon. In an assembly of men new to government this very difficult province fell of itself into the hands of a man whose genius all admitted, and whose probity no one of his enemies would deny. Long before the insurrection took place, any man with information, with authority, or with a special duty to perform, had learnt to regard the Committee as his chief, for the simple reason that no other centre of authority existed. Add to this the incalculable force of secrecy, the power by which the most glaring failures of our cabinets can be hidden by merely saying, "We know what all the rest ignore," and it will appear reasonable to say that by June the Committee could almost, had it wished, have summoned an army to Paris. The Committee then held the power.

In the second place, we must establish, as far as is possible, the aims of the Committee and their method of guiding the insurrection. As was said earlier in this chapter, those aims and methods can only be arrived at by inference; the very nature of a body that deliberates in secret makes this method of inquiry necessary. There is no direct evidence, unless the contradictory anecdotes of a much later period can be given that name. Now we can infer with some accuracy what went on in their deliberations. There should be noted at the outset the document to which I have already referred, and which, if I am not mistaken, is printed for the first time in this book. It was the first of those general Rapports which were delivered by Barrère to the Convention for the next sixteen months, and which so profoundly affected the course of the Revolution. It sums up the result of two months of astonishing labour; everything—all the weakness of France—has been noted with the accuracy of a topographical survey. It gives the equipment, the provisioning, the local difficulties of each army, the detailed condition of the fleet (a most deplorable picture), the result of what is evidently an elaborate spy-system in the department of foreign intrigue, and everywhere the indictment is obvious—"whatever has governed France hitherto has hopelessly failed." There are, indeed, polite references to the ineptitude of the old regime, but side by side with these there is a direct attack on the Girondin Ministers of War, and on the diplomatic, or rather non-diplomatic, methods which had been pursued abroad; indeed, many parts of this report would not be out of place had they appeared in a Compte Rendu drawn up by the victorious insurrection, instead of preceding, as they did, the fall of the Gironde.

Again, there is the date of its appearance. It was not by a coincidence that Barrère was given it to read on the 29th of May. Note this sequence. Isnard made his fatal speech on Saturday the 25th. Monday the 27th was the date of Danton's attempt to dissolve "the twelve;" and his failure followed on Tuesday the 28th, when, by the blindness or firmness of the Gironde, they were reinstated. It is on Wednesday the 29th that Barrère rises at the end of a long and stormy discussion, and, late in the afternoon, presents his report. The vague phrases on the importance of unity which it contains have made some imagine that it was an attempt at conciliation, rapidly devised and thrown out at that critical moment. That opinion is surely erroneous. It is long (some 17,000 words) and carefully prepared; it must have taken some time to draw up, and it has all the appearance of a weapon framed at leisure and held in reserve; it comes at that moment with some such force as this, saying from the Committee, from Danton, to the Gironde—"You have refused to do what France absolutely needed. You have rejected my attempts to save you, the avenues which I opened for your escape; you were given the commission of twelve; you have fatally abused the gift. Will you be convinced at the last moment by this picture of the terrible straits to which you have brought the nation?"

Finally, we can draw a fairly conclusive set of proofs from our knowledge of the men in the Committee and of the public action they took. Of all the nine, Danton was the one commanding personality. Cambon was a specialist, and but for him and Lindet, honest but not an orator, there were Danton and his men only. Barrère, it may be urged, was not a Dantonist; but he was pliant to a degree; his pliancy is notorious, and has ignorantly been given a still worse name. Moreover, Barrère was closeted with Danton day after day; they undertook the same department in the Committee (that of foreign affairs), and they follow exactly the same course in the tribune. In the Department of War was Delacroix, Danton's friend and right hand. Of the report itself, all the last part, and possibly some paragraphs in the middle, were drawn up by Danton. Later we shall see that his preponderance was notorious and a danger to him.

Well, Danton and the Committee being so nearly identical, can we make a description of the motive that urged him? I think we can. Desmoulin's "Histoire des Brissottins" was certainly not of Danton's inspiration. Camille wrote that deadly pamphlet under the eye of Robespierre. But Fabre d'Eglantine at the Jacobins, on May the 1st, calling on the Girondins "to go, and return when all is settled," is almost using Danton's own phrase— "Qu'ils s'en aillent, et qu'ils revennent profiter de notre victoire." All that he and Barrère say, from then to the day of June the 2nd, seems to fall under this formula. He permits the attack of the Commune, while he does everything to moderate its force. He speaks continually for the defence, but he and his Committee refuse to act, and if ever he has spoken a little too strongly, has given the Girondins a little too much power, he retreats somewhat towards the Commune. He resembles a man who is opening a sluice in a dyke of the fen country: behind him is the sea; he admits and plays with its power, but unless his calculation is just it may rush in and overwhelm him. He permitted Paris to strike, and he created a tyranny; both the mob of the capital and the dictatorship were destined to break from his hands.

These are, as I read them, the causes of the fall of the Girondins. I have dealt with them at this length because the passage from the 31st of May to the 2nd of June 1793 is not only one of the most fiercely debated, but also one of the most important in the history of the Revolution. I have not given it too much space, for upon the understanding of what led to and what permitted the insurrection depends, without any question, our final judgment on Danton's position.

Here, then, the Committee, even in its infancy, furnishes the clue to a difficult passage in the Revolution. It is becoming more and more necessary as research progresses to refer the mysteries of the period to that central body; and, as it seems to me, we have in its first general report the first explanation of that most complex movement, the insurrection of the 2nd of June.

The Gironde having disappeared, there was left before Danton a task of extreme difficulty. He was about to attempt the management of men whom he deliberately permitted to engage in battle. It is of the very first importance in our study of his career to appreciate the conditions of this task. Consider for a moment what he has done. He has by arguments, by threats, and finally by the use of the mob, made the Revolutionary Government a reality. It is in this last ally that we find the cause of his future failure. Hitherto he has been battling with particular men, preventing a small group of politicians from obstructing the Revolutionary measures, cajoling on the other hand the extreme members of the Convention by calculated outbursts of sympathy. Such a task no one would find impossible, did he possess at once a clear object and the genius to approach it. But after the 2nd of June it was another matter. He had let loose the storm, and with the pride of a man who felt his strength inwards and outwards (for scheming and for haranguing), he had determined deliberately to ride it. It was a miscalculation. Something resembling a natural force, something like an earthquake or a lava stream, opposed itself to his mere individual will; and Danton, who among the politicians had been like a man among boys, became in the presence of these new forces like a lonely traveller struggling at evening against a growing tempest in the mountains. From this moment we shall see him using in vain against the passions of 1793 the ability, the ruse, the eloquence, the energy which had so long succeeded among the statesmen. They will be swept down like driftwood upon the current of popular madness which he himself has let loose. The Committee will be formed of new members, the Terror will grow from day to day, the Revolution will begin to take on that character of fanaticism which was directly opposed to Danton's plan, and he will retire disappointed and beaten. He will return frankly out of sympathy with the excesses, and in expiation of that fault of sanity he will die.

The months in which he fights this losing battle are the hot months of 1793. I will not deny that during this summer his name is more conspicuous than at any period of his life. I will admit that if we deal with history as a spectacle, the climax of 1793 should be distinguished by his voice and presence. But it is this fascination of the picturesque which has made his life inexplicable, and a biographer dares not leave it so. Although June, July, and August are full of his speeches, his warning, and even his energy, yet I say that he was day after day losing his hold and slipping. He is conspicuous because in the face of such disaster he redoubled his energy; but even that redoubled energy is dwarfed in the face of the spirit that animated the Terror.

First with regard to June: it was still a period of hope, and he still thought himself the master. He had added to the Committee, not thinking them dangerous, but as a kind of sop, five members of the Mountain. Among them were two who were to prove the ruin of his whole system—Couthon and St. Just. Perhaps to temper their action, perhaps merely because he was a friend, he included Hérault de Séchelles. The names were typical of what was to happen in 1794, when, by the power of St. Just, Hérault was to be thrust out of the Committee and sent to die with Danton himself.

Unconscious of what this addition would lead to, unconscious also of what echoes the 2nd of June might arouse in the provinces, Danton pursued his path as though the insurrection had been but one event of many. The minister Le Brun was brought by his guards day after day to aid in the discussions, and taken back to the custody of his own house. One might have thought that the "moral insurrection" of which Robespierre had talked had led only to a "moral suppression" of the Girondins. Moreover, the whole of these days of June are full of Danton's yet remaining supremacy. He goes on with his two principal methods, namely, a strong secret government and moderation in the application of its tyranny, as though the situation was his to mould at his will. Thus, on the 8th, he says with regard to the decree against foreigners: "I will show you such and such an alien established in France who is much more of a patriot than many Frenchmen. I say to you, therefore, that while the principle of watching foreigners is good, you should send this proposal to the Committee and let it be discussed there." Again, two days later, he refuses to admit the violent attitude of the Mountain towards Bordeaux. He even praises that city at a time when it was practically in rebellion, to defend its proscribed members. Within the same week he continues to talk of La Vendée as the only centre of insurrection. He continues to be the Danton of old, although the Girondins are raising the standard of civil war on every side, and he maintains that continuous effort and compromise which had saved so much in the autumn of 1792, and which could do so little now.

Within the Committee they framed the Constitution of 1793—that great monument of democracy, which never took its place in history, nor ever affected the lives of men. It stands like an idol of great beauty which travellers find in a desert place; its religion has disappeared from the earth; no ruins surround it; in the day when it was put up the men who raised it were driven from what should have been the centre of their adoration. That Danton was still in power when the result was debated in the Parliament during the third week of the month is evident from two things: first, that the Constitution, with its broad guarantees of individual liberty and of local autonomy, with its liberal spirit, so nearly approaching the great dream of Condorcet, so opposed to the narrow fanaticism of the Jacobins, was definitely intended to appease the growing passions of civil war. Two-thirds of France, of the country-sides at least, was arming because Paris had dared to touch the representatives of the nation. The Constitution was thrown like a hostage; the men who saw the necessity for a dictatorship said virtually, "The violence that offends you is only for a moment. Here is what we desire with the return of peace." And the document so responded to the heart of France that it succeeded.

The second proof that Danton had still hold of the reins is to be found in this: that the advice which he gives during the discussions on the Constitution is not that of violence, nor of flattery, but of moderate common-sense; and of such advice which the Convention accepts the best example is to be found in the speech on the power of making war. It was a difficult thing to convince the Assembly, in those days of abstractions, that the nation, as a whole, could not exercise such a right without hopeless confusion. Yet Danton had his way. This month of June, then, which was so full of terrible internal danger, during which Buzot had raised a Girondin army sixty miles from Paris, during which Normandy was in full revolt, during which Lyons had attacked the Republic, and during which the counter-Revolution seemed on the point of breaking out—this month was still Danton's own. He was secure in his public position, for the very conquerors of the 2nd of June, the violent extremists, could not prevent him from exercising his diplomacy abroad and his pacificatory compromise in domestic affairs.

He was also secure in that which mattered so much more to him—I mean in his home. His mind had sufficiently steadied after the shock that had maddened him in February for him to follow the advice which his dead wife had left him. On the 17th of June he re-married. The woman was not suited to Danton. She did not love him, nor probably did he love her. There were two young children, whom, in the winter, his first wife, finding herself to be dying, felt she was leaving orphans. The eldest was only three years old. This good woman, Catholic and devout, knowing her husband, and the sheer necessity for a home which his character had shown, determined on a religious education for her sons, and determined on a Catholic woman to be about her husband. She urged him to marry her younger friend, Mdlle.

Gély. An incident, which is doubtful, but which, on the whole, I accept, does not seem to me to prove the violence of an uncontrolled affection, but, on the contrary, to show a kind of indifference, as though Danton said to himself, "The thing must be done, and had better be done so as to offend the family as little as possible." I mean the story of his marriage before a non-juring priest. At any rate, that marriage shows an element of determination and security. He was still master of his fortunes and of himself.

But he had called up a spirit too strong for him. July was to prove it.

June, which had seen the rise of the Girondin insurrection, had also seen its partial appeasement and suppression. It was, as we have said, the Constitution, hurriedly improvised for this purpose, that had been the main cause of such a success, but there remained for July, more dangerous than ever, the foreign invasion and the three outstanding strongholds of the civil war—Lyons, Toulon, and La Vendée. It was against them and their growing success, against the rebels and the invaders, that the Terror was serviceable, and it was on account of their continual progress that the Terror assumed such fearful proportions.

I said earlier in this chapter that Danton inaugurating and strengthening the dictatorship of the Revolutionary Government was like a man deliberately opening a sluice behind which was the whole sea. There was an element of uncertainty upon the chances of which he had staked the success of his effort, and, with the reverses, he soon discovered that the forces which he had let loose were going beyond him. It may be that he thought the results of the 2nd of June would be more immediate than they were. As a fact, it took many months to recover the position which the supineness of the Girondins had lost. In those months the Revolutionary Government crystallised, as it were, became permanent, and fell into the hands of the extremists.

On the very day that the Norman insurrection was crushed at Vernon, a Norman girl stabbed Marat. It is not within the scope of this book to deal at any great length with the fate of the man whom Danton had called "l'individu." That most striking and picturesque episode concerns us only in this matter, that it was a powerful impetus to the system of the Terror, and such an one as Danton, with all his judgment, could not possibly have foreseen. Moreover, on the very day that Marat was killed, the allied forces entered Warsaw, and there can be no doubt that the success of this infamy gave them a freer hand morally, at least upon the French frontier. Mayence fell, and its fall cost the life of Josephine's first husband. The Allies had crossed the Rhine. Five days later, on the 28th of July, Valenciennes fell. At the same moment the Spaniards were pouring in east and west of the

Pyrenees, and the Piedmontese had crossed the Alps. From a little press in Newcastle (the family of the printer yet remain to tell the tale), Pitt was drawing the thousands of forged assignats to ruin the Republic. Five foreign armies were occupying the territory of France, and late in the following month the Spanish and English fleets were admitted to the harbour and arsenal of Toulon. Let it then be granted that, with the possible exception of the Roman power after Cannæ, no power in history was ever so near destruction as was Revolutionary France in that summer.

Let us see how the misfortunes of the country reacted upon the position of Danton. Already, with early July, he felt himself pressed and constrained by the growing power of the Jacobin doctrine and of its high priest. His system of conciliation, his attempts (in large part successful) to coax rather than to defeat the insurrection, were violently criticised in the debate of the 4th. The anger against the Girondins, which the death of Marat was to increase to so violent a degree, produced the report of St. Just upon the 8th of July, which, though history has called it moderate, yet mentions the accusation of Vergniaud and of Gaudet, and to this Danton was forced reluctantly to put his name. Two days afterwards the old Committee to which he had belonged was dissolved and a new one was elected.

It would be an error to regard this as a mere resignation on the part of Danton; it would be equally an error to regard it as a violent censure on the part of the Convention. It is certain that he chose to withdraw because the fatal necessity of things was giving power to men of whom he had no opinion. Thus Robespierre joined the Committee on the 27th of July—Robespierre, of whom Danton could say in private, "The man has not wits enough to cook an egg." Yet this was the man who was so worshipped by the crowd, that, once within the Committee, he was destined to become the master of France. It may be remarked in passing that something fatal seemed to attach to the date on which a man entered and began to lead the Committee. On the day that Danton entered in '93, on that day was he guillotined in '94. On the day that Robespierre entered in '93, on that day in '94 he fell.

Danton remained, for a little longer than a month, more and more separate from the management of affairs, more and more out of sympathy with the men who were conducting the government. Nevertheless, he stands almost as an adviser and certainly with pure disinterestedness throughout the month of August. He was alone. Desmoulins was more with Robespierre than with him at that moment. Westermann, his great friend and ally on the 10th of August 1792, was under censure for his defeat in Vendée. But standing thus untrammelled, Danton for the moment appears with an especial brilliancy. Indeed there is no act of his public life so clear, so typical of his method, or so successful as his great speech on the 1st of August. It was as though, divorced from the pre-occupations of political intrigue and free from the responsibility of executive power, he was able for the first time in his whole life to speak his mind fully and clearly. The speech is a précis, as it were, of all his pronouncements on the necessity for a dictatorship and the methods it should employ. It turns round this sentence, "I demand that the Committee of Public Safety should be erected into a Provisional Government." He said openly that while he asked for absolute powers for the Committee, he refused ever to join it again. He pointed out to them the necessity of uniting all power in the hands of one body, of making a unique command for a nation at war. To men who had been lost for so long in the discussion of constitutional checks and guarantees, he talked of the necessities as a general would to his staff. If you will read this speech through, you will find it to be the clearest exposition in existence of the causes and of the methods of the action of France in all her dangers from that day to our own. This speech, which is the climax of his career, and which stands at the fountain-head of so much in the modern nation, was followed throughout the month by many a piece of practical and detailed advice. He talks always quietly, and always with a specific object in view, on the educational proposals, on the great conscription (14th of August), on the enforcement of an absolute military discipline (15th of August), and so forth. But while he is still in this position, of which the brilliancy and success have deceived some into thinking that it was the centre of his career, two things were at work which were to lead to the strange crisis in which he lost his life. First, the Terror was beginning to be used for purposes other than those of the National Defence. Secondly, there was coming upon him lethargy and illness. He seems to have remained for a whole month, from the middle of September till the middle of October, without debating. There had come a sudden necessity for repose into his life, and until it was satisfied he gave an impression of weakness and of breaking down.

This was emphasised by a kind of despair, as he saw the diplomatic methods abandoned in dealing with foreign nations and the personal aims of the mystics, the private vengeance of the bloodthirsty, or the ravings of the rank madmen capturing the absolute system which he had designed and forged at the expense of his titanic powers. It was during this period that Garat saw him, and has left us the picture of his great body bowed by illness, and his small deep eyes filled with tears, as he spoke of the fate that was following the Girondins, and of how he could not save them. It was then also that, walking slowly with Desmoulins at sunset by the Seine, he said with a shudder that had never taken him before, "The river is running blood."

With October the Terror weighed on all France by the decree of the month before. The suspects were arrested right and left, and the country had entered into one of those periods which blacken history and leave gaps which many men dare not bridge by reading. He broke down and fled for quiet to his native place. From thence the Great Mother, of whom in all the Revolution he had been the truest son, sent him back to fulfil the mercy and the sanity of Nature as he had up till then fulfilled her energies.

This book is the life of a man, and a man is his mind. Danton, who has left no memoirs, no letters even—of whose life we know so little outside the field of politics—can only be interpreted, like any other man, by the mind. We must seek the origin, though we have but a phrase or two to guide us. What was that meditation at Arcis out of which proceeded the forlorn hope of the "Vieux Cordelier" and of the "Committee of Indulgence"?

He was ill already; the great energies which had been poured out recklessly in a torrent had suddenly run dry. Garat saw him weak, uncertain, refusing to leave his study, troubled in the eyes. The reins were out of his hands; all that he thought, or rather knew, to be fatal to the Republic was succeeding, and every just conception, all balance, was in danger. This, though it was not the cause of his weariness, coincided with it, and made his sadness take on something of despair. There had always been in his spirit a recurrent desire for the fields and rivers; it is common to all those whom Nature has blessed with her supreme gift of energy. He had at this moment a hunger for his native place, for the Champagne after the harvest, and for the autumn mists upon the Aube. It was in this attitude, weary, despairing, ill, and needing the country as a parched man needs water, that he asked and obtained permission to leave the Convention. It was upon the 12th of October, just as the worst phase of the Terror was beginning, that he left the violence and noise of the city and turned his face eastward to the cool valley of the Marne.

Starting from this point, his weariness and his longing for home, we can trace the movement of his mind during the six weeks of his repose. He recovered health with the rapidity that so often characterises men of his stamp; he found about him the peaceable affection, the cessation of argument and of self-defence which his soul had not known since the first days of 1789. His old mother was with him, and his children also, the memories of his own childhood. The place refreshed him like sleep; he became again the active and merry companion of four years before, sitting long at his meals, laughing with his friends. The window of the ground-floor room opened on to the Grande Place, and there are still stories of him in Arcis making that window a kind of little rendezvous for men passing and repassing whom he knew, his chatting and his questions, his interests on every point except that political turmoil in which the giant had worn himself out. The garden was a great care of his, and he was concerned for the farm in which he had invested the reimbursement of his pre-revolutionary office. He delighted to meet his father's old friends, the mayor, the functionaries of the place. This man, whom we find so typical of his fellow-countrymen, is never more French than in his home. The little provincial town, the *amour du clocher*, the prospect of retirement in the province where one was born—the whole scene is one that repeats itself upon every side to-day in the class from which Danton sprang.

Moreover, as quiet took back its old place in his soul, he saw, no longer troubled, but with calmness and certainty, the course that lay before the Republic. The necessity of restraint, which had irritated and pursued him in his days of fever in Paris, was growing into a settled and deliberate policy; he began to study the position of France like a map; no noise nor calumny was present to confuse him, and his method of action on his return developed itself with the clearness that had marked his first attitude in the elections of Paris. How rapidly his mind was working even his friends could not tell. One of them thought to bring him good news, and told him of the death of the Girondins. Danton was in his garden talking of local affairs, and when this was told him, the vague reputation which he bore, the "terrible Danton," and the fear he had inspired, led them to expect some praise. He turned as though he had been stabbed, and cried sharply, "Say nothing. Do you call that good news? It is a terrible misfortune.... It menaces us all." And no one understood what was passing in his mind. It was the note that Garat had heard, and later Desmoulins: "I did my best to save them; I wish to God I could have saved them!"

Whatever other news reached Arcis in those terrible months served only to confirm him more strongly in his new attitude. Had he been tinged in the slightest degree with the mysticism that was common to so many in that time he would have felt a mission. But he was a Champenois, the very opposite of a mystic, and he only saw a task, a thing to be planned and executed by the reason. Perhaps if he had had more of the exaltation of the men he was about to oppose he might have succeeded.

It was upon the 21st of November that he returned to Paris. His health had come back, his full vigour, and with the first days of his reappearance in politics the demand for which the whole nation was waiting is heard. And what had not the fanatics done during the weeks of his silence! Lyons, the Queen, the Girondins, Roland's wife—the very terms of politics had run mad, and he returned to wrestle with furies.

Let me describe the confusion of parties through which Danton had to wade in his progress towards the re-establishment of liberty and of order. As for the Convention itself, nominally the master, it was practically of no power. It chose to follow now one now another tendency or man; to be influenced by fear at this moment, by policy at that, and continually by the Revolutionary formulæ. In a word, it was led. Like every large assembly, it lacked initiative. Above it and struggling for power were these: First, the committees, that of Public Safety, and its servant, that of General Security — the Government and the police. It was Danton, as we know, who desired to make the committees supreme, who had raised them as the institution, the central government. But by this time they were a despotism beyond the reach of the checks which Danton had always desired. To save so mighty an engine from the dangers of ambition, he had resigned in July. His sacrifice or lethargy did not suffice. The Committee which had once been Danton was now the Triumvirate — Robespierre, Couthon, St. Just. It pursued their personal objects, it maintained by the Terror their personal creed. Still Danton did not desire to destroy it as a system. He wished to modify its methods and to change its personnel, to let it merge gradually into the peaceable and orderly government for which the Revolution and the Republic had been made. By a strange necessity, the workers, the men who were most like Danton in spirit, the practical organisers on the Committee, such as Carnot, Prieur, and Lindet, could not help defending it in every particular. They knew the necessity of staying at their post, and they feared, with some justice, that if the Robespierrian faction was eliminated their work might be suddenly checked. It was because they were practical and short-sighted that they were opposed to the practical but far-sighted policy of Danton. They feared that with the cessation of the Terror the armies would lack recruits, the commissariat provisions, the treasury its taxes.

Against the Committee was the Commune. Hébert at its worst; Clootz at its most ideal; Pache at its most honest. This singular body represented a spirit very close indeed to anarchy. It preached atheism as a kind of dogma; it was intolerant of everything; it was as mad as Clootz, as filthy as Hébert. It possessed a curious mixture of two rages — the rage for the unity and defence of France, the rage for the autonomy of Paris. In the apathy that had taken the voters this small and insane group held command of the city. But the Committees were not what the Girondins had been. You could not bully or proscribe Carnot, St. Just, Cambon, Jean Bon. With the fatal pressure of the stronger wrestler the Committee was pressing the Commune down. The Terror remained in either case. But with the Committee supreme it was a Terror of system striking to maintain a tyranny, a pure despotism working for definite ends. Had the Commune succeeded, it would have meant the Terror run mad, the guillotine killing for the sake of killing—and for ever.

The third party in the struggle was Robespierre. He also desired the Terror, but he intended to use it, as he did every power in France, towards a definite end—a certain perfect state, of which he had received a revelation, and of which he was the prophet. Of his aims and character I shall treat when I come to his action after the fall of Danton. It suffices to point out here that of the three forces at work Robespierre alone had personality to aid him. He had a guard, a group of defenders. They were inside, and led the Committee itself; they were the mystics in a moment of strong exaltation, and unreal as was the dream of their chief, the Robespierrians were bound to succeed unless the force of the real, the "cold water" that came with Danton's return, should destroy their hopes. Therefore, as a fact, though no one, though Danton himself, did not see it, it was between him and Robespierre that the battle would ultimately be fought out.

For what was Danton's plan? He put into his new task the ability, the ruse, the suppleness that he had only lost for a moment in the summer. First, Hébert and the "enragés" must go—they were the vilest form of the spirit that he perceived to be destroying the Republic. Then the Committee must be very gradually weakened. In that task he hoped, vainly enough, to make Robespierre his ally. And finally, the end of all his scheme was the cessation of the Terror. He had created a dictatorship for a specific purpose; that purpose was attained. Wattignies had been won, Lyons captured; soon La Vendée was to be destroyed, and even Toulon to fall. It was intolerable that a system abnormal and extreme, designed to save the State, should be continued for the profit of a few theorists or of a few madmen. How much had not his engine already done?—this machine which, to the horror of its creator, had found a life of its own! It had killed the Queen after a shocking trial; it had alienated what was left of European sympathy; it had struck the Girondins, and Danton was haunted by the inspired voice of Vergniaud singing the "Marseillaise" upon the scaffold; it had run to massacre in the provinces. He feared (and later his fears proved true at Nantes) that September might be repeated with the added horror of legal forms. The Terror finally had reopened the question that of all others might most easily destroy the State. A handful of men had pretended to uproot Catholicism for ever, and what Danton cursed as the "Masque Anti-Religieuse" had defiled Notre Dame. This flood he was determined to turn back into the channels of reason; he was going, without government or police or system, merely by his voice and his ability, to realise the Revolution, to end the dictatorship, and to begin the era of prosperity and of content.

The first steps taken were successful. On the very night of his return, Robespierre was perorating at the Jacobins against atheism and on the great idea of God, but within twelve hours, on the morrow, Danton's voice gave the new note. It was in the discussion upon the pension to be paid to the priests whom the last decree had thrust out of their regular office and of its salary. Danton spoke with the greatest decision on this plain matter, and the Convention heard with delight the fresh phrases to which it had so long been a stranger. He says virtually, "If you do not pay this sum you are persecutors." There are in this speech such sentences as these: "You must appreciate this, that politics can only achieve when they are accompanied by some reason.... I insist upon your sparing the blood of men; and I beg the Convention to be, above all, just to all men except those who are the declared and open enemies of the Republic." Four days later he went a little further, and the Convention still followed him. On the question which he had most at heart he spoke plainly. Richard complained of Tours. He said that the municipality of that town were arresting "suspects" right and left, and had even attacked himself. Danton said in a speech of ten lines: "It is high time the Convention should learn the art of government. Send these complaints to the Committee. It is chosen, or at least supposed to be chosen, from the élite of the Convention." Later in the same day he spoke on a ridiculous procession such as the violence of the time had made fashionable. It was a deputation of Hébertists bringing from a Parisian church the ornaments of the altar. Already, it will be remembered, the Commune had ordered the churches in Paris to be closed, and the attempt to enforce such scenes were being copied in all the large towns of France. He said: "Let there be no more of these mascarades in the Convention.... If people here and there wish to prove their abjuration of Catholicism, we are not here to prevent them ... neither are we here to defend them.... The Terror is still necessary, the Revolutionary Government is still necessary, but the people does not demand this indiscriminate action. We have no business save with the conspirators and with those who are treating with the enemy." There was a protest from Fayan, who cried, "You have talked of clemency!" for all the world as though such talk was blasphemy. But Danton was getting back his old position and was leading the Convention. His success seemed certain. On the 3rd of December (14th Frimaire) he was violently attacked at the Jacobins, but he managed to hold his own. Robespierre defended him in a speech which has been interpreted as a piece of able treachery, but which may with equal justice be regarded as an attempt to hold himself between the opposing parties; and within a fortnight after his return Danton, who had in him a directness of purpose and a rapidity of action that prefigured Napoleon, had gained every strategic point in his attack.

Events helped him, or rather he had foreseen them. The Vendeans, moving more like a mob than an army, were caught at Le Mans on the 13th of December. On the 7th of December the genius of Bonaparte had driven the English and Spanish from Toulon. On the 26th the news came to the army of which Hoche had just been given the command, and, as though the name Bonaparte brought a fate with it, the lines of Wissembourg were carried, Landau was relieved, the Austrians passed the Rhine.

All these victories were the allies of the party of indulgence. The men who said, "The Terror has no *raison d'être* save that of the national defence," found themselves expressing what all France felt. After such successes it only remained to add, "The nation is safe; the Terror may end." Already Danton had called up a reserve, so to speak, in the shape of the genius of Desmoulins. The first issue of "Vieux Cordelier" had appeared, and the journal was read by all Paris.

That club, in which we saw the origin of Danton's fame, was now the Hébertists, and nothing more. The pamphlets which Camille issued under the leadership of Danton were given a name that might recall its position and its politics of the old days. And indeed the two men most concerned in the new policy of clemency had been, from their house in the Cour du Commerce, the heart of the "République des Cordeliers." There are not in the history of the Revolution, in all the passages of its eloquence and genius, any words that strike us to-day as do the words of these six pamphlets which spread over the winter of the year II. It is a proof of Danton's clear vision, of his strong influence, that a distant posterity, far removed from the passions of 1793, should find its own expression in the appeals which his friend wrote, and which form the Testament of the Indulgents.

The first two numbers were an attack upon the Hébertists alone. Robespierre, from his position in the Committee of Public Safety, from the spur of his own ambition, was willing to agree. He himself corrected the proofs. But on the 15th of December appeared the famous Numero III., which ran through Paris like a herald's message, which did for reaction something of what the great speeches had done for liberty in clubs during the early days of the Revolution. Few men cared to vote, but every man read the "Vieux Cordelier." To those who had never so much as heard of Tacitus the pen of Tacitus carried conviction. A crowd of women passed before the Parliament crying for the brothers and husbands who filled the prisons; the "Committee of Clemency" was within an ace of being formed; and, coinciding with the victories and with Danton's reappearance, the demand of Desmoulins was dragging after it, not France only (for France was already convinced), but even the capital. It was then that the Committee, who alone were the government, grew afraid. Robespierre still hesitated. He could only succeed through the committees; but Desmoulins was his friend; there was an appeal to "the old college friend" in the "Vieux Cordelier" that touched his heart and his vanity; they had sat together on the benches of the Louis le Grand, and Robespierre seems to have made an honest attempt to aid him then. A fourth number had appeared on the 20th, a fifth (written on Christmas Day) appeared on January 8th.

The Jacobins denounced Camille, and Robespierre, the eyes of whose mind looked as closely and were as short-sighted as the eyes of his body, grew afraid. The men determined on rigour had warned him in the Committee; now when he tried to defend Camille he saw the Jacobins raging: what he did not see was France. Perhaps, had his sight been longer, he would not have been dragged six months later to the guillotine. He attempted a compromise and said: "We will not expel Camille, but we will burn his journal, punishing his act but not himself." Camille answered with Rousseau, *"Brûler n'est pas repondre."* He would not be defended.

The battle was closely joined. Desmoulins was pushing forward his attack with the audacious infantry of pamphlets; Danton, from the Convention, was giving from time to time the heavy blows of the artillery; the advance was continuous; when there was felt a check that proved the prelude to disaster and that showed, behind the opposing lines, the force of the Committees. In the middle of January, just after Desmoulins's defence at the Jacobins, Fabre D'Eglantine, the friend and old secretary of Danton, was arrested. It was in vain that Danton put into his defence all the new energy which he had discovered in himself. It was in vain even that he called for "the right of the deputy to defend himself at the bar of the house." Like all organised governments, the Committee could give reasons of State for this silent action. Danton was overborne, and the Convention for the first time since his return deserted him.

He had yet seven weeks to live. Desmoulins still attacked, but Danton knew that the action was lost. He knew the strength of that powerful council whose first efforts he himself had moulded, and when he saw it arise in support of continuing the Terror, when he saw it and Robespierre allied, he lost hope. The policy of the Committee grew more and more definite. One member of it, (Hérault de Séchelles) was Danton's friend: they expelled him. Silently, but with all their strength, they disengaged the government from either side. The Committee and Robespierre determined to strike at once, when the occasion should arise, both those in the Commune who desired to turn the Terror to their own ends and those of the Convention—the Dantonists, who desired to end it altogether.

Danton still speaks in the tribune, but the attack is no longer there. He defends modestly and well the practical propositions that appear before the Parliament on education, on the abolition of slavery, on the provisions for the giving of bail under the new judiciary system, and so forth. But there is in his attitude something of expectancy. He is waiting for a sudden attack that must come and that he cannot prevent. He holds himself ready, but the Committee is working in the dark, and he does not know on which side to guard himself. A last personal interview with Robespierre failed, and there was nothing left to do but to wait and see whether they feared him so much as to dare his arrest. It was with Ventose, that is, with the first days of March, that the blow fell.

The Hébertists, chafing under three months of growing insults—insults which their old ally the Committee refused to avenge—broke out into open revolt. Carrier was back from his truly Hébertist slaughtering at Nantes, and it was felt at the Cordeliers that the public execration would destroy them unless they rose. In the autumn they would have had the Committees on their side, but the strong action of the Indulgents had broken the alliance. They determined on insurrection. The Commune this time was, once and for all, to conquer the government. The decision was taken at the Cordeliers on the 4th of March—within ten days they were arrested. The Committee pushed them through the form of a trial. Less than three weeks after the first talk of revolt, Hébert, Clootz, and the rest were guillotined.

There were many among the Dantonists who thought this the triumph of their policy. "The violent, the enragés are dead. It is we who did it." But Danton was wiser than his followers. He knew that the Committee were waiting for such an opportunity, and that a blow to the right would follow that blow to the left. Both oppositions were doomed. Only one chance remained to him—they might not dare.

On the occasion of the arrest of the Hébertists he made a noble speech on the great lines of conciliation and unity, which had been his constant policy—a speech which was all for Paris, in spite of the faction.

But that week they determined on his arrest and that of his friends. Panis heard of it, and sent at once to warn him. He found him in the night of the last day of March 1794 sitting in his study with his young nephew, moody and silent. His wife was asleep in the next room. On the flat above him Camille and Lucille were watching late. The house was silent. Panis entered and told him what the Committee had resolved. "Well, what then?"

said Danton. "You must resist." "That means the shedding of blood, and I am sick of it. I would rather be guillotined than guillotine." "Then," said Panis, "you must fly, and at once." But Danton shook his head still moodily. "One does not take one's country with one on the soles of one's boots." But he muttered again to himself, "They will not dare—they will not dare." Panis left him, and he sat down again to wait, for he knew in his heart that the terrible machine which he himself had made, and which he had fought so heroically, could dare what it chose. They left him silent in the dark room. From time to time he stirred the logs of the fire; the sudden flame threw a light on the ugly strength of his face: he bent over the warmth motionless, and with the memories of seven years in his heart.

CHAPTER VII
THE DEATH OF DANTON

In the night the armed police came round to the Passage du Commerce; one part of the patrol grounded their muskets and halted at the exits of the street, the other entered the house.

Desmoulins heard the butts falling together on the flagstones, and the little clink of metal which announces soldiery; he turned to his wife and said, "They have come to arrest me." And she held to him till she fainted and was carried away. Danton, in his study alone, met the arrest without words. There is hardly a step in the tragedy that follows which is not marked by his comment, always just, sometimes violent; but the actual falling of the blow led to no word. Words were weapons with him, and he was not one to strike before he had put up his guard.

They were taken to the Luxembourg, very close by, a little up the hill. We have the story of how Danton came with his ample, firm presence into the hall of the prison, and met, almost the first of his fellow-prisoners, Thomas Paine. The author of "The Rights of Man" stepped up to him, doubtless to address him in bad French.[140] Danton forestalled him in the English of which he was a fair master.

"Mr. Paine," he said, "you have had the happiness of pleading in your country a cause which I shall no longer plead in mine." He remembered Paine's sane and moderate view on the occasion of the king's trial, and he envied one whose private freedom had remained untrammelled with the bonds of office; who had never been forced to a 2nd of June, nor had to keep to an intimate conversation his fears for the Girondins. Then he added that if they sent him to the scaffold he would go gaily. And he did. There was the Frenchman contrasted with his English friend.

Beaulieu, who heard him, tells us that he also turned to the prisoners about him and said, "Gentlemen, I had hoped to have you out of this, and here I am myself; I can see no issue."

So the prisoners came in, anxiously watched by reactionaries, to whom, as to many of our modern scribblers, one leader of the Revolution is as good as another—Lacroix, Westermann (the strong soldier with his huge frame overtopping even Danton's), and Desmoulins. As they passed to their separate cells, for it was determined to prevent their communication, a little spirit of the old evil[141] used the powerful venom of aristocracy, the unanswerable repartee of rank, and looking Lacroix up and down, said, "I could make a fine coachman of that fellow." He and his like would have ruined France for the sake of turning those words into action.

Till the dawn of the 11th Germinal broke, they were kept in their separate rooms. But the place was not built for a prison. Lacroix and Danton in neighbouring rooms could talk by raising their voices, and we have of their conversation this fragment. Lacroix said, "Had I ever dreamt of this I could have forestalled it." And Danton's reply, with just that point of fatalism which had forbidden him to be ambitious, answered, "I knew it;" he had known it all that night.

There was a force stronger than love—private and public fear. It is a folly to ridicule, or even to misunderstand that fear. The possessions, the families of many, the newly-acquired dignity of all, above everything, the new nation had been jeopardised how many times by a popular idol turned untrue. The songs of 1790 were all for Louis, many praised Bailly; what a place once had Lafayette! Who had a word to say against Dumouriez eighteen months before? The victories had just begun—barely enough to make men hesitate about the Terror. The "Vieux Cordelier" had led, not followed opinion, as it was just that the great centre of energy should lead and not follow the time. And, men would say, how do we know why he has been arrested, or at whose voice? How can we tell where the sure compass of right, our Robespierre, stands in the matter? and so forth. Nothing then was done; but Paris very nearly moved.

There were thus two gathering forces; one vague and large, one small but ordered, and on the result of their shock hung the life of Danton—may one say (knowing the future) the life of the Republic?

Now the struggle with Europe had taught the Committee a principal lesson. Perhaps one should add that the exuberant fighting power of the nation and of the age had forced the Committee to a certain method, apparent in the armies, in the measures, in the speeches: it was the method of detecting at once the weakest spot in the opposing line, and of abandoning everything for the purpose of concentrating all its strength and charging home. So their descendants to-day in their new army practise the marvellous massing of artillery which you may watch at autumn in the manœuvres.

What was the opposing line? A vague ill-ordered crowd—Paris; the undisciplined Convention, lacking leaders, ignorant of party rule. Where was its weakness? In the want of initiative, in the fact that, till some one spoke, no one could be sure of the strength of the corporate feeling. Also, on account of the public doubt, during that time men were grains of dust; but the dust was like powder, and speech was always the spark which permitted the affinities of that powder to meet in fierce unity and power. A sudden blow had to be struck and the fire stamped out before it had gathered power; this is how the check was given.

In the morning of the 12th Germinal the Convention met, and each man looked at his neighbour, and then, as though afraid, let his eyes wander to see if others thought as he did. At last one man dared to speak. It was Legendre the butcher;[142] he vacillated later before a mixture of deceit in others and of doubt in himself, but it should be remembered to his honour that he nearly saved the Revolution by an honest word. "Let Danton be heard at the bar of the Convention," was his frank demand; common-sense enough, but it fatally opened his guard, and gave an opportunity to the thrusts most dangerous in the year II.—an accusation of desiring privilege, and an accusation of weakening that government which was visibly saving the state on the frontiers.

Tallien was President that day, and he gave the reply to Robespierre. Now Robespierre was no good fencer. The supreme feint, the final disarming of opinion, was left to an abler man. He had gone home from the Committee to Duplay's house in the early morning; a monomaniac hardly needing sleep, he reappeared at the early meeting of the Convention. But, poor debater as he was, he could take advantage of so easy an opportunity. In a speech which was twice applauded, he asserted that Legendre had demanded a privilege. He struck the note which above all others dominated those minds. "Are we here to defend principles or men? Give the right of speech to Danton, and you give rein to an extraordinary talent, you confuse the issue with a hundred memories, you permit the bias of friendship. Let the man defend himself by proofs and witnesses, not by eloquence and sentiment." Yet he did not add—perhaps he hardly knew—that the memories and friendship would but have balanced a direct enmity, and that witnesses and proofs would be denied. Again he used that argument of government—had not they saved France? were they not the head of the police? did not they know in the past what they were doing? He assured them that a little waiting would produce conviction in them also. It did not, but time was gained; already half the Convention doubted.

Legendre, bewildered, faltered a reply; he admitted error, and begged Robespierre not to misunderstand. He could have answered for Danton as for himself, but the tribunal was of course to be trusted. It was almost an apology.

On that changing, doubtful opinion came with the force of a steel mould the hard, high voice of St. Just.

St. Just spoke rarely. There has been mention in an earlier part of this book of the speech against the Girondins. There will be mention again of a vigorous and a nearly successful attempt to save Robespierre. That he should have been given the task of defending the Committee's action that day is a singular proof of the grip which they had of the circumstances. Barrère could never have convinced an unsympathetic public opinion. Robespierre could meet a rising enthusiasm with nothing but dry and accurate phrases. But St. Just had the flame of his youth and of his energy, and his soul lived in his mouth.

The report, even as we read it, has eloquence. Coming from him then, with his extreme beauty, his upright and determined bearing, it turned the scale. The note of the argument was as ably chosen as could be; moreover it represented without question the attitude of his own mind: it was this. "The last of the factions has to be destroyed; only one obstacle stands between you and the appreciation of the Republic.[143] Time and again we have acted suddenly, but time and again we have acted well and on sufficient reasons—so it is now. If you save Danton you save a personality— something you have known and admired; you pay respect to individual talent, but you ruin the attempt in which you have so nearly succeeded. For the sake of a man you will sacrifice all the new liberty which you are giving to the whole world." There follows a passionate apostrophe in which he speaks to Danton as though he stood before him, as striking as the parallel passage in the fourth Catiline Oration.[144] Had Danton been present he would have been a man against a boy: a loud and strong voice, not violent in utterance, but powerful in phrase and in delivery, a character impressing itself by sheer force of self upon vacillating opinion. Had Danton spoken in reply, his hearers would have said with that moral conviction which is stronger than proof, "This man is the chief lover of France."

But such is rhetoric, its falsity and its success—the gaps of silence grew to a convincing power. The accusations met with no reply; they remained the echo of a living voice; the answers to them could be framed only in the silent minds of the audience. The living voice won.

And there was, as we have said, intense conviction to aid St. Just. He was a man who would forget and would exaggerate with all the faults of passion, but he believed the facts he gave. Not so Robespierre. Robespierre had furnished the notes of St. Just's report,[145] and Robespierre must have known that he had twisted all to one end. Robespierre was a man who was virtuous and true only to his ideal, not to his fellow-men. Robespierre had not deceived himself as he wrote, but he had deceived St. Just, and therefore the young "Archangel of Death" spoke with the added strength of faith, than which nothing leaps more readily from the lips to the ears. Can we doubt it? There is a phrase which convinces. When he ends by telling them what it is they save by sacrificing one idol, when he describes the Republic, he uses the phrase common to all apostolates, the superb "les mots que nous avons dits ne seront jamais perdus sur la terre"—the things which they had said would never be lost on earth.

It ended. No one voted; the demand of the Committee passed without a murmur. The Convention was never again its own mistress; it had silenced and condemned itself.[146]

Meanwhile at the Luxembourg the magistrate Dénizot was making the preparations for the trial. Each prisoner was asked the formal question of his guilt, and each replied in a single negative, but Danton added that he would die a Republican, and to the question of their defence replied that he would plead his own cause. Then, at half-past eleven they were transferred to the Conciergerie.

From that moment his position becomes the attitude of the man fighting, as we have known it in the crisis of August 1792 and of the calling up of the armies. Ready as he had always been to see the real rather than the imaginary conditions, he recognised death with one chance only of escape. He knew far better than did poor Desmoulins the power of a State's machinery; he felt its grasp and doubted of any issue. The people, for Desmoulins, were the delegators of power; for Danton the people were those who should, but who did not rule. To live again and enter the arena and save the life of the Republic the people must hear his voice, or else the fact of government would be more strong than all the rights and written justice in the world.

He was like a man whose enemy stands before him, and who sees at his own side, passive and bewildered, a strong but foolish ally. His ally was the people, his enemy was Death.

Therefore we have of his words and actions for the next four days two kinds: those addressed to death and those to his ally. Where he desires to touch the spirit of the crowd—in what was for their ears—we have the just, practical, and eloquent man apologising for over-vehemence, saying what should strike hardest home—an orator, but an orator who certainly uses legitimate weapons.

But there is another side. In much that he said in prison, in all that he said on his way to the scaffold, he is simply speaking to Death and defying him. The inmost thing in a man, the stock of the race, appears without restraint; he becomes the Gaul. That most un-northern habit of defiance, especially of defiance to the inevitable and to the strongest, the custom of his race and their salvation, grows on his lips.

He insults Death, he jests; his language, never chaste or self-conscious, takes on the laughter of the Rabelaisian, and (true Rabelaisian again) he wraps up in half-a-dozen words the whole of a situation.

Thus we see him leaning against the window of his prison and calling to Westermann in the next cell, "Oh! if I could leave my legs to Couthon[147] and my virility to Robespierre, things might still go on." And again when Lacroix said, "I will cut my own hair at the neck, so that Sanson the executioner shall not meddle with it," Danton replied, "Yet will Sanson intermeddle with the vertebræ of your neck." So he meets death with a broad torrent of words; and that a civilisation accustomed rather to reticence should know what this meant in him, my readers must note his powerful asides to Desmoulins and to Hérault, coinciding with the fearful pun in which he tried to raise the drooping courage of D'Eglantine.

Also in his prison this direct growth of the soil of France "talked often of the fields and of rivers." Shakespeare should have given us the death scenes of so much energy, defiance, coarseness, affection, and great courage.

In the Conciergerie they spent the rest of the day waiting for the trial, and this time Danton was next to Westermann, to whom and to Desmoulins he said, "We must say nothing save before the Committees or at the trial." It was his plan to move the people by a public defence, but his enemies in power had formed a counter-plan, and, as we shall see, forestalled him.

Desmoulins, "the flower that grew on Danton," was still bewildered. So he remained to the end; at the foot of the scaffold he could not understand. "If I could only have written a No. VII. I would have turned the tables."[148] "It is a duel of Commodus; they have the lance and I have not even a reed." To that man, his equal in years,[149] but a boy compared with him in spirit, Danton had always shown, and now continued to show, a peculiar affection. He treated him like a younger brother, and never made him suffer those violent truths with which all France and most of his friends were familiar in his mouth. So now, and in the trial, and on the way to the scaffold, his one attempt was to calm the bitter violence and outburst of Camille.

There are two phrases of Danton's which have been noted on this first day passed at the Conciergerie, and which cannot be omitted, though in form they have not his diction, yet in spirit they might be his; they are recollections presumably of something of greater length called to Westermann.

The first: "On such a day[150] I demanded the institution of the Revolutionary tribunal. I ask pardon of God and of man."

The second: "I am leaving everything at sixes and sevens; one had better be a poor fisherman than meddle with the art of governing men." There you have the real Danton—a reminiscence of some strong and passionate utterance put into this undantonesque and proverbial form. A real sentiment of his—all of him; careless of life, intense upon the interests of life, above all upon the future of the Revolution and of France, knowing the helpless inferiority of the men he left behind. And in the close of the phrase it is also he; it is the spirit of great weariness which had twice touched him, as sleep an athlete after a day of games. It was soon to take the form of a noble sentence: "Nous avons assez servi—allons dormir."

On the 13th (April 2, 1794), about ten in the morning, they were led before the tribunal.

The trial began.

It must not be imagined that the Dantonists alone came before the tribunal to answer for their particular policy. There had originated under Robespierre (and later when he alone was the master it was to be terribly abused) the practice of confusing the issues. Three groups at least were tried together, and the Moderates sat between two thieves—for D'Eglantine on a charge of embezzlement alone, Guzman, the Freys as common thieves and spies to the Republic, were associated on the same bench. Fourteen in all, they sat in the following order:—Chabot, Bazire, Fabre, Lacroix, Danton, Delaunay, Hérault, Desmoulins, Guzman, Diederichsen, Phillippeaux, D'Espagnac, and the two Freys. D'Eglantine occupied "the armchair," and it will be seen that the *five*—the Moderates—were carefully scattered.

The policy was a deliberate one; it was undertaken with the object of prejudicing public opinion against the accused. Nor was it permitted to each group to be separate in accusation and in its method of defence. They were carefully linked to each other by men accused of two out of the three crimes.

Herman was president of the tribunal, and sat facing the prisoners; on either side of him were Masson-Denizot, Foucault and Bravé, the assistant-judges. They say that Voullaud and Vadier, of the lower committee, appeared behind the bench to watch the enemies whom they had caught in the net. Seven jurors were in the box to the judges' left, by name Renaudin (whom Desmoulins challenged in vain), Desboisseaux, Trinchard, Dix-Aout, Lumière, Ganney, Souberbielle,[151] and to these we must add Topino-Lebrun, whose notes form by far the most vivid fragment by which we may reconstruct the scene. The jury of course was packed.[152] It was part of the theory of the Revolutionary Government that no chance element should mar its absolute dictatorship. It was practically a court of judges, absolute, and without division of powers.

At a table between the President and the prisoners sat Fouquier-Tinville, the public prosecutor; and finally, on the judges' right was the open part of the court and the door to the witnesses' room.

Here was a new trial with a great and definite chance of acquittal, a scene the like of which had not been seen for a year, nor would be seen again in that room. The men on the prisoners' bench had been the masters, one of them the creator, of the court which tried them; they were evidently greater and more powerful than their judges, and had behind them an immense though informal weight of popularity. They were public men of the first rank; their judges and the public prosecutor were known to be merely the creatures of a small committee. More than this, it was common talk that the Convention might yet change its mind, and even among the jury it was certain that discussion would arise.

By the evidence of a curious relic we know that the Committee actually feared a decree or a coup-de-main which would have destroyed their power. This note remains in the archives, a memorandum of a decision arrived at in the Committee on the early morning of the 13th or late in the night of the 12th.

"*Henriot to be written to, to tell him to issue an order that the President and the Public Prosecutor of the Revolutionary Tribunal are not to be arrested.*"

Then in another hand:

"*Get four members to sign this.*"

Finally, the memorandum is endorsed in yet another hand:

"*13th Germinal.—A policeman took this the same day.*"[153]

It will thus be seen that the Committee was by no means sure of its ground. It had indeed procured through St. Just the decree preventing Danton from pleading at the bar of the Convention and permitting his trial, but it would require the most careful manœuvring upon their part to carry through such an affair. As we shall see, they just—and only just—succeeded.

The whole of the first day (the 13th Germinal, 2nd of April 1794) was passed in the formal questions and in the reading of accusations. Camille, on being asked his age and dwelling, made the blasphemous and striking answer which satisfied the dramatic sense, but was not a true reply to the main question.

Danton gave the reply so often quoted: "I am Danton, not unknown among the revolutionaries. I shall be living nowhere soon, but you will find my name in Walhalla." The other answers, save that of Hérault, attempted no phrases.

Yet Guzman would have made more point of his assertion if he had chosen that moment to say, "I am Guzman, a grandee of Spain, who came to France to taste liberty, but was arrested for theft;" while the two Freys missed an historic occasion in not replying, "We are Julius and Emanuel Frey, sometime nobles of the Empire under the title of Von Schönfeld, now plain Jews employed by the Emperor as spies."

The public prosecutor read the indictment. First at great length Amar's report on the India Company. The details of the accusations which cost Fabre his life need not be entered into here. Suffice it to say that it was an indictment for corruption, for having suppressed or altered for money the decree of the Convention in the autumn before, and being accomplice in the extra gains which this had made possible—one of those wretched businesses with which Panama and South Africa have deluged modern France and England. It is an example of the methods of the tribunal that Fouquier managed to drag in Desmoulins's name because he had once said, "People complain of not being able to make money now, yet I make it easily enough."

The second group, the Freys, Guzman, the unfrocked priest D'Espagnac, and Diederichsen the Dane, were accused of being foreigners working against the success of the French armies, and at the same time lining their pockets. In the case of three of them the accusation was probably true. It was the more readily believed from the foreign origins of the accused, for France was full of spies, while the name of a certain contumacious Baron de Bartz made this list sound the more probable.

Finally, the small group at which they were really aiming (whose members they had already mixed up with the thieves) was indicted on nothing more particular than the report of St. Just—virtually, that is, on Robespierre's notes. Danton had served the King, had drawn the people into the place where they were massacred in July 1791, did not do his duty on the 10th of August, and so forth—a vapid useless summary of impossible things in which no one but perhaps St. Just and a group of fanatics believed. With that the day ended, and they were taken back to prison.

On the next day, the 14th Germinal (3rd of April 1794), Westermann, who, though already arrested, had only been voted upon in Parliament the day before, appeared on the prisoners' bench, and sat at the end after Emanuel Frey. He was the last and not the least noble of the Dantonists, with his great stature, his clumsy intellect, and his loyal Teutonic blood.

"Who are you?" they said. "I am Westermann. Show me to the people. I was a soldier at sixteen, and have been a councillor of Strasbourg. I have seven wounds in front, and I was never stabbed in the back till now."

This was the man who had led the 10th of August, and who had dared, in his bluff nature, to parley with the Swiss who spoke his language.

It was after some little time passed in the interrogation of the prisoners who had been arrested for fraud, especially of D'Espagnac, that the judge turned to Danton.

In the debate and cross-questioning that followed we must depend mainly upon the notes of Lebrun,[154] for they are more living, although they are more disconnected, than the official report. We discover in them the passionate series of outbursts, but a series which one must believe to have had a definite purpose. There was neither hope of convincing the tribunal nor of presenting a legal argument with effect. What Danton was trying to do in this court, which was not occupied with a trial, but merely in a process of condemnation, was to use it as a rostrum from which he could address the people, the general public, upon whose insurrection he depended. He perhaps depended also on the jury, for, carefully chosen as they were, they yet might be moved by a man who had never failed to convince by his extraordinary power of language. He carries himself exactly as though he were technically what he is in fact—a prisoner before an informal group of executioners, who appeals for justice to the crowd.

He pointed at Cambon, who had sat by him on the Committee, and said, "Come now, Cambon, do you think we are conspirators? Look, he is laughing; he believes no such thing." Then he turned, laughing himself, to the jury and said, "Write down in your notes that he laughed."

Again, he uses phrases like these: "We are here for a form, but if we are to have full liberty to speak, and if the French people is what it should be, it will be my business later to ask their pardon for my accusers." To which Camille answered, "Oh, we shall be allowed to speak, and that is all we want," and the group of Indulgents laughed heartily.

It was just after this that he began that great harangue in answer to the questions of the judge, an effort whose tone reaches to this day. It is, perhaps, the most striking example of a personal appeal that can be discovered. The opportunities for such are rare, for in the vast majority of historical cases where a man has pleaded for his life, it has either been before a well-organised court, or before a small number of determined enemies, or by the lips of one who was paid for his work and who ignored the art of political oratory. The unique conditions of the French Revolution made such a scene possible, perhaps for the only time in history.

The day, early as was the season, was warm, the windows of the court, that looked upon the Seine, were open, and through the wide doors pressed the head of a great crowd. This crowd stretched out along the corridor, along the quays, across the Pont Neuf, and even to the other side of the river. Every sentence that told was repeated from mouth to mouth, and the murmurs of the crowd proved how closely the great tribune was followed. In the attitude which had commanded the attention of his opponents when he presented the first deputation from Paris three years before, and that had made him so striking a figure during the stormy months of 1793, he launched the phrases that were destined for Paris and not for his judges. His loud voice (the thing appears incredible, but it is true) vibrating through the hall and lifted to the tones that had made him the orator of the open spaces, rang out and was heard beyond the river.

"You say that I have been paid, but I tell you that men made as I am cannot be paid. And I put against your accusation—of which you cannot furnish a proof nor the hint of a proof, nor the shadow nor the beginning of a witness—the whole of my revolutionary career. It was I who from the Jacobins kept Mirabeau at Paris. I have served long enough, and my life is a burden to me, but I will defend myself by telling you what I have done. It was I who made the pikes rise suddenly on the 20th of June and prevented the King's voyage to St. Cloud. The day after the massacre of the Champ de Mars a warrant was out for my arrest. Men were sent to kill me at Arcis, but my people came and defended me. I had to fly to London, and I came back, as you all know, the moment Garran was elected. Do you not remember me at the Jacobins, and how I asked for the Republic? It was I who knew that the court was eager for war. It was I, among others, who denounced the policy of the war."

Here a sentence was heard: "What did you do against the Brissotins?"

Now Danton had, as we know, done all in his power to save the men who hated him, but whom he admired. It was no time for him to defend himself by an explanation of this in the ears of the people who had never understood, as he had, the height of the men who followed Vergnaud; but he said what was quite true: "I told them that they were going to the scaffold. When I was a minister I said it to Brissot before the whole cabinet."

He might have added that he had said to Guadet in the November woods on the night before he left for the army, "You are headstrong, and it will be your doom."

Then he went back again to the list of his services. "It was I who prepared the 10th of August. You say I went to Arcis. I admit it, and I am proud of it. I went there to pass three days, to say good-bye to my mother, and to arrange my affairs, because I was shortly to be in peril. I hardly slept that night. It was I that had Mandat killed, because he had given the order to fire on the people.... You are reproaching me with the friendship of Fabre

D'Eglantine. He is still my friend, and I still say that he is a good citizen as he sits here with me. You have told me that my defence has been too violent, you have recalled to me the revolutionary names, and you have told me that Marat when he appeared before the tribunal might have served as my model. Well, with regard to those names who were once my friends, I will tell you this: Marat had a character on fire and unstable; Robespierre I have known as a man, above all, tenacious; but I—I have served in my own fashion, and I would embrace my worst enemy for the sake of the country, and I will give her my body if she needs the sacrifice."

This short and violent speech, which I have attempted to reproduce from the short, disjointed, ill-spelt notes of Lebrun, hit the mark. The crowd, the unstable crowd, which he contemned as he passed to the guillotine, moved like water under a strong wind; and his second object also was reached, for the tribunal grew afraid. These phrases would soon be repeated in the Convention, and no means had been taken to silence that terrible voice. The President of the court said to him that it was the part of an accused man to defend himself with proofs and not with rhetoric. He parried that also with remarkable skill, saying in a much quieter tone which all his friends (they were now growing in number) immediately noted: "That a man should be violent is wrong in him I know, unless it is for the public good, and such a violence has often been mine. If I exceeded now, it was because I found myself accused with such intolerable injustice." He raised his voice somewhat again with the words, "But as for you, St. Just, you will have to answer to posterity," and then was silent.

When the unhappy man who had taken upon his shoulders the vile duty of the political work that day, when Herman was himself upon his trial, he said, "Remember that this affair was out of the ordinary, and was a political trial," when a voice rose from the court, "There are no political trials under a Republic." He would have done well, obscure as he is before history, to have saved his own soul by refusing a task which he knew to involve injustice from beginning to end.

It was at the close of that day that three short notes passed between Herman and the public prosecutor, Fouquier-Tinville. Herman wrote, "In half an hour I shall stop Danton's defence. You must spin out some of the rest in detail." Tinville answered, "I have something more to say to Danton about Belgium;" and Herman replied, "Do not bring it in with regard to any of the others." This little proof of villany, which has survived by so curious an accident (it is in the Archives to-day),[156] closed the proceedings of that hearing.

The next day, the 15th of Germinal (4th April), Danton himself said little. It was given over mainly to the examination of Desmoulins; and as with Danton it had been rumours or opinions, so with Desmoulins only the vague sense of things he had written were brought in to serve as evidence in this tragic farce.

Fouquier, the distant cousin of Camille, to whom he owed the post in which he was earning his bread by crime,[157] tried to put something of complaint against the nation and of hatred to the Republic into his reading of the Old Cordelier. Even in his thin unpleasant voice there was only heard the noble phrase of Tacitus, and—it is a singular example of what the tribunal had become—they dared not continue the quotation because every word roused the people in the court. But Camille, so great with the pen, had nothing of the majesty or the strength of Danton. His defence was a weak, disconnected excuse, and, like all men who are insufficient to themselves, he was inconsistent.

Hérault made on that same day a far finer reply. Noble by birth, holding by his traditions and memories to that society which he himself had helped to destroy, and of which Talleyrand has said, "Those who have not known it have not lived;" accustomed from his very first youth to prominence in his profession and to the favour of the court, he remained to the last full of contempt for so much squalor, and he veiled his eyes with pride.

"I understand nothing of this topsy-turvydom. I was a diplomat, and I made the neutrality of Switzerland, so saving 60,000 men to the Republic. As for the priest you talk about, who was guillotined in my absence at Troyes, I knew him well. He was a Canon, if I remember, and by no means a reactionary. You are probably joking about it. It is true he had not taken the oath, but he was a good man; he helped me, and I am not ashamed of my friendship. I will tell you something more. On the 14th of July two men were killed, one on either side of me." He might have added, "I was the second man to scale the Towers."

It was not until the day's proceedings had been drawn out for a considerable time that a sentence was spoken, the full import of which was not understood at the time, but which was, as a fact, the first step in those four months of irresponsibility and crime which are associated with the name of Robespierre, and which hang like a weight around the neck of the French nation. Lacroix had just said with a touch of legal phraseology, "I must insist that the witnesses whom I have demanded should be subpœnaed, and if there is any difficulty about this, I formally demand that the Convention shall be consulted in the matter;" when the public prosecutor answered, "It is high time that this part of the trial, which has become a mere struggle, and which is a public scandal, should cease. I am about to write to the Convention to hear what it has to say, and its advice shall be exactly followed."

Both the public prosecutor and the judge signed the letter. The first draft which Fouquier had drawn up was thought too strong, and it appears that Herman revised it.[158] "Citoyens Représentants,—There has been a storm in the hall since this day's proceedings began. The accused are calling for witnesses who are among your deputies.... They are appealing to the people, saying that they will be refused. In spite of the firmness of the president and of all the tribunal, they continue to protest that they will not be silent until their witnesses are heard, unless by your passing a special decree." [This was false, and was the only part of the letter calculated to impress the Parliament.] "We wish to hear your orders as to what we shall do in the face of this demand; the procedure gives us no way by which we can refuse them."

But note the way in which the letter was presented to a Parliament in which there yet remained so much sympathy for the accused, and the way in which it was received. St. Just appeared in the tribune with the letter in his hands, and, instead of reading it, held it up before them and made this speech:—

"The public prosecutor of the Revolutionary Tribunal has sent to tell you that the prisoners are in full revolt, and have interrupted the hearing, saying they will not allow it to continue until the Convention has taken measures. You have barely escaped from the greatest danger which has yet menaced our new liberty, and this revolt in the very seat of justice, of men panic-stricken by the law, shows what is in their minds. Their despair and their fury are a plain proof of the hypocrisy which they showed in keeping a good face before you. Innocent men do not revolt. Dillon, who ordered his army to march on Paris, has told us that Desmoulins's wife received money to help the plot. Our thanks are due to you for having put us in the difficult and dangerous post that we occupy. Your Committees will answer you by the most careful watching," and so forth. When the Convention had had laid before them every argument and every flattery which could falsify their point of view, he proposed the decree that any prisoner who should attempt to interrupt the course of justice by threats or revolt should be outlawed.

As they were about to vote, Billaud Varennes added his word, "I beg the Convention to listen to a letter which the Committees have received from the police concerning the conspirators, and their connection with the prisoners." The letter is not genuine. Even if it were, it depends entirely upon the word of one obscure and untrustworthy man (Laflotte), but it did the work. The Committees, as we know, were names to conjure with. Their secret debates, their evident success, the fact that their members had been chosen for the very purpose of guarding the interests of the Republic, all fatally told against the prisoners. The decree passed without a vote. Robespierre asked that the letter might be read in full court, and his demand was granted. It was from that letter, from this obscure and uncertain origin, that there dated the legend of the "conspiracy in the prisons" which was to cost the lives of so many hundreds.

It was at the very close of this day, the 4th of April, that the decree of the Convention was brought back to the tribunal. Amar brought it and gave it to Fouquier, saying, "Here is what you wanted." Fouquier smiled and said, "We were in great need of it." It was read in the tribunal. When Camille heard the name of his wife mentioned in connection with St. Just's demand he cried out, "Will they kill her too?" and David, who was sitting behind the judges, said, "We hold them at last."[159]

The fourth day, the 16th Germinal (5th April), the court met at half-past eight in the morning, instead of at the ordinary hour of ten. Almost at once, before the accused had time to begin their tactics of the day before, the decree was read. The judge, relying on the law which had already been in operation against others, and which gave the jury the right to say after three days whether they were satisfied, turned to them, and they asked leave to deliberate.

Before the prisoners had passed into the prison Desmoulins had found time to tear the defence which he had written into small pieces, and to throw them at the feet of the judge. Danton cried out, and checked himself in the middle of his sentence. All save poor Camille had kept their self-control. He, however, clung to the dock, determined on making some appeal to the people, or to the judges, or to posterity. Danton, who calmed him a few hours later at the foot of the scaffold, could do nothing with him then, and it was in the midst of a terrible violence that the fifteen disappeared.

The prisoners were taken back to the Conciergerie, but in their absence occurred a scene which is among the most instructive of the close of the Revolution. One of the jury could not bring himself to declare the guilt of men whom he knew to be innocent. Another said to him, "This is not a trial; it is a sacrifice. Danton and Robespierre cannot exist together; which do you think most necessary to the Republic?" The unhappy man, full of the infatuation of the time, stammered out, "Why, Robespierre is necessary, of course, but——" "It is enough; in saying that you have passed judgment." And it came about in this way that the unanimous verdict condemned the Indulgents. Lhuillier alone was acquitted.

Of what passed in the prison we only know from the lips of an enemy,[160] but I can see Danton talking still courageously of a thousand things; sitting in his chair of green damask and drinking his bottle of Burgundy opposite the silver and the traps of D'Eglantine.[161] They were not taken back to hear their sentence; it was read to them, as a matter of form, in the Conciergerie itself. Ducray read it to them one by one as they were brought into his office. Danton refused to hear it in patience; he hated the technicality and the form, and he knew that he was condemned long ago. He committed himself to a last burst of passion before summoning his strength to meet the ordeal of the streets, and followed his anger by the insults which for days he had levelled at death. Then for a few hours they kept a silence not undignified, save only Camille, unfitted for such trials, and moaning to himself in a corner of the room, whom Danton continually tried to console, a task in which at the very end of their sad journey he succeeded. It was part of his broad mind to understand even a writer and an artist, he who had never written and had only done.

It was between half-past four and five o'clock in the evening of the same day, the 5th of April 1794, that the prisoners reappeared. Two carts were waiting for them at the great gate in the court of the Palais—the gate which is the inner entrance to the Conciergerie to-day.[162] About the carts were a numerous escort mounted and with drawn swords, but the victims took their seats as they chose, and of the fifteen the Dantonists remained together. Hérault, Camille, Lacroix, Westermann, Fabre, Danton went up the last into the second cart, and the procession moved out of the courtyard and turned to the left under the shadow of the Palais, and then to the left again round the Tour de l'Horloge, and so on to the quay. They passed the window of the tribunal, the window from which Danton's loud voice had been heard across the river; they went creaking slowly past the old Mairie, past the rooms that had been Roland's lodgings, till they came to the corner of the Pont Neuf; and as the carts turned from the trees of the Place Dauphine on to the open bridge, they left the shade and passed into the full blaze of the westering sun within an hour of its setting.

Early as was the season, the air was warm and pleasant, the leaves and the buds were out on the few trees, the sky was unclouded. All that fatal spring was summerlike, and this day was the calmest and most beautiful that it had known. The light, already tinged with evening, came flooding the houses of the north bank till their glass shone in the eyes. There it caught the Café de l'École where Danton had sat a young lawyer seven years before, and had seen the beauty of his first wife in her father's house; to the right the corner of the old Hotel de Ville caught the glow, to the left the Louvre flamed with a hundred windows.

Where the light poured up the river and came reflected from the Seine on to the bridge, it marked out the terrible column that was moving ponderously forward to death. A great crowd, foolish, unstable, varied, of whom some sang, some ran to catch a near sight of the "Indulgents," some pitied, and a few understood and despaired of the Republic—all these surging and jostling as a crowd will that is forced to a slow pace and confined by the narrowness of an old thoroughfare, stretched from one end of the bridge to the other, and you would have seen them in the sunlight, brilliant in the colours that men wore in those days, while here and there a red cap of liberty marked the line of heads.

But in the centre of this crowd and showing above it, could be seen the group of men who were about to die. The carts hidden by the people, the horses' heads just showing above the mob, surrounded by the sharp gleams that only come from swords, there rose distinguished the figures of the Dantonists. There stood Hérault de Séchelles upright, his face contemptuous, his colour high, "as though he had just risen from a feast." There on the far side of the cart sat Fabre D'Eglantine, bound, ill, collapsed, his head resting on his chest, muttering and complaining. There on the left side, opposite Fabre, is Camille, bound but still frenzied, calling loudly to the people, raving, "Peuple, pauvre Peuple!" He still kept in his poet's head the dream of the People! They had been deceived, but they were just, they would save him. He wrestled with his ropes and tore his shirt open at the bosom, clenching his bound hands—clutched in his fingers through all the struggle shone the bright hair of Lucille. Danton stood up immense and quiet between them. One of those broad shoulders touched D'Eglantine, the other Desmoulins; their souls leant upon his body. And such comfort as there was or control in the central group came out like warmth from the chief of these friends.

He had been their leader and their strength for five years; they were round him now like younger brothers orphaned. The weakness of one, the vices of another, came leaning for support on the great rock of his form. For these were not the Girondins, the admirable stoics, of whom each was a sufficient strength to his own soul: they were the Dantonists, who had been moulded and framed by the strength and genius of one man. He did not fail them a moment in the journey, and he died last to give them courage.

As they passed on and left the river, they lost the light again and plunged into shadow; the cool air was about them in the deep narrow streets. They could see the light far above them only, as they turned into the gulf of the Rue St. Honoré, down which the lives of men poured like a stream to be lost and wasted in the Place de la Revolution. Up its steep sides echoed and re-echoed the noise of the mob like waves. They could see as they rolled slowly along the people at the windows, the men sitting in the cafés or standing up to watch them go by. One especially Danton saw suddenly and for a moment. He was standing with a drawing-book in his hand and sketching rapidly with short interrupted glances. It was David, an enemy.

Then there appeared upon their left another sight; it was the only one in that long hour which drove Danton out of his control: it was the house of Duplay. There, hidden somewhere behind the close shutters, was Robespierre. They all turned to it loudly, and the sentence was pronounced which some say God has executed—that it should disappear and not be known again, and be hidden by high walls and destroyed.

The house was silent, shut, blockaded. It was like a thing which is besieged and which turns its least sentient outer part to its enemies. It was beleaguered by the silent and unseen forces which we feel pressing everywhere upon the living. For it contained the man who had sent that cartload of his friends to death. Their fault had been to preach the permanent sentiments of mankind, to talk of mercy, and to recall in 1794 the great emotions of the early Revolution—the desire for the Republic where every kind of man could sit and laugh at the same table, the Republic of the Commensales. They were the true heirs of the spirit of the Federations, and it was for this that they were condemned. Even at this last moment there radiated from them the warmth of heart that proceeds from a group of friends and lovers till it blesses the whole of a nation with an equal affection. Theirs had been the instinct of and the faith in the happy life of the world. It was for this that the Puritan had struck them down; and yet it is the one spirit that runs through any enduring reform, the only spirit that can lead us at last to the Republic.

In a remote room, where the noise of the wheels could not reach him, sat the man who, by some fatal natural lack or some sin of ambition unrepented, had become the Inquisitor—the mad, narrow enemy of mercy and of all good things.

For a moment he and his error had the power to condemn, repeating a tragedy of which the world is never weary—the mean thing was killing the great.

Nevertheless, if you will consider the men in the tumbril, you will find them not to be pitied except for two things, that they were loved by women whom they could not see, and that they were dying in the best and latest time of their powerful youth. All these young men were loved, and in other things they should be counted fortunate. They had with their own persons already transformed the world. Here the writer knew that his talent, the words he had so carefully chosen and with such delight in his power, had not been wasted upon praise or fortune, but had achieved the very object. There the orator knew and could remember how his great voice had called up the armies and thrown back the kings.

But if the scene was a tragedy, it was a tragedy of the real that refused to follow the unities. All nature was at work, crowded into the Revolutionary time, and the element that Shakespeare knew came in of itself—the eternal comedy that seems to us, according to our mood, the irony, the madness, or the cruelty of things, was fatally present to make the day complete; and the grotesque, like a discordant note, contrasted with and emphasised the terrible.

Fabre, who had best known how omnipresent is this complexity—Fabre, who had said, "Between the giving and taking of snuff there is a comedy"—furnished the example now. Danton hearing so much weakness and so many groans from the sick man said, "What is your complaint?" He answered, "I have written a play called 'The Maltese Orange,' and I fear the police have taken it, and that some one will steal it and get the fame." Poor Fabre! It is lost, and no one has the ridicule of his little folly. Danton answered him with a phrase to turn the blood: "Tais toi! Dans une semaine tu feras assez de vers," and imposed silence. Nor did this satisfy Fate; there were other points in the framework of the incongruous which she loves to throw round terror. A play was running in the opera called the "10th of August;" in this the Dantonists were represented on the stage. When the Dantonists were hardly buried it was played again that very night, and actors made up for Hérault and the rest passed before a public that ignored or had forgotten what the afternoon had seen. More than this, there was already set in type a verse which the street-hawkers cried and sold that very night. For the sake of its coincidence I will take the liberty of translating it into rhymed heroics:—

> "When Danton, Desmoulins, and D'Eglantine
> Were ferried over to the world unseen,
> Charon, that equitable citizen,
> Handed their change to these distinguished men.
> 'Pray keep the change,' they cried; 'we pay the fare
> For Couthon, and St. Just, and Robespierre.'"[163]

Danton spared only Camille, and as he did not stop appealing to the people, told him gently to cease. "Leave the rabble there," he said, "leave them alone." But for himself he kept on throwing angry jests at death. "May I sing?" he said to the executioner. Sanson thought he might, for all he knew. Then Danton said to him, "I have made some verses, and I will sing them." He sang loudly a verse of the fall of Robespierre, and then laughed as though he had been at the old café with his friends.

There was a man (Arnault of the Academy) who lived afterwards to a great age, and who happened to be crossing the Rue St. Honoré as the carts went past. In a Paris that had all its business to do, many such men came and went, almost forgetting that politics existed even then. But this batch of prisoners haunted him. He had seen Danton standing singing with laughter, he hurried on to the Rue de la Monnaie, had his say with Michael, who was awaiting him, and then, full of the scene, ran back across the Tuilleries gardens, and pressing his face to the railings looked over the great Place de la Révolution. The convoy had arrived, the carts stood at the foot of the guillotine, and his memory of the scene is the basis of its history.

It was close on six, and the sun was nearly set behind the trees of the Étoile; it reddened the great plaster statue of Liberty which stood in the middle of the Place, where the obelisk is now, and to which Madame Roland delivered her last phrase. It sent a level beam upon the vast crowd that filled the square, and cast long shadows, sending behind the guillotine a dark lane over the people. The day had remained serene and beautiful to the last, the sky was stainless, and the west shone like a forge. Against it, one by one, appeared the figures of the condemned. Hérault de Séchelles, straight and generous in his bearing, first showed against the light, standing on the high scaffold conspicuous. He looked at the Garde Meuble, and from one of its high windows a woman's hand found it possible to wave a farewell. Lacroix next, equally alone; Camille, grown easy and self-controlled, was the third. One by one they came up the few steps, stood clearly for a moment in the fierce light, black or framed in scarlet, and went down.

Danton was the last. He had stood unmoved at the foot of the steps as his friends died. Trying to embrace Hérault before he went up, roughly rebuking the executioner who tore them asunder, waiting his turn without passion, he heard the repeated fall of the knife in the silence of the crowd. His great figure, more majestic than in the days of his triumph, came against the sunset. The man who watched it from the Tuilleries gate grew half afraid, and tells us that he understood for a moment what kind of things Dante himself had seen. By an accident he had to wait some seconds longer than the rest; the executioner heard him muttering, "I shall never see her again ... no weakness," but his only movement was to gaze over the crowd. They say that a face met his, and that a sacramental hand was raised in absolution.[164]

He stood thus conspicuous for a moment over the people whom he had so often swayed. In that attitude he remains for history. When death suddenly strikes a friend, the picture which we carry of him in our minds is that of vigorous life. His last laughter, his last tones of health, his rapid step, or his animated gesture reproduce his image for ever. So it is with Danton; there is no mask of Danton dead, nor can you complete his story with the sense of repose. We cannot see his face in the calm either of triumph or of sleep—the brows grown level, the lips satisfied, the eyelids closed. He will stand through whatever centuries the story of the Revolution may be told as he stood on the scaffold looking westward and transfigured by the red sun, still courageous, still powerful in his words, and still instinct with that peculiar energy, self-forming, self-governing, and whole. He has in his final moment the bearing of the tribune, the glance that had mastered the danger in Belgium, the force that had nailed Roland to his post in September, and that had commanded the first Committee. The Republic that he desired, and that will come, was proved in his carriage, and passed from him into the crowd.

When Sanson put a hand upon his shoulder the ghost of Mirabeau stood by his side and inspired him with the pride that had brightened the death-chamber of three years before. He said, "Show my head to the people; it is well worth the while." Then they did what they had to do, and without any kind of fear, his great soul went down the turning in the road.

They showed his head to the people, and the sun set. There rose at once the confused noise of a thousand voices that rejoiced, or questioned, or despaired, and in the gathering darkness the Parisians returned through the narrow streets eastward to their homes.

CHAPTER VIII
ROBESPIERRE

I desire in this additional chapter to show what place Danton filled in the Revolution by describing the madness and the reaction that followed his loss; and the extent to which his influence, in spite of these, was permanent.

When Danton disappeared, one man remained the master of the terrible machine which he had created. It remains to show what were the fortunes of his work when death had come to complete the results of his abdication.

The genius of the dead man had foreseen a necessity, had met it with an institution, and that institution had proved his wisdom by its immense success. France was one within, and was beginning on her frontiers the war whose success was not to end until it had rebuilt all Europe. This unprecedented power dominated a country long used to centralisation, and was strengthened by the accidents of the time, by the even play of the government over a surface where all local obstacles had broken down, by the tacit acquiescence of every patriotic man (for it was the thing that saved the nation), by the very abuse of punitive measures. This power was destined to change from a machine to a toy.

They say the children of that time had little models of the guillotine to play with. The statement is picturesque and presumably false, but it will serve well for a simile. A man unused to action, dreaming of a perfect state which was but a reflection of his own intensely concentrated mind, acquired the control of the guillotine. Unfortunately the model was of full size.

The punishment of death had hitherto been inflicted, for the most part, with a clear and definite, though often with an immoral, object. In the hands of Robespierre it was used to defend a theory and a whim. The men of the time loved their country ardently, and believed with the firmness of a large and generous faith in those principles upon which all our civilisation is at present based. France and the Republic were, in their minds, one thing, and a thing which they spared no means to make survive the most terrible struggle into which any nation has ever dared to enter. They killed that they might be obeyed in a time which verged on anarchy, and they desired to be obeyed because, but for obedience to government, France and all her liberties would have perished. Such a motive for punishment is just, and its execution is honest.

By the side of this and beyond it were the excesses, those excesses in protest against which Danton himself had died. Execrable as were these, infamous as will ever remain their most conspicuous actors, Hébert and Carrier, they were prompted by a motive which is of the commonest and the most easily understood in human affairs. They were actions of revenge. Danton had said once and sincerely, "I can find no use for hate." It was the key to his successful effort, by far the most creative in a time when all was energy, that no part of his strength was lost in personal attack, hardly any in personal defence. This could no more be said of his contemporaries than it can be said of the bulk of men in any nation, even in times of order and of peace. And everywhere, in Nantes, in Lyons, in the Vendée, in the accusation of Marie Antoinette, from the very beginning of the Terror, this hate had surged and broken. The Girondins were put to death on a charge full of the spirit of revenge; and as the autumn grew into winter, in the very crisis of that oppression by which the nation had been saved, the accusations became trivial, the process of justice more and more of a personal act, depending in the provinces on the temper of an emissary, in Paris upon the summary judgment of the Committee and the Tribunal.

But all this had so far been comprehensible. With the advent of Robespierre to full power we have to deal with a phase of history which will hardly be understood in happier times. Danton, who saw straight, who understood, and who, when the victories began, found leisure to pity, is a type whose extremes are the romance, whose moderation is the groundwork of history. We have to deal in him with an enthusiast who is also a statesman, in whom the mind has sufficient power to know itself even in its violence, and to return deliberately within its usual boundaries after never so fantastic an excursion. With Hébert again we know the type. Those are not rare in whom passions purely personal dominate all abstract conceptions, and whose natures desire the horrible in literature during times of peace, and satisfy their desire by action during their moments of power.

But with Robespierre an absolutely different feature is presented: the man who could laugh and the man who could hate, the right and the left wing have disappeared, and there is left standing alone a personality which had gradually become the idol of the city. He could neither laugh nor hate; the love of country itself, which illuminates so much in the Revolution, and which explains so many follies in the smaller men, even that was practically absent in the mind of Robespierre. His character would have fitted well with the absence of the human senses, and should some further document discover to historians that he lacked the sense of taste, that he was colour-blind, or that he could not distinguish the notes of music, these details would do much to complete the imperfect and troubling picture. For in the sphere that is above, but co-ordinate with, physical life, all those avenues by which our fellow-beings touch us more nearly than ideas were closed to him.

It is possible that he may take, centuries hence, the appearance of majesty. He had the reserve, the dignity, the intense idealism, the perfect belief in himself, the certitude that others were in sympathy—all the characteristics, in fine, which distinguish the Absolutists and the great Reformers. In his iron code of theory we seem to hear the ghost of a Calvin, in his reiterated morals and his perpetual application of them there is the occasional sharp reminiscence of a Hildebrand. The famous death cry, "I have loved justice and hated iniquity, therefore I die in exile," is not so far distant from "... *de mourir pour le peuple et d'en être abhorré.*"

We are accustomed to clothe such figures with a solemn drapery, and to lend them, at great distances of time, a certain terrible grandeur. Robespierre is too near us, he is too well known, and his reforms failed too utterly, for this to be now the case with him. Yet it may well happen that some one else treading in the same path, and succeeding, will see fit to build a legend round his name.

What then was the ideal which he pursued—this "one idea," which stood so perpetually before him as to exclude the sight of all human things, of sufferings, of memories, of patriotism itself? It was the civic ideal of Rousseau, in so far as he conformed to it, and nothing more.

The ideas of the great reformers must of their nature be simple—unworkably simple. But Robespierre's idea was less than simple—it was thin. Now and again in the history of upheavals a type has been defined with special formulæ, which in its original shape could never have survived the conditions of active existence, but which was real enough to receive accretions, and robust enough to bear moulding until at length it became the living nucleus of a new society, changed, transformed in a thousand details, yet in its main lines the ideal of the founder. With all the great reforms of the world some such type has been present; the Puritan, the knight of chivalry, were at first but a faint figure realised in a few phrases.

Rousseau himself had created such a type, and it has survived; for what permanent fortunes a century is insufficient to show. The Republican citizen of Jean-Jacques stood in the generation which succeeded him the centre of a new society; in a thousand shapes he really lived. Thomas Jefferson, William Cobbett, were living men to whom this ideal stood for model; not in its details, but in its main lines. Such noble men are to be met to-day on every side.

But Robespierre saw reflected in his mind a figure at once more detailed and less human, and one too sharply defined to be capable of any moulding or of any transference into the real world. For him this ideal citizen was nevertheless the one good thing, the one sound basis of a State. This ideal citizen existed (did men only know it) in each individual; all men could be made to approach the type; only a very few were opposed to its success, and it was a sacred duty to break their criminal effort. The figure stood ever before him, it dominated his every thought, it was the sacred thing before which his essentially mystical mind was perpetually at worship. But he could see nothing beyond or on either side of it; concrete impressions faded on the unhealthy retina of his mind. For there was a mirror held up before his eyes, and the figure on which he dwelt was himself.

Thus intensely concentrated upon a certain individual type, it was in his nature to forget the reactions of a community. He saw in society a few evils prominent, authority without warrant, arbitrary rule (that hateful thing), servility in the oppressed (the main impediment to any reform). He was blind to the interplay, the organic quality in a State, which our own time so ridiculously exaggerates, but which the eighteenth century as a whole neglected. Rousseau had put admirably the metaphor of contract as explaining the bond of society. Robespierre, interpreting him, conceived of contract as the simple and all-sufficient machinery of a State. The error gave his attempt a mechanical and an inhuman appearance over and above its rigidity of dogma. Rousseau, like all the great writers, gave continual glimpses of the insufficiency of language; he let his audience see in a hundred phrases, in a recurrence of qualifications, that his words were no more than the words of others, hints at realities, at the best metaphors brought as near as possible to be the true reflection of ideas. Robespierre read him, and has remained among the words entangled and satisfied. Rousseau was perpetually insisting upon a point of view, calling out, "Come and see." He had discovered a position from which (as he thought) the bewildering complexity of human affairs appeared in a just and simple perspective. But Rousseau never asserts that such a view will have the same colouring to all men; on the contrary, at his best he denies it. He trusts to the main aspect of his theory for a main result in the State, to an agreement among men of good-will for the harmonising of conflicting details. Robespierre, as the high-priest of that gospel, had come and had seen, but the perfect citizen and the perfect state of his vision must be realised in every tittle as he had observed them. Once again a great message was destined to be sterilised and almost lost through the functionary of its creed.

Such was the man who had slowly supplanted Danton. A mind whose type of aberration is common to all nations had supplanted the typical

Frenchman who had organised the defence of France, and in the place of one whom his enemies perpetually reproach with an excess of vigour and manhood, a theorist of hardly any but intellectual emotions was master.

What gave him his great ascendancy, his practically absolute power? It was due, in the first place, to the popularity whose growth was the feature of the later Revolution. That popularity was real in the number of his followers and in the sincerity of their profession. It must be remembered that hitherto he had stood on the side of leniency in public action, while in words he had expressed always accurately, sometimes nobly, the ideals upon which the nation was bent. He had, from a constitutional incapacity for real work, been only in the background of those crises which had left behind them an increasing crowd of malcontents. Not he, but Danton, had made the 10th of August. No one had connected his name with the massacres of September. The necessity of government was not *his* interpretation of the defeats in Belgium; the creation of that government was another's; its latent benefits reflect no merit upon him now; its immediate rigours exposed him to no special vengeance at the time. Not he, but Marat, is the obvious demagogue whom the visionary Girondin girl marks out as the enemy. To Carnot would turn the hatred of those whom the great conscription oppressed. The Christian foundation of France had others than Robespierre to curse for the Masque of Reason and for the suppression of public worship. He had stood behind Desmoulins when the reaction of Nivose and Frimaire was at work; he had approved and was thought the author of that trial and execution in which Hébert had suffered the sentence already pronounced upon him by the best of France. In fact, he had stood in nothing as the extremist or as the tyrant till the day when he permitted the arrest of Danton. He had been rather the voice of a strong public opinion than the arm which, when it acts at the orders of unreason, becomes hated by its own furious master. Thus upon the negative side there was nothing to prevent his sudden attainment of power.

In the second place, his name had been the most present and the most familiar from the earliest days of the Revolution. He had sat in the Assembly of the Commons five years before, a notable though hardly a noted figure, with some stories surrounding him, with quite a reputation in his provincial centre; he had been, since first the Jacobin Club became the mouthpiece of the pure Republicans, the conspicuous leader of the Society. The force of continuity and tradition counts for little in the history of this whirlwind, but such as it is it explains to a great degree the ascendancy of Robespierre. He alone was never absent, he alone remained to chant a ceaseless chorus to the action of the drama. His name was familiar to excess; but it was hardly an epoch at which men grew weary of hearing a politician called "the just."

Besides this familiarity with his name, certain virtues—and those the most cherished of the time—were in fact or by reputation his. None could accuse him of venality; his sincerity was obvious—indeed, it was the necessary fruit of his narrow mind. The ambition from which we cannot divorce his name was apparent to but few of his contemporaries, and was not fully seized even by his enemies till he had started on that short career of absolute power which has stamped itself for ever upon the fortunes of his country. Thus habit, the strongest of forces, was his ally.

In the third place, circumstances quite as much as his own action had left him (as far as one can follow the mysteries of the Committee) sole director of an exceptional executive. On account of the illusions and necessities of the people such a position was not immediately recognised as tyrannical. The machine was theirs, working for them and made by them; all the better if an idol of theirs held the levers; he would make the most trusty of servants. Robespierre was not master in theory. Even committees were not the masters in theory. Theory was everything to France in the year II., and in theory the Convention was master. Nay, even the Convention was only master because—in theory again—the sovereign, the nation, was behind it. The majority of the Convention, and it alone, is the technical authority. Robespierre's name was not to be discovered at the foot of those lists of the condemned which his monstrous policy constructed, and at the end of his four months he fell because the theoretical master, the Convention, acted as it chose, and no sufficient force dared to deny its right.

He starts then upon the closing act of the play, the one figure whom all regard, and into whose hands the police, the committees, the juries, and (by their own disorder) the majority of the Convention itself have fallen.

The new reign began on the 6th of April, exactly a year to a day since the Committee of Public Safety had been established. It was Germinal, the month of seeds that grow under ground, the most significant and the most terrible of the new names. M. Zola has chosen it for the title of his greatest work; it was the other day on the dying lips of a poor wretch in Spain whose madness also turned upon social injustice.

The following of Robespierre did not hesitate to show at once its tendencies and even its dogmas—for it held a religion. That same day, the 6th of April—17th Germinal of the year II.—Couthon came from the Committee with a proposition for the Parliament to discuss the establishment of a national worship of God. A new note had been heard in the clamour; soon in the clear silence of suspense it is to be the only sound, saving the dull accompaniment of the two guillotines. This or that occasional freak of theory or dramatised ribaldry the Terror had already known; unlimited power defended by inexorable severity had developed many strange decrees, dissociated from the general life and dying as they rose—absurdities whose chief purpose would seem to be the interest they have afforded to foreigners. But in these there had been no system. The Mass was being said on all sides when the churches were supposed to be closed. Even as the Feast of Reason was being held at Notre Dame, vespers were chanted at St. Germains. One thing alone had been the purpose and had given the motive force to nine months of agony endured—the salvation of Revolutionary France. But when Couthon spoke it was not France, nor common rights and liberties which were proposed as the object of the defence—it was Robespierrian Rousseau. In two months we shall have the worship of the Supreme Being, in three the reaction; in less than four the high-priest of this impossible system is to fall; yet his dream and his power will be almost enough in their fall to drag down the Republic.

Five days more saw "the rest of the factions" sacrificed to this new personal terror. Gobel, who had always been afraid, and whose conscience had been turned like a weathercock away from the nearest pike; the wives of Desmoulins and of Hébert (for women, as the Terror increased, were suspected, sometimes rightly, of being the best at plotting); Chaumette, who had helped Hébert to put up his theatricals in Notre Dame—they were all tried, and in this trial it is again not the Revolution, but Robespierre pure and simple whom we hear arguing and condemning through the mouths of the court.

One of the accused "has wished to efface the idea of the divinity." Another has "interfered with the worship of his fellow-citizens" (this was said to Chaumette, who must have thought it even at that moment something of a platitude). To a third the reproach is made of "changing the mode of worship without authority." We are on the highroad to those last six weeks in which trial of any kind and definite accusation itself was absent. The details of one man's opinion are become the numberless dogmas of a creed, and of a creed that kills unmercifully. And yet even as he asserted his creed its mechanical impotence appeared in violent contrast with the humanity that the Puritan was persecuting. For Lucille lighted her face radiantly when she was condemned, and said, "I shall see him in a few hours."

Three days more—the 17th of April—and the machinery was further centralised. St. Just demanded that the political prisoners should be taken from every part of France to be judged in Paris. The popular commissions—mere gatherings to denounce without proofs and without forms—were actively used all over the Republic. In Paris the commission was to be the feeler for the central machine. And such was the incapacity of the Dreamer, "who had not wits enough to cook an egg," that this new feature in the machinery was not even organised: it was a government of mere rigid absolutism resting on bases that were rapidly becoming mere anarchy. But even as the system, such as it was, developed, as the central power grew more rigid, and the thing to be governed more decayed, Danton, who had been killed that it might exist, pursued it. It was due to his work that the wrestling on the frontier was showing a definite issue. The advance had begun.

With his death the diplomacy of France had ceased. The phrase of Robespierre's, which he had so successfully combated, had reappeared in vigour: the "nation would not treat with her enemies." But the organisation of her armies, the levies, the rigid discipline, the arms were telling. That aspect of the national energy had grown more healthy as the central brain grew more diseased and vain. Robespierre was threatening Carnot vaguely in the Committee, but Carnot was at work and was saving France. St. Just himself, when he is upon the frontier, appears in a capacity worthy of admiration, for he has there to deal with a thing in action. His energy is as fierce as ever, but its object is victory over a national enemy, and not the triumph of a jejune idea. He had better have remained with the soldiers.

In Paris the Commune had been seized. The enemy whom all had feared, whom even Danton had to the last conciliated, was fearlessly grasped. The mayor was broken simply, and replaced by a servant of the rulers; the Sections protested with the last of their vitality, but the Club denounced them, and they disappeared—even an attempt at martyrdom is to give the idol yet more gilt. Then the news of Turcoing came to Paris. It was little more than a happy rumour, a battle whose importance seems greater to us now than it did to contemporaries. But Pichegru, the peasant, had prepared a good road for Jourdan, and Fleurus was the direct result of Turcoing. Barrère long after called these victories "the Furies," which swept upon and destroyed the fanatic in power.

With every point of good news the Terror was less necessary, yet Robespierre's action grew as the national danger disappeared. Even Lord Howe's great victory of the 1st of June did little to check the sentiment of relief. The *Vengeur* went down and left a force of many ships to the French navy for ever. The food reached port, and the eyes of Frenchmen were not directed to the sea, whose command they knew themselves to have gained and lost before then with but little resulting change; they turned, as they have always and will ever turn, to the frontier of the north-east, the wrestling-ring upon whose fair level was to be decided the fate of all their sacrifice and of all their ideals, and Paris every day grew more hopeful of the result, Robespierre more blind to everything except his vision. On the 8th of June—the 20th Prairial—he capped the edifice of his national religion with the Feast of the Supreme Being; on the 10th he forged the last piece of the machinery which was to make that religion the moral order of the new era by force.

In the connection of these dates we see the whole man and the time. Three weeks pass from the first definite victory against the allies to the law of the 22nd Prairial. That short time widened the breach between the armies and the government till it became an impassable gulf. The fruit of that schism was to appear much later, but already its elements were clear. Of the two parts of Danton's work one had become national, healthy, representative; the other, which had been designed for similar action, had finally become a thing of personalities and of theories. The armies were in full success, the Terror was menaced, and was doomed.

In this feast of the Almighty, Robespierre was insanely himself. He wore his bright-blue coat, perhaps to typify the bright sky which we have all worshipped for so many thousand years. In his little white hand, that never had been nor could be put to a man's work, he held the typical offerings of fruit and corn. His head was bent forward a little, and he looked at the ground. The men who stood up boldly in the attitudes of Mirabeau and of the Tribunes were dead or in the armies.

Remove the scene by hundreds of years, and tell it of a primitive people in some mountain valley, it assumes a simplicity and a grandeur as legend. Their old traditions (let us say) have been lost or stolen from them. They are casting about for a lawgiver and for a starting-point. A pure idealist is found, draconian in his method, but ascetic and sincere in his life, laying down as necessary for the state a clear and simple morality, basing all ethics on the recognition and the worship of God. If we make that picture we have some idea of what passed through the mind of the little clique which still surrounded Robespierre, some conception of the picture which still half-fascinated the crowd. For Robespierre himself it was intensely true; he lived æons and myriads of leagues away in time and space from humanity, intent upon his dream.

But in sight of the mummery stood Notre Dame. Not a man there but had been baptized in the Christian faith; a history more complex and more eventful than that of perhaps any other nation was the inheritance and the future of that crowd. And even as the game was being played, the real France on the Sambre and in the plains of Valenciennes was carrying out the oldest of struggles in defence of the first of rights. The scene has been laughed at and despised sufficiently by aliens within and without the French nation; let it suffice for this book to insist upon its unreality, and to assert that its principal actor was genuine because he lived in the unreal.

The law of the 22nd of Prairial followed this feast. It was the establishment of a pure despotism, arbitrary, absolute, personal. Already the trials were centralised in Paris since the demand of St. Just had been made. The Commune had been captured, the popular commissions used, even the Presidency of the Convention had become the appanage of one man and his associates. This new law proposed the final step. After it was passed the trials were to be conducted without proofs, and without witness or pleading, for they were to be nothing more than a formal process. The Committee once satisfied of guilt, the tribunal was merely to condemn. To be upon the lists was virtually to be dead. It was the end of civil government, the declaration of a state of siege. And that at the moment when the armies sent every day better and better news. The Convention debated with Robespierre in the chair; it hesitated and it nearly condemned the proposal. There was a conflict in the minds of some between the admiration—almost the adoration—of a man; in the minds of others, between fear and the necessity apparent to all of relaxing the machinery which only the national danger had called into being.

Robespierre came down from the chair and spoke. The even, certain voice which carried away his admirers, which terrified his opponents, succeeded, and the law was passed. Those who find it easy to judge the time, who think it may all be explained by the baseness or the pusillanimity of the Parliament, should note the appeal which he made to the *Moderates* even then—an appeal which had always been successful, which, when his death drew near, he made at last (and for the first time) in vain.

For the Moderates, the Plain, the "Marsh," saw in him a kind of saviour, the just man, the slayer of the Mountain, the master who would be terrible only for a little time, and would soon restore peace when he had established a dogma of moral order. Were Moderates ever slow to give full power for the sake of order?

The next day some one saw that the new law touched the Parliament itself. Self-defence, the most sacred, perhaps the only, right of a prince, occurred to them, and they protested. They passed a resolution that no member could be taken before the Revolutionary Tribunal without their consent. The following day Robespierre again appears, again appeals to the "Marsh." The men of order saw at once that no danger applied to them, that the disorderly fellows up on the benches of the Left alone were in danger. The resolution was repealed. On that day, the 24th of Prairial of the year II.—12th of June 1794—the whole of France was at his feet, save the armies.

The France which had made the Revolution, and which Danton had loved, defended, and saved, was in the Ardennes and before Ypres. There were two main bodies. One, on the left, in the plains by the frontier towns, was opposed to a united force of English and Austrians; the other, on the right, in the woods and deep ravines of the Ardennes, was opposed to a strong series of Austrian posts. These armies were not separated, but the enemy held the angle between them. Away on the extreme right Jourdan held the Moselle valley. Pichegru had come back to the army of the left, which in his absence had won Turcoing, and at whose head Soudham, Moreau, and Macdonald had fought and succeeded. On the right St. Just was throwing into the attack upon the Sambre all the energy which had saved, before this, the army of Alsace. Five times the attempt had been made to pierce the Austrian lines, and five times it had failed. Coburg lay on both sides of the river; Charleroy, on the right bank, was his strong place. The Deputies on mission, St. Just and Lebas, the same whom we shall see standing by Robespierre at the end, were present at the last decisive check before Charleroy itself. With the Sambre thus held, the southern army was immobilised; the successes of the army of the north seemed almost valueless, for Coburg held the angle between the two. Nevertheless, Turcoing bore great fruit, for it convinced the Austrians that reinforcements were needed to meet the French advance in the north. The allies were like a man fighting with a sword in each hand against two opponents. Wounded in the right hand, he must cross rapidly with the sword in his left, and so expose his left side. Thus Coburg left the Sambre a little more exposed in order to provide temporary reinforcements against the army that had just won Turcoing. St. Just and Carnot were enemies; the young Robespierrian was planned to replace the organiser whom Danton had recognised; nevertheless, they agreed at this supreme moment upon the necessary action. St. Just from the army, Carnot from the Ministry of War at Paris, called up Jourdan from the Moselle with over forty thousand men.

They are wrong who imagine that Napoleon invented the attack by concentration on the weakest point; so far as the large lines of a campaign go he inherited it from the early Republican generals. Leaving strong places unoccupied, careless of holding (for example) this position on the Moselle, the hurried march northward was determined on, and a supreme effort against the Austrian lines.

By this junction was formed that "Army of the Sambre-et-Meuse" which to this day gives a theme for one of the noblest marching-songs of the French soldiery. Under Jourdan were men whose names alone have something of the quality of bugle-calls. Ney, and Kleber, and Marceau were leading them. There ran through this new army a kind of prescience, the foreknowledge of victory, an unaccustomed feeling of expansion and of hope. Soult speaks of it as his awakening; and there is a fine phrase in the memoir of a contemporary which gives us some echo of its enthusiasm: "We always seemed to be marching into the dawn;" they felt in every rank that the balance was turning, and that France was to be saved.

A sixth attempt was for a sixth time foiled. The seventh succeeded. The Austrian line was broken and Charleroy surrounded; in a week it fell. The capitulation was hardly achieved when the army of Coburg appeared to the north-east upon the heights that command the left bank of the river, a plateau called that of Fleurus.

It was upon the 25th of June that the armies met and fought with blazing hay about them and ripe harvest that had caught fire. Kleber recovered the left wing, as Cromwell at Naseby, after it had given way. Marceau obstinately held the right in front of Fleurus, as Davoust did at Austerlitz ten years later. And towards evening the watchers in the balloon above the French ranks saw in regular and stiff retreat the last army of the old world. By the end of Messidor the English were in Holland, the Austrians upon the Rhine, the whole of Belgium was in the hands of the Republic.

The sun which set upon the death of Danton had risen again.

So in Robespierre's own country his fall was prepared by circumstances. At Arras, his birthplace, one could almost hear the guns of Fleurus; he and his thin soul belonged to those plains of the north where the Norman and the Burgundian, and the Provençal and the Gascon, born in more generous places, were driving the enemy before them.

St. Just came back from the front. He at least had seen on what Revolutionary France was really bent, and in what she was vigorous. With the superb courage that belonged to his energy and his youth he had led the charges. Living with the soldiers, he had seen more closely, and with more accuracy than is common in visionaries, the needs of an army. Why did he come back to continue the insane drama whose seven weeks of action count more with the enemies of France than all her centuries?

Because the armies and their victories, though affording proof of what the nation was and of what it required, could afford that proof only to a just and even mind. The soldiers themselves did not express a political opinion; their whole mind was bent upon the breaking of the line, the attempt in which they had succeeded. Of Paris, Revolutionary in the last few months, they knew little. They judged it as our contemporaries do—on hearsay; and it seemed to them that there stood in the capital a powerful Committee full of patriots, who had by an intense, an almost furious energy, saved them—the soldiers. Men who risk their lives every day and see death constantly are not likely to be horror-stricken at an excess of rigour in government. In their eyes a number of men had fallen, places had changed, the central power was surrounded by a tumult, but *they* had been clothed and fed almost by a miracle—their battles had been made possible. The year since the great conscription had drawn them from their homes had been for them a struggle of continual promise, ending in a great achievement. Already the soldier was half-professional; the eager volunteer of 1792, full of his politics, had given place to a type which the wanton policy of the old regime was forging to its own destruction. For it was forging the veterans who cared more and more for the Revolutionary thing, and less and less for the discussions and the theories, till at last they produced the Empire.

St. Just therefore could not warn Robespierre. St. Just himself had learnt no lesson. His ideal was still in his eyes the salvation of France, and even of the world; the victory of Fleurus only made it the more possible to carry his ideal out in action. He had seen the emigrants who were taken in that battle spared for the first time by the French soldiery, but he did not recognise the tremendous import of this, nor appreciate what our own time has thoroughly learnt, that it is the success or the failure of the national defence which rules the temper of a nation.

When the news of Fleurus became known in Paris the law of Prairial had been in action for nearly three weeks. By the time the victory and its meaning had fully sunk into the mind of the capital half the short period of Robespierre had expired. How much was due to fear upon his part, how much to mere blindness, we cannot tell, but the very moment when the necessity for the Terror patently disappeared was the moment chosen by him for the aggravation of his system.

He attacked the Mountain.

It will be remembered that the Convention had feared for itself when it gave the full power into his hands. On the 11th of June Bourdon from the Oise had carried a motion which would have defended the deputies, but which Robespierre had caused to be cancelled upon the following day.

With an attack, however, appearing as a reality instead of remaining as a threat, even the "Marsh" grew afraid. He put into his speech an excellent maxim, that "not success of armies abroad or on the frontier are the greatness of a nation, but the virtue of its private citizens within" (21st Messidor)—a truth appearing perhaps at the very worst moment, for it translated itself at once in the minds of his audience into "the victories mean nothing to me; the guillotine is for the defence not of the nation but of my dogmas." And his faith went on sacrificing its innumerable victims.

Another and a final element was added to the forces against him. The Committee began to refuse his leadership. It must be remembered that Robespierre was not absolute master in the sense in which (for example) an

English general would be master of an Indian province after the suppression of a mutiny. Circumstances, immense popularity, above all the kind of men who composed the great Committee, are the explanation of his power. His power was a fact, but a fact based on no theoretical right, and therefore possessed of no elements of endurance. Even the Committee was in the eyes of all the governed, and of some of its own members, only the servant of the national welfare. Two men upon it were Robespierrians—Couthon and St. Just; one was a turncoat by nature—Barrère; two more were men of the Hébertian type, most unreliable for an idealist to deal with—Billaud and Collot. Finally there remains Carnot, the worker, and four others—the two Prieurs, Lindet and St. André.

Robespierre could be virtually a master, but a master only on the tolerance of superior though latent force. He could inspire terror by the common knowledge that the machinery was in his hands, that its terrible punishment was practically his to inflict at pleasure. But something put it into his hand, and something could take it away. It cannot be too often repeated, if we wish to understand the Revolution, that from the fall of Lafayette to the 13th of October 1795 there was no disciplined armed force at the service of the Government, there was nobody better armed or better drilled than the man in the street—not even gunners, the first necessity of modern masters, for the very artillery was amateur; above all, there was no armed body whose members obeyed without question, who were, as a good army must be, a rigid instrument of government framed upon a device which multiplies a hundredfold the strength of each man in the public service. The "strong men" of history, whom our reactionaries delight to honour, have always had such an instrument at their disposition, but when there is no one to fire at a command, your strong man is like any other, save that he is a little weaker for shouting.

What then was the ultimate master which permitted Robespierre to rule? It was composed of several forces, and in its division is to be found the secret of its inertia.

Firstly, the Convention, mutilated as it was, was granted by all to be the nearest representative of the nation. What the majority voted was done. It exercised a very great moral influence, and if it had shown that influence so slightly, it was because its organisation was contemptible—a mass of individuals, with no traditions of action or of grouping, a crowd in which the fear of each that another might be his enemy caused the sum of its individual cries to be anything but the integrate expression of its corporate will. Well, this crowd had had one formidable enemy. The *right* of the Convention had been combated by the *force* of the well-organised

Commune. The Commune used to be a mirror of at least half of Paris; it had lost this character. It was nothing now but a group of Robespierrians, and the Convention was the stronger for the change.

Secondly, there was the material force—the populace of Paris. They had not risen hitherto save for one or two motives—the establishment of the national defence, the prevention of a political reaction; and they had been more turbulent and more dangerous where the first than where the second was their cause for action.

Thirdly, the regular initiative was in the hands of a majority of the Committee of Public Safety.

The moment therefore that the majority of the Committee refused to follow Robespierre's lead, he would have had to ascend the tribune of the Convention, and in one of those speeches which carried to some such genuine conviction, but to many others such still more genuine fear, he would have had to obtain a majority for the reconstruction of the great Committee.

Now a deliberative Assembly which is not strictly organised upon party lines, which has no aristocratic quality and no great (because traditional) corporate pride, is very strongly influenced by what we call "Public Opinion." It hears reports from the whole nation, is composed of every kind of man, regards itself moreover as in duty bound to listen to the voices outside, meets in its lobbies and during its recesses every species of expression.

Such a jury is therefore the very worst before which a popular idol could present itself when some strong adverse action had just shown his reputation to be falling. Outvoted in Committee, condemned in Parliament, the man who had but just now been supreme would have to turn to whatever he could find of physical force to support him.

But that physical force in the case of Robespierre was only the populace of Paris, and a populace moreover whose one organising centre—the Commune—had been weakened by himself. Once suppose him forced to depend upon a rising of the people, and the weakness of his position is apparent; even were he still the politician of the majority, it would be a long step from approving of his policy to risking one's life in a civil tumult, conscious that one was attacking every form of constituted authority, and presumably the opinion of the whole nation, for no principle, from no necessity, but to save a man. As we shall see, the rising to defend him comprised but a small knot of men, and totally failed.

The man who had not the wits to cook an egg prepared his own ruin. Carnot, whose one idea was to work and save the frontier, he openly menaced. Robespierre meditated the inconceivable folly of replacing Carnot's science by the blind activity of St. Just. In alienating Carnot and losing that possible ally, Robespierre lost five of his colleagues on the Committee. The end of Messidor saw him in a kind of voluntary isolation, letting the fatal machine work on, while he stood off from the levers.

He seems to have just felt two doubts disturbing the serenity of his fanatical complacency. First, whether after all he was going down to posterity as he saw himself to be—the maker of a new France, "the terror of oppressors and the refuge of the oppressed." (One day his eyes filled when the noise of the tumbrils reached him, and he said, "I shall be remembered only as a slayer of men." So wrapped up in himself, he had not yet heard an echo of what all men were saying.) Secondly, he wondered whether his perfect state was so near as he had thought. The killing went on, and he got no nearer. The "anti-patriots," the "anti-revolutionaries," the "anti-Robespierres" (though he did not think of them so) passed perpetually eastward and westward daily from the prisons to the two guillotines.

By the irony of whatever rules and laughs at men, events caused the first mutterings to rise among the Extremists. The Terror was too mild, and above all the men with hearts of beasts—the remainder of the Hébertists—hated a policy which included, however fantastically, the ideal and the worship of God. They hated his half-alliance with whatever was Christian in the Convention, and his perpetual appeals to the Moderates.

The Lower Committee had a partially independent life. It was known to be the policy of Robespierre to submit this body, as he had submitted all the other organs of government, to the great Committee of Public Safety. Hence it was in this Lower Committee of General Security—menaced as a function and as individuals, thoroughly in touch, by its position, with the police—that the conspiracy arose. The majority of its members joined it, and from the Higher Committee Billaud and Collot adhered. On the 7th of Thermidor (25th of July 1794) the storm burst. Barrère read his report to the Convention, and it was an open menace to Robespierre.

The origins of that report merit a certain discussion. We have seen that from the first the reports, directed by the Committee, were usually written by Barrère, and were read to the Convention by him. On the other hand, we can discover usually in the style, and always in the opinions of the reports, the action of whoever led in the councils of the Committee. Thus, in the document of this nature of which so much mention is made in chapter vi., the spirit, and evidently many of the actual phrases, are the work of Danton.

Who drew up Barrère's report, whether (possibly) it was his own work, when he saw opinion shifting away from Robespierre, or whether, as is more probable, it was inspired by Billaud and Collot, and permitted by the five neutrals, we cannot tell. The main fact is this, that the Committee had at least permitted to be made in its name a public declaration hostile to the man who, through the Committee, had ruled France.

The report repudiated in detail the policy of the past seven weeks; it insisted on the importance of the victories, on the iniquity of further lists of victims. For the first time in four months the Convention acted freely; it ordered the report to be printed and to be sent to all the Communes of France.

On the next day Robespierre came for the last time into his accustomed place. He gave his last speech to the Parliament. He was to appear once more, but never again as the orator and the leader. Reading, as was his wont, not declaiming, in the slow even voice that had compelled such attention, such enthusiasm, and such fear, he made the last of his declarations. This speech, if no other, should be read to understand the man. Here a theory stated with power and with precision; there a description of those without whose condemnation the theory could not be realised. A noble ideal based upon the scaffold; a dogma and a detailed persecution side by side. He read it slowly from end to end, proving to himself, and, as he thought, to his audience, the perfection of his ideal, and the necessity of the terrible road towards it. But his audience heard nothing of the ideal; they heard only the description of themselves.

Men of all kinds, the mere demagogues, were in that summary, the personal enemies, the financiers. It seems that on the manuscript from which he read even Cambon's name was written. But in this extreme crisis, when he was denouncing the first men in order to save his own position, he was no longer Robespierre. It made no difference to his fate, yet we judge him with more accuracy when we know that he omitted the name of Cambon, and that he did not pronounce that of Carnot, whom he had threatened in private. It was an attempt at compromise.

The Convention heard him and his threat. Of his theories they had heard enough for years. Yet such was the power of his slow clear utterance, of the reverence which his following commanded, and of the idea which he expressed so well, and in which all at heart believed, that they voted the printing and the dissemination of the speech. Cambon and Billaud-Varennes rose to demand the repeal of the vote. The great unwieldy assembly, or rather its great unwieldy neutral faction, hesitated, conferred, and yielded to the demand. Then Robespierre was doomed.

As he was reading, as the distribution of the speech and then its repeal were being voted, there hung above his head and that of the Parliament the flags taken in the new victories from the English and Austrians at Turcoing, at Landrecies, at Quesnoy, at Condé, at Valenciennes, at Fleurus, and it was they that turned the scale.

When the evening came the Club met, the little society of the Jacobins, which was still the most independent and the most vital force in Paris. It had dared to elect a president for its debates whose whole policy was antagonistic to Robespierre; yet now it heard him and remembered its old idol. He re-read, in the same tone, but in a more familiar surrounding and with ampler diction, the speech of the morning, and his hearers grew wild with enthusiasm. They hissed and they turned out Billaud and Collot, who had dared to be present; they cried out to Robespierre that they would follow him always towards the perfect Republic; and David, an excellent artist and a bad man, cried to him from the back, "I will drink the hemlock with you!" but he was afraid even to acknowledge his master when Robespierre came to die.

The Jacobins that night were ready to rise for Robespierre. As so many minorities have been in that city of convictions and of intense enthusiasms, they were ready to impose themselves and their creed upon the capital and upon France; but they did not know to what a handful they had been reduced in the last seven weeks. All night the conspiracy against Robespierre worked hard. Boissy D'Anglas, the leader of the "Marsh," was brought over. To him and his followers Robespierre was pointed out as the tyrant; to what was left of the Mountain he was denounced as the moderate and the compromiser. But, above all, he was, to the great bulk of the Convention, the enemy who had destroyed all civil order in pursuit of his mad theories, and who had even held the victories of no account.

The Parliament met the next morning, on the 9th of Thermidor (27th of July). It was a year to a day since Robespierre had joined the great Committee; but it was for the condemnation of Robespierre that they met. The great hall waited for a coming tumult. First into the tribune went St. Just, with his beautiful face and strong bearing, determined in oratory as in the battles to strike at once and lead a charge. He was eloquent, for he was trying to save his friend; he boldly attempted argument, a compromise, anything; called it "saving the Republic." "Let us end his domination if you will, but let the government still be that of the Revolution, and let us draw up such rules as shall save us from arbitrary power without destroying the motive force of the national demand." The sentiment was precisely that of the Convention, but the speaker was known to be merely the young bodyguard of their enemy.

Tallien called out from the right, "Pull back the curtain," and, though the fellow was an actor, he had struck the right note. St. Just could never defend Robespierre; it would have been a cloak for continuing the Terror. The Convention applauded, and from applause turned to crying down St. Just in a public roar of fear and hatred.

Then twice Robespierre tried to speak; the hubbub silenced him. During a lull in the storm they voted the arrest of Henriot. It meant the transference of such pitiful armed force as he commanded from the hand of a friend to that of an enemy. Robespierre made a last effort to rescind that order. He was not heard.

Tallien was given the tribune by the Speaker (Collot was Speaker that day, and Collot had been turned out by the Jacobins the night before). Tallien spoke theatrically, as he always did, but to the point. Robespierre, he said, had plotted to destroy the assembly for his purposes; he quoted the speech of the day before. While Barrère, the turncoat, stood looking this way and that, not knowing how things would turn. Once more Robespierre attempted a reply; he only raised a storm that drowned his voice.

When he saw that full speech was denied him, he turned from the place where he stood towards the "Marsh," the Moderates, and said, "I appeal to you who are just and who are not conspiring with these assassins;" but the "Marsh" was lost to him—they also cried him down.

A little silence followed. They saw Robespierre attempting for a fifth time to speak, but the agony of the night and the fearful struggle of the morning had overcome him at last: his voice could not be heard though he tried to articulate. Garnier of the Aube called to him across the floor of the hall, "The blood of Danton chokes you." It was the truest thing said in that wild meeting.

Before the silence was broken, Louchet, an unknown man, rose and proposed the arrest, saying openly what all thought: "No one will deny that Robespierre has played the master; let us vote his arrest." Then Robespierre found his voice. He went up four steps above his usual seat, to a place where, high up and from the left, from the summit of what had been the Mountain in the old days, he could see the whole of that multitudinous assembly, with whose aid he had hoped to regenerate France and to save mankind. Beneath him as a host, like the dim pictures of Martin's Milton, rank on rank, he saw so many heads that it must have seemed to him a nation. He remembered all his dreams of a perfect state, of men living in equality, with no one oppressed and no one oppressing, of a government based upon the clear will of all, and upon the civic virtues which he had preached, till there should rise the perfect Republic, an exemplar for all the nations. He saw that he was doomed, and with him all his dreams. Perhaps, also, he saw the armed despotism which he had twice prophesied coming in his place. To the last he did not understand his folly, and he replied to the demand of Louchet, "Vote for my death."

Le Bas, who had been with St. Just in the Ardennes, who had helped to make the great army of Sambre-et-Meuse, and Robespierre the younger, another honest man, came and did what David failed to do—they said they would die with him, and took his hands in theirs. The Committee passed to the vote, and the three were taken away with St. Just and with Couthon. The scene that follows is the end of the Revolution in Paris.

Twice at least in the course of the preceding five years Paris had risen against the law and had removed an obstacle or a man for the sake of the Revolution. The random Municipality of 1789 (which for all its disorder was the parent of the puissant modern system of Communes) is an example in point; the 2nd of June is another. Ultimately the people of Paris were the only force on which government rested, and it was to them that the final appeal was made.

The Commune possessed the initiative in this matter—it was the sole centre of Paris in theory; and now that the clubs were all in decay (save the Jacobins), now that the great orators were exiled or dead, and that the Sections themselves did not meet, the Commune was also the only centre in fact. But the Commune, it will be remembered, had become a Robespierrian thing. It determined to rise against the Convention.

The Convention had ordered the arrest of Henriot, who was commander of the armed force (such as it was) of the town. It sent his successor, Hesmart to do the work. But the head of a number of pikes and guns would not submit to a man who represented only the law, and instead of Hesmart arresting Henriot, it was Henriot who arrested Hesmart.

Meanwhile the other officers of the Commune displayed the same energy, the same rapidity of execution and design which under better leaders and for a better cause had hitherto succeeded. Lescot-Payot (the Robespierrian mayor who had been put into the place of Pache on the 21st of Floréal), and Payan the national agent, were at the head of the movement. They sent orders to the prisons to refuse the arrested deputies, they gave Henriot the formal order to employ his full force and act. They raised the Jacobins. They formed a committee of nine who were to take over the government; they ordered the arrest of their principal enemies in the Convention, and most important of all, they convened the Sections.

They had only a night to work in—the 9th Thermidor to the 10th—and *their* work had the energy of a fever; but the greatest factor of all was lacking—the fever did not spread. The inertia of the people, even their disapproval, was evident as they proceeded; the majority of such Sections as did meet stood aloof from or condemned the cause of Robespierre.

While it was still just light, between eight and nine in the evening, Robespierre, whom the keepers of the Luxemburg prison had refused, was brought to the Mairie, and there one after the other all the arrested deputies came, profiting by the official routine; for the Mairie was the "right place" officially for prisoners when a difficulty arose as to imprisonment within Paris. But official routine had a strange bedfellow that night, for while the officials took the prisoners there, the small band of rebels, who knew of no place more friendly, brought there also those whom they had delivered by force. Robespierre was again with the strongest of his friends—his brother, St. Just, Couthon; he was surrounded by an organised and legal body, the Commune, which had risen in his defence; they passed to the Hotel de Ville, and outside, on the Place de Grève, there gathered between ten o'clock and eleven a fairly large group of the National Guard. But there was no order among them, nor any accurate knowledge among their officers as to what was to be done. From the windows of the room where Robespierre and his companions sat, there could be dimly seen a moving crowd of mingled citizens and guards, discussing rather than preparing for action.

Robespierre refused to put himself at the head of the movement; at least it is only thus that we can explain the delay and the confusion. He was to the last the strange mixture of lawyer and pedant and idealist. He would not act without the legal right, for his pedantry forbade it, nor move with an armed minority, because, judged by his theories, it would have been a crime. Perhaps at the very last he decided to move: there exists a document authorising a march on the Convention, and at its base the first three letters of his name—the signature unfinished, interrupted.

Meanwhile the Convention had found a new energy and a power of corporate action to which it had been long a stranger—each man there was defending his life. Legendre, with a small force, went and closed the Jacobins. Barras was given the command of such armed men as could be gathered; the two committees sent emissaries who appealed with success to the Sections. The Convention was the law which had always meant so much to the people; it was the authority of the constitution. Its majority, obeyed when it was in lethargy, could not but be successful when it awoke. All Paris defended it.

At midnight one of the sudden thunder-showers which are common in the Seine valley at that season cleared what was left of the crowd before the Hotel de Ville. They had discussed both sides, and they had not decided—

hardly an army for rebellion; they had doubted what business they had there, and with the rain they went home. Yet it was not till two hours after, in the early morning, that the little band of the Convention came into the square. They found it almost empty, with here and there a small group standing on the wet cobble-stones, sleepy but curious.

Bourdon and a few policemen went into the Hotel de Ville and found no defenders. They went up to the room where the conspirators sat.

Robespierre was on the ground with his jaw broken by a pistol-shot.

At half-past seven in the evening of that day (the 10th Thermidor) twenty-two of the Robespierrians were taken in three carts to the guillotine. Robespierre himself, half-unconscious from his wound, stood propped against the side of the cart, his head bandaged, his arms bound, his chin upon his breast. Ropes also bound his body to the sides of the tumbril. He passed the house where Duplay had sheltered him, and where he had hidden himself, so as not to hear the noise of the executioners' carts. Now beneath him the heavy wheels were making the same sound on the ruts of the Rue St. Honoré. At a cross-street the cart stopped to let pass the funeral of Madame Aigué, who had killed herself the day before from fear of Robespierre.

As they neared the Place of the Revolution, where Louis and Danton had suffered, probably at the turning of the Rue St. Honoré, where the guillotine came in sight and where Danton had sung his song, a woman came forward from the crowd—doubtless some one whom his tyranny had directly bereaved—and struck Robespierre a blow. For sixteen hours he had not spoken nor made a sign, but when he felt through this blow the popular hatred, he made a gesture of contempt and of despair; he shrugged his shoulders, but kept his innumerable thoughts within the bandages. "*De mourir pour le peuple et d'en être abhorré.*"

Then—so the greatest of French historians tell us—France marched down a broad road to the tomb where she has left two millions of men.

But the armies of the great twenty years cannot be stated in the terms of one man's ambition, nor summed up in any of the simple formulæ which a just hatred of Cæsarism has framed to explain them. At the root of every battle of the Empire was the organisation and the enthusiasm of 1793. The tactics of Austerlitz and of Jena were learned in Flanders; the enthusiasm of the Guard itself came in clear descent from the exaltation of the Sambre-et-Meuse.

In this book we have attempted to judge the first man of a great crisis in relation to his time; it is still more essential that, when we consider the after-effects of his action, a whole nation under arms should stand in the right historical framework, its gigantic effort part and parcel of a supreme necessity.

We can understand, we can speak rationally, and therefore truly, of Danton, when we show him above all loving and defending France and the Revolutionary Thing: that same appreciation will make us follow clearly the continuous development of his action. It is hardly too much to say that, until Tilsit, the French had to advance or be crushed—nation, creed, and men.

The men and the armies must be for us the men and the armies that gave a new vigour to Europe; the details of their action should not be the matter of our judgment, but their relation to the whole community—its needs, its defence, its faith.

As the time grows greater between that period and our own, a just proportion imposes itself. The flame which, close at hand, burnt in a formless furnace is beginning to assume a certain shape. From a standpoint so distant that no living memory bridges the gulf, we can measure the light, the heat, and even the fuel of that flame.

As to its final meaning in our society, every day makes that clearer; and, to change the metaphor, this much becomes more and more apparent, that through whatever crises the Western civilisation is to pass, and whatever form its edifice will finally take, when the noise of the building is over, the corner-stone, with its immense strength and its precision of line, was planned by the philosophy and was hewn by the force of the Revolution. Civilisations die, and ours was dying before that wind swept across Europe.

It would have been a poor excuse for leaving unremoved the rubble, the dust, and the putrescence of the old world to have pleaded that the decay was the action of centuries, and that old things alone were worthy of reverence. Old things alone are worthy of reverence, but old things which have grown old upon just and sure foundations, to which time has added ornament and the satisfaction of harmonious colour, without destroying the main lines, and without sapping the strength by which they live.

The new foundations alone stand at the present day. They are crude, they satisfy nothing in us permanently, they are very far from affording that sentiment of content which is the first requisite of a happy civilisation. But time will do in this case, as it has always done in every other, the work of harmony and of completion. The final society will not be without its innumerable complexity of detail, its humour, and its inner life. Certainly it will not long remain a stranger to the unseen; but it will be built upon 1793.

Meanwhile the light grows on the origins. The personal bitterness which the struggle produced has passed. It is a pious memory in this or that family in France to give itself still the name of a Revolutionary faction; but the hatred that has produced confusion in honest critics, and that has furnished such ample material for false history, that hatred is disappearing in France. The vendettas have ceased, and the grosser of the calumnies are no longer heard. The history of the Revolution began to be possible when Louis Blanc sat down to curse the upheaval that had killed his father, and ended by producing the work which more than any other exalted the extreme Revolutionary ideal.

The story of that time is now like a photographic negative, which a man fixes, washing away the white cloud from the clean detail of the film. Point after point, then more rapidly whole spaces, stand out precise and true. And the certitude which he feels that the underlying picture is an accurate reminiscence of Nature comes to us also when we make out and fix some passage in the Revolution, cleared of its mass of hearsay, of vituperation, of ignorance, and of mere sound.

We are beginning to see a great picture, consonant in its details, and consecutive in its action. The necessity of reform; the light of the ideal striking men's minds after a long sleep, the hills first and afterwards the plains; privilege and all the interests of the few alarmed and militant; the menace of attack and the preparation of defence; the opposition of extremes on either side of the frontier, growing at an increasing speed, till at last, each opposite principle mutually exciting the other, as armatories their magnets, from a little current of opinion rose a force that none could resist. The governments of the whole world were for the destruction of the French people, and the French people were for the rooting out of everything, good and evil, which was attached, however faintly, to the old regime.

The rhetoricians passed in the smoke of the fire, unsubstantial, full of words that could lead and inspire, but empty of acts that could govern the storm. From their passing, which is as vague as a vision, we hear faintly the "Marseillaise" of the Girondins.

The men of action and of the crisis passed. They burnt in the heat they themselves had kindled, but in that furnace the nation was run, and forged, and made. Then came the armies: France grown cold from the casting-pit, but bent upon action, and able to do.

Wherever France went by, the Revolutionary Thing remained the legacy of her conviction and of her power. It remains with a kind of iron laughter for those who judge the idea as a passing madness. The philosophers have decided upon a new philosophy; the lawyers have clearly proved that there has been no change; the rhetoric has been thoroughly laughed down, enthusiasm has grown ridiculous, and the men of action are cursed. But in the wake of the French march citizens are found who own the soil and are judged by an equal code of laws; nationalities have been welded, patriotism has risen at the call of the new patriotic creed; Germany, Austria, Hungary, Bohemia, Italy have known themselves as something more than the delimitations of sovereigns. Nor was there any abomination of the old decay, its tortures, its ignominies, its privileges, its licensed insults, or its slaveries, but she utterly stamped them out. In Germany, in Austria, in Italy, they disappeared. Only in one dark corner they remained—the great Northern field, where France herself grew powerless from cold, and from whence an unknown rule and the advance of relentless things menaces Europe now.

But with the mention of that frozen place there comes a thought older than all our theories—the mourning for the dead. Danton helped to make us, and was killed: his effort has succeeded, but the tragedy remains. The army at whose source he stood, the captain who inherited his action, were worn out in forging a new world. And I will end this book by that last duty of mourning, as we who hold to immortality yet break our hearts for the dead.

There is a legend among the peasants in Russia of a certain sombre, mounted figure, unreal, only an outline and a cloud, that passed away to Asia, to the east and to the north. They saw him move along their snows through the long mysterious twilights of the northern autumn in silence, with the head bent and the reins in the left hand loose, following some enduring purpose, reaching towards an ancient solitude and repose. They say it was Napoleon. After him there trailed for days the shadows of the soldiery, vague mists bearing faintly the forms of companies of men. It was as though the cannon-smoke of Waterloo, borne on the light west wind of that June day, had received the spirits of twenty years of combat, and had drifted farther and farther during the fall of the year over the endless plains.

But there was no voice and no order. The terrible tramp of the Guard and the sound that Heine loved, the dance of the French drums, was extinguished; there was no echo of their songs, for the army was of ghosts and was defeated. They passed in the silence which we can never pierce, and somewhere remote from men they sleep in bivouac round the most splendid of human swords.

APPENDIX

I NOTE ON THE CORDELIERS

The spot once occupied by the Cordeliers is among the most interesting in Paris, and it is of some importance to sketch its history and to reconstruct its appearance at greater length than was possible in the text.

All the land from St. Germains des Près up northwards along the hillside had belonged to that abbey since its foundation, when the first dynasty of Frankish kings had endowed the foundation with a great estate carved out of what had once been the Roman fiscal lands on the south bank. Round the abbey itself a few houses had gathered, forming the "Faubourg" (or suburb) of "St. Germains"; but the greater part of the estate was open field and meadow. When Philip Augustus built his great wall round Paris it cut through the estate, leaving the Church and Abbey of St. Germains outside the city, but enclosing a small part of the fields within its boundary.

You may trace the line of the wall at this day by noting the street "Rue de Monsieur le Prince," once called "Rue des Fossés Monsieur le Prince," and running on the line of the outer ditch. The wall ran not twenty yards east of the modern street and exactly parallel to it. A portion of it may yet be seen in that neighbourhood, a great hollow round built into the wall of one of the houses, a cobbler's shop in the Cour du Commerce; it is one (the last, I believe) of the half-towers which flanked Philip Augustus's wall.

In the beginning of the thirteenth century, very shortly after the death of St. Francis, the first preachers of the new Order which he had founded came to Paris. It was the moment when the University was climbing up the hill, building its colleges, having possessed its charter for some years, and already a strong, organised, wealthy, and therefore conservative body. This order of preachers, wandering, intensely new, and founded by a mystic whose place in Christendom was not yet finally determined, were bound to come into collision with the spirit of the place. It must be remembered that the thirteenth century was not transitional, but, on the contrary, a time of settled order. For a century it had known the Roman law; it had everywhere the Gothic architecture; it had systemised and made legal the rough accidents of feudal custom; it was wealthy, proud, and successful. On it there falls one of those creations which are only possible in a time of energy, and yet which almost invariably quarrel with the period that has produced them. An Order devoted to simplicity, making of holy poverty the foundation of the inner life, specially created for the poor (whom the growing differentiation of society was beginning to debase), the early Franciscans were essentially revolutionary, because they built on the great foundations of all active and permanent reform—I mean the appetite for primitive conditions, and the determination to break through the net of complexity which the long growths of time weave about a conservative society.

The rich Abbey of St. Germains gave them asylum. It was proud to possess dependants, it was great enough to afford benevolent experiments, and it took pleasure in offending the University, which was an upstart in its eyes, and was beginning to show as a powerful rival in the affairs of the south side of Paris. The Franciscans, therefore—whom the populace already called the "Cordeliers" from the girdle of rope about their habit—were permitted to settle in that little corner of their estate which had been cut off by the building of the town wall, and they occupied a triangle of which the wall formed the south-western, a lane (afterwards called "Rue des Cordeliers") the northern, and an irregular line bounding one of the University estates the south-eastern side.

This was in 1230. St. Louis was still a boy of fifteen. The little foundation was, for the University, nothing but an unwelcome neighbour whom it could not oust, and for the Abbey of St. Germains nothing but a guest. Their provisional tenure did not permit them a peal of bells nor a public cemetery.

St. Louis, however, grew into a manhood which, for all its piety, had a wonderful grasp of the society around it. The saint who was never clerical, and the Capetian who in all things was rather for the spirit than the letter, became their principal support. The Papacy, having once (though reluctantly) recognised the Franciscan movement in the interview between Innocent III. and its founder, continued in the succeeding generation to protect it. From a distance, where the quarrels of the University affected it little, the Holy See decided more than one dispute in favour of the new-comers, and the Franciscans of Paris flourished exceedingly. By 1240 the full privileges of an independent foundation were granted. They have their public service, their cemetery, and their bells. St. Louis helps them to build a new chapel by giving them, in 1267, part of the great fine which he levied on Enguerrand de Coucy. They succeed at last in obtaining the recognition of the University; they are permitted to teach; they number among their lecturers Duns Scotus and St. Bonaventure; and they become one of the most famous of the colleges.

During the Middle Ages (apart from certain minor structures and a few private houses which had been permitted to rise on their land, and which were technically known as the "dépendances"), three principal groups of buildings marked the foundations. First, the monastery itself, a somewhat irregular mass, running (as a whole) north and south, and separated from the Rue des Cordeliers by a little court or garden. Secondly, running from the northern end of this convent, and forming, as it were, a letter L with the main building, was the chapel, lying, of course, east and west, and forming the southern side of the Rue des Cordeliers, upon which was the principal porch. Thirdly, running also east and west, but separated from the other buildings by a short space, was the hall.

This famous monument, the only part of the college that has been preserved, stood well back from the street, and in the middle of the convent grounds. It was on the eastern side of the monastery, and hence in the ground plan balanced (so to speak) the church, which lay to the west of that main building; this was so designed that its western end faced about the middle of the college.

I have called it a hall because its use exactly corresponded to that of our college halls in the English universities. I mean, it was at once a refectory and lecture-room. It was approached by a little lane running up through the grounds under the side of the convent, later hemmed in with houses.

Here not only were the voices of the great scholars heard and the subtleties of the fourteenth century, but also Etienne Marcel called the States General of 1357. From hence that Danton of the mediæval invasion sent out his messengers to the Feudality. Here the District gathered for the elections of 1789; here the Club met in 1791 and urged the debate that finally produced the Republic of the next year. It was here also that the three watchwords of the Republic were devised; here Hérbert veiled the Declaration; and here the last few words of 1794 were spoken. Here the century, which owes more perhaps to that site than to any place in France, has collected a museum of surgery, where you may see anomalies preserved in spirits, skeletons hung on wires, and other objects, interesting rather than sublime.

As for the college and its estate, they continued for some three hundred years—that is, during the fourteenth, fifteenth, and sixteenth centuries—to increase in importance. It is a matter of common knowledge how soon the pure ideals of St. Francis had to compromise with the world. This Order, like all others, became wealthy, rooted, and traditional. The Cordeliers, as Paris grew, found themselves possessed of a most valuable plot, whose ground-value continually increased. They reserved the garden to the west, but for the rest—and especially around the buildings and along the lanes—

houses were built. When the wall of Philip Augustus was first embedded by the growth of the city, and afterwards in part destroyed, the Cordeliers bought an extension to their estate, so that it stretched a little beyond the new street of "the Fossés," which had been built on the site of the ditch. In 1580 their old thirteenth-century chapel (which must have been one of the best bits of early Gothic in Paris) was burnt down, and a larger one in the style of the time was put up by the piety of Henry IV. Throughout the seventeenth century the house seems to have suffered from a decay which continued throughout the succeeding hundred years, and culminated in the disasters of the Revolutionary period. They permitted the alienation of a strip to the west of their grounds, through which the municipality drove in 1673 the new street which, in compliment to the Order, they called "Rue de l'Observance," after the name of their rule.

With this exception no important change occurred to change the aspect of the quarter until the Revolutionary period with which we have to deal.

We are, after this general description, in a position to recognise the site of the Cordeliers in modern Paris. As you go down the Boulevard St. Germains, just before you reach the Boulevard St. Michel (going east), you see a street leading off at a slight angle to the right. It is the Rue de l'École de Médecine, the college after which it is named facing both on this street and on the Boulevard. This street is merely the Rue des Cordeliers broadened and modernised. As you go a few yards up this street, you see on your left the great court of the college, and if you stand at its gate and look at the opposite side of the street, at the new buildings which are now the lecture-rooms and theatres of the Faculty, you are looking at the site of the old church, which has disappeared during this century. The street has been broadened by taking down the southern side, so that the church would actually have overlapped the modern street. Continuing, you pass on your right the open yard leading up to what was the hall of the Cordeliers, and is now the museum of surgery (the Musée Dupuytren), and a few yards farther brings you into the Boulevard St. Michel. Following this very broad avenue for twenty yards at the most, you may note a new street, the "Rue Racine," turning off to the right. This did not exist in Danton's time, but it lies *nearly* on the line that separated the Cordeliers from the Collège d'Harcourt (at present the Lycée St. Louis). As a fact, the line was a trifle to the south of the Rue Racine, and of course more irregular. The Rue Racine in its turn leads you into that old street the "Rue de Monsieur le Prince." If you turn again to the right and go down this some hundred yards, you are still following the boundary of the Cordeliers, till you reach the "Rue Antoine Dubois." This is identical with the old "Rue de l'Observance," spoken of above, and a few steps down this short street leads you to the starting-point in the "Rue de l'École de Médecine." Such a modern itinerary would describe as nearly as is now possible the circumference of the college and estate of the Cordeliers. The quadrilateral comprised by these four streets, the Rue de l'École de Médecine, the Rue Racine, the Rue M. de le Prince, and the Rue Antoine Dubois, is the site of the famous convent and its grounds.

To reproduce the quarter in 1788 we have to imagine the following changes:—The Rue de l'École de Médecine, very narrow, flanked for the greater part of its southern side with the church and old wall of the convent. It leads into a little narrow street called the "Rue de la Harpe," which went right up the hill, and would correspond to a strip taken in the exact centre of the present Boulevard St. Michel. The first few buildings here, notably the Church of St. Come, were still on the Cordeliers' estate. Just above them, however, began the grounds and buildings of the "College d'Harcourt." As we have observed, the Rue Racine did not exist, nor anything corresponding to it. To follow the boundaries of the estate you would have had to let yourself in by a side-door, and then you might have followed a long, irregular wall which separated their land from the College d'Harcourt. This wall, after passing through a great garden, came out on the Rue Monsieur le Prince, and the rest of one's circuit would be much what it is to-day.

Finally, to see the building as Danton saw it, you must imagine a half-deserted place, rich, but somewhat unfrequented, like certain old legal Inns that once stood in London, old walls appearing here and there from between houses of a century's date; a mass of irregular buildings, of garden and of private house hopelessly intermingled; while up a narrow and dark passage stood the Hall, which was still the best preserved part of the college, and with which alone his name is associated.

II NOTE ON CERTAIN SITES MENTIONED IN THIS BOOK

It may be of interest to those who desire to study with some particularity the personal history of Danton to know where are to be found in modern Paris the places with which we have found him personally connected in this book.

His first offices were in the Rue des Mauvaises Paroles. This street has disappeared in the improvements which included the prolongation of the Rue de Rivoli. This office in the Rue des Mauvaises Paroles occupied almost exactly the same spot, which can be recognised to-day in the following manner. As you go along the northern side of the Rue de Rivoli going east, you come to a point 500 yards or so from the Louvre, from whence you begin to see the Tour St. Jacques just peering round the southern side of the street. The shops which are then upon your left hand and the pavement upon which you stand correspond to the position of the old mansard house in which Danton served his apprenticeship. It was here that he had his first offices; it was from this that he bought the business of Monsieur M. de Paisy in the Rue de la Tissanderie.

Concerning the position of these offices in the Rue de la Tissanderie, which he moved into, I have been able to learn nothing. There is a curious little record in the police archives of Paris—Danton complaining that he could not work on account of the noise that a saddle-maker made in the exercise of his trade in the same house. In this little document, which is quoted by Monsieur Clarétie in his "Life of Camille Desmoulins," the house is mentioned as being "just opposite the Rue des Deux Portes"; but as an inference to be drawn from the same record is that he left immediately after for some other lodging in the same street, this does not help us much.

I have said in the text that Danton lived, during the six years which were those of his active political life, in a house of the Passage du Commerce. I have also mentioned in the text the fact that Dr. Robinet mentions a short residence in the Rue des Fossés Saint Germains. I have given, moreover, in the same passage my reasons for following M. Aulard in rejecting this first address. It seems proved that, after he left the Rue de la Tissanderie, he moved with his wife to the corner house of the Passage du Commerce. This was his home during the whole of the Revolution, and it is worth while to describe its position and character with some care.

In the first place, it has disappeared; the construction of the Boulevard St. Germains destroyed all that end of the Cour du Commerce. If you are going along the Boulevard St. Germains from the west towards the University, you pass on the right the statue of Danton. It is erected on an open triangle of ground, formed by the junction of the Boulevard and of the Rue de l'École de Médecine. The apex of this triangle, not twenty yards from the statue, marks the site of the old house in which Danton and Desmoulins lived, and in which they were arrested before their trial.

The old quarter was a network of narrow streets, and where the Boulevard St. Germain now stands, an intricate block of houses, with courtyards and passages, not unlike the similar intricate masses which you will find in the City of London, formed the northern side of the Rue des Cordeliers (that is to say, the modern Rue de l'École de Médecine). A narrow alley, known as the Cour de Commerce, joined this Rue des Cordeliers by a still narrower passage. Danton's house was the corner house, as is proved by the mention in the inventory that some rooms looked upon this passage and some upon the Rue des Cordeliers.

Of course he did not occupy the whole of it, but, in the Parisian custom, which had already obtained for more than a century, he took a flat, and two rooms (used as a lumber and as a servant's bedroom) were added from the entresole below. This flat was just such an apartment as a similar bourgeois householder would have in Paris to-day: a dining-room, two bedrooms, a study, a little library, a drawing-room, a kitchen, and offices, built round the staircase and courtyard or well of the house.

I have been unable to find any mention of the rental which was paid, but a guess at something like £150 a year in that quarter at that time for such a flat would, I think, not be extravagant. The corresponding flat above, Desmoulins took after his romantic marriage in December 1790, but he did not begin to occupy the house until the early part of 1791. It was here that his little Horace was born; it was here that his wife and Danton's passed the terrible night of the 10th of August, and it was here, in the great bedroom overlooking the Rue des Cordeliers, that Danton's wife died in February 1793.

As to the furniture of the little apartment, it may be described as follows:—The drawing-room was not very large, but there had been spent upon it the most considerable sum in the furnishing of the house. It figures for very nearly a third in the valuation, which may be read in Appendix VII. The white furniture, which was the mark of the eighteenth century, was its principal note; it is also worth observing that the household was sufficiently cramped for room to use the cupboards in the drawing-room as wardrobes. The principal bedroom was well furnished, but, as you will find to be the case in such houses in Paris, the study, the dining-room, and the spare room to the side of the study were very bare. It is also remarkable that the lumber-room held nothing but two trunks and an old double bedstead. It was the household of a man who made every effort to maintain his position before his wife's friends, but who was not wealthy, and who had evidently arranged the scale of his expenditure considerably below the probable receipts which an office such as his would have brought in. I should much doubt whether as much as £500 a year would go out on such an establishment, though he was certainly receiving £1000. We know the reason of this; he had to pay off by every means in his power the debt which he had incurred in buying the practice. While he lived in this house, and until the office was suppressed in 1790, he continued to keep his business rooms in the Rue de la Tissanderie. It may be worthy of mention that he kept two servants, and that his apartment was on the first, whilst that of Desmoulins was on the second floor of the house.

As to the Cordeliers, on which the preceding note is written, the hall in which their meetings were first held still exists (as we have said in the text) under the title of Musée Dupuytren. The Church of the Cordeliers, into which they afterwards moved, has disappeared, but the last locale of the club (when the Municipality had turned them out of the church in 1791) still remains, and is to be discovered at No. 105 Rue Thionville. Danton's father-in-law had been master of a café on the Quai de l'École. This house still remains. If I am not mistaken, it was altered slightly during the restorations of the Second Empire. It is the house which now stands at the south-western corner of the Place de l'École, and which faces the quai on one side and the square on the other. The street and quay outside M. Charpentier's café was, however, somewhat oblique to the modern street, and ran less east than west, more south-east than north-west, than it does to-day.

The quay has been raised and the old fountain in the Place de l'École destroyed. Otherwise the quarter is much the same. The café became famous later for its draught players, a reputation that still continues.

III NOTE ON THE SUPPOSED VENALITY OF DANTON

I will not go in this note into any of the general considerations which have led the greater part of modern historians to reject the legend of Danton's venality. These general considerations are by far the strongest arguments upon which we can rely in this matter, but I trust that the character which I have attempted to draw in the text of the book will furnish them in sufficiency.

Neither do I desire to insist in this note upon the unquestionable value of the two principal modern authorities in England and in France (Mr. Morse Stephens and M. Aulard), who both of them regard the question as finally settled in Danton's favour. I have insisted sufficiently upon this in the text. What I shall attempt to do is to quote the contemporary accusations, to determine how much reliance can be placed upon them, to show their character, and to describe in what way and to what extent they are explained by documents which have since come to light.

First of all, a list of those contemporaries who took his venality for certain. It is very formidable.

Mirabeau (letter to Lamarck, Thursday, 10th March 1791).—... "Montmorin has told me ... of particular schemes ... for instance, that Beaumetz and ... D'Andrée dined yesterday alone and got Danton's confidence ... and then proposed to demolish Vincennes in order to make themselves popular. Danton got 30,000 livres yesterday, and I have the proof that Danton inspired the last number of Desmoulins' paper.... If it is possible I intend to risk 6000 livres, but at any rate they will be more innocently distributed than the 30,000 livres of Danton." Here is a categorical statement in which a man says what the court had often said (and Mirabeau was then an agent of the court), "I have managed Danton at such and such a price," and the passage gives us indirectly the name of Montmorin. The date should be noted.

Bertrand de Molleville, a far less practical and a far less careful man than Mirabeau, also a singularly untrustworthy authority, has the following:— Memoirs Particuliers, i. 354.—"By the hands of this man Durand, under the ministry of De Montmorin, Danton received more than 50,000 francs to propose certain motions of the Jacobins. He was fairly faithful in keeping this contract, but stipulated that he should be left free as to the means he employed." ... Again ... "In the first debates upon the king's trial the infamous Danton, whose services had been so dearly paid *out of the Civil List*, was one of those who displayed the greatest violence. I was the more alarmed as this scoundrel was at the moment (Autumn 1792) a most powerful and dangerous man in the Assembly. The ardent zeal which I felt for the safety of the king, and which would have made me think all means legitimate, suggested this means against Danton to neutralise the rage of the monster; and though the method I took required a lie, I did not hesitate to employ it without the least scruple. I wrote to him on the 11th December:—'I must not leave you ignorant, Sir, of the fact that I have found in the papers of the late Monsieur Montmorin notes of the dates of the sums which have been paid out of the secret service money, including a receipt in your handwriting. Hitherto I have made no use of this document, but I warn you that I have enclosed them in a letter which I am writing to the President of the Convention, and I will have them printed and placarded on the corners of the streets if you do not conduct yourself well in the trial of the king.' As a fact, Montmorin had shown me these papers a year before, though he had not given them to me. But Danton knew they existed, and knew how intimate had been my relations with Montmorin. He did not reply to the letter, but I saw in the published prints that he had got himself named deputy in a mission to the army of the North. He only returned at the end of the king's trial, and contented himself with voting for death without giving any opinion." (Particular Memoirs, ii. 288-291.) I would have the reader to specially mark this extract, to which I shall return at the end of my note, as it can be easily proved by internal evidence to be a falsehood. It is, indeed, of more value to any one who desires to write a life of Bertrand himself, than it is to one who is writing the life of Danton.

Thirdly, Lafayette says (Memoirs, iii. 83-85): "Danton, whose receipt for 100,000 francs was in the hands of Montmorin, asked for Lafayette's head; that was running a great risk, but he depended on the discretion of Lafayette and on his keeping a secret. For Lafayette to have spoken would have been to have signed the death-warrant of Montmorin, who had paid Danton in order to moderate his anarchic fury." And again (iv. 328-330), he says of Danton: "He was a vulgar tribune and incapable of turning the masses from evil by persuasion or by respect, but he knew how to flatter their passions, &c. &c.... I knew him from the first week of the Revolution in the district of Cordeliers, whither I had been attracted. After the 6th October he took money from Montmorin, whom he caused in consequence to be assassinated on the 2nd September. In connection with this secret he said to me once, 'General, I know you do not know me, I am more of a Monarchist than you.'... I have learnt since from the person to whom Madame Elizabeth told it that he had received, about the 10th August, a considerable sum to give the movement a direction in the king's favour, and, indeed, he got the royal family sent to the Temple. He said to a friend of the king, 'It is I who will save him or kill him.'"

Fourthly, there is Brissot (iv. 193-194). "Among the stipendiaries of Orleans was ... Danton. I have seen the receipt for 500,000 francs which were paid him by Montmorin. He was sold to the court in order to thrust the Revolution into the excesses which would make it odious to the great bulk of Frenchmen."

Fifthly, Madame Roland (who has so much to say against a character so profoundly antipathetic to her) has this special passage on his corruption (Dauban's edition, 1864, pp. 254-255): "He went to Belgium to augment his wealth, and dared to admit a fortune of 1,400,000 francs, to assume luxury," &c. &c.

Sixthly (if it is worth quoting), among the papers that Robespierre left, in the notes that formed the basis of St. Just's report, are the words—"Danton owed an obligation to Mirabeau; it was Mirabeau who got him repaid the price of his practice. It has even been said that he was paid twice. I heard him admit to Fabre certain thefts of shoes belonging to the army."

Such are the contemporary accusations. There are the following points to be noted with regard to them. No one says that he himself paid money; the sums of money are very various. They are paid, according to some, on a few definite occasions; according to others, upon all occasions. Finally, every accusation that has any definite basis at all pivots round the name of Montmorin. "Montmorin held the receipt," "Montmorin told me," and so forth. Now, if we remember that Montmorin held the receipt for a legitimate and open reimbursement (see Appendix VI.), and then compare the accusations with what we know of the men and of the time, if we then proceed to check these merely general conclusions by matters of absolute knowledge drawn from the valuations upon Danton's estate at various moments of his life, we shall agree with the more modern authorities who have worked with the documents before them, that Danton is innocent of actions to the charge of which his uncertain temper and his lack of solid social surroundings laid him open.

In the first place, let us consider the words of the accusations which appear above, and which include all those of any importance.

That of Mirabeau is what you would expect from such a man; it is quiet, contemptuous, treating of Danton as something on the very last level of the time. But if we take the specific accusation and separate it from all general points of view, we find this much: that Montmorin has been talking to him with regard to what "those fellows" were doing. "In connection with this," says Mirabeau, "Danton got 30,000 yesterday" to work such and such a political move. The grave feature in the quotation is the way in which Mirabeau, who understood men and who had a good grasp of Paris, treats Danton's venality as being something well known, gives a particular example of it, and passes at once to other things. But the specific accusation is hearsay from Montmorin, and, as I have said, it is always Montmorin's name which crops up when this gossip is on foot.

I would, therefore, sum up the value of Mirabeau's accusation somewhat as follows:—If we could prove that Danton was a spendthrift, and that large sums of money passed through his hands for his personal pleasures, then Mirabeau's chance remark, while it would be worthless in a court of law, ought to have some small weight before history. Mirabeau was (on a higher plane) a *bon viveur* such as Danton was reputed to be, and the circles in which the men moved touched each other especially in the point of their good living; but if we can find that Danton did not, as a fact, spend nor invest great sums of money, then the accusation is simply a common error based upon a remark of Montmorin's, suited to the current impression of Danton's character, but disproved by the known facts of Danton's life.

Bertrand de Molleville's accusation is of particular value to any one who is concerned, as I am, in attempting to get to the truth in this matter. It is the only one which is perfectly categorical and detailed. In proportion as it is categorical and detailed it is untrue. If you wish to know whether a man has committed a certain crime, and you hear a number of witnesses against him, one of whom only gives careful evidence with dates, details, and so forth, and if you can then prove that this witness has lied upon all the points which supported his principal accusation, you are in a fair way to winning your case.

De Molleville begins by making the sum 500,000 francs. It seems enormous. It is a sum which no man could receive and spend in a few days' debauch without attracting the attention of the whole city, which no man could invest without leaving some obvious accession of property, and he puts the receipt of this sum as coming under Montmorin's ministry—that is, at a time when public order was secured, when the course of the registries, the transmission of property and so forth, were in the fullest light.

He gives the name of the man who handed him the sum, and calls him Durand. On this point it is impossible to say yes or no, but we can say with absolute certitude that the incident of the letter upon which Bertrand de Molleville makes the whole matter turn, is an untruth added to an untruth. In the first place, he makes Danton "violent in his demands against the king." This accusation is absolutely false.

When the trial of the king was mooted, Danton did speak (notably on the 6th of September), with some decision in favour of the king's being brought to trial upon particular points. He expressed himself in that speech with very great energy upon this particular feature of the trial, that the king merited condemnation because he had obviously and openly betrayed the nation,—a thing which nobody doubted, which nobody denied, and which Louis himself and his advisers would simply have met by saying (at a later epoch of course), "We called in the foreigner as a necessary police in the time of anarchy; we desired to save France by its betrayal." So far, however, from Danton being a leader of the attack on Louis or of the demand for his trial, that attack and that demand were as spontaneous as anything the Convention ever did; and Danton followed rather than led, as a glance at the *Moniteur* can prove.

In the much more important debates wherein the life of Louis was first implicitly and then explicitly at stake, Danton was absent, and in the days of November there is no question at all but that Danton's one preoccupation was to reconcile the Mountain with the Girondins.

De Molleville goes on to give his letter a date—such things are done on purpose, as a rule, in order to give a special character of legal evidence to one's accusations. He says that he wrote the letter on the 11th of December, that Danton on receiving the letter was frightened, and without replying to it got himself put upon the mission to the army of the North.

Now Danton left for the army of the North on the 1st of December, and if the letter was written at all (which I doubt), it was written at a time when Danton, being absent, could not possibly have acted as De Molleville said he did. He could not have "asked" to go on a mission (he did not ask, but was sent), and have started on the 1st in consequence of a letter written on the 11th.

Finally, De Molleville says he came back to vote on the punishment of the king, but had been coerced by the letter into merely voting for death without giving his opinion. This again is a lie. If there is anything remarkable to the historian in the vote Danton gave on the 16th January 1793, and in the speech which he made before his vote, it is that he, by nature so wary, should have discovered in this crisis a violent manifestation of opinion and motive. I have amply shown in the text that we could only reconcile those abnormal days in Danton's life by some extreme shock to the emotions. Some represent him as suffering a violent rebuff from his political opponents; some consider the scene of misery and impending death which he found in his home on returning from his long journey. He demanded a simple majority vote; he spoke violently against the appeal to the people; and when he voted for the death of the king he turned to the Right and said, "I am not a statesman; I am not one of those who are ignorant of the duty of not compromising with tyrants, and who do not know that kings can only be struck on the head, who do not know that we can expect nothing from the kings of Europe save by force and by arms. I vote for the death of the tyrant."

If these are the words, and if that is the action of a man terrorised by a letter into a silent and furtive vote, then evidence has no meaning.

De Molleville, I think, can in this, as in nearly all his historical evidence (with the exception of that which turns upon the personal habits of the king, where he has the details of a valet), be dismissed.

With Lafayette, again, we have that half-truth and half-lie which runs through all his accusations. "The receipt for 100,000 francs was in the hands of Montmorin." This was true. The sum was not quite 100,000, it was 61,000 (Appendix VI.); but the receipt did exist, and to any one who did not know that all the men occupying positions on the Council had been reimbursed, it might look like a receipt for a bribe, or might be twisted into meaning such. It is impossible for us to discover whether Lafayette meant to tell an untruth, as we can prove De Molleville did; he may in this matter have been perfectly loyal, for there was a note found among his papers after his death (Memoirs, iii. 84-85), saying that "a position on the Councils was only worth 10,000, and had been reimbursed at 100,000 as a bribe." We now know from the discovery of so many receipts that from 60,000 to 80,000 was the regular price of reimbursements, but Lafayette might easily have been ignorant of this, and have jumped to a false conclusion.

As to his mention of Madame Elizabeth's having told the man who told him that Danton had been paid before the 10th August, the old man's memory is certainly turning to the remark which many witnesses heard from the lips of that saintly woman just before the attack on the Tuilleries, when she said with simplicity (she knew nothing at all of the characters of the Revolution save what she might hear from the courtiers), "Well, we can count on Danton; he has been paid." That is not evidence. If Danton was paid to make the 10th of August turn in favour of the monarchy, and if, as Lafayette hints, he had attempted to make it so turn, he certainly took the most extraordinary way of defending his employers. One might as well say that Lord Chatham's principal object in the taking of Quebec was the defence of the French power in Canada. For the 10th of August was openly and directly an attack upon the ancient crown of France, to overthrow it and to substitute in its place a new regime, and Danton worked at it as indefatigably as a general before a battle would work.

The remark, "General, I am more monarchist than you," reads to me like truth; it is exactly what Danton would have said. He despised Lafayette as much as any one man can despise another. He believed right up to the moment of the war that the existing fact of the monarchy was worth all the theories in the world as a nucleus for the new regime, and he saw the emptiness of Lafayette's vanity. He may quite probably have met it upon some occasion as direct as that which Lafayette has given us, and Lafayette, in the abundance of his folly, may quite easily have misunderstood the meaning of his criticism.

Brissot is an admirable example of how the false rumours arose. He says: "I have myself seen the receipts which Montmorin held from Danton."

Now, as we have seen, that receipt (to any one who did not know the details of the transaction) might quite honestly appear a damning piece of evidence, and it is without question the document round which the great mass of accusations have been built.

As to Madame Roland, I cannot imagine what flight of feminine inaccuracy made her put down a fortune of £60,000 to her enemy's name. If a witness in any other circumstances than revolution should tell one that a young lawyer and politician had secretly and suddenly become possessed of this sum, he would be reputed mad. In such a time, however, anything seems possible to an enemy, and we must rely upon the simple fact that Danton can be definitely proved neither to have spent, invested, nor left a tenth of such a sum. It seems to me that this accusation of Madame Roland's is on a par with that other extreme remark that she had known "the Dantons living on 16s. a week, which they borrowed regularly from their father-in-law," and this "at the opening of the Revolution," a time when we know him positively to have been defending cases involving half a million pounds in the issue of the trial, and when we know him to have had for clients some of the richest men in France.

Now, the papers that prove Danton's financial position are quite simple. He was cut off suddenly; they were all seized, and they all remain. Unless he spent huge sums in debauch (sums like those of Orleans), or unless he buried the money, he cannot have received much more than what openly appears. He entered his married life with a debt of £2500 secured on his office. He enjoyed a good practice for four years; he was reimbursed to somewhat less than the value of his office, and on his death the sum sequestrated by the State, and later refunded to his sons, tallies with this small fortune.

IV NOTE ON DANTON'S RESPONSIBILITY FOR THE MASSACRES OF SEPTEMBER

The arguments for and against Danton's responsibility in this matter must necessarily be of a more general order than those which can be advanced for and against his character in regard to money matters. There are but one or two really definite facts upon either side, and, as the purport of these notes is to deal with actualities, I will treat of these known facts only.

In the first place, it must be clearly understood that Danton did not shrink from, and was not unsympathetic with, the extreme measures of the Revolution. His position with regard to them is perfectly clear in history, and is simply this—his violence was persuaded that an exceptional time required, almost as a method of government, the most exceptional terrors.

But, on the other hand, Danton was a man to whom not only a useless massacre but a useless anything was detestable. Death in itself, the infliction of death on others, even the death to which he himself was led, never seemed to him a matter of vast moment. It is a common fault in courageous men to have this disregard for the life of others and of oneself, but I deny that you will ever discover Danton causing the death of a single human being unless it is in the furtherance of his policy.

In the second place, consider what is actually known to have proceeded from his mouth. (1) Quite early in the Revolution (in June 1791) he demanded the head of Lafayette, and he probably meant it; (2) he boasted of, or confessed to, being the author of Mandat's death; (3) in the course of speeches which led up to the establishment of the Revolutionary tribunal he speaks in favour of the extreme penalties and of the terror that they would inspire, always as a means to an end, and as a means to be employed without hesitation. Let me quote but one sentence from the speech of the 10th March 1793 to illustrate what I mean:—"I feel to what a degree it is necessary to take judicial measures by which we may punish the counter-revolutionaries. This tribunal should be erected in order to replace for them the supreme tribunal of popular vengeance. It is very difficult to define a political crime, but if a man of the common people for his sort of misdeed gets punished at once, is it not necessary that extreme laws, something out of the common running of our social machinery, should be passed to terrify rebels and to strike the guilty? In this matter the safety of the people demands from you extreme methods and the measures of terror."

Finally, we know that Danton was, on the whole, the guide of that earlier part of the Terror between May and August 1793, in which (as he thought) the system was doing necessary work without which the nation could not have been saved.

Now, let us set against these what we definitely know of Danton's character which would lead us to a conclusion that he would not have countenanced massacre.

No one questions the fact that the leading motive in Danton's mind was the establishment of a strong government around or in the place of a weak monarchy. He was a true descendant of the lawyers of the Code. The massacres of September took place at a moment when he was using the whole of his personal energy in trying as well as may be to supply that Government. He guides the ministry in Paris; he dominates Roland as a man might dominate a woman. It was of supreme importance to such a scheme that the thin ice between government and anarchy in the days that preceded Valmy should not be broken. The massacre of September broke it; there was a week of anarchy in Paris. There is the first great argument against Danton's complicity with the massacres.

It must, however, be remembered that a theory exists, by no means untenable, which would make Danton argue something in this fashion: "Once let the popular fury have full rein against what it regards as the internal enemy, and I shall have the disappearance of that disturbing factor of royalist reaction in Paris, while on the part of the mob I shall have the lassitude and shame that follow excess; they are not difficult to govern." It is only a personal opinion, but it seems to me that in a mind of Danton's type, downright and practical to excess, such a far-reaching and subtle idea as the last would hardly occur, and that the massacres must have produced on him an especial annoyance, because they were the breakdown of a system the support of which occupied his every effort.

Secondly, Danton's allusions to the massacres of September were always of a more definite and more reasonable nature than those of his colleagues. The attitude which he adopts with regard to them after their occurrence is this: "There was no public force, none of that disciplined government which I postulate as the first necessity of the Revolution; nothing on earth could prevent them, and they occurred in spite of every governing power." So much for generalities.

Now let us turn to one or two points which have been made the basis of a definite accusation against Danton in this matter.

Firstly: that he knew that the massacres were coming, and withdrew from prison more than one of his friends on the eve of the uprising. This I take to be true, or rather I am certain of it; but one would have to be very ignorant of the time not to know that all Paris expected the massacres, and that those who were at all in touch with the Commune knew two or three days before that anything illegal might be done. To have worked to prevent them, in which Danton might have employed his energy, would, as I have said in the text, have been to risk that which he most desired, and to risk it for the sake of saving the prisoners. Certainly he did not desire to save them as passionately as he desired to remain at the helm and build up a government; he preferred to keep his influence over the city. That accusation is just.

Secondly, it is affirmed with justice that Danton, from the peculiar position of the ministry which he occupied, filled the prisons, which were afterwards gutted. It is true that on Danton, as Minister of Justice, and above all as a general power in the Cabinet, the responsibility of arresting the prisoners rests; but was this action taken with a knowledge of what the consequences would be nearly a month later? Certainly not. It would show a complete ignorance of what happened in the last fortnight of August to say that an action taken just after the 10th was taken with a view to something that would occur on the 2nd of September. The state of public feeling in those four weeks went through a most violent crisis, and one might say that the intensity of the feeling against the Royalists and the foreigners was not only a hundred-fold greater when Verdun was actually falling than it had been just after the success against the Tuilleries, but different in quality as well.

Thirdly, there is one detailed accusation—the circular which Marat sent out to the Departments. If it can be proved that this circular was approved of, that its distribution was aided by Danton, then we shall have a definite piece of evidence which cannot be overridden. Now let me describe what that circular was, and see how far we must blame circumstances, how far the carelessness, and how far the deliberate act of the minister. All the accounts are much the same. Madame Roland says, "Sent out above the signature of the Minister of Justice." Bertrand de Molleville is also perfectly definite (Memoirs, ix. 310)—"Sent by the minister Danton."

The examination of the documents seventy years later has given more accurate results to history than the memoirs of contemporaries, whether they are truthful and enthusiastic like Madame Roland, or frankly dishonest like

Bertrand de Molleville. Bougeart was at the pains of looking up the original documents at the archives of the police. What appears in this document (Bougeart, pp. 121-122) is a series of signatures, Panis, Sergent, Marat, &c., that is, the Committee of Surveillance appointed by the Commune. There is no trace of any ministerial signature, and even the stamp which was used in the office by the clerks for everything that passed officially through the Ministry of Justice is not attached to the sheet. What did happen was this. The circulars were sent out in envelopes which bore the official mark of the Ministry. It is as though some act of a body in London, let us say, should be distributed to the provinces in the blue envelopes of Her Majesty's Service. That is all, either for or against Danton, that remains of the incident of the circular.

Now it is certain that Danton had not at that time openly broken with Marat. Moreover, Danton had not actually quarrelled with the Commune, though he certainly treated it with contempt. But Danton had no conceivable object in helping Marat to distribute the circulars unless he himself was openly on Marat's side. A man of his character would either have signed, or else, had he known that the circulars were going out, he would have forbidden their distribution; he would have taken some definite line. Why? Because the distribution of the circular was bound to condemn him to a very definite position—here is a man who has stood aloof from a very violent conspiracy, a conspiracy whose authors came out at last in the open day and gloried in what they had done. They wrote the most violent of all their manifestoes, containing such phrases as "the ferocious prisoners have been put to death by the people;" "it was an act of justice indispensable to our Committee," and so forth. It would be quite impossible to send out unwittingly such a circular as that without knowing that one was compromising oneself and definitely entering the most extreme party of the Parisians. It is inconceivable, therefore, that he would have lent official envelopes for the purpose, and have said, "So far I will help you, but I will not help you more than that." You might as well suppose an English official in India, of the stronger kind, saying, "I will allow you, an unofficial personage, to send out the order for an illegal execution from this office, but I will not put my name to it."

Again, how comes it that this document alone, of all those sent from the Minister of Justice at the time, goes out in the official envelope, but bears in itself no mark whatsoever of the Ministry of Justice? How was it that the officials in the country towns, among the mass of papers that they received from the Ministry in Paris, should receive this single one without any stamp or signature, and should then discover that it had proceeded from a body which had nothing on earth to do with the Ministry of Justice? There are but two replies possible to this question—either that the envelopes were taken from the Ministry by one of the clerks (several of whom we know to have been intimately linked with the Commune), or that Danton timidly lent envelopes but refused to do anything further. Of these two replies, the second appears to me absolutely at variance not only with Danton's own character but also with the general routine of a great office. I cannot conceive the Cabinet Minister offering, in the very gravest conditions, a few blue envelopes, when a whole political party desire from him a definite pronouncement on one side or the other.

Finally, it may be asked, could these envelopes go out without his knowledge? To that I answer that such a thing might be done from any government office to-day. It was, moreover, a time of revolution; the whole complicated organism had been shaken and partly transformed; there was confusion in every department of the building, and even under these conditions Danton was doing far more work than depended upon his office. I think, therefore, that it is eminently possible that the circulars should have been sent out by one of the clerks without his knowledge; and the fact that no signature was used, and that the documents did not even pass through one of the many hands whose duty it was to affix the formal stamp, still further corroborates the view that the circulation of the appeal was surreptitious.

As to the accusations such as that of Lafayette (Memoirs, iv. 139, 140), "He commanded the massacre of September and paid the murderers, who went all covered with blood to get their money from Roland," I attach no importance to them at all. Even the phrase in which Danton is supposed to have saluted the return of the murderers from Versailles is very doubtful. It does not occur in any contemporary account; it is not in the *Moniteur*; it is not in the "Révolutions de Paris;" Madame Roland does not quote it, even on hearsay; it is not one of Peltier's inventions, and I have some difficulty in tracing it to its origin.

I think, then, that the general position of Danton during the days of September may be summed up as follows. He did not regard the lives of the prisoners as being of the first importance; he did not use what would have been to his certain knowledge a useless energy in protesting; he did not (as he might conceivably have done) form a special and vigorous tribunal to replace that which was on the point of acquitting L. de Montmorin. By all those, therefore, who would regard public order and a security for life as being more important than the success of a political idea, or the integrity and defence of a nation, he can be accused of a criminal negligence in the matter of the massacres of September. He certainly cannot be accused of having designed them; he cannot be accused on any definite proof of having approved them, and he cannot be accused of having failed to share in the regret and misery which that terrible blunder caused. If we may judge the attitude of his mind by comparing it with that of contemporaries, rather than by comparing it with our own attitude in a time of security and order, we may say that the massacres taught him a more definite lesson than they taught to Roland, for they caused him to pursue a policy of conciliation and to strengthen the government; that, on the other hand, he did less to stop them than Manuel did; and that in a comparison with men whom we know to have been honest, such as Roland himself, or by a contrast with men whom we know to have been evil, such as Hébert, or whom we know to have been frenzied, such as Marat—judged in the midst of all this, Danton will appear responsible to history for having been guilty of indifference at a moment when he might have saved his reputation by protesting, though perhaps his protest would not have saved a single life.

The object of the remainder of this Appendix is to provide for the reader certain documents that illustrate the statements and the line of argument in the text. Of these documents but few have been translated, because only a few appeal to any one but a special student of the Revolution, or are necessary to the understanding of this book.

By far the most important of the documents here printed is the last, Barrère's report of the 29th of May 1793. Hitherto unpublished, it furnishes (to my mind) the most complete explanation of the somewhat complicated manœuvres pursued by the Committee, manœuvres which permitted the revolution of May 31st and June 2nd.

To each document a short preface has been attached for the purpose of explaining its origin and of mentioning the authorities (if any) in which it can be found.

V SHORT MEMOIR by A. R. C. de St. ALBIN

This memoir was published for the first time as an article in the *Critique Française* of the 15th of March 1864. It was so published by the author himself, and, though appearing seventy years after Danton's death, is not without importance. De St. Albin, who is better known by his first name of Rousselin, had some personal acquaintance with Danton (though he was but a boy at the time) and he lived to a great age. He had, moreover, an acquaintance with the family after the Revolutionary period. These circumstances make his testimony decisive on all non-controversial points and valuable on many others.

The criticisms to be made against his account are obvious. It is too florid; it errs also in giving an amiable and somewhat mediocre character to the statesman himself and to all his relatives and surroundings. We have in it but a poor expression of the energy that was Danton's chief character, and which the writer's own mind cannot reflect. It was, moreover, written so very long after the events which it describes that in more than one place an error of date or number has been committed; especially in the incident of Barentin at the close of the memoir, with which M. Aulard finds so much fault, and in the amount of his wife's dowry, which was not 40,000 but only 20,000 livres. On the other hand, it is fresh, full of personal recollections, written by a trustworthy man, and gives many interesting details on the earlier and less known part of Danton's life.

"La famille de Danton n'a point à se prévaloir d'une antique noblesse. Le nom de Danton est commun dans la contrée d'Arcis-sur-Aube, il est apparu avec un certain bruit, en 1740, dans les querelles du jansénisme. Parmi les pièces de théâtre destinées à populariser ces discussions théologiques, il en est une intitulée *La Banqueroute des marchands de miracles*, qui est signée du P. Danton. On a supposé, non sans raison, qui cet ecclésiastique était un grand-oncle du conventionnel.

"Georges-Jacques Danton naquit à Arcis-sur-Aube le 26 octobre 1759. Il était fils de Jacques Danton, procureur au bailliage d'Arcis, qui avait épousé, en 1754, Jeanne-Madeleine Camut. Le père mourut le 24 février 1762, âgé d'environ quarante ans, laissant sa femme enceinte et quatre enfants en bas âge, deux filles et deux garçons, Georges-Jacques Danton resta sous la tutelle de sa mère, femme douée de toutes les qualités qui commandent l'estime. C'est par la sensibilité et la douceur du caractère que la mère de Danton élevait et gouvernait sa jeune famille. Georges, celui de ses enfants dont l'extérieur indiquait le plus de force et de volonté, était le plus docile envers elle. Se jeune indépendance était bien vite soumise quand sa mère parlait à son cœur. La tendresse obtenait ce que la crainte aurait vainement tenté d'arracher. Madame veuve Danton eut un heureux auxiliaire pour le soutien de sa maison dans son père, entrepreneur des ponts et chaussées de la province de Champagne. Celui-ci donna les premières leçons à son petit-fils: il voyait avec joie ses mâles dispositions.

"Il est intéressant de noter quel fut le milieu dans lequel Danton passa ainsi ses premières années, et nous avons trouvé, dans un auteur contemporain, le passage suivant qui nous semble curieux:

"'La ville d'Arcis-sur-Aube est composée d'hommes indépendants; l'air y est vif, les hommes sont robustes; la rivière de l'Aube, qui traverse le pays, est navigable en tout temps, le commerce maritime occupe les natifs; quand les marins ne sont pas occupés à l'eau, ils font des bas; ils sont laborieux, industrieux. Arcis n'est comparable à aucune partie de la Champagne; les lois y sont observées comme si elles n'existaient pas, par le seul sentiment de l'ordre; les seigneurs de l'ancien régime avaient toujours rencontré des opposants dans des hommes chez qui l'amour de la liberté est inné.'

"L'enfance de Danton n'eut rien de remarquable; il fut élevé, suivant l'usage du pays, à peu près comme un enfant de la nature.

"Il avait été nourri par une vache, ce qui est usité en Champagne, quand les mères ne sont pas assez fortes pour allaiter leurs enfants. La vache nourrice de Danton fut un jour aperçue par un taureau échappé, qui se précipita sur elle et donna au pauvre enfant un coup de corne qui lui arracha la lèvre. C'est à cette cicatrice que tenait la difformité de sa lèvre supérieure.

"En grandissant, Danton, comme tous les êtres doués d'une force extraordinaire, éprouvait le besoin de l'exercer. Il voulut un jour faire preuve de vigueur, prendre sa revanche et lutter contre un taureau. Il était difficile qu'il sortit vainqueur de la lutte. Un coup de corne lui écrasa le nez.

"Ces accidents auraient dû le rendre prudent, mais il n'y a guère de prudence là où il y a grande surabondance de vie. Un jour le robuste enfant croit pouvoir faire marcher devant lui les porcs de la ferme qui obstruaient l'entrée de la maison. Il les attaque à coups de fouet; mais son pied glisse, il tombe, et les porcs devenus furieux, se ruent sur lui et lui font une terrible blessure, assez semblable à celle dont Boileau fut victime dans son enfance, au dire d'Helvétius, qui attribuait à cette blessure la disette de sentiment qu'il prétendait remarquer dans les ouvrages du poète. Quel que soit le mérite de cette appréciation, elle ne serait pas applicable à Danton. Sa virilité avait été compromise, non perdue, et il conserva toute son énergie et toute sa hardiesse. Rien ne l'arrêtait: chaque jour il donnait de nouvelles preuves de témérité. A peine fut-il rétabli de ce malheureux accident, qu'entraîné par sa passion pour la natation, il faillit se noyer et fut atteint d'une fièvre maligne, à laquelle vint se joindre une petite vérole très grave, accompagnée du pourpre. Tout semblait ainsi se réunir pour le défigurer.

"Pour faire contracter à son enfant quelques habitudes de discipline, la mère de Danton le remit d'abord à la surveillance d'une maîtresse d'école; celle-ci n'avait pas le temps ou la volonté d'user avec lui d'indulgence. Danton trouva quelque différence dans la comparaison de ce nouveau régime avec les tendresses de sa mère et de son aïeul: non moins sévère que la demoiselle Lambercier de J.-J. Rousseau, la maîtresse d'école croyait ne pouvoir se passer de verges pour diriger les enfants, et Danton lui avait paru avoir les premiers droits à ses corrections. Tous ses contemporains se souvenaient de l'avoir vu faire trop souvent l'école buissonnière et employer les heures de classe à barboter dans l'Aube. Il préférait la liberté de vivre à l'ennui de répéter les caractères de l'alphabet. Il avait cependant d'heureuses aptitudes et apprenait rapidement; mais toute habitude réglée était antipathique à sa nature.

"A huit ans, il fut débarrassé de la rigoureuse maîtresse, et *transvasé*, comme il le dit lui-même, dans une institution supérieure. Le chef de cette institution croyait savoir assez de latin pour en enseigner les éléments. Quand les premiers principes de la grammaire ne sont pas montrés avec une habile méthode aux jeunes intelligences, elle leur offre peu d'attrait.

"Danton en avait peu-être un peu moins pour *Lhomond* que pour le jeu de cartes. A peine le devoir terminé, en hâte il courait avec quelques camarades dans un coin pour faire sa partie. Des billes ou des gâteaux étaient le bénéfice du gagnant. Souvent vainqueur, il partageait toujours avec le vaincu. Quand il se trouvait seul, il lisait ou allait se promener ans les bois ou dans les champs.

"Pour modifier cette humeur un peu sauvage, les parents de Danton crurent devoir le mettre dans une maison religieuse.

"Quoiqu'il ne fût point destiné à l'état ecclésiastique, on le plaça d'abord au petit séminaire de *Troyes*; mais la monotonie de cette maison lui devint bientôt pénible. Pendant tout le temps qu'il y resta, il observa la règle, mais il ne pouvait souffrir que sa récréation fût subitement interrompue par un coup de cloche. *Cette cloche*, disait-il, *si je suis encore forcé de l'entendre longtemps, finira par sonner mon enterrement.*

"Un reproche mal fondé et reçu publiquement du supérieur décida Danton à solliciter sa sortie du séminaire.

"Le fait suivant peut être raconté comme trait de caractère: La pension, dans cette maison, était modique. Les élèves n'avaient de vin qu'en le payant séparément à la fin de chaque année. Tous les dimanches on distribuait des cartes, qui étaient une espèce de billet au porteur. En présentant cette carte au distributeur, on recevait une mesure de vin appelée *roquille*. Danton était généreux, et un de ses grands plaisirs alors était de régaler ses camarades en leur passant des cartes de *roquilles*, surtout à ceux qu'il savait n'avoir pas la bourse bien garnie. Sa générosité alla si loin, que, lorsqu'on fit le compté général et la proclamation publique de tous ceux qui avaient bu du vin, il se trouva être celui qui avait fait une plus grande consommation de *roquilles*. La veille du départ pour les vacances, le supérieur du petit séminaire adressa ces paroles à Danton: *Mon ami, vous pouvez vous flatter d'être le plus grand buveur de la communauté.* A ces mots, tous les rires d'éclater sur lui; il ne répondit pas, mais il se promit bien de ne plus boire de roquilles au petit séminaire. Malgré une véritable bonté, Danton était peu endurant, et on l'avait surnommé *l'anti-supérieur*, et même *le républicain*.

"A peine revenu à Arcis-sur-Aube, il déclara à sa mère qu'il ne rentrerait plus au petit séminaire: "Il y a là, dit-il, des habitudes qui ne me vont pas, et que je ne pourrai jamais comprendre." L'année suivante, on le mit dans une pension laïque. Ses études n'y perdirent rien, car il eut depuis des succès qu'il n'avait pas obtenus auparavant. Il fit ainsi sa seconde, et y remporta la presque totalité des prix....

"Nous arrivons au mois de juin 1775. On apprend que le sacre de Louis XVI. va s'accomplir à Reims. Danton avait déjà plus d'une fois entendu les imprécations dont toute la France couvrait la mémoire de Louis XV. A l'âge de seize ans il en savait assez pour abhorrer l'emploi des lettres de cachet, qui étaient si prodiguées sous ce règne scandaleux. Le professeur avait annoncé qu'il donnerait l'événement du sacre du nouveau monarque comme texte d'amplification: *Pour bien se pénétrer de son sujet*, dit Danton d'un ton décidé, *il faut se servir de ses yeux. Je suis curieux de voir comment se fait un roi.*

"Son projet n'est confié qu'à quelques fidèles camarades qui lui prêtent de l'argent pour sa route. Il part sans prévenir son maître; il traverse son pays d'Arcis sans voir ses parents, dans la crainte de les trouver opposés à son pèlerinage. Après avoir franchi vingt-huit lieues sans encombre, il arrive à Reims, se glisse partout; il suit attentivement toutes les cérémonies du sacre, et il entend le jeune monarque, la main sur l'Évangile, prononcer le serment *de régner par les lois et pour le bonheur de la nation*. Que des réflexions fait naître un pareil spectacle dans un cerveau ardent, déjà prompt à concevoir de rapprochements!

"A son retour de Reims, les amis de Danton étaient impatients de l'entendre raconter tout ce qu'il avait vu. Cet appareil ne l'avait pas émerveillé, la richesse des décors de la cathédrale ne l'avait pas séduit. Il raisonnait assez déjà pour sentir que ce n'était guère plus qu'une pompe vaine, encore dispendieuse pour la France déjà si obérée. Le jeune voyageur s'égayait en parlant de ce nombreux essaim d'oiseaux de toute espèce auxquels on avait donné la volée dans l'église: "*Plaisante liberté*, disait-il, *que de voltiger entre quatre murs, sans avoir de quoi manger ni poser son nid!*" Il comparait aussi les oiseaux babillards aux courtisans qui entouraient déjà le nouveau roi, par continuation de leur dévouement pour le défunt. A l'entendre débiter avec autant de simplicité que de malice ses réflexions sur le luxe, on peut entrevoir que l'écolier moraliste, devenu grand, ne sera pas sans quelque exigence envers la royauté, et sans quelque sévérité envers les agents qui vivent des abus.

"Danton, revenu à Troyes, éprouva des difficultés pour rentrer à sa pension. Sa sortie, à l'insu du maître, avait indisposé celui-ci. Le voyageur, soumis et repentant, proteste *qu'il na été à Reims que pour se mettre en mesure de faire en connaissance de cause son devoir d'amplification sur le sacre.* Il produit effectivement un morceau des plus brillants, mais où il se défend d'introduire les observations hardies échappées dans la familiarité de conversation, qui ne peuvent se présenter dans une narration écrite, dont les convenances sont la première règle. Le maître, satisfait et surpris du mérite de l'œuvre, en fait lecture à ses élèves. Il dit *qu'il aurait donné la première place à l'auteur s'il n'avait fait l'école buissonnière.* Les camarades de Danton s'unissent avec enthousiasme à l'appréciation du maître; ils admirent comment l'enfant prodigue, leur ayant fait un récit aussi piquant, aussi jovial de son voyage, avait pu en même temps mettre dans son style autant de réserve et de noblesse. C'est ainsi que Danton fait admettre ses excuses, et sa grâce est devenue une espèce de triomphe. Il reprend sa classe, dont les travaux allaient bientôt se terminer. L'époque des compositions pour les prix annuels approchait; se fiant à sa facilité, Danton ne semble pas se préparer au concours. Mais dès que les sujets de composition sont donnés, il rassemble tous les efforts de son intelligence et obtient toutes les couronnes. Il déploie d'admirables moyens dans le discours français, la narration latine et la poésie. Imagination, jugement, exactitude, saillie dans la pensée, force, élégance, originalité dans l'expression, rien ne lui manque, et le 18 août 1775 fut peut-être le plus beau jour de sa vie. Le nom de *Danton-Camut* (qui était celui de sa mère pour le distinguer d'un homonyme son condisciple) fut répété au bruit des fanfares. Si le lauréat fut heureux, ce fut surtout en apportant ses lauriers à sa mère, objet de son culte et de son amour; cette piété filiale, dès lors le plus vif de ses sentiments, demeurera la même dans son cœur pendant tout le cours de sa vie, quelles qu'en soient les violences ou les distractions; plus tard, il la montra mieux encore, et l'homme auquel il voua la haine la plus tenace fut un misérable soupçonné d'avoir manqué de respect à Madame Danton.

"Lorsqu'un écolier se distinguait au collège, on songeait à la carrière que lui ouvriraient ses talents. *Il faut en faire un prêtre ou un procureur.* Le curé de Barberey, près Troyes, désignait déjà Danton pour qu'il lui succédât dans son presbytère; mais le moment de séjour que Danton avait fait au séminaire ne lui avait pas inspiré la vocation ecclésiastique. Il avait besoin de liberté, il lui fallait les franches allures, l'indépendance. Il demandait une profession libérale, il désirait être avocat.... Démosthènes et Cicéron, qu'il venait de commencer à connaître n'étaient-ils pas des avocats? La famille réunie ayant déféré au vœu de Danton, il fut décidé qu'il irait à Paris et qu'il travaillerait chez un procureur pour y apprendre la procédure en même temps qu'il ferait ses études de droit, pour se préparer au barreau.

"Ici vient se placer une circonstance intéressante qui fait honneur à Danton et qui fournit une nouvelle preuve de sa tendresse pour ses parents. Madame veuve Danton, demeurée seule avec sa nombreuse famille, s'était remariée pour lui donner un soutien. Elle avait épousé M. Recordin, estimable négociant, dont la bonté est restée proverbiale dans le pays: *bon et brave comme Recordin*. Par suite de sa facilité dans ses relations, les affaires de la maison Recordin se trouvèrent embarrassées. Danton, loin d'exiger les comptes qu'il avait droit de demander de la fortune qui lui revenait de son père, fut le premier à offrir des secours à son beau-père; il mit à sa disposition tout ce qui lui appartenait; il alla jusqu'à engager la portion du bien de ses tantes qui devait lui échoir un jour, ne craignant pas d'aliéner son présent en son avenir. *Il faut mettre ses affaires en règle*, disait-il, *quand on fait un grand voyage.*

"Tels furent les préparatifs du départ.

"Tous les témoignages de ses camarades, parents et amis, déposent de la délicatesse de Danton sous tous les rapports; à l'exception du prêt de quelques écus qui lui furent offerts par ses camarades pour le voyage de Reims, il n'a jamais demandé d'argent à qui que ce soit, dans les moments où, soit comme écolier, soit comme clerc de procureur, il a pu éprouver de ces gênes de jeune homme qui rendent hardi aux emprunts.

"Danton arrive à Paris en 1780 dans la voiture du messager d'Arcis-sur-Aube, qui était l'ami de sa famille, et qui voulut lui faire la conduite gratuitement. Il se logea à l'auberge du *Cheval noir*, tenue rue Geoffroy-Lasnier par un nommé Layron, qui était l'hôte le plus fréquenté par les Champenois. Danton avait très peu de fonds, et il dut se mettre immédiatement au travail: il entra chez un procureur appelé Vinot. Ce procureur commença par lui demander un modèle de son écriture, qu'il ne trouva pas belle. Les procureurs de ce temps-là voulaient de ces écritures promptes et faciles, propres à produire de larges grosses, de longues requêtes. Le jeune Champenois déclara franchement *qu'il n'était pas venu pour être copiste*. Ce ton d'assurance imposa au procureur Vinot. Il dit: *J'aime l'aplomb, il en faut dans notre état.*

"Danton fut admis comme clerc, avec la nourriture et le logement. Il étudia la procédure non sans quelque dégoût; il fut chargé, comme on dit dans le métier, *de faire le palais*. C'est la première initiation des jeunes clercs aux affaires. Elle commence à les mettre en relation avec les choses et les personnes du monde judiciaire, et leur donne les éléments de la pratique par de petits plaidoyers sommaires et des explications contradictoires qui leur ouvrent les idées et leur apprennent à se conduire dans le labyrinthe où ils sont destinés à vivre.

"Danton remplissait sa fonction de clerc avec intelligence et exactitude; ses récréations les plus habituelles étaient toujours l'escrime, la paume et la natation, sa passion favorite! dont il usait fréquemment; c'était le besoin même de son tempérament. Il était assez habile à cet exercice pour être cité au premier rang; il y trouva un encouragement digne de son émulation. Il sauva plusieurs fois de la mort des camarades qui auraient péri s'il n'était venu au secours de leur imprudence et de leur faiblesse. Quelques-uns d'entre eux ont raconté les tours de force véritables que Danton exécutait dans les courants les plus difficiles de la rivière. De l'endroit même où ils prenaient leurs ébats, on voyait les tours de la Bastille, et plus d'une fois les baigneurs ont entendu Danton, dressant sa tête comme un triton, jeter une menace du côté de la prison d'État et s'écrier de sa voix vibrante: *Ce chateau fort suspendu sur notre tête m'offusque et me gêne. Quand le verrons-nous abattu? Pour moi, ca jour là, j'y donnerais un fier coup de pioche!*

"Les constitutions les plus robustes sont souvent les plus exposées, parce que cette exubérance de force donne plus de sécurité. Danton, à la suite d'une double partie de natation et d'escrime, fut encore atteint d'une grave maladie. Longtemps retenu au lit, alors que son corps était réduit à l'inaction, il ne pouvait se livrer à ses exercices habituels, mais son imagination ne restait point inactive. Avec son infatigable ardeur de lecture, il s'obstina à lire *l'Encyclopédie* tout entière, et il avait achevé ce labeur si considérable avant que la convalescence fût terminée. Il trouvait encore le temps de lire les grands publicistes dont les principes et la morale politique commençaient à devenir les guides du siècle. Montesquieu qu'il devait souvent citer, fut de sa part l'objet d'une étude tout particulière, et, après avoir lu *l'Esprit des lois*, il disait: *Quel horizon nouveau s'ouvre devant moi! Je n'ai qu'un regret, c'est de retrouver dans l'écrivain qui vous porte si loin et si haut, le président d'un parlement.* De Montesquieu, Danton passa bientôt à Voltaire, à J.-J. Rousseau, puis à Beccaria, qui apparaissait alors. Danton ne tarda pas à savoir par cœur l'admirable petit ouvrage de cet auteur, le traité *Des délits et des peines*, qui allait réformer la législation criminelle du monde; afin de se préparer des couleurs de style pour le jour où il aurait à parler aux foules, afin d'apprendre, à revêtir les questions sociales des belles images de la nature, Danton étudia particulièrement *l'Histoire naturelle* de Buffon: au moyen de sa puissante mémoire il en retenait et récitait des pages entières. Voilà d'amples provisions d'instruction qui pourront trouver un jour un utile emploi dans la carrière de l'homme public! Tout en dédaignant la littérature frivole et n'ayant jamais lu de romans que les chefs-d'œuvre consacrés qui sont des peintures de mœurs, Danton apprit en même temps la langue italienne assez pour lire le Tasse, l'Arioste et même le Dante. Il faisait aussi des vers avec facilité, quelques-uns même adressés, en tout bien et tout honneur, à une personne qui n'était pas indigne de les lui inspirer, à la femme de son procureur.

"Mais tous ces délassements littéraires étaient en dehors de la profession qu'il voulait exercer. Ils ne lui firent point négliger l'apprentissage de la procédure et du droit.

"Il lui restait maintenant à devenir de licencié avocat, et comme il avait gardé un bon souvenir de la ville de Reims, il alla se faire recevoir avocat dans cette ville. Champenois de cœur, il était heureux de contribuer de tous ses moyens à l'honneur de son pays natal. Il avait toujours de bonnes saillies à son service, et ne manquait pas une occasion de citer des hommes distingués dans les lettres et les arts de diverses époques qui appartenaient à la province de Champagne. Parmi les contemporains, Danton pouvait du reste trouver plus d'un exemple à l'appui de son patriotique enthousiasme: c'est ainsi qu'il parlait souvent de quelques notabilités qu'il connaissait, tels que le savant *Grosley*, l'avocat *Linguet*.

"De retour de Reims à Paris, Danton, après avoir achevé son stage, s'essaya au barreau de la capitale pendant quelque temps. Chargé d'une affaire, entre autres, pour un berger contre le seigneur de son village, il eut l'occasion de produire, en cette circonstance, quelques-uns des sentiments qu'il devait plus tard développer davantage sur un grand théâtre. Il réclama avec autant de vigueur que d'adresse les principes de l'égalité devant la loi. Il gagna sa cause devant la cour de parlement qui, comme on se le rappelle, n'était alors composée que de nobles et de privilégiés. Nous ne sommes encore qu'en 1785. Le factum de Danton fut imprimé: il était concis, substantiel, énergique—nous n'avons pu en retrouver la trace.—Cette première lutte soutenue par Danton fit sensation au palais et valut au jeune avocat des témoignages d'estime de Gerbier, Debonnière, Hardouin et toutes les sommités du barreau de cette époque. Linguet, qui se connaissait en style, et qui, nous l'avons vu, était de Reims, lui adressa à ce sujet de vifs encouragements.

"Mais les témoignages de ces hommes éminents, qui assuraient à Danton un succès d'honneur, ne le menaient point à la fortune; il s'en éloignait même à mesure que son talent aurait dû l'en rapprocher davantage, car il recherchait la clientèle du pauvre autant que d'autres recherchaient la clientèle du riche. Il pensait qu'en thèse générale le pauvre est le plus souvent l'opprimé, qu'ainsi il a le droit de priorité à la défense. D'après ce principe de conduite, ceux qui ont dit que Danton n'avait point fait fortune au barreau, pouvaient ajouter qu'il ne l'y aurait jamais faite....

"S'ennuyant peut-être un peu, comme on a pu l'entrevoir, dans sa profession d'avocat, Danton ne demandait point de distraction à des plaisirs qui auraient pu prendre sur les ressources nécessaires à son existence. Gagnant fort peu dans ses travaux de palais, il n'aurait pas voulu ajouter à la gêne de sa position en contractant des dettes; il était fort rangé, toujours avec une petite réserve d'économies qui lui permettait de rendre des services sans en demander lui-même. Après son frugal repas chez un traiteur, dont la maison était nommée l'*Hôtel de la Modestie*, il prenait une demi-tasse de café et jouait quelques parties de dominos. Ajoutez, de temps en temps, le spectacle d'une tragédie classique au Théâtre-Français, voilà toute la defense et tous les amusements du jeune avocat.

"Un café où se rendait le plus habituellement Danton s'appelait *Café de l'École*, parce qu'il était situé sur ce quai, presque au coin de la place qui a conservé ce nom. C'était un rendez-vous très fréquenté par les hommes de loi qui se trouvaient rapprochés du Châtelet et du Palais de Justice. La rigueur du costume et de la coiffure, espèce de signalement perpétuel, avait cet avantage qu'on n'était pas tenté de se commettre.

"Les maîtres des cafés, alors peu nombreux dans Paris, étaient eux-mêmes des bourgeois d'honnête allure. Ils maintenaient le bon ton de leur maison par leur civilité. Ils faisaient rarement fortune, à l'exception de deux ou trois qui étaient de premier rang. Le *Café de l'École* n'était pas précisément à ce niveau; mais il était l'un de ceux qui avaient la meilleure réputation. Nous croyons voir encore le maître de la maison avec sa petite perruque ronde, son habit gris et sa serviette sous le bras. Il était rempli de prévenances pour ses clients, et il en était traité avec une considération cordiale. Une femme des plus recommandables et fille de la maison, aussi douce que gracieuse, tenait le comptoir. Parmi les habitués, qui paraissaient s'arrêter avec un intérêt particulier à ce comptoir, on put remarquer un jeune avocat qui, d'abord fort gai et jovial, parut quelque temps après plus sérieux. Ce jeune avocat était Danton; il avait cru d'abord ne causer que généralement et sans conséquence avec les dames du comptoir; son cœur s'y était pris, et Danton était amoureux. Mademoiselle Gabrielle Charpentier n'avait pas songé à se défier des assiduités de Danton; elle se trouva bientôt, à son insu, préoccupée du même sentiment. Sans être dans le secret de cette inclination, le père et la mère Charpentier ne furent pas très surpris quand la main de leur fille leur fut demandée par le jeune avocat. La vivacité de son caractère leur fit craindre un moment de consentir à cette union; mais il avait su toucher le cœur de Gabrielle. Lorsqu'on disait: *Qu'il est laid!* elle répétait, presque comme l'avait dit une femme au sujet de Lekain: *Qu'il est beau!* Elle admirait son esprit, que l'on trouvait trop piquant; son âme, que l'on trouvait trop ardente; sa voix, que l'on trouvait forte et terrible, et qu'elle trouvait douce.

"Il fallait cependant prendre des renseignements sur ce prétendant. M. Charpentier visita particulièrement les procureurs chez qui Danton avait travaillé, et les avocats avec lesquels il avait été en rapport au barreau. Il n'y eut qu'une voix en sa faveur. D'après des renseignements aussi satisfaisants, les bons parents ne s'informèrent point de sa fortune; ils y tenaient peu, quoique en ayant eux-mêmes une assez modeste. Pourtant, ils donnaient en mariage à leur fille une somme de 40,000 francs, ce qui était pour l'époque une dot considérable. Ils imposaient à leur gendre une seule condition, c'est qu'il exerçât un état; c'est qu'il fût *occupé*. La profession d'avocat au parlement était sans doute une profession honorable et libre, mais trop libre peut-être, et qui ne commandait pas un travail assez assidu. Danton promit de remplir les vœux de son beau-père; il s'exprima dans des termes si chaleureux, que le père et la mère Charpentier se mirent à aimer Danton presque autant que leur fille.

"Des amis de Danton lui conseillèrent d'acheter une charge d'avocat aux conseils. M. et Madame Charpentier offrirent généreusement la dot de leur fille; mais ce n'était que 40,000 francs, et il en fallait 80,000! Des Champenois dévoués proposèrent de compléter ce qui manquait pour le payement de la charge.

"Ils s'en rapportaient tous à la délicatesse et à la probité de Danton; sa bonne conduite était sa caution. Le mariage n'ayant plus de cause de retard, les bans publiés, le consentement de sa mère arrivé d'Arcis-sur-Aube, Georges-Jacques Danton et Gabrielle Charpentier furent unis, et le même jour il entra, comme il le disait gaiement, *en puissance de femme et en charge d'officier ministériel; le même jour, mari et avocat aux conseils*.

"Les avocats aux conseils réunissaient les doubles fonctions d'avocats et de procureurs; ayant peu de procédure à faire, ils avaient l'avantage de rester maîtres de leurs affaires et de ne pas subir, comme les avocats des autres cours, la loi d'un procureur préoccupé du désir d'attirer à lui tous les bénéfices. Les fonctions des avocats aux conseils avaient aussi quelque chose d'éminemment propre à élever l'âme des jeunes gens; leur mission consistait souvent à redresser les torts du parlement et des cours supérieures. Ils communiquaient journellement avec les maîtres des requêtes, avec les conseillers d'État, avec les hommes du plus haut rang, qui étaient obligés de recourir à leur ministère pour lutter contre les usurpations dont ils avaient à se plaindre.

"Les avocats aux conseils avaient ainsi l'occasion, en discutant avec les ministres eux-mêmes, soit pour les attaquer, soit pour les défendre, d'apprendre à connaître les rapports des autorités entre elles, la vraie distinction des pouvoirs, l'organisation civile dans toute son étendue, l'ordre social dans son ensemble: c'était une excellente école pour créer des économistes, des politiques, des législateurs.

"En exposant le rôle et la mission des avocats aux conseils, nous aurions peut-être dû expliquer que tels étaient au moins la pensée et le droit de l'institution. Faut-il constater maintenant ce qu'était en fait l'institution? Sur le nombre de soixante membres composant l'honorable confrérie, on voyait plusieurs hommes distingués qui sentaient la dignité de leurs fonctions, traitaient leurs clients avec générosité et délicatesse, les affaires avec science, application et courage. Mais tous, il faut bien le dire, n'avaient pas un sentiment aussi élevé de leurs devoirs, et il en était quelques-uns dont l'émulation consistait à faire beaucoup de *grosses*.

"Au moment où Danton fut reçu avocat aux conseils, c'était en 1787; il avait vingt-huit ans, sa femme en avait vingt-cinq. Dans ce moment, l'Ordre était divisé en trois partis plus ou moins actifs.

"Les anciens voulaient créer un *syndicat*, à la tête duquel ils auraient été tout naturellement placés.

"Les jeunes arrivants appartenaient aux idées nouvelles, et ne voulaient être ni conduits ni éconduits.

"Un troisième parti se composait des hommes modérés et pacifiques qui, aimant le repos avant tout, et, comme on a dit depuis, *la paix partout et toujours*, ne voulaient se mêler à aucune action et préféraient laisser faire le mal à leur détriment plutôt que de se mouvoir en aucun sens et se laisser déranger même par un progrès qui leur eût été utile, mais qui aurait pu les *déshéurer*.

"On a déjà pressenti à quel parti Danton avait dû se rallier. Il ne méconnaissait pas la discipline qui doit présider à la bonne organisation d'une compagnie judiciaire; mais il croyait que la force et la puissance réelles des compagnies sont dans leur indépendance, comme le talent même des membres de ces corporations ne peut se passer de la dignité du caractère.

"L'homme qui, en entrant dans une compagnie, dessine ses opinions avec une énergique rudesse, peut s'attendre à rencontrer bien des luttes et bien des hostilités.

"Voulant juger la valeur du nouvel arrivant, les avocats, sous prétexte de bienvenue, et sans l'avoir averti à l'avance, lui firent subir une épreuve en latin. On lui imposa pour sujet l'exposé de la situation morale et politique du pays dans ses rapports avec la justice. C'était, comme Danton l'a dit depuis, *lui proposer de marcher sur des rasoirs*.... Il ne recula point. Saisissant même comme une bonne fortune la difficulté inattendue dans laquelle on croyait l'enlacer, il s'en tira avec éclat, et laissa ses auditeurs dans l'étonnement de sa présence d'esprit et de la décision de son caractère. Il ne craignit point d'aborder la politique qui commençait a pénétrer en toute affaire, et qui était peut-être ici une cause secrète du piège qui lui était tendu. On espérait surprendre en défaut un jeune avocat qui levait la tête et annonçait des principes d'indépendance. Danton, en homme de talent habile à triompher des plus grandes difficultés, osa parler des choses les plus actuelles; il dit que, comme citoyen ami de son pays, autant que comme membre d'une corporation consacrée à la défense des intérêts privés et publics de la société, il désirait que le gouvernement sentît assez la gravité de la situation pour y porter remède par des moyens simples, naturels et tirés de son autorité; qu'en présence des besoins impérieux du pays, il fallait se résigner à se sacrifier; que la noblesse et le clergé, qui étaient en possession des richesses de la France, devaient donner l'exemple; que, quant a lui, il ne pouvait voir dans la lutte du parlement, qui éclatait alors, que l'intérêt de quelques particuliers puissants qui combattaient les ministres, mais sans rien stipuler au profit du peuple. Il déclarait qu'à ses yeux l'horizon apparaissait sinistre, et qu'il sentait venir une révolution terrible. Si seulement on pouvait la reculer de trente années, elle se ferait amiablement par la force des choses et le progrès des lumières. Il répéta dans ce discours, qui ressemblait au cri prophétique de Cassandre: *Malheur à ceux qui provoquent les révolutions, malheur à ceux qui les font!*

"Plusieurs fois les vieux avocats qui avaient tendu ce piège à Danton voulurent interrompre son improvisation. Ils avaient cru entendre des mots qui les effrayaient, tels que *motus populorum, ira gentium, salus populi suprema lex*.... Les jeunes gens qui, récemment sortis des collèges, avaient le droit de comprendre le latin mieux que les anciens, qui l'avaient oublié ou ne l'avaient jamais su, répondaient à leurs vieux confrères qu'ils avaient mal entendu, que le récipiendaire était resté dans une mesure parfaite, irréprochable.

"Espérant constater plus facilement dans le texte d'une rédaction écrite les pensées imprudentes qu'ils avaient cru saisir en écoutant ses paroles, les anciens demandèrent que Danton déposât son discours de réception sur la table de la chambre du conseil. Danton répondit qu'il n'avait rien écrit. Il avait déjà pour système d'écrire le moins possible. Ainsi qu'il l'a dit depuis, on n'écrit point en révolution. Il ajouta d'ailleurs que si l'on désirait porter un jugement sur les paroles qu'il avait prononcées, il ne prétendait pas s'y opposer. Il était assez certain de sa pensée et de sa mémoire pour répéter avec fidélité toute son improvisation.... Le remède eût été pire que le mal. L'aréopage trouva que c'était déjà bien assez de ce qu'on avait entendu, et la majorité s'opposa avec vivacité à la récidive.

"Le cabinet acheté par Danton était loin, au moment où il en devint titulaire, de posséder une clientèle nombreuse. Il n'en fut pas moins toujours d'un grand désintéressement vis-à-vis de ses clients.

"Il se montrait peu exigeant dans la question des honoraires, même lorsqu'il avait gagné sa cause. Lorsque son client venait s'acquitter envers lui, il lui arrivait souvent de dire: *c'est trop*, et de rendre ce qu'il appelait *le trop*. Dans certaines affaires perdues, il refusait toute rémunération. 'Je n'ai point de déboursés, disait-il, puisque je n'ai point fait d'écritures, et que j'ai laissé à la régie son papier timbré.' Il lui arrivait, bien qu'il ne fût pas riche, de donner lui-même des secours d'argent à des clients malheureux.

"Une pareille conduite ne mène pas rapidement à la fortune. Cependant le cabinet de Danton s'améliora en très peu de temps. En dirigeant dignement ses affaires, il gagnait de vingt à vingt-cinq mille francs par an; son sort de père de famille était assuré.

"Dans ce temps où la France était encore divisée en provinces, les classes inférieures pouvaient se réclamer des grands seigneurs de leur pays, et ceux-ci aimaient souvent par vanité autant que par humanité à protéger leurs vassaux. La maison de Brienne était de Champagne, près Arcis-sur-Aube. Danton était connu du comte de Brienne, ancien ministre de la guerre, et de l'archevêque de Sens, alors premier ministre. Il comptait parmi ses clients M. de Barentin. Il avait des conférences avec lui pour ses affaires particulières, et plusieurs fois, après les avoir traitées, M. de Barentin s'entretenait avec son avocat des affaires publiques. La manière supérieure dont Danton voyait les choses avait frappé M. de Barentin et lui avait laissé une vive impression de sa capacité.

"Devenu garde des sceaux, M. de Barentin se souvint aussitôt de son avocat et lui fit demander s'il voulait être secrétaire de la chancellerie? Danton, dans un long entretien qu'il eut avec ce ministre, lui exposa avec détails un plan qu'il croyait pouvoir éloigner les déchirements que l'opposition des parlements allait enfanter. Quelques-uns de ces parlements venaient d'être exilés: Danton pensait que leur rappel n'était pas une chose de la plus grande urgence. Il fallait avant tout les enlacer dans la participation aux réformes; ils en étaient autant les adversaires que la noblesse et le clergé, dont ils faisaient en quelque sorte partie et dont ils avaient les privilèges. Tous les privilégiés enfin, quels que fussent leurs costumes, qu'ils eussent un manteau de noblesse, une soutane de prêtre ou une robe de palais, tous, selon l'opinion de Danton, devaient contribuer aux charges qui ne pesaient que sur le tiers État, c'est-à-dire sur l'immense majorité; la nation attendait l'allégement du fardeau intolérable qu'elle ne pouvait plus supporter, la résignation était épuisée....

"Si ces idées étaient acceptées, le roi, étant à leur tête, se trouverait conquérir dans l'intérêt de tous une puissance supérieure à tous les intérêts particuliers. Il pourrait réaliser les demandes de la raison et donner, par un progrès réel, toute satisfaction aux lumières du siècle et à la philosophie, interprète des vrais besoins de l'humanité.

"En résumé, le plan conçu par Danton tendait à faire accomplir par le roi une réforme progressive qui, laissant en place les pouvoirs établis, les rendit, à leur insu ou malgré eux, les instruments de cette équité pratique qui aurait fortifié à la fois tous les organes du mécanisme social. M. de Barentin parla du projet de Danton à l'archevêque de Sens. On parut l'approuver. Dans l'intervalle, la cour répudia ce système trop net et trop décisif pour ses allures. Le parlement fut rappelé. Brienne croyait en avoir gagné les principaux membres.

"Mais trois mois après—novembre 1787—lorsque le roi fut obligé de venir à Paris tenir un lit de justice à ce même parlement pour obtenir l'enregistrement d'un édit portant création de divers emprunts jusqu'à concurrence de 450 millions, Louis XVI rencontra la plus violente opposition dans cette cour qu'on croyait réduite. Il voulut vaincre l'opposition en exilant les plus récalcitrants, les conseillers Fréteau, Sabatier, de Cabre et le duc d'Orléans.... Au mois de mai suivant, 1788, le même parlement rendit un arrêt qui réclama avec véhémence 'les lois fondamentales de l'État; le droit de la nation d'accorder des subsides, le droit des cours du royaume de vérifier les édits, de vérifier dans chaque province les volontés du roi, et de n'en accorder l'enregistrement qu'autant qu'elles seraient conformes aux lois constitutives de la province, ainsi qu'aux fondamentales de l'État; l'immovabilité et l'indépendance des magistrats, le droit pour chaque citoyen de n'être jamais traduit en aucune manière devant d'autres juges que ses juges naturels désignés par la loi; le droit, sans lequel tous les autres sont inutiles, de n'être arrêté, par quelque ordre que ce soit, que pour être remis sans délai entre les mains des juges compétents; protestant la cour du parlement contre toute atteinte qui serait portée aux principes exprimés.'

"M. de Barentin proposa de nouveau a Danton d'être secrétaire du sceau. Celui-ci remercia en disant que l'état de la question politique était changé. 'Nous n'en sommes plus aux réformes modestes; ceux qui les ont refusées ont refusé leur propre salut; nous sommes, dit-il plus nettement que jamais, à la veille d'une révolution. Eh quoi! ne voyez-vous pas venir l'avalanche?...

A. R. C. de Saint-Albin."

VI EXTRACTS FROM DOCUMENTS
Showing the Price Paid for Danton's Place at the Conseils du Roi, the Sources from which he Derived the Money for its Payment, and the Compensation Paid on its Suppression in 1791.

The three documents from which I quote below are of the utmost importance to a special study of Danton, because they give us most of our evidence as to the value of his post at the Conseils du Roi, and permit us to understand his financial position during the first years of the Revolution.

They are three in number:—

(*a*) The deed of sale by which Danton acquired the post from Me. Huet de Paisy. This deed was discovered by Dr. Robinet (from whose "Vie Privée de Danton" I take all the documents quoted) in the offices of a Parisian solicitor, Me. Faiseau-Jaranne of the Rue Vivienne. This gentleman was the direct successor in his business of the M. Dosfant who drew up the deed seventy years before.

I have quoted only the essential portions of this exceedingly interesting piece of evidence. They give us the date of the transaction (March 29, 1787), the price paid, 78,000 livres, or rather (seeing that Danton acquired the right to collect a debt of 11,000) 67,000 livres net (say £2600); the fact that some £2000 of this was paid down out of a loan raised for him by his relations in Champagne and his future father-in-law, while some £160 he paid out of his savings, and the rest remained owing. The receipt of 1789, which I have attached at the end of the extract, shows us that by that time the balance had been paid over to Me. Huet de Paisy, including interest at 5 per cent. Incidentally there is mention of Danton moving to the Rue de la Tissanderie, whence we shall find him drawing up his marriage-contract.

(*b*) The marriage-contract between Danton and Antoinette Charpentier, contains all the customary provisions of a French marriage-contract, and is witnessed by the usual host of Mends, such as we find witnessing Desmoulins' contract, three or four years later. It tells us, among other things, the position of his stepfather Recordain and the well-to-do connections of the Charpentiers; but the point of principal interest is the dowry—20,000 livres, that is, some £800—of which the greater part (£600) went to pay his debt on the place he held as Avocat ès Conseils, and the fact that he had remaining a patrimony of some £500.

(*c*) The acknowledgment of the sum due as compensation to Danton when the hereditary and purchasable office which he had bought was put an end to. All students of the period know the vast pother that has been raised on this point, the rumour that Danton was overpaid as a kind of bribe from the court, &c. &c. All the direct evidence we have of the transaction is in these few lines. They are just like all the other forms of reimbursement, and are perfectly straightforward.

The amount is somewhat less than we should give in England under similar circumstances, for (1) the State does not allow for the entrance-fees (10,000 livres), which Danton had had to pay, and (2) it taxes him 12 per cent. for the *probable* future taxation which would have fallen by death, transference, &c., on the estate. Finally, he gets not quite 70,000 livres for a place which cost him first and last 78,000.

To recapitulate: the general conclusions which these documents permit us to draw with regard to Danton's financial position are as follows:— The price of the practice he bought was 68,000 livres; of this, 56,000 was paid down, a sum obtained by borrowing 36,000 from Mdlle. Duhattoir (a mortgagee discovered by the family solicitor, Millot), and 15,000 from his future father-in-law, Charpentier, the remaining 5000 being paid out of his own pocket.

He thus remains in debt to Me. Huet de Paisy, the vendor, in a sum of 12,000 livres at 5 per cent. interest.

To this must be added a sum of 10,000 livres entrance-fee, which he presumably pays by recovering a debt of somewhat larger amount (11,000) which he had bought along with the practice.

When he marries, his wife's dowry cancels his debt to Charpentier and leaves him 5000 livres over, he possessing at that time in land and houses at Arcy some 12,000—in all 17,000 livres or their value are in hand in the summer of 1787, and his total liabilities at the same date are the 36,000 to Mdlle. Duhattoir and the 12,000 to Me. de Paisy. He starts his practice, therefore, with 31,000 livres, or about £1200 of net liability. The practice was lucrative; we know that he is immediately concerned with three important chancery cases; he becomes the lawyer of two of the wealthiest men in the kingdom; he lives modestly. We know that he pays the 12,000 with interest in December 1789, and though we do not possess the receipt for Mdlle. Duhattoir's repayment, it is eminently probable that, under such conditions, he could easily have met a debt of less than £800 out of four years' successful practice in a close corporation, which of necessity dealt with the most lucrative cases in the kingdom. I think, therefore, one may regard the reimbursement which he received in 1791 as presumably free from debt, and see him in no financial difficulty at any period of the Revolution. This opinion has the advantage of depending upon the support of all those who have lately investigated the same documents—MM. Aulard, Robinet, earlier Bougeart (but he is a special pleader), and finally Mr. Morse Stephens in England.

(*a*) From the Deed of Sale between Huet de Paisy and Danton, *29th March 1787.*

"Par devant les conseillers du Roi, notaires, &c....

"... Me. Charles-Nicholas Huet de Paisy, écuyer, ancien avocat au Parlement et ès conseils du Roi, demeurant à Paris, Rue de la Tissanderie, paroisse de St. Jean en Grève ... a vendu... a Me. Jacques-Georges Danton, avocat au Parlement, demeurant à Paris, Rue des Mauvaises Paroles, paroisse St. Germain l'Auxerrois ... l'état et office héréditaire d'avocat ès conseils du Roi, faisant un des 70 créés par édit du mois de septembre 1738....

"Ledit Me. Huet de Paisy vend en outre en dit Me. Danton la pratique et clientèle attachées au sous dit office, et consistant en dossiers, liasses, &c....

"Cette vente est faite... par ledit Me. Danton qui s'y oblige d'entrer au lieu... dudit Me. Huet de Paisy.... Moyennant la somme de 78,000 livres... dont 68,000 sont le prix de la pratique et 10,000 les charges accoutumées....

"Ledit Me. Huet de Paisy reconnaît avoir reçu sur les 68,000 livres (prix de la pratique) la somme de 56,000 livres dont autant quittances. Quant au 12,000 livres de surplus Me. Danton promet et s'oblige de les payer dans quatre années du jour de sa reception audit office avec l'intérêt sur le pied du dernier vingt ... (5 per cent.).

"Déclare en outre une ... somme de 11,000 livres lui être légitimement due par.... (*Then follow the details of this debt to the office. Danton consents to pay the 68,000 on condition that he may collect this debt from the client of the office, and specially mentions the fact that, if he is not given full powers to collect, the price shall be not 68,000, but only 57,000 livres*)....

"A ces présentes est intervenu Me. François-Jacques Millot, procureur au Parlement, demeurant à Paris, rue Percée, paroisse St. Séverin. Fondé de la procuration spéciale pour ce qui suit dû, Sieur François Lenoir, maître de poste, et dame Marie-Geneviève Camus, son épouse, de dame Elisabeth Camus, veuve du Sieur Nicolas Jeannet et de demoiselle Anne Camus, fille majeure, demeurant tous à Arcy-sur-Aube, passée en brevet devant Morey notaire à Troyes, en présence de témoins, le deux décembre dernier, l'original de laquelle dûment contrôlé légalisé a été certifié véritable et déposé pour minute à Me. Dosfant, l'un des notaires soussignés par acte du vingt-huit du présent mois. Lequel a, par ces présentes, rendu et constitué lesdits Sieur et dame Lenoir, dame veuve Jeannet et demoiselle Camus, cautions et répondants solidaires dudit Me. Danton envers ledit Me. Huet de Paisy, ce faisant les oblige solidairement avec lui, séparément les uns avec les autres au payement desdites douze mille livres qui restent dues sur ladite pratique, intérêts d'icelle, et au payement des dix mille livres, prix du corps dudit office aux époques ci-dessus fixées, à quoi ledit Me. Millot, audit nom, affecte, oblige et hypothèque sous ladite solidarité, généralement tous les biens, meubles et immeubles, présents et à venir de ses constituants.

"Ledit M. Danton déclare que dans, les cinquante-six mille livres par lui ci-dessus payées, il y a trente-six mille livres qui proviennent des deniers qu'il a empruntés à demoiselle Françoise-Julie Duhauttoir, demoiselle majeure, et quinze mille livres qu'il a empruntées du Sieur François-Jérôme Charpentier, contrôleur des fermes, sous le cautionnement desdits Sieur et dame Lenoir, dame veuve Jeannet et demoiselle Camus.... (*What follows is the receipt in full, signed by Huet de Paisy in December 1789.*)

"Et le trois décembre mil sept cent quatre-vingt-neuf, est comparu devant les notaires à Paris, soussignés, ledit Me. Huet de Paisy, nommé et qualifié en l'acte ci-devant, demeurant à Paris, rue des Couronnes, près de Belleville,—Lequel a reconnu avoir reçu dudit Me. Danton aussi ci-devant nommé, qualifié et domicilié, à ce présent, la somme de treize mille cinq cent livres composée, 1º des douze mille livres qui, sur le prix du traiteé ci-devant, avaient été stipulées payables en quatre années du jour de la réception dudit Me. Danton et sur lesquelles ce dernier devait exercer l'effet de la garantie contractée par ledit Me. de Paisy, par le traiteé ci-devant, relativement à l'affaire du Sieur Papillon de la Grange, de l'effet de laquelle garantie, quoique cette affaire ne soit pas encore terminée, ledit Me. Danton décharge ledit Me. de Paisy; 2º et de quinze cents livres pours les intérêts de ladite somme de douze mille livres échus jusqu'au premier octobre dernier qu'ils ont cessé de courir, de convention entre les parties; de laquelle somme de treize mille cinq cents livres et de toutes choses au sujet dudit traité, ledit Me. Huet de Paisy quitte et décharge Me. Danton;—Dont acte fait et passé à Paris, en l'étude, lesdits jour et an et ont signé."

(b) From the Marriage-Contract of Danton and Mdlle. Charpentier, 9th June 1787.

"Par devant les conseillers du Roi, &c...

"Me. Georges-Jacques Danton, avocat ès conseils du Roi, demeurant à Paris, rue de la Tissanderie, paroisse de Jean en Grève, fils du defunt Sieur Jacques Danton, bourgeois d'Arcis-sur-Aube, et dame Jeanne-Madeleine Camus, sa veuve actuellement épouse du Sieur Jean Reordain négociant audit Arcis-sur-Aube, de présent à Paris, logée chez ledit sieur, son fils, à ce présent, stipulant le dit Me. Danton d'une part.

"Et Sieur François-Jerome Charpentier, controleur des Fermes, et dame Angelique-Octavie Soldini, son épouse... demeurant à Paris, quai de l'École, paroisse de St. Germain l'Auxerrois, stipulant pour... demoiselle Antoinette-Gabrielle Charpentier leur fille majeure... d'autre part.

"... Ont arrêté les conventions civiles dudit mariage ... à savoir...

(*Then follow the names of the witnesses to the contract; their only importance is the idea they give us of the social position of the two bourgeois families concerned. They include Papillon, a surgeon; Dupont, a lawyer of the Châtelet; Duprat and Gousseau, barristers; Wislet, a banker; Mme. Tavaval, widow of a painter to the Court, and so forth.*)...

"... Les biens dudit futur époux consistent:—

"(1°) Dans l'office d'avocat aux conseils... acheté à Me. Huet de Paisy... le 29 mars dernier... moyennant la somme de 68,000 livres qu'il doit en entier soit audit Me. Huet de Paisy, soit aux personnes qui lui ont prêté les sommes qu'il a payées comptant.

"(2°) Dans de terres, maisons et heritages situé audit Arcis-sur Aube et aux environs de valeur de la somme de 12,000 livres....

"Les père et mère de ladite demoiselle lui donnent en dot ... une somme de 18,000 livres... pour s'acquitter de cette somme ils... déchargent ledit Me. Danton de celle de 15,000 livres qu'ils lui ont prêtée, et qui a été employée par lui au payement de partie du prix... attachée à l'office dudit Me. Huet de Paisy....

"Ils ont présentement payé audit Me. Danton les 3000 livres completant les dix huit milles livres.

"Enfin ladite demoiselle future épouse apporte ... la somme de 2000 livres provenant de ses gains et épargnes."

(*The remainder of the document is a statement of the "community property" in marriage and the settlements made in case of decease, the whole regulated by the "custom of Paris." They have no interest for this book.*)

(c) From the Note Liquidating Danton's Place at the Conseils du Roi and his Receipt for the Reimbursement, *8th and 11th of October 1791.* **Held by de Montmorin in his Office.**

"Nous, Louis-César-Alexandre-Dufresne Saint-Léon, commissaire du Roi, directeur général de la liquidation.

"Attendu la remise à nous faite des titres originels... concernant l'office d'avocat ès conseils du Roi dont était titulairé ... le Sieur Georges-Jacques Danton.

"Ledit office liquidé... par décret de l'Assemblée Nationale ... sanctionné par le Roi le deux octobre, à la somme de 69,031 livres 4 sols.... Avons delivré au Sieur Danton... la présente reconnaissance définitive de la dite somme de 69,031 livres 4 sols, qui sera payée a la caisse de l'extraordinaire....

"M. Georges-Jacques Danton, avocat ès conseils, en présence des soussignés... a reconnu... la liquidation... de l'office d'avocat ès conseils du Roi dont été titulairé... ledit Georges-Jacques Danton... savoir.

"(1°) 78,000 livres... principale moyennant laquelle il a acquis l'office le 29 Mars 1787.

"(2°) 240 livres pour le remboursement du droit de mutation.

"(3°) 416 livres 4 sols pour celui du Marc d'or.

"(4°) 125 livres pour celui des frais de Sceau.

"Deduction faite de 9750 pour le huitième du prix retenu.... Au moyen du paisement effectif qui sera fait audit Sieur Danton de ... 69,031 livres 4 sols ... quitte et décharge l'état, M. Dufresne de Saint-Léon et tous autres de ladite somme de 69,031 livres 4 sols ... &c." (*The remainder of the document is the mention of the original deed of sale having been shown to the liquidator, and the correction of certain clerical errors in a former document.*)

VII EXTRACTS FROM DOCUMENTS
Showing the Situation of Danton's Apartment in the Cour de Commerce, its Furniture and Value, &c.

The extracts given below are of a purely personal interest, and do not add anything material to our knowledge of the Revolution. On the other hand, they are of value to those who are chiefly concerned with Danton's personality, and with the details of his daily life. They show what kind of establishment he kept, with its simple furniture, its two servants, its reserve of money, &c., and enable us to make an accurate picture of the flat in which he lived, and of its position. It is from them that I have drawn the material for my description of the rooms in Appendix II. on p. 329. Incidentally, they tell us the profession of M. Charpentier's brother (a notary), give us a view of the religious burial practised in the spring of 1793, show us, as do many of his phrases elsewhere, the entire absence of anti-clericalism in Danton's family as in his own mind, the number of the house, the name of its proprietor, Danton's wardrobe, his wine, the horse and carriage which he bought for his hurried return from Belgium, and many other petty details which are of such interest in the study of an historical character.

Like most of the documents quoted in this Appendix, they are due to the industry and research of Danton's biographer, Dr. Robinet, and will be found in his Memoir on Danton's private life. They are three in number:—

(*a*) The various declarations of Thuiller, the justice of the peace for the Section du Théâtre Français. He put seals upon the doors and furniture (as is the French custom) upon the death of Danton's first wife. This death occurred on February 11, 1793, while Danton was away on mission in Belgium, and the visit of the justice of the peace is made on the following day, the 12th. Danton returns at once, and the seals are removed on various occasions, from the 24th of March to the 5th of April, in the presence of Danton himself, or of his father-in-law, Charpentier.

(*b*) The inventory which accompanied the sealing and unsealing of the apartments.

(*c*) The raising of the seals which were put upon the house after Danton's execution. Interesting chiefly for the astonishing writing and spelling of the new functionaries.

All the three were obtained by Dr. Robinet from the lawyers who have succeeded to, or inherited from, the original "Etudes" where the documents were deposited.

"Cejourd'hui douze février mil sept cent quatre-vingt-treize, l'an deuxième de la République française, dix heures du matin, nous, Claude-Louis Thuiller, juge de paix de la section du Théâtre-Français, dite de Marseille, à Paris, sur ce que nous avons appris que la citoyenne Antoinette-Gabrielle Charpentier, épouse du citoyen Georges-Jacques Danton, député à la Convention Nationale, était décédée le jour d'hier en son appartement, rue des Cordeliers, cour du Commerce, dans l'étendue de notre section, et attendu que ledit citoyen Danton est absent par commission nationale, nous sommes transporté avec le citoyen Antoine-Marie Berthout, notre secrétaire-greffier ordinaire, en une maison sise à Paris, rue des Cordeliers, cour du Commerce, et parvenus à l'entrée de l'escalier qui conduit à l'appartement dudit citoyen Danton, nous avons trouvé des prêtres de la paroisse de Saint-André-des-Arts et le cortège qui accompagnait l'enlèvement du corps de la d. Charpentier, épouse dudit citoyen Danton, et étant montés au premier étage au-dessus de l'entresol et entrés dans l'appartement dudit citoyen, dans un salon ayant vue sur la rue des Cordeliers, nous y avons trouvé et par-devant nous est comparue la citoyenne Marie Fougerot, fille domestique dudit citoyen Danton.—Laquelle nous a dit que ladite citoyenne Antoinette-Gabrielle Charpentier, épouse dudit citoyen Danton, est décédée dans la nuit du dimanche au lundi dernier en l'appartement où nous sommes, par suite de maladie; que ledit Danton est absent par commission de la Convention Nationale; que la mère de ladite défunte Charpentier a envoyé chercher hier son fils encore en bas âge, qu'elle comparante, le citoyen Jacques Fougerot, son frère qui, depuis quinze jours, habite la maison où nous sommes, et la citoyenne Catherine Motin, aussi fille domestique dudit citoyen Danton, sont les seuls qui restent dans l'appartement dudit Danton; que les clefs des meubles et effets étant dans l'appartement où nous sommes ont été prises et emportées par la mère de ladite défunte Charpentier qui était présente à ses derniers moments; qu'elle vient d'envoyer chercher lesdites clefs chez le citoyen Charpentier, qui demeure quai de l'École. Et a signé M. Fougerot.

"A l'instant est comparu le citoyen François-Jérôme Charpentier, demeurant à Paris, quai de l'École, n° 3, section du Louvre.—Lequel nous a représenté un paquet de clefs."

(a) Extracts from the "Apposition des Scellés" by M. Thuiller, Justice of the Peace, on February 12, 1793, and from the "Vacations" by the same.

"Surquoy nous, Juge de Paix susdit ... avons apposé nos scellés comme il suit. Premierment dans le dit salon ayant vu sur la rue des Cordeliers ... dans un petit salon étant en suite ayant même vue ... dans la chambre à coucher étant en suite et ayant même vue....

"Le citoyen Charpentier a fait observer des louis que ledit citoyen Danton avait remis à sa femme pour payer aux mandats de ceux qui viendraient le rejoindre dans la Belgique.—Des scellés ... sur une porte d'un cabinet noir qui communique avec une petite chambre à coucher ... sur la porte d'entrée dudit cabinet noir ... dans une chambre dernière le salon ayant vue sur la cour du Commerce... dans un anti-chambre près de la cuisine ayant vue sur la cour du Commerce.... Dans une chambre de domestiques à l'entresol.... Dans la petite salle audessous.... Dans la salle a manger ayant vue sur la cour du Commerce.... Dans une chambre en suite à toilette.... Dans la cuisine.... Dans la cave....

"Et le 24 février 1793, l'an deuxième de la République française, est comparu devant nous le citoyen Georges-Jacques Danton, député à la Convention ... lequel nous a requis ... de procéder à la levée des dits scellés ... apposés après le décès de la dite dame (*the word "citoyenne" is evidently still a little unfamiliar*) Antoinette Charpentier....

"Ensuite à la réquisition des parties nous nous sommes ... transportés dans une maison, rue du Pæon, Hotel de Tours ... où il a été procédé à l'estimation d'un cabriolet, d'un cheval, d'une jument et harnais.... Le C. Antoine-François Charpentier, notaire, demeurant rue du l'Arbre-Sec, a comparu ... et le C. François-Jerome Charpentier, n°. 3 Quai de l'École...."

(*The rest of the document is a long account of the raising of the seals on various occasions, from March 1 to April 5. It contains nothing of interest.*)

(b) **Summary of the Inventory taken in Danton's House after his First Wife's Death, 25th February 1793.**

"L'an mil sept cent quatre vingt-treize, le deuxième de la République française, le vingt-cinq février, huit heures du matin.

"A la requête de Georges-Jacques Danton, député a la Convention Rationale, demeurant, etc. ... il va être par lesdits notaires a Paris soussignés, procédé à l'inventaire de tous les biens, meubles, &c.... dans les lieux composant l'appartement du premier étage d'une maison située a Paris, rue des Cordeliers, passage du Commerce, appartenant au Sieur Boullenois."

(*Here follow the details of the Inventory, of which I give a summary in English.*)

	Livres
In the Cellar.—Three pieces of Burgundy, 62 bottles of claret, 92 bottles of Burgundy, a small barrel of white wine	600
In the Kitchen.—The usual *batterie de cuisine* of a French household, enumerated in detail, and valued at	208
In the Pantry and Offices of the Kitchen.—A few chairs, a pair of scales, cups, saucers, and so forth	98
In a Bedroom adjoining, and giving on the Cour de Commerce.—The usual furniture; probably a dressing-room. Here was the watch found on Danton after his execution, his writing-table, &c.: the whole, including dishes in the cupboard and a stove	264
In a larger Bedroom giving on the Rue des Cordeliers.—After the usual furniture, a small piano, a guitar, two looking-glasses, and a writing-table	990
In a little Room opening out of this.—Usual furniture of a small study or boudoir, furnished in the white wood of the period	470
In the Drawing-room.—The furniture, mostly grey and white, no piece worth any special mention	992
A large cupboard near the chimney contained some summer clothes put away, and the sword which Danton had worn in the old Bataillon of the Cordeliers. The whole valued at	332

In a little Room looking on an inner court (evidently used as a Library, the list of whose books will be found on p. 380):—Furniture, chiefly bookcases, to the value of	160
In a little Lumber-room.—Three empty trunks and a bed	16
In two little Rooms adjoining.—Furniture (mostly put away)	214

The rest of the inventory mentions the household linen, the clothes, the plate, and the jewels. The summary is as follows:—

Household linen, in all	734
Clothes, including every item	925
Plate, including several wedding presents, marked with initials	291
Knives and forks other than plate	20
Jewellery (including two women's rings, set with brilliants, and a wedding-ring)	509

This gives us the whole value of the furniture, clothing, &c., in the house, and it amounts to a total of just over 9000 livres, that is, about £360. There was £50 in money in the house, which he had left with his wife before going off to Belgium.

(c) Extracts from the Raising of the Seals after Danton's Death.

"L'an trois de la République une et indivisible, cejourd'hui vingt-cinq messidor, neuf heures de matin, à la requête du bureau du Domaine national du département de Paris et en vertu de son arrêté en *datte* du seize susdit mois, signé Rennesson et Guillotin, portant nomination de nous Jourdain, pour en notre qualité de commissaire dudit bureau, à l'effet de nous transporter, assisté de deux commissaires civils de la section du Théâtre-Français, et d'un commissaire de toute autorité constituée qui aurait fait apposer des scellés dans la demeure de feu Jacques-Georges Danton, condamné à mort le seize germinal, an deuxième, par le Tribunal Révolutionnaire établi à Paris, y procéder à la levée d'iceux, et pareillement à celle de ceux dudit bureau du domaine national en ladite demeure, sise rue des Cordeliers, n° 24, le tout en présence du citoyen Charpentier, beau-père dudit feu Danton et tuteur d'Antoine et François-Georges Danton, enfants mineurs dudit *deffunt*, et de la citoyenne feue Antoinette-Gabrielle Charpentier, fille dudit citoyen Charpentier, ayeul et tuteur desdits mineurs; faire ensuite concurremment avec ledit tuteur, et en présence de la citoyenne seconde femme en secondes noces dudit Danton, ou de son fondé de pouvoir, le recollement des meubles et effets dudit *deffunt* sur l'inventaire qui en a été précédemment fait, ensuite mettre le logement cy-dessus désigné, et pareillement les titres et papiers, meubles et effets qui se trouveront à la disposition dudit citoyen Charpentier au nom et qualité qu'il procède, moyennant décharge valable, destituer le gardien préposé à la garde des scellés, duquel remise lui sera faite par extrait de ladite destitution.

"Nous, Jean-Baptiste Jourdain cy-dessus *qualiffié*, demeurant audit Paris, rue de la Liberté, n° 86, section du Théâtre-Français.

"Étant accompagné des citoyens Beurnier et Leblanc, commissaires adjoints au comité civil de la susdite section, requis par nous audit comité civil, sommes ensemble et en vertu de l'arrêté ci-dessus *datté*, transporté en la demeure sus *ditte*, rue des Cordeliers, *ditte* de l'*Écolle* de Santé, audit n° 24, entré de la cour du Commerce, où étant nous avons requis le citoyen Desgranges, gardien, de nous faire ouverture lors de l'intervention dudit citoyen Charpentier et de la citoyenne Gély, seconde femme dudit Danton....

"Clos le présent à deux heures de relevée dudit jour, vingt-cinq messidor, an troisième de la République une et indivisible, et ont lesdits citoyens Charpentier et Gély, ainsi que nos adjoints et ledit citoyen Desgranges, signés le présent avec nous, après lecture, approuvé trente-neuf mots rayés comme nuls, ainsi signés Gély, Charpentier Le Blanc, Desgranges, Jourdain et Beurnier. Plus bas est écrit. Enregistré à Paris, le premier thermidor an 3°. Reçu quatre livres. Signé Caron. Deux mots rayés nuls à la présente.

"Pour *coppie* conforme, délivrée par nous, membres du bureau du Domaine national du département de Paris.

"A Paris, le sept thermidor an troisième de la Republique une et indivisible.

Signé Renesson, Duchatel.

"Collationné à l'original, déposé aux archives de Seine-et-Oise.

L'archiviste,
Sainte-Marie Mévil."

The lack of education in the Robespierrian functionary is worth noting.

VIII CATALOGUE OF DANTON'S LIBRARY

No part of the very scanty evidence we possess upon Danton's personal life and habits is of more value than this little list. It is the small and carefully chosen bookcase of a man thoroughly conversant with English and Italian as well as with his own tongue. He buys a work in the original almost invariably, and collects, in a set of less than two hundred works, classic after classic. He has read his Johnson and his Pope; he knows Adam Smith; he has been at the pains to study Blackstone. It must be carefully noted that every book he bought was his own choice. There were only a few legal summaries at the old home at Arcis, and Danton was a man who never had a reputation for learning or for letters, still less had he cause to buy a single volume for effect. I know of few documents more touching than this catalogue, coming to the light after seventy years of silence, and showing us the mind of a man who was cut off suddenly and passed into calumny. He had read familiarly in their own tongues Rabelais and Boccaccio and Shakespeare.

The following volumes are in English:—

A translation of Plutarch's Lives	8	vols.
Dryden's translation of Virgil	4	"
Shakespeare	8	"
Pope	6	"
Sussini's Letters	1	vol.
The Spectator	12	vols.
Clarissa Harlowe	8	"
A translation of Don Quixote (probably Smollett's)	4	vols.
" " Gil Blas	4	"
Essay on Punctuation	1	vol.
Johnson's Dictionary (in folio)	2	vols.
Blackstone	1	vol.
Life of Johnson	2	vols.
Adam Smith's "Wealth of Nations" (number of vols. given as 23, probably an error)		
Robertson's History of Scotland	2	"
" " America	2	"
Works of Dr. Johnson	7	"

The following are in Italian:—

(The names are not given in Italian by the lawyer, and I can only follow his version.)

Venuti: History of Modern Rome	2	vols.
Guischardini: History of Italy	4	"
Fontanini: Italian Eloquence	3	"
Denina's Italian Revolutions	2	"
Caro's translation of Virgil	2	"
Boccaccio's Decameron	2	"
Ariosto	5	"
Boiardi's edition of the "Orlando Furioso"	4	"
Métastase (?)	8	"
Dalina (?)	7	"
Reichardet (?)	3	"
Davila: History of the French Civil Wars	2	"
"Letters on Painting and Sculpture"	5	"
Il Morgante de Pulci, 12 mo	3	"

The remainder (except one or two legal books and classics) are in French.

Métamorphoses d'Ovide, traduit par Banier, in 4to	4	vols.
Œuvres de Rousseau, 4to	16	"
Maison Rustique, 4to	2	"
Lucrèce, traduit par La Grange, 8vo	2	"
Amours de Daphnis et Chloé, 4to, Paris, 1745		
Œuvres de Lucien, traduit du grec, 8vo	6	"
— de Montesquieu, 8vo	5	"
— de Montaigne, 8vo	3	"
— de Malby, 8vo	13	"
— Complètes d'Helvétius, 8vo	4	"
Philosophie de la nature, 8vo	7	"
Histoire Philosophique, de l'Abbé Raynal, 8vo	10	"
Œuvres de Boulanger, 8vo	5	"
Caractères de la Bruyère, 8vo	3	"
Œuvres de Brantôme, 8vo	8	"
— de Rabelais, 8vo	2	"
Fables de La Fontaine, avec les figures de Fessard, 8vo	6	"
Contes de La Fontaine, avec belles figures, 8vo	2	"
Œuvres de Scarron, 8vo	7	"

— de Piron, 8vo	7	"
— de Voltaire, 12mo	91	"
Lettres de Sévigné, 12mo	8	"
Œuvres de Corneille, 12 mo	6	"
— de Racine, 12mo	3	"
— de Gresset, 12mo	2	"
— de Molière, 12mo	8	"
— de Crébillon, 12mo	3	"
— de Fiévé (sic), 12 mo	5	"
— de Regnard, 12mo	4	"
Traité des Délits, 12mo	1	vol.
Le Sceau Enlevé, 12mo	3	vols.
Tableau de la Révolution Française,	13	cahiers
Dictionnaire de Bayle, folio	5	vols.
César de Turpin, 4to	3	"
Œuvres de Pasquier, folio	2	"
Histoire de France de Velly, Villaret et Garnier, 12mo	30	"
Histoire du P. Hénault, 8vo	25	"
— Ecclésiastique de Fleury, 4to	25	"
— d'Angleterre de Rapin, 4to	16	"
Dictionnaire de l'Académie, 4to	2	"
Corpus Doctorum, 4to	1	vol.
Dictionnaire Historique, 8vo	8	vols.
Abrégé de l'Histoire des Voyages, 8vo	23	"
Dictionnaire d'Histoire Naturelle de Bomard, 8vo	15	"
Virgile de Desfontaines, 8vo	4	"
Œuvres de Buffon, 12mo, figures	58	"
Hérodote de Larcher, 8vo	7	"
Œuvres de Démosthenes et d'Eschyle, par Auger, 4to	4	"
Histoire Ancienne de Rollin, 12mo	14	"
Cours d'Etudes de Condillac, 12mo	16	"
Histoire Moderne, 12 mo	30	"
— du Bas-Empire, 12mo	22	"

Corpus Juris Civilis, folio 2 "
Encyclopédie par Ordre de Matières, toutes les
livraisons excepté la dernière (1).

The whole is valued at just over a hundred pounds (2800 livres).

IX EXTRACTS FROM THE MEMOIR WRITTEN IN 1846 BY THE SONS OF DANTON

This memoir was written by Danton's sons. Both survived him, the one by fifty-five, the other by sixty-four years (1849, 1858). Their fortune was restored to them by the Republic two years after their father's death (13th April 1796). Their guardian, Charpentier (their maternal grandfather), died in 1804; they then were taken in by Danton's mother, Mme. Recordain, who was still living at Arcis. She died in October 1813, a year in which the youngest came of age, and they sold out the greater part of the land in which Danton's fortune had been invested, and appear to have put the capital into one of the new factories which sprang up after the peace. In 1832 we find them partners and heads of a cotton-spinning establishment at Arcis, which they maintain till their deaths. They left, unfortunately, no surviving sons.

The manuscript was written for Danton's nephew, the son of a younger brother. This nephew became inspector of the University of Paris, and lent the MSS. to several historians, among others, Michelet and Bougeart. It finally passed into the possession of the latter, who gave it to Dr. Robinet. This writer printed it in the appendix of the "Vie Privée," from which I take it.

It is not a precise historical document, such as are the official reports, receipts, &c., upon which much of this book depends. Thus, it ignores the dowry of Mdlle. Charpentier and the exact date of the second marriage; it is weak on some points, especially dates, but there attaches to it the interest due to the very quality from which these errors proceed—I mean its familiar reminiscences. While the memory of these men, advanced in life, is at fault in details, it is more likely to be accurate in the motives and tendencies it describes than are we of a hundred years later.

> "Rien au monde ne nous est plus cher que la mémoire de notre père. Elle a été, elle est encore tous les jours calomniée, outragée d'une manière affreuse; aussi notre désir le plus ardent a-t-il toujours été de voir l'histoire lui rendre justice.
>
> "Georges-Jacques Danton, notre père, se maria deux fois. Il épousa d'abord en juin 1787, Antoinette-Gabrielle

Charpentier, qui mourut le 10 février 1793. Dans le cours de cette même année 1793, nous ne pourrions pas indiquer l'époque precise, il épousa, en secondes noces, Mademoiselle Sophie Gély, qui vivait encore il y a deux ans (nous ne savons pas si elle est morte depuis). Notre père en mourant ne laissa que deux fils issus de son premier mariage. Nous sommes nés l'un le 18 juin 1790, et l'autre le 2 février 1792; notre père mourut le 5 avril 1794; nous n'avons donc pas pu avoir le bonheur de recevoir ses enseignements, ses confidences, d'être initiés à ses pensées à ses projets. Au moment de sa mort tout chez lui a été saisi, confisqué, et plus tard, aucun de ses papiers, à l'exception de ses titres de propriété, ne nous a été rendu. Nous avons été élevés par M. François-Jérôme Charpentier, notre grand-père maternel et notre tuteur. Il ne parlait jamais sans attendrissement de Danton, son gendre. M. Charpentier, qui habitait Paris, y mourut en 1804, à une époque où, sans doute, il nous trouvait encore trop jeunes pour que nous puissions bien apprécier ce qu'il aurait pu nous raconter de la vie politique de notre père, car il s'abstint de nous en parler. Du reste, il avait environ quatre-vingts ans quand il mourut; et, dans ses dernières années, son esprit paraissait beaucoup plus occupé de son avenir dans un autre monde que de ce qui s'était passé dans celui-ci. Après la mort de notre grand-père Charpentier, M. Victor Charpentier, son fils, fut nommé notre tuteur. Il mourut en 1810. Quoiqu'il habitât Paris, nous revînmes en 1805 à Arcis, pour ne plus le quitter. La fin de notre enfance et le commencement de notre jeunesse s'y écoulèrent auprès de la mère de notre père. Elle était affaiblie par l'âge, les infirmités et les chagrins. C'était toujours les yeux remplis de larmes qu'elle nous entretenait de son fils, des innombrables témoignages d'affection qu'il lui avait donnés, des tendres caresses dont il l'accablait. Elle fit de fréquents voyages à Paris; il aimait tant à la voir à ses côtés! Il avait en elle une confiance entière; elle en était digne, et, s'il eût eu des secrets, elle les eût connus, et nous les eussions connus par elle. Très souvent elle nous parlait de la Révolution; mais, en embrasser tout l'ensemble d'un seul coup d'œil, en apprécier les causes, en suivre la marche, en juger les hommes et les événements, en distinguer tous les partis, deviner leur but, démêler les fils qui les faisaient agir, tout cela n'était pas chose facile, on conviendra: aussi, quoique la mère de Danton eût beaucoup d'intelligence et d'esprit, on ne sera pas surpris que, d'après ses récits, nous n'ayons jamais connu la Révolution que d'une manière extrêmement confuse...

"Sa mère, d'accord avec tous ceux qui nous ont si souvent parlé de lui pour l'avoir connu, et que notre position sociale ne fera, certes, pas suspecter de flatterie, sa mère nous l'a toujours dépeint comme le plus honnête homme que l'on puisse rencontrer, comme l'homme le plus aimant, le plus franc, le plus loyal, le plus désintéressé, le plus généreux, le plus dévoué à ses parents, à ses amis, à son pays natal et à sa patrie. Quoi d'étonnant, nous dira-t-on? Dans la bouche d'une mère, que prouve un pareil éloge? Rien, sinon qu'elle adorait son fils. On ajoutera: Est-ce que pour juger un homme la postérité devra s'en rapporter aux déclarations de la mère et des fils de cet homme? Non, sans doute, elle ne le devra pas, nous ne convenons. Mais aussi, pour juger ce même homme devra-t-elle s'en rapporter aux déclarations de ses ennemis? Elle ne le devra pas davantage. Et pourtant que ferait-elle si, pour juger Danton, elle ne consultait que les 'Mémoires' de ceux qu'il a toujours combattus?...

"On a reproché à Danton d'avoir exploité la Révolution pour amasser scandaleusement une fortune énorme. Nous allons prouver d'une manière incontestable que c'est à très grand tort qu'on lui a adressé ce reproche. Pour atteindre ce but, nous aliens comparer l'état de sa fortune au commencement de la Révolution avec l'état de sa fortune au moment de sa mort.

"Au moment où la Révolution éclata, notre père était avocat aux conseils du Roi. C'est un fait dont il n'est pas nécessaire de fournir la preuve: ses ennemis eux-mêmes ne le contestent pas. Nous ne pouvons pas établir d'un manière précise et certaine ce qu'il possédait à cette époque, cependant nous disons que, s'il ne possédait rien autre chose (ce qui n'est pas prouvé) *il possédait au moins sa charge*, et voici sur ce point notre raisonnement:—

"(1°) Quelques notes qui sont en notre possession nous prouvent que Jacques Danton, notre grand-père, décédé a Arcis, le 24 février 1762, laissa des immeubles sur le finage de Plancy et sur celui d'Arcis, il est donc présumable que notre père, né le 26 octobre 1759, et par consequent resté mineur en très bas âge, a dû posséder un patrimoine quelconque, si modique qu'on veuille le supposer."...

[Here follow guesses as to how he paid for his place in the *Conseils*. They are of no importance now, as we possess the documents which give us this. The only point of interest in the passage omitted is the phrase, "probably our mother brought some dowry." We know its amount, but the sentence is an interesting proof of the complete dislocation which Germinal produced in the family.]

"Nous allons établir que ce qu'il possédait au moment de sa mort n'était que l'équivalent à peu près de sa charge d'avocat aux conseils. Nous n'avons jamais su s'il a été fait des actes de partage de son patrimoine et de celui de ses femmes, ni, si, au moment de la confiscation de ses biens, il en a été dressé inventaire, mais nous savons très-bien et très-exactement ce que nous avons recueilli de sa succession, et nous allons le dire, sans rester dans le vague sur aucun point, car c'est ici que, comme nous l'avons annoncé, nos arguments vont être basés sur des actes authentiques.

"Nous ferons observer que l'état que nous allons donner comprend sans distinction ce qui vient de notre père et de notre mère.

"Une loi de février 1791 ordonna que le prix des charges et offices supprimés serait remboursé par l'État aux titulaires. La charge que Danton possédait était de ce nombre. Nous n'avons jamais su, pas même approximativement, combien elle lui avait coûté. Il en reçut le remboursement sans doute, car précisément vers cette époque, il commença à acheter des immeubles dont voici le detail:—

"Le 24 mars 1791, il achète aux enchères, moyennant quarante-huit mille deux cents livres, un bien national provenant du clergé, consistant en une ferme appelée Nuisement, située sur le finage de Chassericourt, canton de Chavanges, arrondissement d'Arcis, département de l'Aube, à sept lieues d'Arcis.... Danton avait acheté cette ferme la somme de quarante-huit mille deux cents, ci

48,200 liv.

— — —

A reporter 48,200 liv.

"12 avril 91.—Il achète aux enchères du district d'Arcis, par l'entremise de maître Jacques Jeannet-Boursier....

[Then follows a list of purchases made in the month of April 1791, of which the most important is an extension to the house at Arcis—the total of these is 33,600 livres; and in October 1791 a few acres of land in the town and a patch of wood for 3160 livres. Then follows the sum total.]

"Total du prix de toutes les acquisitions d'immeubles faites par Danton en mil sept cent quatre-vingt-onze: quatre-vingt-quatre mille neuf cent soixante livres, ci

84,960 liv.

"On doit remarquer qu'il est présumable que la plus grande partie de ces acquisitions a dû être payée en assignats qui, à cette époque, perdaient déjà de leur valeur et dont, par conséquent, la valeur nominale était supérieure à leur valeur réelle en argent, d'où il résulterait que le prix réel en argent des immeubles ci-dessus indiqués aurait été inférieur à 84,960 livres.

"Depuis cette dernière acquisition du 8 novembre 1791 jusqu'à sa mort, Danton ne fit plus aucune acquisition importante:—...

[Here then is what Danton left.]

"(1°) La ferme de Nuisement (vendue par nous le 23 juillet 1813);

"(2°) Sa modeste et vieille maison d'Arcis, avec sa dépendance, le tout contenant non plus 9 arpents, 3 denrées, 14 carreaux (ou bien 4 hectares, 23 ares, 24 centiares) seulement, comme au 13 avril 1791, époque où il en fit l'acquisition de Mademoiselle Piot, mais par suite des additions qu'il y avait faites, 17 arpents, 3 denrées, 52 carreaux (ou bien 786 ares, 23);

"(3°) 19 arpents, 1 denrées, 41 carreaux (898 ares, 06) de pré et saussaie;

"(4°) 8 arpents, 1 denrée, 57 carreaux (369 ares, 96) de bois;

"(5°) 2 denrées, 40 carreaux (14 ares, 07) de terre située dans l'enceinte d'Arcis.

"Nous déclarons à qui voudra l'entendre et au besoin nous déclarons *sous la foi du serment*, que nous n'avons recueilli de la succession de Georges-Jacques Danton, notre père, et d'Antoinette-Gabrielle Charpentier, notre mère, rien, absolument rien autre chose que les immeubles dont nous venons de donner l'état, que quelques portraits de famille et le buste en plâtre de notre mère, lesquels, longtemps après la mort de notre second tuteur, nous furent remis par son épouse, et que quelques effets mobiliers qui ne méritent pas qu'on en fasse l'énumeration ni la description, mais que nous n'en avons recueilli aucune somme d'argent, aucune créance, en un mot rien de ce qu'on appelle valeurs mobilières, à l'exception pourtant d'une rente de 100 fr. 5 p. 100 dont MM. Defrance et Détape, receveurs de rentes à Paris, rue Chabannais, n° 6, ont opéré la vente pour nous le 18 juin 1825, rente qui avait été achetée pour nous par l'un de nos tuteurs....

"On pourra nous faire une objection qui mérite une réponse; on pourra nous dire: Vous n'avez recueilli de la succession de votre père et de votre mère que les immeubles et les meubles dont vous venez de faire la déclaration, mais cela ne prouve pas que la fortune de votre père, au moment de sa mort, ne se composât que de ces seuls objets; car sa condamnation ayant entraîné la confiscation de tous ses biens sans exception, la République a pu en vendre et en a peut-être vendu pour des sommes considérables. Vous n'avez peut-être recueilli que ce qu'elle n'a pas vendu.

"Voici notre réponse:—

"Les meubles et les immeubles confisqués à la mort de notre père dans le département de l'Aube et non vendus, furent remis en notre possession par un arrêté de l'administration de ce département, en date du 24 germinal an IV. (13 avril 1796), arrêté dont nous avons une copie sous les yeux, arrêté pris en conséquence d'une pétition présentée par notre tuteur, arrêté basé sur la loi du 14 floréal an III. (3 mai 1795), qui consacre le principe de la restitution des biens des condamnés par les tribunaux et les commissions révolutionnaires, basé sur la loi du 21 prairial an III. (9 juin 1795), qui lève le séquestre sur ces biens et en règle le mode de restitution; enfin, arrêté basé sur la loi du 13 thermidor an III. (31 juillet 1795), dont il ne rappelle pas les dispositions.

"L'administration du département de l'Aube, dans la même délibération, arrête que le produit des meubles et des immeubles qui ont été vendus et des intérêts qui ont été perçus depuis le 14 floréal an III. (3 mai 1795), montant à la somme de douze mille quatre cent cinq livres quatre sous quatre deniers, sera restitué à notre tuteur, en bons au porteur admissibles en payement de domaines nationaux *provenant d'émigrés seulement*. Nous ne savons pas si notre tuteur reçut ces bons au porteur; s'il les reçut, quel usage il en fit; nous savons seulement qu'il n'acheta pas de biens d'émigrés. Il résulte évidemment de cet arrêté de l'administration du département de l'Aube, que dans ce département le produit des meubles et immeubles provenant de Danton et vendus au profit de la République, ne s'est pas élevé au-dessus de 12,405 livres 4 sous 4 deniers. C'était le total de l'état de réclamation présenté par notre tuteur dans sa pétition, et tout le monde pensera, comme nous, qu'il n'aura pas manqué de faire valoir tous nos droits. On peut remarquer que dans cet arrêté il est dit que ces 12,405 livres sont le montant du produit des meubles et des immeubles vendus, et des *intérêts* qui ont été perçus depuis le 14 floréal an III. (3 mai 1795).... Mais si d'un côté on doit ajouter 12,405 livres, d'un autre côté on doit retrancher 16,065 livres qui restaient dues aux personnes qui ont vendu à notre père les immeubles dont nous avons hérité....

"Il est donc établi d'abord que dans le département de l'Aube, le prix des meubles et des immeubles qui ont été vendus n'a pas pu s'élever au-dessus de 12,405 livres; ensuite que notre père, au moment de sa mort, devait encore 16,065 livres sur le prix d'acquisition des immeubles qu'il y possédait....

"Maintenant nous allons citer quelques faits *authentiques* qui pourront faire apprécier la bonté de son cœur. Nous avons vu précédemment que ce fut en mars et en avril 1791 qu'il acheta la majeure partie, on pourrait même dire la presque totalité des immeubles qu'il possédait quand il mourut.

"Voici un des sentiments qui agitaient son cœur en mars et en avril 1791. Il désirait augmenter la modeste aisance de sa mère, de sa bonne mère qu'il adorait. Veut-on savoir ce qu'il s'empressa de faire à son entrée en jouissance de ces immeubles qu'il venait d'acheter? Jetons un regard sur l'acte que nous tenons dans les mains. Il a été passé le 15 avril 1791 (deux jours après la vente faite à Danton par Mademoiselle Piot) par-devant Mᵉ Odin que en a gardé la minute, et Mᵉ Étienne son collègue, notaires à Troyes. Danton y fait donation entre-vifs, pure, simple et irrévocable, à sa mère de six cents livres de rentes annuelles et viagères, payables de six mois en six mois, dont les premiers six mois payables au 15 octobre 1791. Sur cette rente de 600 livres, Danton veut qu'en cas de décès de sa mère, 400 livres soient reversibles sur M. Jean Recordain, son mari (M. Recordain était un homme fort aisé lorsqu'il épousa la mère de Danton; il était extrêmement bon, sa bonté allait même jusqu'à la faiblesse, puisque, par sa complaisance pour de prétendus amis dont il avait endossé des billets, il perdit une grande partie de ce qu'il avait apporté en mariage, néanmoins c'était un si excellent homme, il avait toujours été si bon pour les enfants de Jacques Danton, qu'ils le regardaient comme leur véritable père; aussi Danton, son beau-fils, avait-il pour lui beaucoup d'affection). Le vif désir que ressent Danton de donner aux donataires des marques certaines de son amitié pour eux, est la seule cause de cette donation. Cette rente viagère est à prendre sur la maison et sur ses dépendances, situées à Arcis, que Danton vient d'acquérir le 13 avril 1791. Tel fut son premier acte de prise de possession.

"On remarquera que cette propriété, au moment où Mademoiselle Piot la vendit, était louée par elle à plusieurs locataires qui lui payaient ensemble la somme de 600 livres annuellement. Si Danton eût été riche et surtout aussi riche que ses ennemis ont voulu le faire croire, son grande cœur ne se fût pas contenté de faire à sa mère une pension si modique. Pour faire cette donation Danton aurait pu attendre qu'il vint à Arcis; mais il était si pressé d'obéir au sentiment d'amour filial qu'il éprouvait que, dès le 17 mars 1791, il avait donné à cet effet une procuration spéciale à M. Jeannet-Bourcier, qui exécuta son mandat deux jours après avoir acheté pour Danton la propriété de Mademoiselle Piot. Aussitôt que la maison était devenue vacante et disponible, Danton, qui aimait tant être entouré de sa famille, avait voulu que sa mère et son beau-père vinssent l'habiter, ainsi que M. Menuel, sa femme et leurs enfants (M. Menuel avait épousé la sœur aînée de Danton).

"Au 6 août 1792 Danton était a Arcis; on était à la veille d'un grand événement qu'il prévoyait sans doute. Au milieu des mille pensées qui doivent alors l'agiter, au milieu de l'inquiétude que doivent lui causer les périls auxquels il va s'exposer, quelle idée prédomine, quelle crainte vient l'atteindre? Il pense à sa mère, il craint de n'avoir pas suffisamment assuré son mort et sa tranquillité; en voici la preuve dans cet acte passé le 6 août 1792 par-devant Me Finot, notaire à Arcis. Qu'y lit-on? 'Danton voulant donner à sa mère des preuves des sentiments de respect et de tendresse qu'il a toujours eus pour elle, il lui assure, sa vie durant, une habitation convenable et commode, lui fait donation entre-vifs, pure, simple et irrévocable, de l'usufruit de telles parts et portions qu'elle voudra choisir dans la maison et dépendances situées à Arcis, rue des Ponts, qu'il a aquise de Mademoiselle Piot de Courcelles, et dans laquelle maison sa mère fait alors sa demeure, et de l'usufruit de trois denrées de terrain à prendre dans tel endroit du terrain qu'elle voudra choisir, pour jouir desdits objets à compter du jour de la donation. Si M. Jean Recordain survit à sa femme, donation lui est faite par le même acte de l'usufruit de la moitié des objets qu'aura choisis et dont aura joui sa femme....

"Voici encore une pièce, peu importante en elle-même à la vérité, mais qui honore Danton et qui prouve sa bonté: c'est un pétition en date du 30 thermidor an II. (17 août 1794), adressée aux citoyens administrateurs du département de Paris, par Marguerite Hariot (veuve de Jacques Geoffroy, charpentier à Arcis), qui expose que par acte passé devant Me Finot, notaire à Arcis, le 11 décembre 1791, Danton, dont elle était la nourrice, lui avait assuré et constitué une rente viagère de cent livres dont elle devait commencer à jouir à partir du jour du décès de Danton, ajoutant que, de son vivant, il ne bornerait pas sa générosité à cette somme. Elle demande, en conséquence, que les administrateurs du département de Paris, ordonnent que cette rente viagère lui soit payée à compter du jour du décès et que le principal en soit prélevé sur ses biens confisqués au profit de la République. Nous ne savons pas ce qui fut ordonné. Cette brave femme, que notre père ne manquait jamais d'embrasser avec effusion et à plusieurs reprises chaque fois qu'il venait à Arcis, ne lui survécut que pendant peu d'années.

"La recherche que nous avons faite dans les papiers qui nous sont restés de la succession de notre grand'mère Recordain, papiers dont nous ne pouvons pas avoir la totalité, ne nous a fourni que ces trois pièces *authentiques* qui témoignent en faveur de la bonté de Danton dans sa vie privée. Quant aux traditions orales que nous avons pu recueillir, elles sont en petit nombre et trop peu caractéristiques pour être rapportées. Nous dirons seulement que Danton aimait beaucoup la vie champêtre et les plaisirs qu'elle pent procurer. Il ne venait à

Arcis que pour y jouir, au milieu de sa famille et de ses amis, du repos, du calme et des amusements de la campagne. Il disait dans son langage sans recherche, à Madame Recordain, en l'embrassant: 'Ma bonne mère, quand aurai-je le bonheur de venir demeurer auprès de vous pour ne plus vous quitter, et n'ayant plus à penser qu'à planter mes choux?'

"Nous ne savons pas s'il avait des ennemis ici, nous ne lui en avons jamais connu aucun. On nous a très-souvent parlé de lui avec éloge; mais nous n'avons jamais entendu prononcer un mot qui lui fût injurieux, ni même défavorable, pas même quand nous étions au collège; là pourtant les enfants, incapables de juger la portée de ce qu'ils disent, n'hésitent pas, dans une querelle occasionnée par le motif le plus frivole, à s'adresser les reproches les plus durs et les plus outrageants. Nos condisciples n'avaient donc jamais entendu attaquer la mémoire de notre pere, il n'avait donc pas d'ennemis dans son pays.

"Nous croyons ne pas devoir omettre une anecdote qui se rapporte à sa vie politique. Nous la tenons d'un de nos amis qui l'a souvent entendu raconter par son père, M. Doulet, homme très recommandable et très digne de foi, qui, sous l'Empire, fut longtemps maire de la ville d'Arcis. Danton était à Arcis dans le mois de novembre 1793. Un jour, tandis qu'il se promenait dans son jardin avec M. Doulet, arrive vers eux une troisième personne marchant à grands pas, tenant un papier à la main (c'était un journal) et qui, aussitôt qu'elle fut à portée de se faire entendre, s'écrie: Bonne nouvelle! bonne nouvelle! et elle s'approche.—Quelle nouvelle? dit Danton.—Tiens, lis! les Girondins sont condamnés et exécutés, répond la personne qui venait d'arriver.—Et tu appelles cela une bonne nouvelle, malheureux? s'écrie Danton à son tour, Danton, dont les yeux s'emplissent aussitôt de larmes. La mort des Girondins une bonne nouvelle? Misérable!—Sans doute, répond son interlocuteur; n'était-ce pas des factieux?—Des factieux, dit Danton. Est-ce que nous ne sommes pas des factieux? Nous méritons tous la mort autant que les Girondins; nous subirons tous, les uns après les autres, le même sort qu'eux. Ce fut ainsi que Danton, le Montagnard, accueillit la personne qui vint annoncer la mort des Girondins, auxquels tant d'autres, en sa place, n'eussent pas manqué de garder rancune....

"La France aujourd'hui si belle, si florissante, te placera alors au rang qui t'appartient parmi ses enfants généreux, magnanimes, dont les efforts intrépides, inouïs, sont parvenus à lui ouvrir, au milieu de difficultés et de dangers innombrables, un chemin à la liberté, à la gloire, au bonheur. Un jour enfin, Danton, justice complète sera rendue à ta mémoire! Puissent tes fils avant de descendre dans la tombe, voir ce beau jour, ce jour tant désiré."

Danton.

X NOTES OF TOPINO-LEBRUN, JUROR OF THE REVOLUTIONARY TRIBUNAL

The interest of these notes is as follows:—They are the only verbatim account of the trial which we possess. There are of course the official accounts (especially that of Coffinhal), and upon them is largely based the account in M. Wallon's *Tribunal Révolutionnaire*; but these rough and somewhat disconnected notes, badly spelt and abbreviated, were taken down without bias, and as the words fell from the accused. Topino-Lebrun, the painter, was at that time thirty-one years of age, a strong Montagnard of course; he hesitated to condemn Danton, but was overborne by his fellows, especially by his friend and master David.

These notes were kept at the archives of the Prefecture of Police until the year of the war. In 1867 M. Labat made copies, and gave one to Dr. Robinet, and one to M. Clarétie. Each of these writers has used them in their works on the Dantonites. The original document was burnt when, in May 1871, the Commune attempted to destroy the building in which they were preserved.

There are given below only those portions which directly refer to Danton and his friends.

Au président, qui lui demande ses nom, prénoms, âge et domicile,
il répond: Georges-Jacques Danton, 34 ans, né a Arcis-sur-Aube, département de l'Aube, avocat, député à la Convention. Bientôt ma demeure dans le néant et mon nom au Panthéon de l'histoire, quoi qu'on en puisse dire; ce qui est très sûr et ce qui m'importe peu. Le peuple respectera ma tête, oui, ma tête guillotinée!

Seance de 14 Germinal (13 Avril).

[Westermann having asked to be examined, the judge said it was "une forme inutile."]

Danton. Nous sommes cependant ici pour la forme.

Vest. insiste. Un juge vas (*sic*) l'interroger.

Danton dit: Pourvu qu'on nous donne la parole et largement, je suis sûr de confondre mes accusateurs; et si le peuple français est ce qu'il doit être, je serai obligé de demander leur grâce.

Camille. Ah! nous aurons la parole, c'est tout ce que nous demandons (grande et sincère gaieté de tous les députés accusés).

Danton. C'est Barrère qui est patriote à present, n'est-ce-pas? (Aux jurés)—C'est moi qui ai fait instituer le tribunal, ainsi je dois m'y connaître.

Vest. Je demanderai à me mettre tout nu devant le peuple, pour qu'on me voye. J'ai reçu sept blessures, toutes par devant; je n'en ai reçu qu'une par derrière: mon acte d'accusation.

Danton. Nous respecterons le tribunal, parceque, &c.... Danton montre Cambon et dit: Nous crois-tu conspirateurs? Voyez il rit; il ne le croit pas. Écrivez qu'il a rit....

Danton. Moi vendu? un homme de ma trempe est impayable! La preuve? Me taisais je lorsque j'ai défendu Marat; lorsque j'ai été décrété deux fois sous Mirabeau; lorsque j'ai lutté contre La Fayette?—Mon affiche, pour insurger, aux 5 et 6 octobre! Que l'accusateur (Fouquier-Tinville) qui m'accuse d'après la Convention, administre la preuve, les semi-preuves, les indices de ma vénalité! J'ai trop servi; la vie m'est à charges. *Je demande des commissionaires de la Convention pour recevoir ma dénonciation sur le système de dictature.*

J'ai été nommé administrateur par un liste triple, le dernier, par de bons citoyens en petit nombre [that is, substitute in December 1790].

Je forçai Mirabeau, aux Jacobins, de rester à son poste; je l'ai combattu, lui qui voulait s'en retourner à Marseille.

Où es ce patriote, qu'il vienne, je demande a être confondu, qu'il paraisse, j'ai empêché le voyage de Saint-Cloud, j'ai été décrété de prise de corps pour le Champ de Mars.

J'offre de prouver le contraire [that is, the contrary of St. Just's statement that he was unmolested when he fled to Arcis] et lisez la feuille de l'orateur: Des assassins furent envoyés pour m'assassiner à Arcis, l'une a été arrêté.—Un huissier vint pour mettre le décret à execution, je fuyais done, et le peuple voulut en faire justice.—J'etais à la maison de mon beau-père; on l'investit, on maltraita mon beau-frère pour moi, je me sauvais (*sic*) à Londres, je suis revenu lorsque Garran fut nommé. On offrit à Legendre 50,000 écus pour m'égorger. Lorsque les Lameth ... devenu partisans de la cour, Danton les combattit aux Jacobins, devant le peuple, et demanda la République.

Sous la législature je dis: la preuve que c'est la cour qui veut la guerre c'est qu'elle a [a word illegible] l'initiative et la sanction. Que les patriotes se rallient et alors si nous ne pouvons vous vaincre nous triompherons de l'Europe (?).

—Billaud-Varennes ne me pardonne pas d'avoir été mon secrétaire. Quelle proposition avez-vous faite contre les Brissotins?—La loi de Publicola! Je portai le cartel à Louvet, qui refusa. Je manquai d'être assassiné à la Commune.— J'ai dit a Brissot, en plein, Conseil, tu porteras la tête sur l'echafaud, et je l'ai rappelé ici à Lebrun.

—J'avai préparé le 10 août et je fus à Arcis, parce que Danton est bon fils, passer trois jours, faire mes adieux à ma mere et régler mes affaires il y a des témoins.—On m'a revu solidement, je ne me suis point couché. J'étais aux Cordeliers, quoique substitut de la Commune. Je dis au ministre Clavières, que venait de la part de la Commune, que nous allions sonner l'insurrection. Après avoir réglé toutes les opérations et le moment de l'attaque, je me mis sur le lit comme un soldat, avec ordre de m'avertir. Je sortis à une heure et je fus à la Commune devenue revolutionnaire. Je fis l'arrêt de mort contre Mandat, qui avait l'ordre de tirer sur le peuple. On mit le maire en arrestation et j'y restais (*sic*) suivant l'avis des patriotes. Mon discours à l'Assemblée législative.

—Je faisais la guerre au Conseil; je n'avais que ma voix, quoique j'eusse de l'influence.

—Mon parent, qui m'accompagna en Angleterre [Mergez, a volunteer in 1792, and later a general of Napoleon's] avait dix huit ans.

—Je crois encore Fabre bon citoyen.

—J'atteste que je n'ai point donné ma voix à d'Orléans, qu'on prouve que je l'ai fait nommer.

—J'eûs 400 mille f. sur les 2 millions pour faire la rev., 200 mille livres pour choses secrètes. J'ai dépensé devant Marat et Robespierre pour tous les commissaires des departements. Calomines de Brissot. J'ai donne 6000 a Billaud pour aller à l'armée. Les autres 200 mille, j'ai donné ma comptabilité de 130 mille et le reste je l'ai remis.

... Fabre la disponibilité de payer les commissaires, parce que Billaud-Varenne avait de refusé (sic).

Il n'est pas à ma connaissance que Fabre prêcha la fédéralisme.

—J'embrasserais mon ennemi pour la patrie, à laquelle je donnerais mon corps à dévorer.

Je nie et prouve le contraire. Ce fut Marat qui m'envoya un porte feuille et les pièces, et j'avais fait arrêter Duport. Se a été jugé à Melun, d'après une loi. Liu et Lameth out voulu me faire assassiner. Ministre de la Justice, j'ai fait executer la loi. Pour mon fait, je n'avais pas de preuves judiciaires.

—La guerre feinte n'est que depuis quinze jours, et le Brissotins m'ont pardieu bien attaqué. Lisez le *Moniteur*. Barbaroux a fait demander par le bataillon de Marseille ma tête et celles de Marat et de Robespierre. Marat avait son caractère volcanisé, celui de Robespierre tenace et ferme, et moi, je servais à ma manière.—Je n'ai vu qu'une fois Dumourier, qui me tâta pour le ministre: je repondis que je ne le serais qu'on bruit de canon. Il m'ecrivit ensuite.—Placé là, Kelerman (sic) voulait passer la Marne et Dumourier ne le voulait pas; embarrassé et mon dictateur, je soutins le plan de Dumourier, qui reussit.—Craignant la jalousie de deux généraux, j'envoyai Fabre, etc.... avait vu Vesterman, au 10, le sabre à la main.

—Je talonnai Servan et Laenée; je n'ai connu de plan militaire que celui de Dumourier et de Kelerman, et Billaud fut nommé par moi pour surveiller Dumourier; il eu a rendu compte à la législature et aux Jacobin. Ordre d'examiner ce que c'etait... cette retraite (sic). La Convention a envoyé trois commissaires.

—Moi, ministre, j'embrassais la masse et les détails de la Justice.

—Billaud m'a dit qu'il ne savait pas si Dumourier était un traître; d'ailleurs c'était une surabondance de patriotisme.

—Sur, la Belgique, répète son dire aux Jacobins.

—Le piège des Brissots était de faire croire que nous desorganisions les armées.

—On me refuse des temoins, allons je ne me défends plus!

—Je vous fais d'ailleurs mille excuses de ce qu'il y a de trop chaud, c'est mon caractère.

—Le peuple dechirera par morceaux mes ennemis avant trois mois.

Séance du 15 Germinal (4 Avril).

Hérault. Sur le petit Capet, nie le fait.—Il fut nommé pour la partie diplomatique avec Barrère. Déclare que jamais il ne s'est mêlé de negociations. Nie avoir jamais fait imprimer aucune chose en diplomatie. Deforgues envoya Dubuisson.

Hérault. Je ne conçois rien à ce galimathias. Je me suis opposé a l'envoi de Salavie. C'est un moyen employé par nos ennemis. Envoyé dans le Bas-Rhin par le Comité, je travaillè (*sic*) avec Berthelemy (*sic*) à la neutralité de la Suisse et j'ai sauvé à la Republique un armée de soixante-mille hommes.—Jamais je n'ai communiqué a Proly rien en politique, il n'y en avait pas. Au surplus, il fallait me confronter avec Proly.—J'ai été trompé comme j'a jaie st fois [J. Jay St. Foix] comme la Convention, comme jam bon [this does not mean *ham*, but Jean-Bon St. André], qui le voulait emmener secretaire, comme Colot. Comme Marat, Proly a été porté en triomphe. La Convention, par un decret solennel, a reçu mes explications. Anacharsis me dit vient (*sic*) dîner avec moi, dîner avec Dufourni, etc.... J'ai laissé la veuve Chemineau, etc. L'huillier! c'est à l'instigation de Clootz.

J'ai connu l'abbé guillotiné en troie [that is, in Troyes] (*sic*), dans mon exil il était chanoine et non refractaire. C'est donc un plaisanterie. Il n'etait pas soumis au serment, il m'avait assisté dans mon exil.

Au 14 juillet, à la Bastille, j'ai eu deux hommes tués à mes côtés. Maltraité par mes parents, j'ai voyage, j'ai été incarceré trois semaines en Sardaigne et je suis revenu.

Camille. Lors de sa dispute avec Saint-Just, celui-ce lui dit qu'il le ferait périr,—j'ai denoncé Dumourier avant Marat; d'Orleans, le premier, j'ai ouvert la Revolution et ma mort va la fermer.—Marat s'est trompé sur Proly. Quel est l'homme qui n'a pas eu son Dilon? Depuis le n° 4 [that is, of the *Vieux Cordelier*] je n'ai écris (*sic*) que pour me rétracter. J'ai attaché le grelot à toutes les factions. On m'a encouragé! écrit (*sic*) etc. demasque la faction Hébert, il est bon que quelqu'un le fasse.

Lacroix. Sur la déclaration de Miajenski, rappelle qu'il l'a confondu, que la Convention a été satisfaite, et qu'il n'a pas été accusé pour cela. Il dit: je fus envoyé a Liége pour connaître des reproches faits à la Tresorerie, et vice-versà. Nous étions trois. Jamais je n'ai vu Dumourier en présence de Dumourier (au lieu de Miacrinski?). J'ai dit a Miajenski, sa legion manquant de tout, que je appuyerais devant mes collègues, mais qu'il etait étonnant que sur le pays ennemi ou ne décrétât pas que les troupes étrangerès fussent payées. Je n'ai ni bu, ni mangé avec Dumourier. Vu pendant six à sept jours toujours ensemble. Danton, Gossuin et moi nous avions visité toutes les caisses de la Belgique pour examiner les faits.—Dumourier ne voulait point prêter les mains au decrêt, je me levai et lui déclarai que s'il ne signait pas à l'heure, nous le ferions garrotter, etc. Il signa l'ordre à Ronsin.—La seconde fois nous nous rendîmes à Bruxelles, Dumourier était en Hollande.—Tous mes collègues ont attesté que je preposai de me laisser aller auprès de Dumourier l'observer et le tuer mes collègues ne furent pas de cet avis.

.. 1900 et 600 livres de linge acheté par Brune en présence des collègues, pour la table. Il etait à bon marché. Il dut être chargé sur les voitures que ramenaient en France les restitutions des effets pillés par les generaux, c'était contenu dans une malle à mon addresse. Je l'ai declaré alors au comité de Salut. Alors je l'ai réclamée. Ne confondez pas la première voiture d'argenterie qui fut pillé, elle etait expédiée par tous nos collègues.

Danton. J'avais défié publiquement d'entrer en explication sur l'imputation des 400,000. Il résulte du procès-verbal qu'il n'y a à moi que mes chiffons et un corset molleton. *Le bas,* sommé, m'a donné communication.

Appelé aux Jacobins par mes collègues, je déclarais (*sic*) que le renouvellement était contre-revolutionnaire: ce que portait (*sic*) les pouvoirs des envoyés des sociétés populaires.—Billaud-Varennes m'appuya et je fus chargé de faire la proposition le 11 à la Convention.—Hébert, le lendemain, me dénonça dans sa feuille; et voilà le principe de la calomnie.

Je fus indigné, au 31 mai, de voir un officier qui disait: il n'y a ni Marais, ni Montagne; qui distribuait de l'argent au bataillon de Courbevoie; je ... témoin Panis, Legendre, Robespierre, Pache, Robert-Lindet. Alors je montais (*sic*) à la tribune, etc. ... que nous n'etions pas libres. Au Comité, devant Pache, le 2 juin, j'ai improuvé la mesure maladroite de Hauriot. Nous l'avions prévenu qu'en rentrant nous décréterions les 32, mais que ce n'était pas assez pour la chose publique, qu'il fallait purger la Convention, et a proposé 500,000 livres pour l'armée de Paris que avait sauvé la patrie. Barère s'y opposa. C'est Barère qui a proposé le décret d'accusation contre Hauriot; c'est moi qui ai défendu Hauriot contre cela. Qu'on entende les témoins, la Convention a été trompée.

—J'ai appelé l'insurrection en demandant cinquante revolutionnaires comme moi. La Convention m'appuya, l'avais dit trois mois avant, il n'y a plus de paix avec les Girondins, ai-je la face Hypocrite?

Hanriot crut que j'etais opposé à l'insurrection et alors je lui dis: vas toujours ton train, n'aie pas peur, nous voulons constater que l'Assemblée est libre.

—Je n'ai jamais bu ni mangé avec Mirande, et je proposai à mes collègues de l'arrêter, il s'y opposerent.

Je pris la main à Hanriot et lui dis: tiens bon.

Hérault. C'est moi qui ai découvert l'ordre signé au crayon par Hauriot pour laisser passer la Convention, ainsi, etc.

Philippeaux. Arrivé de mon dépt j'ignorais les intrigues, je fus trompé par Roland. Je me suis rétracté à temps. —Lorsque je m'aperçus du piége tendu dans l'appel au peuple, je montai à la tribune et j'abjurai et votai de suite comme la Montagne. J'ai voté pour Marat (c'est faux, il n'a voté ni pour ni contre). Le Comité ne répondant point à mes lettres, je suis venu ici. Le Comité ne m'a point entendu. Alors, pour remplir mon devoir, j'ai écrit à la Convention, et l'événement, sur Hébert, a prouvé, etc. On a fait contre moi des adresses contre moi (*sic*) etc. On a envoyé de chez moi trois commissaires pour connaître les faits et Levasseur les a fait arrêter.

Vesterman. Lorsque Dumouriez etait en Belgique j'etais au Hollande. Abandonné entre les ennemis, vivant de pillage, je suis arrivé à Envers (*sic*) avec ma legion. Le regiment de cavalrie fut attaqué. Je repoussai l'ennemi.

Accusé de venir deux et trois fois apporter les dépêches de Dumourier à Gensonné.

L'armée manquait de souliers, je fus envoyé par Dumourier au Conseil, et je les rapportai à l'armée.

Dumourier lui montra la lettre de roi de Prusse pour son secretaire, qu'il avait renvoyé, je courus après lui et l'arrêtai de mon pouvoir. Le second voyage pour porter le pli des articles arrêté (*sic*) entre les généraux.

Il a encore été envoyé en otage à Mons, lors de l'evacuation.—Troisième voyage pour amener Malus et d'Espagnac, et porta un pacquet (*sic*) au président du comité diplomatique.—J'ai denoncé au (*sic*) Jacobins, au Comité le fils naturel de Proly, et on me rit au nez. Il engagea au déjeuné (*sic*) pour rétablien Dumourier aux Jacobins. Pourquoi ne m'a-t-on pas appelé lors de la déposition de Miajenski? J'etais ici, mandé à la barre. Dumourier m'a toujours éloigné de lui. A protesté sur la capitulation d'Anvers. Sur le fait de Lille.

Avant d'arriver à Menhem Proly me denonca. Ici, on me mis (*sic*) hors de la loi et un officier prussien me montra la feuille de la Convention et m'engagea à rester, qu'on me payerait, et chercha à m'effrayer en disant que les autres généraux avaient été massacrés. Voir au comité militaire. Je fus à Lille avec ma troupe. Je trouvai Mouton et vint (*sic*) prendre son ordre pour venir à la barre.—J'ai prêté serment avant, à Douai. Le décret du 4 mai dit qu'il n'y avait lieu à m'accuser. J'étais dénoncé aur comités, je ne connais point Talma.

Danton. C'est Barère qui est patriote à present et Danton aristocrate. La France ne croira pas cela longtemps.

Danton, dans la chambre des accusés.—Moi conspirateur? Mon nom est accoté de toutes les institutions révolutionnaires: levée, armée rév., comité rév., comité de salut public, tribunal révolutionnaire, C'est moi qui me suis donné la mort, enfin, et je suis un modéré!

[Topino-Lebrun left no notes of the following day, the 16 Germinal.]

XI REPORT OF THE FIRST COMMITTEE OF PUBLIC SAFETY TREATING OF THE GENERAL CONDITION OF THE REPUBLIC, AND READ BY BARRÈRE TO THE CONVENTION ON WEDNESDAY, MAY 29, 1793

This report is the most important appendix not only to this book, but to any description of the two days that expelled the Girondins. It is here published for the first time, and, though of some length, will well repay the reading for any student of the Revolution.

I have dwelt sufficiently on its importance in the text, and I can dismiss it here with a short introduction.

It is the first great result of the Committee which Danton had helped to create, and of which he was the soul. It is the first step taken by this new organ of government towards that dictatorship to exercise which it had been called into existence. The enormous amount of detailed work necessary to produce it shows us the number of agents which the Committee must have possessed, and their activity, as well as the industry of the members themselves, for it had been at work but eight weeks.

Danton undoubtedly inspired the tone and direction of the report, but the somewhat florid style is Barrère's own. Dr. Robinet thinks, however, that the last pages, from the section on Public Instruction onwards, are in Danton's manner, and M. Boruard would even put it at the section on the Colonies, two pages earlier. Even if this is the case, some sentences at least were put in by Barrère, for they betray his inimitable verbiage, to which Danton was a stranger.

Of the important part the report played in the complicated history of the week May 26-June 3, 1793, enough has been said in the text; it is only necessary to add here that no speech or memoir contains such an indictment of the Girondin misgovernment as is given indirectly by this list of ascertained facts in the condition of France.

The reading of the report is mentioned in the *Moniteur* of May 31, but, contrary to their custom, they did not print it on account of its great length. It seems to have been read in the afternoon from about two to four, just before Cambon's motion was put to the vote. I give the more important passages, about half the full length of the document.

CONVENTION NATIONALE

RAPPORT GÉNÉRAL

SUR

L'ÉTAT DE LA RÉPUBLIQUE FRANÇAISE

Fait, au nom du Comité de Salut Public, dans la seance du mercredi 29 mai, l'an second de la République:

Par Barrère,

Député du département des Hautes-Pyrénées

Imprimé par ordre de la Convention Nationale

Citoyens,—Chargés par les représentans du peuple de leur parler aujourd'hui des grands intérêts qui les rassemblent, et des moyens que nous avons employés depuis deux mois pour le salut de la patrie en péril; nous réclamons d'abord de votre justice de remonter par la pensée, à l'èpoque de notre nomination, et de vous rappeler en quel état se trouvaient alors la République et toute les parties d'administration nationale.

Quoiqu'accablés par la tâche périlleuse et grande que vous nous avez imposée, nous avons dû obéir. Votre confiance, notre zèle et l'amour de notre pays ont dû nous tenir lieu de facultés.

Au-dehors se présentait une guerre terrible à soutenir sur des frontières d'une étendue immense et sur des côtes indéfendues. Audedans, se propageaient des dissensions civiles, portant avec elles les deux caractères les plus funestes, le fanatisme royal et religieux, secouru par des perfidies multipliées dans l'intérieur, et par des intelligences combinées audehors.

What follows is a general indictment of the results of Girondin rule, with special and particular attacks on the Ministry of War and on their fear of responsibility.

On voyait dans toutes nos armées des besoins impérieux et sans cesse renaissans; des secours nuls ou tardifs; des approvisionnemens insuffisans ou de mauvaise qualité et des administrations dévorantes, dont quelques-unes, n'ont d'autre but réel que d'agrandir la fortune de beaucoup d'agioteurs et de quelques capitalistes. Dans nos ports des travaux ralentis et une inertie coupable; partout des trahisons ourdies et des coalitions préparées; des états-majors à refaire ou à épurer; des armées à organiser ou à improviser; des fonctionnaires civils et militaires à surveiller ou à remplacer; des forces à créer sur tous les points menacés par les troubles; des armes à fabriquer; des canons à fondre; la marine à créer; l'esprit public à remonter avec énergie; l'anarchie à attaquer; la discipline à rétablir; des mouvemens contra-révolutionnaires à comprimer et un cahos d'intérêts, de plaintes, de passions, d'abus, de prétentions et de préjugés à débrouiller, au milieu d'une correspondance journalière et centuplée par ces circonstances actuelles. Quel vast génie ou quel courage inépuisable il eût fallu pour répondre tout à coup à des circonstances aussi extraordinaires ou pour dominer des évènemens aussi imprévus? Nous avons borné notre tâche à parcourir d'abord toutes les parties du gouvernement provisoire, et à nous frayer ensuite une route au milieu de cet assemblage énorme de forces et de résistances, de bons et de mauvais principes.

Le premier obstacle qui s'est présenté à nous, est venu du changement dans le ministère de la guerre, que avait précédé notre établissement.

Le second obstacle était dans le ministère de la marine négligé, anéanti même, par un série de ministries royaux, et dont nous avons été forcés de faire changer le chef et plusieurs adjoints.

Là s'est rompue, pour nous, la chaîne des opérations de ces deux départemens, les plus importans dans un temps de guerre de terre et de mer; et nous nous sommes vus privés, tout à coup, de toutes les ressources de l'expérience. Nous n'avons pu recueillir, dans l'agglomération des affaires de cette partie de l'administration publique, que des états inexacts ou des lumières incertaines.

Un aperçu des délibérations du conseil exécutif nous a montré, d'un côté, des travaux incohérens qui n'ont pu avoir aucune espèce de succès à cause des évènemens qui les dominaient; de l'autre, des négligences funestes et des fautes graves que les évènemens suivants ont mieux fait sentir. Depuis les bouches de l'Escaut, ouvertes par un usurpation de la puissance souveraine, jusqu'aux extrémités de la Méditerranée, qui ont été le théâtre de nos revers, et de la versatilité ministérielle, nous n'avons vu ni cette suite d'opérations qui assurent les succès, ne cette prévoyance des mesures qui diminuent les revers. Point d'ensemble, point de conceptions vastes, point de vues hardies, point de plan arrêté, point d'énergie, et partout la terreur de la responsabilité, marchant en avant du ministère, tandis qu'il s'agit de marcher fièrement à la liberté, sans regarder en arrière.

Au mois d'octobre, la résistance à l'ennemi avait donné des conceptions et des forces au conseil exécutif.

Les succès du mois de novembre ont amolli le conseil. Jemmappes a été pour les ministres (sic) la Capoue qui a détruit son énergie et atténué ses travaux.

Le département de l'intérieur, machine trop lourde, trop compliquée pour un homme, quand il serait plein de talens et de moyens d'exécution, avait refroidi pendant longtemps l'esprit public et engourdi les corps administratifs. Il était impossible que la main d'un seul homme pût remuer cette machine énorme surchargée de details, d'une administration immense, d'opérations mercantiles dont le succès est douteux, dont le résultat exige de grands sacrifices, et dont le secret appelle la défiance. La seule ressource que ce ministère disproportionné pouvait trouver, était dans les administrateurs départementaires, dont la plupart, insoucians sur les travaux qui leur sont confiés, négligent de correspondre, ou dont la conduite exagérée et sans mesure leur faisait méconnaître toute subordination.

Le département de la guerre, dans lequel chaque ministre a porté ses préjugés et ses assertions, ses routines et ses haînes; le ministère de la guerre désorganisé sans cesse par la fréquente mutation de ses agens et par la diversité de leurs principes ou de leurs opinions, présentait et présent encore un chaos inextricable, des abus sans nombre, et une impuissance réelle dans tout homme que ne serait pas né très actif dans la manière d'ordonner et entreprenant sur tous les moyens de défense.

In what follows note the hand of Danton, almost his phraseology in the second paragraph.

Le ministère des affaires étrangères, couvert d'obscurités politiques, ne pouvant avoir au milieu des défiances produites par la révolution et des mouvemens irréguliers de la guerre, ni fixité dans les opérations, ni vues suivies, ni projets déterminés, ni secrets dans les plans, a saisi seulement le fil de quelques affaires importantes, et redonne maintenant de l'activité aux moyens nombreux dont l'intérêt de plusieurs gouvernemens prépare le succès.

C'est de l'audace dans les conceptions politiques, c'est de l'ensemble dans les mesures, c'est de la promptitude dans les moyens d'exécution, que dépend la diplomatie nouvelle d'un peuple qui naît à la liberté.

Again, a direct attack on the Girondins, especially in the characteristic phrase, "the paralysis of honesty."

> Le ministère de la marine enrayé longtemps dans les opérations par une probité paralytique, et par des sous-ordres inexpérimentés ou suspects, n'ayant donné ni protection au commerce, ni défense pour nos côtes, ni moyens au succès de la course, ni activité aux grands armemens dans nos ports, ni approvisionnemens suivis pour les flottes, reprend sous un ministre nouveau son activité, nous promet une défense et une marine....

Here again is a half-concession to the Girondins, which was part of the policy I have spoken of in the text.

> Le conseil exécutif en sent lui-même la nécessité: et nous lui devons la justice de dire, que ne se dissimulant pas cette caducité politique, amenée par les circonstances, par des dénonciations multipliées, et par la presqu'impossibilité de tenir régulièrement le gouvernail au milieu de la tempête; le conseil exécutif désire et sollicite le renouvellement du ministère....
>
> DE L'ETAT MILITAIRE.
>
> Pressés entre la nécessité de pourvoir sans délai aux besoins des armées, et l'impossibilité d'approfondir en si peu de temps des plans généraux, nous avons recherché d'abord des armes....
>
> Des arrêtés du comité ont ordonné l'envoi des commissaires pour dénombrer subitement les armes et les canons qui se trouvaient dans les fabriques et les manufactures nationales, et pour les faire transporter aux armées et dans les départemens les plus dénués de ce genre de secours. Saint-Etienne, Ruel, Mont-Cénis, Indret, Toulouse, Lyon, Charleville, Sedan, Maubeuge, ont reçu des ordres pressants sur cet objet....
>
> Divers arrêtés ont ordonné le transport de vieilles armes qui se trouvent dans diverses fabriques ou arsenaux, pour les faire raccommoder dans les diverses villes dont la population offrait des ouvriers, et surtout dans les départemens limitrophes des pays révoltés....
>
> Les ministres et les assemblées nationales ont mis trop peu d'importance à la manufacture de Saint-Etienne, depuis le commencement de la révolution.

Les ouvriers brûlaient du désir de travailler pour la république, mais le prix de l'arme ayant toujours été fixé au-dessous des déboursés du fabricant, ils ont travaillé pour les corps administratifs, dont la concurrence a augmenté la valeur. Le fer et le salarie de l'ouvrier sont augmentés de prix.

Des commissaires du pouvoir exécutif viennent de requérir tous les fabricans de porter à la commission de verification, toutes les armes qui sont en leur pouvoir, pour être expédies pour Bayonne, Perpignan, et Tours. Les livraisons se font chaque jour.

Les commissaires s'occupent de redonner la plus grande activité à la manufacture d'armes de Saint-Etienne, qui secondée par le patriotisme des ouvriers et de la municipalité, portera la fabrication à quatre ou cinq cents fusils ou pistolets par jour.

Il y a à Tulle un grand nombre d'armes à réparer, le comité en a fait distribuer à plusieurs départemens méridionaux; le ministre de la marine donne de l'activité à la manufacture de Tulle, pour armer nos marins. Dans ce moment, le commissaire Bouillet, envoyé par le conseil exécutif, est a Tulle, pour accélérer la fabrication des armes nécessaires à la marine, et pour connaître l'état des vieilles armes qu'on a entassés dans ce dépôt....

The following passages indicate the motives of what was to be the Terror, a system based, of course, upon the necessity for commissariat.

VIVRES.

Les vivres sont aussi nécessaires que les armes; on se plaint dans quelques armées organisées trop lentement, ou improvisées trop à la hâte, pour que tout ce qui leur était nécessaire fût préparé, et ces plaintes sont justes; nous accélérons l'approvisionnement des armées, autant qu'il est en nous, par le ministre et les administrations qui en dépendent. La latitude des pouvoirs donnés à vos comités, peut suppléer la faiblesse du ministère de la guerre l'insuffisance de ses agens, et la malveillance ou la torpeur de ses régies. Il est cependant des obstacles éprouvés par les régisseurs et par leurs agens, à cause des craintes propagées sur le manque de subsistances, et le comité s'est occupé de faire cesser ces obstacles.

L'administration chargée de l'approvisionnement des places de guerre a présenté au comité des états de situation rassurante sur l'approvisionnement des places les plus menacées: il lui a montré les dispositions générales prises pour les fournitures de subsistances dans toutes les divisions. Il en résulte que les évènemens imprévus de la Belgique, en ramenant subitement l'ennemi sur nos frontières, ont contrarié des calculs et nous ont privé des approvisionnements faits d'après un autre système; mais le comité presse les directeurs de pourvoir aux approvisionnements, et avertit sans cesse le ministre des autres besoins des armées, à mesure que ces besoins se démontrent ou que les plaintes nous parviennent. Un changement dans cette administration, dont vous nous avez renvoyé l'examen, mérite toute notre sollicitude, et se trouve être la suite inévitable des changements perpétuels dans le ministère de la guerre; changement qui entraîne celui de ses principes et de ses moyens.[165]

Le partie de l'habillement et de l'équipement, qui a coûté tant de trésors à la nation, a été mal fournie, mal administrée, et pillée dans la Belgique avec autant d'impudeur que de trahison.

Les fournisseurs, plus avares que patriotes, ont distribué à toutes les armées des étoffes de mauvaise qualité. Un force de prodigalité nationale payait les habits à l'avarice agioteuse qui les fournissait, et le soldat, au milieu des fatigues et des perils de la guerre, était sans habits ou en portait qui n'étaient pas de long usage.

Ces jours derniers il a défilé devant vous un détachement de braves soldats du régiment ci-devant Conti, qui allait vers les départemens révoltés. On n'aurait pas présenté au plus petit prince d'Allemagne, ou au plus pauvre de l'Italie, des troupes aussi mal vêtues; elles ont paru devant les représentans d'une nation qui dépense pour la guerre, chaque mois, plus de millions que plusieurs rois de l'Europe n'ont de revenu dans un an....

L'armée des Ardennes, réunie à celle du Nord, se forme sous les regards de commissaires actifs, et les recrues y abondent à un point que votre comité a cru devoir les faire refluer vers l'armee du Nord.

The next allusion is interesting as showing us the appreciation of what was to be the reinforcement of the army of Sambre-et-Meuse.

L'armée de la Moselle a pris des positions avantageuses. Réunie à celle du Rhin, elles annoncent que Mayence pourra devenir le tombeau des hordes prussiennes. L'esprit est bon dans cette armée, distinguée par la discipline, et les recrues s'y encadrent tous les jours.

On s'occupe à faire camper et exercer l'armée des Alpes, dont le recrutement est entièrement effectué. On fortifie tous les points de défense, et on augmente la garnison des places. Les recrues nombreuses qui y sont arrivées ont fourni un excédant de vingt-un mille hommes; vous avez disposé de huit mille contre les départemens révoltés. Les treize mille restans renforceront l'armée d'Italie, diminuée pour servir à la défense de la Corse, formeront une réserve ou renforceront l'armée des Pyrénées orientales.

Le département du Mont-Blanc s'est empressé d'organiser plusieurs bataillons et de prouver ainsi son attachement à la République; ils réclament des armes, et nous espérons qu'avec des moyens mis déjà en activité ils seront bientôt armés.

La révolte de Thonnes est appraisée et les coupables jugés. C'était la mêche d'une mine préparée sous le Mont-Blanc, et dont l'explosion était combinée avec la prochaine attaque des Piémontais et des Autrichiens.

L'armée d'Italie se prépare à défendre ce que la valeur et la liberté ont conquis à Nice. Mais des agitateurs y ont causé de la fermentation, comme dans l'armée des Alpes; ils y tenaient des propos injurieux à la Convention nationale; ils y parlaient de royauté, et se servaient du moyen de la paye en assignats pour altérer le bon esprit des troupes; des alarmes ont été jetées sur les subsistances, dont le comité s'occupe dans ce moment.

Le général de l'armée d'Italie a pris les moyens propres à découvrir les agitateurs et à les faire conduire au tribunal extraordinaire.

L'armée des Pyrénées a été la plus négligé et la plus mal pourvue en armes et en munitions, et c'est contre les troupes les plus féroces et les plus fanatiques qu'elles doivent défendre les plus belles contrées de la République.

Aussi nous sommes accablés tous les jours par des relations malheureuses qui ne sont que le triste résultat de la négligence de deux anciens ministres de la guerre qui n'ont jamais su penser qu'il existât une armée des Pyrénées....

The whole of the above is an interesting example of the detailed methods of the Committee, with its reiteration against the Girondin management of the war. It continues in much the same spirit.

Du côté de l'Océan, la trahison de quelque chef des Miquelets et la lâcheté d'une partie du régiment vingtième ont livré un point de la frontière. Une terreur panique produite par le mot de trahison et par des malveillans semés dans les petits camps formés sur l'extrême frontière, a désorganisé le peu de force qui y étaient arrivées, a découragé ceux qui y accouraient et forcé d'abandonner Andaye et tout le pays qui se trouve entre la rivière de Nivelle et la frontière pour ne former qu'un seul camp à Bidarre.

La discipline à rétablir, le courage à relever, étaient les premiers besoins de cette armée.

Nos commissaires se sont vus forcés d'établir provisoirement un règlement sévère de discipline. Ils nous disent que l'ennemi abat partout l'arbre de la liberté, fait les incursions sur les maisons des patriotes dans la partie française abandonnée; mais les habitans des campagnes ont le courage de ne pas obéir aux requisitions du général espagnol.

Il paraît qu'il n'est fort que de notre faiblesse, et que si des secours d'armes et d'artillerie sont portés a nos frères, notre territoire sera bientôt évacué. Le commandement de Bayonne est confié au patriote Courpon, et la citadelle de Saint-Esprit est défendue par des républicains. Vingt canons et quatre compagnies des canonniers de Paris y ont été envoyés en poste, et doivent avoir secouru cette frontière le 14 de ce mois; le camp de Bidarre se forme avec succès.

La division de l'armée des Pyrénées en deux grands parties, nous donnera plus de force pour une défense active au besoin: la terre y produit des bataillons d'hommes libres; nous leur devons des secours abondans, car ils ont été oubliés jusqu'à présent. On eût dit, en voyant l'état de ces frontières, que le complot était prêt, que la force devait envahir le Nord, tandis que la perfidie et l'indéfense livreraient le Midi. Mais l'intrépidité et l'enthousiasme des Méridionaux pour la liberté, est un obstacle invincible au succès des négligences ministérielles, des trahisons intérieures, et des succès que le perfide Pitt a promise à l'Espagne. Le camp se forme devant Bayonne et il a repris du terrain du côté d'Andaye; l'armée reprend l'attitude qui convient à des phalanges républicaines, et l'artillerie commence à y arriver avec des provisions.

L'affaire de la Vendée n'a été envisagée trop longtemps que comme une affaire de police, ou une querelle élevée dans un coin d'un département.

There follows a further indictment based upon a special case. L'armée des côtes n'a jamais existé; l'état-major n'avait pas même été formé; quelques chefs militaires avaient été envoyés avec de faibles moyens et de simples requisitions. On avait donné des ordres pour que des cadres y fussent transportés; ils ont été arrêtés dans leur marche par la crainte ou l'impuissance momentanée que nous avait donné la trahison de Dumouriez. Des recrues y ont été rassemblées, sans y trouver ni cadres, ni armes, ni un nombre suffisant d'officiers généraux....

Voilà l'état où se trouvaient les armées au 10 mai, époque à laquelle le comité a demandé inutilement la parole....

Then a summary, the detail of which is well worth following.

VOICI LE DERNIER ÉTAT.

Il arrive des troupes à Bayonne ainsi que des canons. Le camp qui était à Bidard entre Bayonne et Saint-Jean de Luz a été porté, depuis vendredi, entre Saint-Jean de Luz et Andaye.

L'armée des Pyrénées orientales qu'on espérait, au moyen des recrutemens, mettre en état de contenir au moins l'Espagnol, a essuyé presque consécutivement deux échecs qui compromettent la sûreté de cette partie de la frontière. Cette défaite n'est due qu'à la gendarmerie nationale; mais un exemple prompt et sévère mettra un terme à cette lâcheté ou à cette trahison.

Aux Alpes nous venons d'être menacés d'une attaque très prochaine exécutée par des forces très considérables, surtout dans la partie du Var, débouché par lequel l'ennemi peut menacer aussi Marseille et Toulon. Le comité de salut public a dû prendre la seule mesure qui était en son pouvoir; il a ordonné au général Kellerman, le seul qui eût une connaissance suffisante des points de défense et de nos moyens militaires dans cette partie, de s'y rendre avec la plus grande diligence, afin de prévenir, s'il est possible, les malheurs que le moindre retard pourrait amener. Le général de l'armée d'Italie a paru craindre que la cour de Naples ne vienne renforcer la coalition dans le midi. Mais le ministre des affaires étrangères vient de communiquer des dépêches qui détruisent ces nouvelles.

Kellerman s'est fait précéder par un courrier extraordinaire qui a porté à ses lieutenans les ordres préparatoires des opérations auxquelles l'ennemi peut le forcer. Ce général, investi de votre confiance et de celle des troupes, ne pouvait être remplacé. On vous avait annoncé d'abord qu'il se rendrait dans la Vendée; mais les avantages remportés un instant sur les révoltés, et la certitude de la prochaine arrivée de Biron dans les départemens révoltés, ont du faire changer la première destination de Kellerman. L'armée d'Italie a des subsistences assurées pour quelque temps. On a pris des mesures pour la mettre à l'abri de la disette.

Au Rhin, une action qui n'a servi qu'à la destruction des hommes, sans avancer les affaires d'aucun parti, y laisse les choses à peu près dans la même situation qu'auparavant, avec cette différence, que le changement de général qui a été en partie forcé, peut influer sur nos succès. Il est bon d'observer que nos armées dans cette partie se trouvent avoir en tête des forces les plus manœuvrières, et commandées par les généraux les plus accrédités de l'Europe.

Nos généraux, au contraire, portés au commandement pour la première fois, ne peuvent avoir la même habitude et les mêmes avantages que ceux auxquels les grands mouvemens de guerre sont familiers. Les approvisionnemens dans cette partie et les subsistances sont bien assurés.

Dans le Nord, notre situation est très alarmante, et la Convention doit connaître tous ces maux; elle a besoin d'être instruite par le malheur, et de sentir les tristes effets de ses divisions.

Notre armée, repoussée entre Combrai et Bouchain, quittant son camp de Famars pour prendre plus loin celui de Coefar, abandonnant à leurs propres forces Condé et Valenciennes, perdant ses communications avec Douay et Lille d'un côté, et de l'autre avec Maubeuge et le Quesnoy, est exposée à de nouveaux revers, si la présence du général Custine, qui a dû y arriver le 25, ne lui rend pas la discipline qui lui manque et la confiance sans laquelle il n'est point de succès à obtenir dans la guerre.

Si les efforts de ce général ne sont pas promptement secondés par l'union des représentans du peuple, la Convention doit s'attendre à tomber dans une situation plus embarrassante qu'au moment où, pendant la dernière campagne, les esclaves allemands entraient en Champagne, et menaçaient Paris et la liberté. Alors d'heureux hasards, ou plutôt cette destinée qui semble conduire la France, ont disparaître des dangers aussi imminens; mais doit-on compter sur une nouvelle faveur de l'aveugle fortune? ne devons-nous pas craindre une nouvelle invasion, et pouvons-nous nous flatter que toutes nos villes imiteront le généreux dévouement de celle de Maubeuge, qui nous écrit le 26 de ce mois:—"Ici on bat la générale dans cet instant: on a envoyé une partie de notre garnison dans la Vendée; nous restons; nous déjouerons nos ennemis extérieurs et intérieurs, ou nous mourrons libres. La ville sautera si nos murs abattus permettent à l'ennemi de souiller notre enceinte."

Quant aux besoins de cette armée du Nord, peut-être croira-t-on difficilement que, malgré toutes nos dépenses, la demande qui vient d'être faite au comité, qui a été arrêtée par le commissaire général de l'armée du Nord, et visée par les commissaires de la Convention, monte à la somme de 49 millions.

L'armée qui doit anéantir les révoltés s'organise; il arrive un grand nombre de bataillons à Tours; les postes de la rive droite de la Loire se renforcent, et l'on fait défiler des troupes en poste. Si les rebelles menacent cette rive, ils sont hors d'état d'exécuter ce project; leurs forces ce divisent, mais ils rentrent dans les pays couverts. Les principaux chefs des révoltés sont subordonnés aux prêtres; c'est une véritable croisade; mais les habitans des campagnes commencent à se lasser de cette horrible guerre, et murmurent.

D'un autre côté, on nous écrit qu'il est parti, depuis notre dernier succès, un courier de Bruxelles à Londres, pour engager le cabinet de Saint-James à accélérer un armement tendant à porter sur les côtes de Bretagne des troupes, des armes, des munitions, et à vomir sur nos rivages un corps considérable d'émigrés de Jersey et Guernsey.

Le transfuge Condé a envoyé à Jersey tous les émigrés bretons pour être déposés sur nos côtes et y seconder un des rejetons de la famille de nos tyrans. On se plaignait presque partout des commissaires des guerres ce corps essentiel des armées va être changé, amélioré sur de nouvelles bases et épuré par des choix patriotiques.

Quant à la suppression de la paie en numéraire, toutes les armées de la République l'ont reçue sans peine; ils sacrifient à chaque instant leur vie à la liberté, comment s'occuperaient-il d'intérêts pécuniaires? mais aussi ils ont droit à plus de surveillance pour les approvisionemens et pour les subsistances. Quelques compagnies de l'armée d'Italie seulement ont montré de la résistance; mais les agitateurs seront déjoués par la surveillance qui y a été établie, et par les soins de vos commissaires.

Dans le choix des officiers généraux, nous avons dû quelquefois obéir aux défiances populaires et aux dénonciations individuelles; mais c'est là un des maux attachés à la révolution, qui use beaucoup d'hommes, qui en éloigne un plus grand nombre, et qui présente plus d'accusations que de ressources. Sans doute après les odieuses trahisons qui ont affligé et qui affligent encore la république et désorganisé deux fois les armées, on peut, on doit même devenir défiant et soupçonneux; mais la ligne qui sépare la défiance et la calomnie, est trop facile à dépasser; et si la dénonciation juste est une action civique, l'accusation intéressée est la honte de nos mœurs et la ressource de la haine....

Le comité, pour ne rien négliger dans cette terrible partie de la guerre, a interrogé des militaires instruits; il s'est environné de leur expérience pour faire un plan de guerre auquel se rattacheraient des plans de campagne pour chacune des armées. Jusqu'à présent la guerre de la liberté a été faite sans plans, sans suite, sans prévoyance même; il est plus que temps de tracer les limites dans lesquelles la guerre sera soutenue, dans quelle partie elle sera défensive, dans quelle autre elle sera offensive, assigner à chaque armée la portion de frontières qu'elle a à défendre, les points des ennemis qu'elle doit attaquer ou couvrir.

In what follows regarding the Navy, we see the attempt of the Committee, which we know was foredoomed to failure, but which was a fine one, to meet the English Power. The "error," as English critics have called it, of rapidly putting in new officers was an unfortunate necessity.

DE LA MARINE.

Ici nous devons accuser ce système perfide de Bertrand et de ses semblables, qui, depuis plusieurs années, semblait préparer, de concert avec l'Angleterre, l'abaissement de la France, et assurer à nos plus constans ennemis l'empire des mers.... C'est par la réunion des forces navales, que nos ennemis out espéré d'attaquer plus sûrement notre indépendance, et de nous dicter de lois. Quoique par cette coalition l'on ait tenté aveuglement de faire passer la balance du pouvoir à une nation maritime, déjà trop puissante pour l'intérêt du continent; ... quoique, par la désorganisation passagère de notre marine, par le dénuement de nos ports, par le ralentissement des travaux, on ait espéré de changer la destinée de la république française, ne craignons pas que l'on parvienne à faire rétrograder la plus belle des révolutions.

La surveillance constante du comité, le zèle du ministre, et le dévouement de l'armée navale qui se forme, feront oublier tant de trahisons ou de négligences, mais les moyens ne peuvent être que lents.

Des expéditions hardies, et confiées à des hommes courageux sont préparées; les plaintes du commerce ont été enfin entendues d'après le dernier rapport du ministre, le cabotage va être protégé dans l'Océan par 34 canonnières, 12 corvettes, 18 lougres, cutters ou avisos, et dans la Méditerranée, par 18 corvettes, ou cannonières et 5 avisos, indépendamment des frégates dont il est inutile de faire connaître le nombre et les stations, sans trahir les intérêts de la défense de la république....

Il existe beaucoup d'officiers capables; l'abaissement des vains préjugés qui séparaient l'armée commerciale de l'armée navale, nous assure des ressources, mais il faut les surveiller et punir sévèrement la désobéissance ou la malversation; avant de choisir les officiers, examen et impartialité; après le choix, confiance entière, mais responsabilité impérieuse. Le secret accompagnera nos opérations, si les inquiétudes du commerçant ou les soupçons du zèle patriotique ne viennent pas les altérer ou les contrarier; les corps civils ne doivent pas s'immiscer dans le secret des opérations navales, ou bien nos ennemis le sauront bientôt, et nous vaincrons sans nous laisser sortir de nos ports. Le comité s'occupe des lois répressives que la discipline navale réclame avec plus d'intérêt que jamais. Une grande force s'organise dans les ports de la Méditerranée, qui par notre position, doit être le canal de navigation du commerce français....

On s'occupe des moyens les plus propres à retirer les colonies de l'état malheureux où elles se trouvent, depuis qu'une cour perfide voulait faire la contre-révolution en France, par les malheurs de l'Amérique; et si, à côté de nous, des Français veulent se rappeler qu'ils descendant de Guillaume, tous les calculs de la politique insulaire pourront être dérangés.

Le comité ne peut vous offrir aucun résultat précis et détaillé dans ce moment; il serait même impolitique de la publier. Mais tout se prépare, et quoique les forces de la république soient très inférieures à celles des ennemis coalisés, le patriotisme les dirigera de manière à rappeler le courage des filibustiers, et les exploits des Bart et des Dugay-Trouin....

In foreign affairs we have the Dantonesque idea of pitting the Powers against one another, which, unfortunately for France, fanatics who were in power later abandoned. The remark on the impolitic nature of the decree of the 19th of December should be specially noted: it comes direct from Danton.

DES AFFAIRES ÉTRANGÈRES.

... Le ministère anglais est forcé, malgré son influence et son orgueil avare, de voir Dantzick passer au pouvoir de la Prusse, sans réclamation; de voir la Pologne, se partager sans sa participation; et de se compromettre vis-à-vis la morale et l'esprit public de la nation anglaise. Aussi l'intrigant Pitt, qui ne peut se dissimuler que le ministre qui fait la guerre, traite rarement de la paix, surtout chez une nation éclairée et trompée sur cette guerre par l'astuce profonde de son gouvernement, ne cesse d'invoquer sans cesse auprès de la ligne, la cause générale des cours....

Le comité a cherché à resserrer le lien qui attache déjà, par les relations commerciales, le peuple suisse et le peuple français; et l'ambassadeur que la Suisse a reçu suit constamment le vœu témoigné par la Convention nationale, de s'allier avec les gouvernemens justes et les peuples libres.

Nous apprenons que les peuples neutres et amis reçoivent avec reconnaissance le décret du 15 avril, qui eut servi plus utilement la liberté, s'il eut été d'une date plus reculée, et si le décret impolitique du 19 décembre n'eût pas donné un nouveau prétexte à la perfidie des cours étrangères.

Ce décret par lequel vous aviez déclaré que la France ne souffrirait jamais qu'aucune puissance semêlât de sa constitution et de son gouvernement, et qu'à son tour, elle ne s'immiscerait en rien sur les autres gouvernemens; ce décret a augmenté subitement le nombre de nos partisans dans la Suisse; et le témoignage d'un peuple simple et libre a son prix auprès des républicains.

Des négociations d'alliance ne sont plus des chimères pour la France libre. Il est des puissances qui ont senti que l'élévation ou la ruine d'une nation intéressent toutes les autres et que celles même qui sont le plus éloignées du théâtre de la guerre, sont souvent les victimes de leur modération ou de leur indifférence. Il est des alliés pour leur propre sûreté, peuvent soutenir nos intérêts, avec autant de chaleur que de bonne foi. Il est d'autres alliances que la politique doit vous assurer, et d'autres qui seront dues en grande partie à votre état républicain; votre commerce ne peut que s'en féliciter.

L'Italie voit avec intérêt le signe de la République arboré dans ses villes, si j'excepte les villes gouvernées encore par un prêtre et par la maison d'Autriche....

Nous apprenons que la Russie a fait faire à la Porte la demande officielle du passage d'une flotte, menaçant de regarder le refus qu'on pourrait lui en faire comme une déclaration de guerre. La réponse a été dilatoire et sera négative; les usurpations de la Russie trouveront enfin des bornes. C'est à la politique européenne à aider le maître des Dardanelles à les poser....

Une suite de coalisation faite contre la France, avait jeté des obstacles à l'arrivée des chebecs à Alger. On voulait encore vous aliéner cette puissance, amie de la République; mais nous recevons la nouvelle que le dey a reçu, avec le plus vif intérêt, les deux chebecs que la République lui a renvoyés, et qu'il a témoigné les dispositions les plus favorables à la France....

There follows the French criticism of the Alien Bill.

> Un bill infâme, qui insulte à l'humanité et aux droits des nations, a été promulgué par le gouvernement anglais, et traduit en espagnol à Madrid et dans les villes hanséatiques, par les intrigues de l'ambassadeur anglais. Ce bill, dont la haine pour la convention a dicté les clauses horribles contre les Français, vous portera sans doute à user du droit de représailles. Le comité vous fera un rapport sur cet objet, ainsi que sur les diverses mesures à prendre contre la gouvernement anglais. Des agens nombreux sont disséminés dans l'Europe, pour connaître les complots de nos ennemis au dedans et au dehors, et pour s'assurer des véritables amis de la république.
>
> Il résulte enfin, de toutes nos relations, que Dumouriez et ses aides-de-camp, chassés du Stoutgard, n'ont pas reçu un meilleur accueil à Vursbourg, par ordre de l'électeur, quoique évêque. Ainsi, les traîtres ne trouvent pas d'asyle même chez les despotes à qui ils se sacrifient.

Matters concerning the Interior are comparatively vague, for here the Committee wished to compromise with the Gironde; but they are strong against civil war.

DE L'INTÉRIEUR.

> ... Quant aux approvisionnemens des armées et de la marine, les commissaires éprouvent des obstacles, en ne pouvant, d'après le dernier décret, acheter que dans les marchés.
>
> Le comité s'est occupé ensuite de sonder la plaie et de connaître la source de toutes les agitations qui tourmentent la république.
>
> Ici des vérités doivent nous être déclarées; car, vous êtes sur le bord d'un abyme profond, et la Convention Nationale, au milieu de ses divisions, a oublié qu'elle marchait entre deux écueils, et qu'elle était conduite par l'aveugle anarchie.
>
> D'un côté, l'exécrable plan de la guerre civile, secondé par l'Anglais, et sans doute dirigée de Londres, de Rome et par des agens correspondans à Paris, étendait ses ramifications sur toute la France, et principalement dans les pays qui étaient, depuis la révolution, infestés de fanatisme, ou qui avaient été le théâtre des troubles fanatiques et des complots contre-révolutionnaires.

D'un autre côté, une alarme générale s'est répandue parmi les propriétaires d'un territoire de vingt-sept mil de lieues quarrées, et ces craintes ont eu pour base des motions exagérées, des journaux feuillantisés et des propos sauguinaires; le mécontentement né de nos discussions personnelles a altéré la confiance, mais vous êtes nécessaires: les aristocrates, redoutant les passions des patriotes, ont excité les hommes énergiques contre les modérés auxquels ils se rattachent sourdement; ils ont préparé des mouvemens contraires....

Marseille, Bordeaux, Lyon, Rouen, prenez garde, la liberté vous observe sur votre marche dans la révolution; elle ne vous croira jamais contraire à ses vues; mais craignez d'être stationnaires dans le mouvement de l'opinion publique; écrasez avec nous les révoltés, les anarchistes et les brigands; mais aussi craignez le modérantisme et les intrigues de l'aristocratie qui veut vous effrayer sur les propriétés et sur le commerce, pour vous redonner des nobles, des prêtres et un roi....

Au moment où le comité a été formé, presque partout les administrations trop faibles ou trop au dessous des circonstances se ressentaient de l'influence meurtrière des passions particulières qui y correspondaient...

A Lyon, l'aristocratie a un foyer plus profond qu'on ne peut le penser; elle est secondée par l'égoïsme et l'indifférence....

Mais les campagnes et les villes de department de Rhône et Loire, surtout Villefranche, présente un autre esprit, et là surtout paraissent ces signes heureux, là sont entendues ces acclamations énergiques qui caractérisent le patriotisme.

A Marseille où tout annonce l'ardeur républicaine, à Marseille où l'on voit presque à chaque pas un arbre de la liberté ou une inscription civique, à Marseille où le pain, égal pour tout et de mauvaise qualité, se vend sept sols la livre, cette calamité est supportée sans murmurer, où l'on entend des plaintes contre les traîtres, les égoïstes, les intrigans; où les seuls malheurs dont on soit afflige sont ceux qui frappent la République entière, Marseille a éprouvé des convulsions violentes; mais si la répression de quelques excès de la démagogie a fait craindre à de bons citoyens que le modérantisme ne prévalût, le républicanisme n'en triomphera pas moins des passions individuelles. Croyons que cette grande cité ne dégénérera pas de sa renommée.

Nous avons à gémir sur des excès commis à Avignon et à Aix; ce qui s'est passé d'irrégulier à Toulon, relativement aux officiers de la marine, vous sera rapporté quand le comité aura fait le travail de cette partie.

Le meilleur esprit règne dans ce moment à Perpignan; la vieille antipathie nationale contre l'Espagnol, y réchauffé l'esprit républicain que le département des Pyrénées orientales avait déjà montré avec tant d'énergie le 21 Juin 1791.

Bayonne se rattache aux bons principes. Les trahisons lui ont donné de l'énergie; mais si cette place est dans ce moment menacée de près par l'ennemi, le zèle des républicains méridionaux la défendra contre les ennemis du dedans et du dehors.

Bordeaux ne cesse de fournir à la liberté et a ses armées des trésors et des soldats; elle va défendre en même temps les Pyrénées et les Deux-Sèvres.

Les intentions manifestées à Nantes ne se ressentent pas assez de l'enthousiasme civique qui doit animer dans ce moment tous les citoyens. Ses moyens auraient pu être plus efficaces; il y a du mécontentement et des craintes sur les effets des divisions intestines.

A Orléans, l'esprit public s'améliore, depuis que l'aristocratie a été frappée par la loi révolutionnaire; mais cette ville a le droit d'obtenir que les procédures faites par les commissaires soient bientôt jugées, les coupables punis et les bons citoyens rassurés.

Dans le département de l'Allier, une correspondance interceptée a fait découvrir des traînes contre la liberté, elles étaient ourdies par des prêtres déportés, de concert avec leurs agens à Moulins. Les corps administratifs, qui vivent dans la plus heureuse harmonie, ont mis en lieu de sûreté les ci-devant que leur conduite avait rendus suspects et les y font garder avec soin et humanité, jusqu'à ce que la République n'ait plus rien à craindre de ses ennemis intérieurs et de ces enfans dénaturés. Le peuple a partout applaudi à cette énergie de ses magistrats, et il les a secourus, parce que le peuple veut franchement la liberté.

A Roanne, le modérantisme est réduit en système, et dans la crise où nous sommes, cette apathie politique est le plus grand fléau de la République, qui ne peut s'établir que par le développement de toute l'énergie nationale.

A Tain, dans le département de la Drôme, des patriotes, que n'étaient qu'aisés dans leur fortune (le patriotisme se trouve rarement avec la fortune), se sont cotisés, et, de concert avec le Maire, ont fait, sans y être contraints par la loi, mais par amour pour la patrie, une cotisation, dont le produit a été employé à fournir du pain à un prix modéré, pour les citoyens peu fortunés. C'est ainsi que dans les provinces méridionales, les mœurs et l'humanité font plus que les lois et le cœur des riches dans les grandes cités....

A Tours, l'administration d'Indre et Loire, apprenant que les ennemis étaient à Loudun, et marchaient à Chinon, a pris la résolution, par un mouvement civique et spontané, de se transporter toute entière au milieu des dangers qui les menaçaient, et décidée à s'ensevelir sous les ruines de la ville, plutôt que de se rendre. Une commission y est restée. Loudun a demeuré sans défense. Quelques aristocrates en ont été heureusement chassés.

Poitiers, trop influencé par des fanatiques et par des hommes de l'ancien régime, peut donner des espérances aux révoltés, et déjà l'administration nous a fait craindre le résultat du mauvais esprit d'une partie de ses habitants, malgré l'énergie connue des patriotes qu'elle renferme.

Paris qu'on accuse sans cesse, qu'on agite presque toujours, tantôt par des crimes, tantôt par des intrigues, tantôt par des passions personnelles, tantôt par des intérêts secrets et étrangers, et plus souvent encore par l'action prolongée ou l'exaltation des passions révolutionnaires; Paris, réceptacle de tant d'étrangers, de tant de conspirateurs, doit attirer vos regards.

The following passage on the Commune of Paris is noteworthy for its non-committal character, in keeping with the attempt to get rid of the Gironde, if possible, without an insurrection.

Vous devez contenir le conseil général de la commune de Paris dans les limites que l'unité et l'indivisibilité de la République exigent et que la loi lui prescrit. C'est à vous qu'il appartient seul de dominer toutes les ambitions politiques, de détruire toutes les usurpations législatives; c'est à vous de répondre à la France du dépôt de pouvoir qui vous a été religieusement confié.

Vous devez aviser aux movemens inégaux et anarchiques que des intrigans font passer dans plusieurs sections peuplées de bons citoyens, et aux mouvemens aristocratiques qu'on pourrait cependant leur communiquer.

Vous devez surveiller également le moderantisme qui paralyse tout et prépare la perte de la liberté, et les excès le la démagogie dont les émigrés et les ambitieux, déguisés parmi nous, tiennent le secret et le prix journalier.

L'esprit des habitants de Paris est bon, malgré les vices de l'égoïsme, de l'avarice et de l'apathie d'un certain nombre de ses habitans. L'amour de la liberté, qu'on a voulu tant de fois y neutraliser, sort victorieux de toutes les épreuves; et nous pensons que Paris n'appartiendra jamais qu'à la liberté; Paris qui à détruit le trône, ne souffrira pas qu'aucune autorité usurpe le pouvoir national, qui est la propriété de tous, et qui est le véritable lieu de tous les départemens.

Malgré toutes les intrigues par lesquelles on a cherché à empêcher Paris de prononcer son patriotisme en marchant contre les révoltés, chaque section a fourni ou s'occupe de fournir son contingent pour former douze ou quatorze bataillons de mille hommes....

I quote certain portions which show the fear of the Committee, so often justified, with regard to foreign intrigue.

FINANCES.

Il a agioté le numéraire pour avilir l'assignat; il a fait hausser les changes, par ses opérations à la bourse.

DISSENTIONS CIVILES.

Il a alimenté le fanatisme de la Vendée; il a fourni des hommes, des armes et des munitions.[166]

ROYALISME.

C'est l'anglais, qui a combiné les regrets et ravivé les espérances, par l'excès du républicanisme qu'il a fomenté, par les motions des lois agraires, dont il cherchait ensuite à faire imputer les projets à des patriotes connus....

GÉNÉRAUX.

Celui qui avait acheté Arnold en Amérique, a acheté Dumouriez en Europe, et il a dû traiter de même les militaires qui n'aiment pas la république....

DE L'ORGANISATION SOCIALE.

L'anglais a semé l'effroi dans l'âme des propriétaires par des motions sur les partages des terres, et dans le cœur des commerçans par le pillage des magasins....

L'anglais a imaginé de la bloquer, de l'affamer, de l'incendier dans ses ports, dans ses édifices publics; de détruire son industrie; il armé tour à tour l'aristocrate contre le patriote, et le patriote contre l'aristocrate; enfin, le peuple contre le peuple, espérant que le spectacle de nos troubles ôtera au peuple anglais le courage de détruire chez lui le despotisme royal.

PERTE DE PARIS.

C'est au cœur que les assassins frappent; c'est sur les capitales que les conquérans dirigent leurs coups. On ne pouvait perdre Paris par les armés; on a voulu perdre Paris par les départemens; on y a semé dès terreurs pour le ruiner par la fuite des propriétaires et des riches; on a semé des idées de suprématie, pour séparer, pour isoler les départemens de Paris.

The danger of civil war and vigorous methods for meeting it are the subject of the passages that follow.

DIVISION DU TERRITOIRE.

L'anglais enfin a espéré diviser la France pour la morceler ou la ruiner. Dans son délire, il a espéré de voir une monarchie impuissante s'établir dans le nord, et des républiques misérables et divisées se former dans le midi.

J'ai dévoilé le gouvernement britannique; il n'est plus à craindre.

Dans un très grand nombre de départemens on a procédé à la réclusion des personnes notoirement suspectes d'incivisme et soupçonnées d'entretenir des intelligences avec les émigrés et les contre-révolutionnaires. On en accuse généralement les prêtres et les moines, les émigrés rentrés impunément sur notre territoire, et les correspondants qui les soutenaient de leurs fortunes et de leurs espérances.

On a dû prendre des mesures sévères, alors que tous les aristocrates correspondaient à la Vendée, et que des lettres interceptées annonçaient un rassemblement à Nantes.

Des arrestations nombreuses ont dû être la suite de ces méfiances, de ces trahisons disséminées dans toute la France; l'autorité, dans les temps de révolution, a plus d'yeux et de bras que d'entrailles; mais le législateur doit à tous les citoyens cette justice exacte qui vient régulariser les premiers mouvemens et faire statuer sur la liberté individuelle avec les précautions que les circonstances peuvent admettre. Vous devez abattre également toutes les aristocraties et toutes les tyrannies; vous devez approuver vos commissaires s'ils ont bien fait, les blâmer et les punir s'ils ont violé les droits des citoyens. Le comité pense que le comité de législation et de sûreté générale doivent proposer incessamment une loi qui règle le mode de jugement de la légitimité de ces arrestations, et qui renvoie aux tribunaux les coupables ou laissât en réclusion ceux qui ne sont que notoirement suspects.

Le département de l'Ain voit l'esprit public se rétablir parmises habitans.

La conspiration qui a éclaté dans l'Ouest semblait se montrer dans les départemens de l'Ardèche, du Gard, de la Haute Loire et du Cantal; mais les administrateurs et vos commissaires sont parvenus à les réprimer. Ces troubles de la Lozère ont un caractère plus fort; mais le patriotisme de ce département et de ses voisins y mettra bientôt un terme.

Les tribunaux ont sévi contre les coupables; nous avions craint que vos commissaires n'eussent dépassé leurs pouvoirs dans le département de l'Ardèche, et nous les aurions déféré à votre sévère justice pour donner l'exemple de la punition de ceux qu'on affecte d'appeler des proconsuls, pour empêcher le bien qu'ils peuvent faire ou en empoisonner les résultats; mais un décret avait déjà mis hors de la loi les coupables complices de Defaillant.

La trahison de Dumouriez que tout annonce avoir eu des branches très étendus, a été un trait de lumière; elle a frappé es administrations et les citoyens d'un coup électrique. Tous nos moyens ont centuplé par cet évènement destiné à les paralyser; mais de tous les maux préparés insensiblement dans les départemens frontières comme dans le centre,

comme au milieu de nous le plus grand, le plus effrayant par ses progrès, est la marche imprévue des contre-révolutionnaires nobiliares, sacerdotaux et émigrés qui, du fond de la Vendée et du Morbihan remontent la Loire, menacent nos cités de l'intérieur, et emploient à la fois, des moyens de terreur et de persuasion....
Les révoltés ont plusieurs corps de rassemblement. Le principe qui s'était porté a Thouars, était, suivant les uns, de quinze mille suivant la dernière relation envoyée par un de nos commissaires, il était de vingt à vingt-cinq mille hommes armés, partie de piques, partie de fusils; ils traînent avec eux, treize pièces de canon, selon les uns, et d'après le dernier succès de Thouars, trente pièces d'artillerie.

Ils sont commandés par des ci-devant nobles et accompagnés par des prêtres; toutes leurs femmes leur servent d'espions; ils se battent pour des fiefs et des prières. Les agriculteurs fanatiques combattent avec fureur et ne pillent pas; ils composent la moitié de la troupe.

Un quart est composé de gardes-chasses, d'échappés des galères et de faux sauniers. Ils pillent, dévastent, égorgent, et sont bien dignes de leurs chefs.

L'autre quart est formé d'hommes pusillanimes ou indifférens, que la violence force de marcher, mais qui, à la première défaite des brigands, se retireraient, et forment, pour ainsi dire, la propriété du premier occupant. C'est à la liberté de s'en emparer par des succès.

Il n'y a que les émigrés, les ci-devant, et les prêtres qui voudraient mettre de l'ordre dans les rassemblemens, et de la tactique dans cette guerre. Ils paient, les rebelles deux tiers en numéraire.

Les chefs connus sont les ci-devant de Leseur, Laroche-Jacquelin, Beauchamp, Langrenière, Delbecq, Baudré-de-Brochin, Debouillé-Loret, un abbé appelé Larivière. Domengé est colonel-général de la cavalerie; Demenens et Delbecq commandent l'armée catholique-royale.

Le comité a pourvu journellement par des arrêtés pressans, à ce que cette guerre intestine fût efficacement comprimée....

Déjà l'armée s'organise à Tours; une commission centrale est établie à Saumur; déjà des troupes de ligne ont dépassé Paris pour s'y rendre, et le renfort considérable que le comité avait requis, est en route pour s'y rendre. Les voitures des riches, les équipages du luxe, auront du moins servi une fois à la défense de la patrie et de la liberté. Une armée est dirigée en poste sur les rives de la Loire. C'est ainsi qu'un des plus fameux guerriers du nord alla écraser en 1757 les autrichiens à la bataille de Liffa ou Leuten, avec une armée arrivée en poste sur le champ de bataille....

Le comité prépare un rapport sur les agens périodiques de l'opinion publique, et sur les arrêtés violateurs de la liberté de la presse.

Tel est le tableau de l'intérieur de la république, d'après les rapports et la correspondance des commissaires et des corps administratifs. Nous devons le terminer par une réflexion sur les commissaires, dont on cherche trop à effrayer les citoyens, et même plusieurs membres de la convention....

The influence of Cambon is apparent in what follows.

DES CONTRIBUTIONS PUBLIQUES.

Quant aux contributions, rien ne prouve mieux le désir de voir fonder la République, et de voir renaître l'ordre social le paiement des impositions, au milieu des ruines et de débris de l'ancien gouvernement; s'il y a de l'arriéré, ce n'est que par les fautes des administrations qui n'ont pas encore terminé la confection des rôles; quelques-unes ont arrêté tout envoi de fonds. Mais un moyen de salut public, appartient à cette partie de l'administration, c'est de vous occuper sans relâche, des lois concernant les contributions publiques, de l'accélération de la vente des biens d'émigrés, et des maisons ci-devant royales, objets qui semblent encore attendre leurs anciens et coupables possesseurs; et des moyens de retirer de la circulation, une certaine masse d'assignats. Vous devez cette loi au peuple, qui a vu s'augmenter par une progression effrayante et ruineuse, le prix des subsistances; vous le devez à tous les créanciers de la République et à tous ceux qu'elle salarie, afin de rétablir la balance rompu trop rapidement, par la masse énorme de cette monnaie. La portion du peuple qui mérite avant toutes les autres l'attention de ses représentants, est celle qui souffre tous les jours au surhaussement du prix des denrées.

Les contributions indirectes, perçues au milieu des mouvemens de la révolution, et des défiances semées sur son succès, par des mécontens et des ennemis publics, alimentent abondamment le trésor national. Déjà dans les trois derniers mois de Janvier, Février et Mars, la perception des impôts indirects excède de plusieurs millions l'estimation qui en a été faite. Le total des trois mois, se porte a 52,182,468 livres en y comprenant 5,400,000 livres, de l'adjudication des bois. Que serace dans un temps de paix et de prospérité? Quelle confiance la République doit avoir de ses forces et de ses moyens?

Nous avons vu avec regret, parmi les produits de l'imposition indirecte, des droits qui devraient être inconnus à des peuples libres, des droits de bâtardise et de déshérence, et que les sauvages de l'Amérique repousseraient.

From henceforward Danton's hand is apparent throughout the report. Some matters on the Constitution and on Public Construction, which have little to do with the insurrection of June 2nd, have been omitted, but the Dantonian policy of framing a constitution which should reconcile enemies is printed in full.

DES COLONIES.

Nous ne disons encore rien des colonies, quoique nous ayons reçu des mémoires et des vues sur cet objet important et malheureux, d'où dépend la prospérité publique, et l'agrandissement de la marine française. Peut-être eût-il mieux valu de ne pas plus parler dans les assemblées nationales, des colonies que de la religion, jusqu'à ce que la révolution du continent eût été à son terme. Perfectionner dans ces contrées lointaines le commissariat civil, adoucir les effets du régime militaire, détruire insensiblement le préjugé des couleurs, améliorer par des vues sages et des moyens progressifs le sort de l'espèce humaine dans ces climats avares, etait peut-être la mesure la plus convenable; mais la révolution a fait des progrès terribles sous ce soleil brûlant. Saint-Domingue est aussi malheureux que les îles des vents sont redevenues fidèles, et ses malheurs ne paraissent pas rès de leur terme.

On examinera un jour s'il est des moyens de rattacher les colonies à la France, par leur propre intérêt, c'est-à-dire, par la franchise absolue de leur commerce avec nous, et une disposition générale des droits perçus sur le commerce étranger, dans ces mêmes colonies. De pareilles lois qui nous défendraient mieux que des escadres, demandent d'être méditées.

Cette partie de l'intérêt national, doit être traitée séparément et avec une forte sagesse; le comité est chargé de préparer en attendant ce rapport, des mesures propres à diminuer les maux que cette belle colonie souffre encore.

DE LA FORCE PUBLIQUE DE L'INTÉRIEUR.

Elle se ressent partout de l'anarchie que règne. Là, elle délibère; ici, elle agit au gré des passions. Disséminée dans toutes les sections de l'empire, elle semble avoir une versatilité de principes et d'actions, qui peut effrayer la liberté. Dans une ville, les citoyens riches et les égoïstes, se font remplacer; défendre ses foyers, semble être encore une corvée plutôt qu'un honneur, une charge plutôt qu'un droit. Dans une autre cité, le service public frappe des artisans peu aisés ou des ouvriers, qui ont besoin du repos de la nuit, pour le travail qui alimente leur famille, il est plus que temps d'effacer ces lignes de démarcation intolérable dans un régime libre. La nature seule a décrit des différences; elle est dans les âges; les jeunes citoyens depuis seize ans jusqu'à 25, sont les premiers que la patrie appelle; moins occupés et plus disponibles, c'est à eux de voler aux premiers dangers. Cette première force est-elle insuffisante (car il ne faut pas penser à la défection) l'autre âge plus fort et plus sage, présente à la société ses moyens, c'est l'âge de 25 à 35; la troisième classe sera de 35 à 45; la dernière réquisition doit frapper tout ce qui peut porter les armes. Alors, la société appelle à son secours, tous ceux qui partagent la souveraineté; une exception favorable se présente pour les pères nourrissant leur famille du produit de leur travail. Une exception contraire doit frapper les célibataires et les hommes veufs sans enfans.

C'est à la législation et à la morale à flétrir ceux qui ne paient cette dette ni à la nature ni à la République.

C'est ainsi qu'il convient aux Français, d'organiser le droit de réquisition. Cet exemple est sorti des besoins de la liberté, dans les terres américaines. La réquisition est l'appel de la patrie aux citoyens; cet appel peut être fait par les généraux, quand la loi le leur a confié momentanément, et dans les cas de guerre; cet appel peut être fait par le pouvoir civil dans toutes les autorités constituées, et encore plus par les assemblées nationales, qui sont à la fois pouvoir civil, législatif et national.

Le comité a pensé qu'il devait présenter un mode uniforme, de requérir la force publique dans toutes les parties de la République, et de la part de toutes les autorités, afin que chaque fonctionnaire et chaque citoyen, connaisse l'étendue de son pouvoir ou de son obligation....

D'ailleurs, on trouverait plusieurs avantages à borner ainsi la constitution aux articles nécessaires.

(1°) Une plus grande espérance qu'elle sera acceptée par le peuple.

(2°) Une plus grande espérance encore que les citoyens ne demanderont point si promptement, une réforme de la constitution.

(3°) On détruirait par cette seule résolution, même avant que la constitution fût faite, une partie des espérances de nos ennemis, parce qu'alors, ils commenceraient à croire que la Convention donnera une constitution à la France, ce que jusqu'à présent ils ne croient pas.

En effet, il est difficile de ce tromper dans des articles généraux importants, sur ce qui convient véritablement à la nation française, et l'on n'a pas à craindre ces difficultés, cette presqu' impossibilité d'exécution qui, si on se livre aux détails, pourraient faire désirer la réforme d'une constitution, d'ailleurs bien combinée.

On pourrait donc proposer de borner la constitution à ces articles essentiels, dans le nombre desquels on sent que doit être compris le mode de réformer la constitution, lorsqu'elle cessera de paraître, à la majorité des citoyens, suffisante pour le maintien de leurs droits; et si l'assemblée adoptait cet avis, elle chargerait quatre ou cinq de ses membres, adjoints au comité de salut public de lui présenter un plan de constitution, borné à ces seuls articles, et combiné de manière que ces articles puissent être soumis immédiatement à la discussion.

Le travail de ce comité ne prendrait qu'une semaine, et l'assemblée pourrait suivre ses discussions sur la constitution, car rien ne serait plus facile que de placer dans ce plan, les points déjà arrêtés par la Convention.

Ce travail même serait utile, quand même l'assemblée voudrait se livrer ensuite à plus de details:

(1°) Parce qu'il en résulterait un meilleur ordre de discussions;

(2º) Parce qu'on aurait toujours alors, un moyen d'accélérer le travail, selon que des circonstances impérieuses l'exigeraient.

C'est d'après cette idée simple que nous vous proposerons de décréter que la Convention charge une commission, composée de cinq de ses membres, adjoints au comité de salut public, de lui présenter dans le plus court délai, un plan de constitution, réduit aux seuls article qu'il importe de rendre irrévocables par les assemblées législatives, pour assurer à la République son unité, son indivisibilité et sa liberté, et au peuple l'exercice de tous ses droits.

Reprenons donc avec constance le travail de la constitution, et discutons-en le petit nombre d'articles vraiment constitutionals, avec cette sagesse qui n'exclut pas l'énergie, et avec ce talent qui ne flétrisse pas les défiances.

Songez que le dernier article de la constitution sera le commencement du traité de paix avec les puissances. Il leur tarde de savoir avec qui elles peuvent traiter, quelle que soit la forme de notre gouvernement....

There follows a strong attack upon the Federal idea, showing the Committee to be definitely anti-Girondin in its sociology.

Mais cette inscription sera-t-elle donc toujours mensongère? verra-t-on sans cesse, dans le palais de l'unité, les fureurs de la discorde, et 44 mille petites républiques y agitant leurs dissensions par des représentans?...

Il faut qu'à votre voix, tous les Français se prononcent, que l'égoïste et l'avare soient flétris par l'opinion, et punis dans leurs richesses. Ne vous y méprenez pas, il n'y a plus de gloire et de bonheur pour vous, que dans le succès de la liberté, dans le rétablissement de l'ordre, et dans l'affermissement des propriétés.

Voilà la base de toutes les sociétés politiques, et le législateur qui la méconnaîtra, sera en horreur à ses contemporains et à la postérité.

Il sera aussi exécré le législateur qui aura méconnu les droits du peuple, et qui n'aura pas écouté la plainte des malheureux.

Si vous perdez cette occasion d'établir la république, vous êtes tous également flétris, et pas un de vous n'échappera aux tyrans victorieux, quelle que soit la nuance de votre opinion ou le principe de vos actions. Le glaive exterminateur frappera les appelans au peuple, et les votans pour la mort du tyran; et c'est la seule égalité que vous aurez fondée. Vos noms ne passeront à la postérité que comme ceux des rebelles et des coupables: vous aurez reculé le perfectionnement des sociétés humaines; vous aurez perdu les droits des peuples, vous aurez fait périr 300 mille hommes, et dilapidé des trésors que la liberté avait déposés dans vos mains pour son affermissement; vous aurez rétrograder la raison publique; vous serez complice de la tyrannie des rois et de la barbarie de l'Europe, et l'on dira de vous; la convention de France pouvait donner la liberté à l'Europe, mais par ses dissensions, elle riva les fers du peuple, et servit le despotisme par ses haines....

FOOTNOTES

[1] C. W. Oman, "History of England," p. 581.

[2] Taine, "La Révolution," preface.

[3] Victor Hugo, "Quatre-vingt-treize." Illustrated edition of 1877. Paris, pp. 136-150.

[4] *E.g.* he says the "gentry" of France should imitate the gentry of England. But to do this it is necessary to own the houses of the peasantry; and even then the system does not always suit the Celtic temperament, they say.

[5] For example, the island of Serque.

[6] Bonaparte may have had a noble ancestry. But so had more than one true bourgeois whose family had had neither the means nor the desire to insist upon the privileged rank in the past.

[7] For the sake of clearness I do not mention the large class who had purchased fiefs, all technically noble, many practically bourgeois.

[8] Lyons was, of course, a frontier town of the empire, but locally it is the centre of its own country the "Lyonnais."

[9] All biographers agree. The first publication of the extract from the civil register was obtained by Bougeart in August 1860. It was furnished to him by M. Ludot, the mayor at the time. There is a ridiculous error in the *Journal de la Montagne*, vol. ii. No. 142, "né à *Orchie* sur Aube."

[10] The date is given in the extract mentioned in the preceding note.

[11] See the action of the relatives in No. VI. of the Appendix.

[12] Bougeart. A Danton, who was presumably the son of this brother, was an inspector of the University under the second Empire.

[13] See Appendix No. V.; also *Théâtre de l'Ancien Collège de Troyes*, Babeau, published by Dufour-Bouquet, Troyes, 1881.

[14] See list of his library, Appendix VIII., and his interview with Thomas Payne, at the beginning of Chapter VII.

[15] Speech of August 13, 1793. Printed in *Moniteur* of August 15.

[16] M. Béon.

[17] *Danton, Homme d'État,* p. 29.

[18] See "Notes of Courtois de l'Aube" in Clarétie's "Desmoulins."

[19] *Danton, Homme d'État,* p. 30.

[20] An excellent reading is afforded by the *Avocat aux Conseils du Roi* of M. Bos (Machal & Billaud, Paris, 1881), quoted more than once in this work.

[21] Since 1728 membership of this body had been purchasable and hereditary; a striking example of how wrongly society was moving.

[22] See Appendix VI.

[23] M. Bos, quoted above.

[24] Ibid.

[25] See Appendix V.

[26] See Appendix II. on Danton's lodgings in Paris.

[27] See Robinet, *Danton vie Privée,* p. 284.

[28] See Appendix VI.

[29] By nature his nose was small. His was one of those faces rarely seen, and always associated with energy and with leadership, whose great foreheads overhang a face that would be small, were it not redeemed by the square jaw and the mouth. Thus Arnault, "une caricature de Socrate."

[30] I refer to the English reformer who, on taking ship at Bristol, cast his perruque into the water, crying, "I have done with such baubles," and sailed bald to the New World.

[31] See Appendix VIII.

[32] See Appendix IX.

[33] From the *Almanack Royal* of 1788. Dr. Robinet, whose opportunities of information are unique, tells us that he first moved into the Rue des Fossés St. Germains, and later into the Cour du Commerce, some time in 1790. The statement as to the first direction is unaccompanied by any authority, but Dr. Robinet possesses a letter with this address on it; now here the definite information of an official list seems to me of the greatest weight.

[34] See Appendices II. and VII. Some rooms look on the Rue des Cordeliers, some on the Cour du Commerce.

[35] De Barentin. See preceding chapter and Appendix V. He became Danton's client just before the decree that summoned the States-General.

[36] Sécretaire du Sceau.

[37] See Appendix V., Rousselin. The anecdote is little esteemed by Aulard, but is admitted to be of value by other biographers. Aulard relies for his opinion upon the undoubted errors in the matter of date. But Rousselin may have been right in the main, though (writing many years after) mistaken in the matter of a month or so.

[38] E. Champion, *La France en 1789*. Esprit des Cahiers in *La Révolution* (*Hist. Générale*, viii.).

[39] Ibid.

[40] Aulard, who quotes Chassin, *Les Elections de Paris*, vol. ii. p. 478. M. Aulard tells us that M. Chassin saw the document himself before the war.

[41] Less than six hundred.

[42] Appendix V.

[43] This description is taken from a contemporary water-colour sketch which I have seen in the collection of Dr. Robinet.

[44] See Appendix I.

[45] See the discussion of the somewhat meagre authorities in Robinet, *Danton, Homme d'État*, pp. 37-40.

[46] *Documents authentiques pour servir à l'Histoire de la Révolution Française Danton*, par Alfred Bougeart. Brussels, 1861 (La Croix, Van Meenen & Cie.).

[47] Aulard, who quotes Charavay, *Assemblée electorale de Paris*.

[48] Chassin, *Les Elections et les Cahiers de Paris*, iii. 580-581, on which this whole scene is based.

[49] Aulard, *Revue de la Révolution Française*, February 14, 1893.

[50] See the figures given in the petition against Danton's arrest.

[51] This decree was passed by the Cordeliers on Tuesday, July 21, 1789. It is not so unreasonable as it might seem, for but two days afterwards (July 23rd) the informal municipal body recognises the necessity of new city elections.

[52] Signed 21st September; promulgated 3rd November.

[53] An excellent example is on p. 45 of *Danton, Homme d'État*.

[54] Their names were Peyrilhe, De Blois, De Granville, Dupré, Croharé. They can be found, with all the decrees touching this business, in *Danton, Homme d'État* (Robinet, 1889), p. 248. Printed, like all the Cordeliers' decrees, by *Momoro* in the Rue de la Harpe, and signed, "d'Anton."

[55] It may be remembered that Bougeart (p. 69) claims the presidency for Danton at the very beginning of '89. The error of this has been pointed out. On the other hand, Aulard says he was not President till October. This is another error. There is at least one earlier document, that of September, quoted on the preceding page.

[56] They had sat for a while at the Evéché; on the Island of the Cité, while the Manège was being prepared.

[57] *Rev. de Paris*, xxiii. p. 20.

[58] November 11th and 12th.

[59] 22nd of December.

[60] 12th November and 14th of December.

[61] 31 against 20 (Aulard, from *Journal de la Cour et de la Ville*, p. 518).

[62] *Danton, Homme d'État*, pp. 256, &c. Signed, "d'Anton."

[63] Danton, his friend Legendre, Testulat, Sableé, and Guintin. Several authorities have placed Danton's election in September 1789 instead of January 1790, an error due (probably) to following Godard's list, which was published in 1790, but bore the title, "Members of the Commune elected since September 1789."

[64] Marat's presses were hidden in a cellar of the Cordeliers now situated under the house of the concierge of the Clinique.

[65] January 19th.

[66] The Rue des Fossés was (and is, under its new name) remarkably straight for an old street. Cannon could be used.

[67] Their names were Ozanne and Damien; the same Damien, I believe, who committed the blunder of September 13, 1791.

[68] Article 9 of the decree of October 8 and 9, 1790.

[69] "Notables-adjoints," to the number of seven in each district. Danton himself was elected on to such a body in May or June 1790, and served for a few months.

[70] That is, till his election as substitute to the Procureur in December 1791.

[71] January 25, 28; February 4, 16; March 3, 5, 13, 19; June 15, 19, 23. Aulard, *Rev. Française*, February 14, 1893, pp. 142, 143.

[72] It is this warrant which has probably misled one biographer as to the date of the "Affaire Marat." (*Danton, Homme d'État*, p. 67: "En *mars* survint l'affaire Marat.")

[73] That is, of course, the inclusion of Paris into the general scheme of December 1789—a scheme that enfranchised the peasants, but created an oligarchy in the towns.

[74] He received 12,550 votes, the great bulk of the limited suffrage. Forty-nine odd votes were cast for Danton, but he was obviously not a candidate (Aulard).

[75] *Ami du Peuple*, No. 192.

[76] *Révolutions de France et Brabant*, tom. x. p. 171.

[77] There is a misprint (a very rare thing with this careful historian) in footnote No. 3, p. 231, of M. Aulard's article on Danton in the *Rev. Française* for March 14, 1893. For "November" we should read "September," for we know that the voting was over on September 16. See Robiquet, *Personnel Municipal*, p. 373, and the evidence on all sides that a new poll was ordered on September 17 in his Section.

[78] This big building in the island next Notre Dame disappeared in the restorations of Viollet le Duc. It was often used in the revolutionary period for public meetings, and even the Assembly sat there for a few days after entering Paris in October, and while the Riding-School was being prepared for it.

[79] *Moniteur*, Old Series, No. 316 (1790).

[80] M. Aulard says "somewhere between the 10th and the 15th," and "nous n'avons pas la date precise." He has probably overlooked *L'Ami du Peuple*, No. 290, "Le 14 de ce mois Danton a été nommé à la place du Sieur Villette."

[81] Aulard. The other biographers all assume that he did not resign.

[82] *Orateur du Peuple*, vol. iii. No. 24.

[83] Ibid., vol. vi. No. 27.

[84] The letter will be found in M. Etienne Charavay's *Assemblée Electorale*, p. 437.

[85] I quote from M. Aulard, *Rev. Française*, March 14, 1893.

[86] Note that Lafayette in his Memoirs (vol. iii. p. 64) talks of Danton "at the head of his battalion." I doubt an error on the part of a soldier whose business it was to know his own command.

[87] *e.g.* that of the quarter of the Carmelites (ibid.).

[88] *Révolutions de France et Brabant*, No. 74.

[89] See his Collected Works, vol. xii. pp. 264, 265.

[90] M. Aulard points out an error in Condorcet's own note (xii. p. 267), where it is mentioned as the 12th of July; but the *Bouche de Fer* of the 10th gives us the above date over these two speeches.

[91] He wrote a funny little letter (among other things) to the *Républicain* of July 16, describing a "mechanical king," "who is practically eternal."

[92] See *Société des Jacobins*, vol. ii. p. 541.

[93] *Moniteur*, July 16, 1791.

[94] *Ami du Peuple*, June 22, 1791.

[95] *Révolutions de France et de Brabant*, No. 82.

[96] This is not a rhetorical exaggeration. It indicates, as will be seen later in the chapter, the very number that finally formed the garrison of the palace—a point not hitherto noticed, and well worth remembering, for it shows how Lafayette's accusations are half the truth. He had approached Danton, and he had told him many of his plans. Danton had not acceded, but he used the knowledge.

[97] *Révolutions de France et de Brabant*, No. 82.

[98] Appendix II.

[99] On June 24.

[100] I follow Aulard in this as to the general scheme, and largely as to authorities also.

[101] Aulard is my authority for the fact that the actual text of this second petition disappeared in 1871, when the Hotel de Ville was burnt by the Commune, but that Berchez saw it before that event, and carefully drew up a list of the principal names. Danton is not among them.

[102] The *Courrier Français* of July 22 asks if "the man in holland trousers and a grey waistcoat was Danton," but says nothing more.

[103] See the letter published in the *Rev. Française*, April 1893, p. 325.

[104] *Orateur du Peuple*, viii. No. 16. Not over-trustworthy.

[105] Possibly later. Beugnot seems to speak as though Danton was still in Troyes on at least as late a date as the 6th of August (*Mémoires*, i. pp. 249-250).

[106] Since writing the above I notice that M. Aulard in the same article quotes a remark of Danton's in the Electoral Assembly of September 10th. This is taken from the *procès verbal* of the Assembly, and M. Charavay communicated it to M. Aulard.

[107] His election was not declared till the 7th, but was known on the 6th.

[108] January 20, 1792.

[109] I see in that phrase all Danton's attitude upon the war.

[110] There was a minority of seven.

[111] Perhaps as early as the evening of the 28th.

[112] This account is translated from the *Moniteur*, August 3, 1792.

[113] *Journal des Débats*, 183.

[114] I take this document from Robinet, *Danton, Homme d'État*, pp. 109, 112; but neither he nor Aulard (who quotes it) gives the authority. The circular is quoted often under the date of August 19; it was issued on that Sunday, but was drawn up and dated on the Saturday to which I have assigned it.

[115] Aulard, who quotes from the *Moniteur*, xii. 445.

[116] The scene can be reconstructed from his testimony at the trial of the Girondins and from his speech at the Jacobins on the 5th of November.

[117] I take all this from Aulard's article in the *Révolution Française* of June 14, 1893.

[118] The votes of the 30th, 31st, and 2nd.

[119] The word "illegally" is just, for the constitution of the Commune and all its acts were legally dependent on the Assembly. On the other hand, the Commune had given this committee right to add to its numbers, but such men as Marat, who was not a member of the Commune, were surely not intended.

[120] First *La Poissonnière*, then the *Postes* and the *Luxembourg*.

[121] It is possible that this sentence, including the preceding phrase, "le tocsin qui va sonner," &c., are the only part of the speech that has been literally reported. The *Logotachygraphe* was not founded till January, and while the *Moniteur* and the *Journal des Débats* give much the same version, the latter calls it a "summary."

[122] "Appel à l'impartiale posterité." Madame Roland had the great historical gift of intuition, that is, she could minutely describe events which never took place. I attach no kind of importance to the passage immediately preceding. If Danton and Pétion were alone, as she describes them, her picture is the picture of a novelist. The phrase quoted above may be authentic—there were witnesses.

[123] *Moniteur*, January 25, 1793. Speech of January 21st.

[124] Speech of January 21, 1793.

[125] The accusations against Danton in this matter are given and criticised in Appendix IV., where the reasons are also given for omitting any mention of Marat's circular in the text.

[126] For the figures and very interesting details as to Egalité's election see *Révolution Française* August 14, 1893, second note, page 129.

[127] More than 700 and less than 1000 died. The common exaggeration is Peltier's 12,000.

[128] As a fact, his successor, Garat, was not elected till the 9th of October, and did not begin to act till the 12th. Danton seems to have remained at the Ministry till the evening of the 11th.

[129] October 23.

[130] *Michelet*, 1st edition, vol. iv. pp. 392-394.

[131] October 10 and 11.

[132] He made a speech on the 6th of November demanding (of course) the trial of the King, but not with violence. He left for Belgium with Delacroix on the 1st of December.

[133] This Dannon was a friend of Danton's. He began, but did not complete, a collection of his speeches, &c., and an inquiry into his accounts. He was a member for Pas de Calais. It is not easy to get his name accurately spelt. I follow the spelling of a list of the Convention published in 1794. Dannon voted for banishment.

[134] I must not omit to mention one phrase which is far more characteristic of him—that spoken after Lepelletier's assassination: "It would be well for us if we could die like that."

[135] The proofs of the connection with Talleyrand are based only on inference. They will be found discussed in Robinet's *Danton Emigré*, pp. 12-16 and pp. 270, &c. As for Priestley's correspondence, it was sympathetic and deep, and continued in spite of the massacres of September. There is a draft of a Constitution in the French archives which some believe to be Priestley's, but I am confident it is not in his handwriting.

[136] *Moniteur*, March 9, 1793.

[137] *Ibid.* March 10, 1793.

[138] See *Patriote Français*, No. 1308.

[139] See *Moniteur*, March 13, 1793.

[140] Paine's ignorance of French was such that his speech on Louis's exile was translated for him.

[141] La Roche du Maine.

[142] Levasseur tells us that Delmas spoke first, and that his remarks took the form of a definite motion for the appearance of the Committees to account for their action. Legendre is mentioned here because he alone is agreed upon by all the eye-witnesses (and by the *Moniteur*) as being the principal defender of Danton. We must not underestimate his courage; it was he who with a very small force shut the club of the Jacobins on the night of the 9th Thermidor, and so turned the flank of the Robespierrian faction.

[143] "Quand les restes de la faction ... ne seront plus ... vous n'aurez plus d'exemples à donner ... ils ne restera que le peuple et vous, et le gouvernement dont vous êtes le centre inviolable."

[144] "Mauvais citoyen, tu as conspiré; faux ami, tu disais, il y a deux jours, du mal de Desmoulins que tu as perdu; méchant homme, tu as comparé l'opinion publique à une femme de mauvaise vie, tu as dit que l'honneur était ridicule ... si Fabre est innocent, si D'Orléans, si Dumouriez furent innocents tu l'est sans doute. J'en ai trop dit—tu repondras à la justice."

[145] Robespierre's notes for St. Just's report were published by M. France in 1841 among the "Papiers trouvés chez Robespierre."

[146] "La Convention Nationale après avoir entendu les rapports des Comités de Sureté générale et du Salut Public, décrète d'accusation Camille Desmoulins, Hérault, Danton, Phillippeaux Lacroix ... en conséquence elle declare leur mise en jugement." These were the last words of St. Just's speech, and formed his substantive motion.

"Ce décret est adopté à l'unanimité et au milieu des plus vifs applaudissements." —*Moniteur*, April 2, 1794 (13th Germinal, year II.).

[147] Couthon was a cripple. Once (later) in the Convention it was called out to him "Triumvir," and he glanced at his legs and said, "How could I be a triumvir?" The logical connection between good legs and triumvirates was more apparent to himself than to those whom he caused to be guillotined.

[148] We have the fragments of this "No. VII.," which was not published. See M. Clarétie's *C. Desmoulins*, p. 274 of Mrs. Cashel Hoey's translation.

[149] Danton would have been thirty-five in October. Desmoulins had been thirty-four in March—*not* thirty-three, as he said at the trial. I give this on the authority of M. Clarétie, who in his book quotes the birth-certificate, which he himself had seen (March 2, 1760).

[150] March 10, 1793. Exception has been taken to the whole sentiment by Dr. Robinet, but great, or rather unique, as is his authority, I cannot

believe that an appeal—especially an exclamatory appeal of this nature—was foreign to his impetuous and merciful temper.

[151] Wallon, *Tribunal Révolutionnaire*, vol. iii. p. 156.

[152] It is known that Fleuriot and Fouquier were alone when the jury were "chosen by lot." This appeared at the trial of Fouquier. For the notes of Lebrun, see Appendix X.

[153] Wallon, *Tribunal Révolutionnaire*, vol. iii. p. 155.

[154] See Appendix X. The speeches which I have written here are reconstructed from these notes, and I must beg the reader to check the consecutive sentences of the text by reference to the disjointed notes printed in the Appendix.

[156] Wallon, *Tribunal Révolutionnaire*, iii. 169, quotes *Archives*, W. 342, *Dossier* 641, 1st Part, No. 34.

[157] Fouquier had written a letter to his distant relative Desmoulins, begging for some employment, on August 20, 1792, just after the success of Danton's party, in which Desmoulins had of course shared. It is by no means dignified and almost servile. See Clarétie, *Desmoulins*, English edition, p. 318.

[158] This is M. Wallon's opinion, who gives both versions, and from whom I take so much of this description. See *Tribunal Révolutionnaire*, iii. 177.

[159] All this appears in the trial of Fouquier.

[160] They are given in Clarétie's *Desmoulins* in the Appendix.

[161] See the list of the prisoner's effects in Clarétie's *Desmoulins*.

[162] This gate may be seen to-day just to the right of the great staircase in the court of the Palais de Justice. It has an iron grating before it.

[163] The original of this I take from Clarétie, who quotes P. A. Lecomte, *Memorial sur la Révolution Française*.

> "Lorsqu'arrivés au bords du Phlégéton
> Camille Desmoulins, D'Eglantine et Danton,
> Payèrent pour passer ce fleuve redoutable
> Le nautonnier Charon (citoyen équitable)
> A nos trois passagers voulait remettre en mains
> L'excédant de la taxe imposée aux humains.
> 'Garde,' lui dit Danton, 'la somme toute entière;
> Je paye pour Couthon, St. Just et Robespierre.'"

[164] It was Madame Gély who told this to Despoi's grandfather. Clarétie has mentioned it. But Michelet must have heard from the family about this same priest (Kerénavant le Breton), for according to Madame Gély it was he who married Danton for the second time.

[165] Ce qu'il y a de certain d'après le résultat donné par la commission des subsistances militaires, c'est que les armées sont approvisionnées jusque vers le premier octobre; l'armée d'Italie, la plus mal approvisionnée, a des subsistances pour quelques mois, et l'on a déjà préparé pour elle d'autres approvisionnements.

[166] Des traîtres se sont mêlés dans les rangs des patriotes et dans les convois de l'artillerie qui allaient combattre les révoltés; le comité en a fait arrêter la marche, et le comité de surveillance retient les principaux auteurs de ce nouveau complot. Malgré tant de surveillance, quelques soldats français, indignes de ce nom, ont trahi leur devoir et sont allés grossir la horde des rebelles. Partout les obstacles se multiplient; partout les administrations veulent régler les mouvemens des troupes et les commissaires veulent faire les fonctions de généraux, des communes arrêtent à leur gré des armes qui ont une autre destination, et c'est ainsi que toutes les forces s'atténuent et que les brigands ont des succès.

Mais du moins les rives qui correspondent aux perfides de George III. sont garanties. Les trois divisions commandées par le général Canclaux, qui occupent les ports intermédiaires entre les Sables et Nantes, entretiennent la communication entre ces deux villes, et contiennent les brigands à une certaine distance des côtes.

La communication par terre, entre Nantes et Angers, est libre, on travaille à rétablir la libre navigation de la Loire entre ces deux villes. Quelques bateaux armés de canons sont préparés, et suffiront pour cette protection.

Déjà une victoire signalée vient de raviver toutes les espérances de la patrie. A Saint-Mexent, l'artillerie et les approvisionnemens des révoltés sont le prix de la première victoire signalée que les patriotes viennent de remporter.

INDEX

Agriculture, depression of, before Revolution
Amelinau case, Danton's opinion in
Antoinette, Marie, see "Marie Antoinette."
Arcis-sur-Aube, Danton born at, in 1759
position of
effect on Danton's politics
visited by Danton in 1791
again in August 1792
last retirement of Danton to
Army, condition of, at Valmy
Danton's first mission to
second mission
third
position of on Sambre in June 1793
of "Sambre et Meuse,"
attitude towards Robespierre
Arnault, witness of Danton's death
Arrest of D'Eglantine
of Hébert
of Desmoulins and Danton
Artisans, loss of influence of Church on
their disfranchisement
causes of their discontent, the guild, the octroi
character of before Revolution, numbers, influence of
Assembly, National, see "States General."
Bailly, of the professional class

opposition of Cordeliers to

elected mayor of Paris

resignation of

Barbarian invasions of ninth century

Barentin, de, intimacy with Danton

Barrère, a Bourgeois

his action on first committee with Danton

Report against Robespierre

Bastille, fall of

effect of this,

Battles, of Valmy

of Jemappes

Neerwinden

Turcoing

Fleurus

Belgium, Danton proposes annexation of

Bourgeoisie or middle class, effect of Revolution on, definition of

produces most of the revolutionaries

Brienne, de, client of Danton's

Brissot, draws up petition of Jacobins

attacked by Desmoulins

Brunswick, Duke of, his manifesto

his hesitation

Burning at stake in United States

by Parliament of Strasbourg in 1789

Cahiers, their nature

that of Cordeliers destroyed

Carnot, a Bourgeois

in first Committee of Public Safety

Robespierre's attack on

Centralisation, of pre-revolutionary France

quality of
before Revolution, examples of
pre-revolutionary fails to raise revenue
used as a practical engine of reform, rapid raising of armies
Charlemagne, marks the end of settled Roman order
Imperial tradition of in France
Charleroy, stronghold of Coburg
captured
Charpentier, his Café des Écoles
his daughter marries Danton, Mlle., see "Wife."
Châtelet, impossibility of reforming it
nature of
issue warrant against Marat
against Danton
Church, its loss of power in villages during eighteenth century
loss of influence over citizens
not main cause of egalitarian feeling in France
intention of making Danton a priest in
Cicé, de, Danton as orator of municipal deputation demands resignation of
Civil constitution of clergy, see "Clergy."
Class system, vigour of, before Revolution
Classes, social, five principal, before Revolution
Clergy, Danton's defence of
civil constitution of
its vast importance
its details
passes the Assembly
Louis ratifies
Coburg, his position on Sambre
is defeated at Fleurus
Collot d'Herbois, attacked by Danton in Jacobins

beaten by Danton in election for Substitute Procureur

Committee of Public Safety, first, proposed by Isnard, Danton elected

determines overthrow of Girondins

Danton resigns from

Robespierre elected on

powerful force in winter of 1793

determination to continue Terror in spite of Danton

abandons Robespierre

Commune before August 1792, (*see* "Municipality"), insurrectionary of, August 1792

increases in power

Marat joins its "Comité de Surveillance,"

its quarrel with Gironde

opposes committee in winter of 1793

attacked by Danton

captured by Robespierre

attempts to save him and fails,

Condorcet, of the professional class

example of balance of two French tendencies

demands Republic

Conseils du Roi, Old Court of Appeals, nature of

Danton enters at Bar of

Contrat social, written just after Danton's birth

Convention, elections of Paris to, Danton elected to

its parties

its appearance on first meeting

declares Republic

debate on king's death in

votes arrest of Girondins

Legendre defends Danton in

St. Just attacks Danton in

subservience to Robespierre

outlaws him,

Cordeliers, district of, social character

position of Convent Hall in

meets after elections, importance of this

petitions against Danton's arrest

merged in section of Théâtre Français

Cordeliers, club of, contrasted with Jacobins

their numbers and character

opposition to new municipality

determine on independent use of their guard

attack municipality again

create *Mandat Imperatif*

manifesto to march on Versailles

oppose Lafayette's discipline in National Guard

oath of their deputies

victory of club over municipality

campaign against restriction of suffrage

Danton leaves them for Jacobins

Republican declaration of, on king's flight

petition of, on king's flight, not signed by Danton

Cordelier, Vieux, published by Desmoulins to protest against Terror

Court, relations of nobles to

form party to influence king at Versailles

last stand in the Tuilleries

Courts of Law, before Revolution

Couthon, a Bourgeois

proposes law on worship of God

supports Robespierre in committee

Dannon, his name mistaken for Danton's, Le Gallois's misprint, Michelet's error based on this

Danton, a Bourgeois

very typical of nation, his attitude towards Paris

his rise during the war

preliminary summary of his career

forerunner of Napoleon

retirement and death

born at Arcis-sur-Aube, 1759, age compared with contemporaries

effect of birthplace on his politics

his father Procureur at Arcis

family of, house of, social position of father, death of father, fortune of, his mother and aunts

to be made a priest

educated by Oratorians, their influence, destined for Bar

character as boy

coronation of Louis XVI. seen by

his stepfather Recordain, apprenticed to Vinot, solicitor in Paris, called to Bar at Rheims

practice in lower courts

at bar of Conseils du Roi

his Latin oration

his opinion in Montbarey case, Du Barentin his client, and De Brienne, his income at Bar

frequents Charpentier's Café des Écoles, marriage, dowry of wife

physical appearance

energy, style of oratory, knowledge of English and Italian

reading, pre-revolutionary politics

private life

goes to live in Cour du Commerce

Barentin's offer of post to

his relation to masonic lodges

summary of his condition on outbreak of Revolution

Primary of his District convened

not president of District during elections

at Palais Royal

possibly present at fall of Bastille

action night after, clashes with Lafayette

in Club of Cordeliers

as President of Cordeliers attacks Municipality

creates *Mandat Imperatif*

placards manifesto for march on Versailles

nature of action supporting *Mandat Imperatif*

his success

elected to municipality

defends Marat

discovers error in warrant against Marat

appeals to assembly

false effect of his attitude

sworn in to municipality

with Legendre

goes in deputation to Louis XVI.

warrant for arrest of, issued by Châtelet

district in his favour

his proposition for grand jury, appeal to Assembly, decision in his favour

his policy at close of 1790

rejected at municipal elections of 1790

moderation during affair of Nancy

rejected as candidate for Notables

orator of city deputation (November 1790)

elected head of his battalion

elected to administration of city (1791)

letter to De la Rochefoucald

appears in Jacobins

attacks Collot d'Herbois in Jacobins

speech on death of Mirabeau

action on April, 1791, Desmoulins' testimony untrustworthy

attitude during Louis XVI.'s flight

attacks Lafayette at Jacobins on king's flight

reads Jacobin petition on Champ de Mars, absence from Cordeliers' manifestation there

Lafayette orders arrest of (August 4, 1791)

his flight to England

his return, sent by his section to electoral college

attempted arrest of

elected substitute to Procureur of Paris (November 1791)

his chances of a prosperous municipal career

opposes war policy

speech at Jacobins describing himself

justice of his opposition to war

retained on committee of insurrection (July-August, 1792)

goes to Arcis to see his mother

leads insurrection of August 10

his position after 0th of August, Minister of Justice

his determination to form a strong government after fall of monarchy, only practical man in executive in August, 1792

addresses Assembly as Minister of Justice, his circular to tribunals

defence of himself in the circular, his power over cabinet

he and Dumouriez see chance of repelling invasion

his interview with Roland and ministers on news of invasion reported by Fabre d'Eglantine

his political attitude just before massacres

he orders domiciliary visits and collection of arms

his speech, the volunteers, its success

why he did not interfere during massacres

anecdote of him during massacres, his future comment on

elected to Convention by Paris

his false position in the Mountain, accused of planning massacres

his appearance on first meeting of Convention

resigns Ministry of Justice

repudiates Marat

his diplomacy secures Prussian retreat after Valmy

his attitude towards Dumouriez, partial reconciliation with Gironde

anecdote of theatre and Madame Roland, of meeting with Marat

his reticence after Jemappes

speech on Catholicism opposing Cambon

attempt to reconcile Girondins in meeting at Sceaux, Guadet's opposition

starts on his first mission to army

debates on Louis XVI.'s death, misprint of Danton for Dannon

what he really did in the debate

unusual violence

caused by his wife's illness

intimacy with Priestley, Talleyrand, his diplomacy spoiled by his own violence on king's death, demands annexation of Belgium

second mission to army in Belgium, change of his politics on his return, despairs of reconciling Girondins and Paris

accounted for by death of his wife

his military policy and appeal to Paris

creates Revolutionary Tribunal

violently attacked for his intimacy with Dumouriez

supports Isnard's proposal of Great Committee, is named on it

compared with Mirabeau

summary of Danton's position in Committee, as it changes

his practical policy impossible with Girondins

difficulty of following his action in April and May, 1793, speech on acquittal of Marat

curious action half in favour of Girondins, proposes committee of twelve through Barrère

but prevents formation of special guard

Danton, through the Committee, overthrows the Gironde

his phrase with regard to Girondins

his difficulty in controlling forces after June 2, 1793

begins to lose his power

still retains enough power at end of June to produce Constitution and to persuade Convention to his policy, his second marriage

reasons for it, he loses power still more in July

puts his name reluctantly to St. Just's report attacking fallen Girondins, he resigns his place on Committee

his brilliancy whilst standing alone, great speeches in August, on army, on strengthening government

his despair and illness, Garat's interview with him, Desmoulins retires to his home at Arcis

his rest at Arcis, its effects

regret for execution of Girondins, returns to the Convention

his new politics against the Terror

his defence of religious liberty and attack on Commune

Robespierre defends him in Jacobins, Desmoulins helps him, publication of "Vieux Cordelier,"

his first check, D'Eglantine arrested, he knows his attempt has failed

still speaks in Convention, last interview with Robespierre

Panis comes to warn him, he is arrested

his trial and death

taken to the Luxembourg with Desmoulins, meets Paine

policy of his defence, of Committee

Legendre defends Danton in Convention

St. Just's report and vote against Danton

his remarks in the prison

trial begins

fear of an armed attempt to save him, his reply to the judges

charges against Danton

Westermann's replies

Danton's speech in his own defence
collusion of judge and prosecutor
Renault's defence
judge and prosecutor appeal to Convention
St. Just's second speech to Convention against Danton
Billaud-Varennes
taken back to Conciergerie, condemned, his action in prison
passage to guillotine
passes David
passes house of Duplay and Robespierre's window
he rallies Fabre d'Eglantine
rhymes sold in Paris same night
his execution
effects of his death
contrasted with Robespierre
Danton, Madame, *see* "Wife."
David, artist, portrait of Danton
animosity against Danton
sketches the condemned
false promise to Robespierre
De Barentin, *see* "Barentin."
De Brienne, *see* "Brienne."
De Cicé, *see* "Cicé."
D'Eglantine, *see* "Fabre."
De Séchelles, *see* "Hérault."
Decree of Dec. 1788, elections
Desmoulins, Camille, house in Cour du Commerce
brings news of Necker's dismissal
member of Cordeliers
testimony as to Danton's action on April 18, 1791
Danton sleeps in his flat before insurrection of Aug. 10, 1792

  his "Histoire des Brissottins," allied to Robespierre
  publishes "Vieux Cordelier,"
  arrested
  his answer to his judges
  his examination in court
  tears up his written defence
  his frenzy going to guillotine
  his death
Districts, Paris divided into sixty
District of Cordeliers, *see* "Cordeliers."
Duke of Brunswick, *see* "Brunswick."
Dumouriez, outflanked before Valmy
  fears to attack
  his political motives, his work with Danton after Valmy
  incident in theatre with Danton
  treason of
  Danton attacked for friendship with
Education, French, effect of, due to Jesuits
  effect of on Robespierre and Desmoulins
  of Danton,
Egalité elected for Paris
Eglantine, d', *see* "Fabre."
Elections to, States General decreed
  to first municipality, elected by Cordeliers
  of priests and bishops
  to Legislative
  of Paris to Convention
  of Danton, Bailly, &c., *see* under their names.
England, Danton's flight to
English constitution, flexibility of
  its vices described by Marat

English language, Danton's acquaintance with
English society, homogeneity of in eighteenth century contrasted with the Continent
Fabre d'Eglantine, poet, member of Cordeliers
escorts officers of Châtelet through mob
reports Danton's interview with other ministers
arrested
trial of with Danton
his luxury in prison
his illness and despair on way to guillotine
his "Maltese orange,"
rhymes on him and Danton
Fear, *see* "Great."
Feudalism, founded in troubles of ninth century
fall of, in July, August, 1789,
Feuillants, club of, represents Lafayette's supporters in Legislative
Flanders, regiment of, arrives to strengthen court in 1789
Fleurus, battle of
Fouquier-Tinville, public prosecutor, his action in Danton's trial,
France, centralisation of, before Revolution
egalitarianism in, is not due to Roman law or Church
material state of, prior to Revolution
before Revolution, character of centralisation in
imperial tradition in
origins of social constitution in
specially suited to growth of Roman law
Paris the bond of
re-made by the Revolution
effect of Rousseau upon
united by monarchy, led by Paris as the king's town
Français, Théâtre, *see* "Section."

Franchise, loss of, by artisans
French, character of, in pursuing political theories
courts of law, nature in Ancien Régime
education, effect of Jesuit influence on
education, effect of on Robespierre and Desmoulins, Danton's speech on
peasantry, owners of land before Revolution
peasantry, effect of Revolution on
peasantry, condition before Revolution
village community, decay of, in eighteenth century
loss of Church in
nobility, origin of, as a definite class in ninth century
French Revolution, *see* "Revolution."
Garat, his interview with Danton
Garran Coulon, Danton's return from England on election of
Girondins, represent the professional class
declare war
opposition to Danton from the beginning of the Convention
momentary reconciliation with
failure of, meeting at Sceaux, Guadet rejects him
outbreak of quarrel with Paris
expulsion of
description of their character, excess of idealism, unworkable with Danton's practical policy
their misgovernment, opposition of Paris
bad news from Vendée weakens them in May 1793
Isnard's menace to Paris
firmness during attack, Lanjuinais' proposal to "break the Commune,"
vote of the twenty-nine arrests
confusion of their fall to be explained by great Committee
Danton's phrase concerning
Vergniaud and Guadet attacked in St. Just's report

Danton's pity for
Gobel, schismatic Bishop of Paris, trial under Robespierre
Great fear, peasants' rising destroys feudality
Guadet, Girondin, rejects Danton at Sceaux
St. Just's report on
Guard, National, *see* "National Guard."
Guard, Swiss, their defence of the Tuilleries
demand for vengeance against, by Parisians
special, proposed for the Convention
weak demand for, by Girondins
Hébert, member of the Cordeliers
his character
with Commune against Committee in winter, 1793
Danton's opposition to his religious persecution
his arrest and execution
Henriot, illegally given command of the city forces by the Commune
at head of attack of Convention
note sent to, by Committee on Danton's trial, to prevent a rescue
attempt to save Robespierre
Hérault de Séchelles, present at taking of Bastille
added to Committee
expelled from Committee
trial of
his death
Herbois, d', Collot, *see* "Collot."
Herman, judge at Danton's trial,
Income, of Danton at Bar, estimated
Institution, the, importance of, to France
provided by the Committee
Insurrection, of July 14, 1789
of August 10, 1792

of June 2, 1793

attempted to save Robespierre

Invasions, siege of Verdun by Brunswick

Beaurepaire's suicide, capitulation of Verdun, ferment in Paris

causes massacre of September

Valmy

Jemappes

defeat of Neerwinden, 1793, allies cross the Rhine, Alps, and Pyrenees, take Valenciennes

Turcoing

battle of Fleurus

Isnard, Girondin, proposes Committee of Public Safety

his threat to destroy Paris

Jacobins, character of

Danton's speech in, on death of Mirabeau

Danton attacks Lafayette in

moderate petition of, to Assembly on king's flight

read by Danton in Champs de Mars

joined by radicals in Legislative

debate on war

Robespierre reads his last speech in

Legendre closes

Jemappes, battle of

Judge, in Danton's trial, *see* "Herman."

Just, St., (*see* "St. Just.")

Justice, Ministry of, Danton put into

his circular from

Kersaint, associated with Danton at period of the flight of the king, present at interview of Danton with other ministers in August, 1793, he believes that Brunswick will reach Paris

King, *see* "Louis."

Lafayette, a seceding noble

first clash with Danton

opposition of Cordeliers to

follows the mob to Versailles

his discipline of National Guard opposed by Cordeliers

sends National Guard to arrest Marat

attacked by Danton on flight of the king

his accusation of Danton's venality

his massacre of the Champs de Mars

again attacked by Danton

threatens civil war

Law, Roman, twelfth century, renaissance of, study of, rise of the universities

— — Courts in France, Conseils du Roi

Lawyers, action of, in preventing reform

become conservative as a body

Legendre, a Bourgeois

a member of the Cordeliers

defends Danton before the Convention

shuts the Jacobins

Legislative, elections to

reconciliation with monarchy

parties in

Lafayette's letter to

receives the Royal Family

quarrels with Commune just before massacres

Danton's great speech in

close of

Louis XVI., age of, compared with Danton

his coronation seen by Danton

his attitude to Assembly

his character

brought back to Paris from Versailles by mob
his attitude after this
thanks presented to, by Danton
accepts Civil Constitution of clergy
lost by death of Mirabeau
his attempt to go to St. Cloud
effect of his flight
depends on success of August 0 to receive allies
takes refuge in Parliament
his secret payments
execution of
effect of, on America
Mandat Imperatif
—— head of National Guard, his death
Manifesto of Brunswick, (*see* "Brunswick.")
Manor or village community alone survives ninth century
its survival and power
Manorial relations, their decay
Manuel, Danton's chief in municipality of 1791
Marat, a Bourgeois
incident of
his character
warrant for arrest of
National Guard sent to arrest
importance of issues involved, Lafayette's action
defended by Danton at Bar of Assembly
his escape
elected to "Comité de Surveillance" before massacres
puts Roland on his list of proscribed
his appearance in the Convention
accused by Girondins, acquitted

stabbed by Charlotte Corday, growth of Terror

Marie Antoinette, age of compared with Danton

forms a court party against the Parliament

power over Louis after Mirabeau's death

her determination to hold the Tuilleries

she alone realises the fall of the monarchy

effect of her death on Danton

her shocking trial and its influence on Danton

Marseillais, their march on Paris

Marseillaise

Massacres of September

precipitated by Montmorin's acquittal

refusal of National Guard to interfere

Danton keeps Ministers at their posts just before

the Comité de Surveillance joined by Marat

begin at the Carmes

causes of Danton's neutrality during

close of the massacres

effect of on politics

Medieval Reform, continuity of

failure of after fifteenth century

Middle class, (*see* "Bourgeoisie.")

Mirabeau, age of compared with Danton

calls August 4 "an orgy,"

his reasons for supporting the "Civil Constitution of the clergy,"

death of

Danton's sympathy with, and speech on death of

compared with Danton

Monarchy, French, causes Paris to become head of towns, realises national unity

character of just before Revolution

clogged by local survivals

election of Hugh Capet

examples of pre-revolutionary centralisation in

gradually ceases to be national

origins of its action

reaches power through local institutions

why it could not reform

Danton's attitude towards in crisis of the king's flight

the fall of

importance of, evident after fall

Montmorin, evidence of Danton's venality quoted by Lafayette in Memoirs, really a receipt for Danton's reimbursement

— — Lucien de, acquittal of, hurries on massacres of September

Mountain, party of Paris in the Convention, Danton's false position in

appearance of members of

attacked by Robespierre

Municipal, system of France

Revolution

Municipality, of Paris, first insurrectionary

its weakness

reconstitution of

quarrel with Cordeliers,

Danton elected to

Bailly elected mayor of

petitions against ministers

insurrectionary Commune plot against

dissolved by insurrectionary Commune

(after Aug. 10, 1792, *see* "Commune").

Nancy, affair of, Danton's moderate action

Nationality, differentiation of, in ninth century

National Guard, formed

Lafayette's plan of
Danton elected head of his battalion
clash with people
divided on April 18
fire on people in Champ de Mars
divided on Aug. 10
Santerre put at head of by Danton
refuse to interfere with massacres
Henriot succeeds Boulanger at head of
attack Convention
do not rise for Robespierre
Necker, position of, in 1789, his dismissal
Nobles, origin of, as a definite class in France in ninth century
great numbers of, definition, relation to court, place in Revolution
poverty of, did not at first oppose reform
why they could not rule France
Notables, Danton rejected as candidate for
Octroi, effect on artisans
Oratorians, educated principal revolutionaries
Osselin, his courage after Montmorin's acquittal
Paine, named in Committee with Danton
meets Danton in prison
Panis, warns Danton before his arrest
Paris, the bond of France
cause of headship, effect of Revolution on
head of urban system because seat of monarchy
makes Danton's career
first elections in
solidarity of, in early Revolution
provisional government during attack on Bastille
organises National Guard

model of municipal movement in France
restriction of suffrage in
restrained by Assembly
Bailly elected mayor of
effect of municipal system on
petitions for dismissal of ministers
effect of king's flight on
Pétion, elected mayor of
anger at first disasters of war
effect of Brunswick's manifesto on
ferment on news of invasion
clamours against arrested monarchists
Danton will not oppose
anarchy in, during massacres
elections to the Convention in
eulogy of by Danton
anger against Girondins
conflict of, with Girondins
Isnard's threats against
used by Committee to expel the Gironde
refuses to rise for Robespierre
Parliament of Paris, nature of
Parliaments (representative), see "States General," "Legislative," "Convention."
Peasantry, French, condition of, before Revolution
ownership of land by, before the Revolution
effect of Revolution on
Pétion, elected mayor of Paris
unable to interfere with the massacres
gets some hold on the city at their close
attempt of Danton to get him elected for Paris

named on Committee with Danton
Petition, of municipality against ministers
of Jacobins on king's flight
of Cordeliers
Pitt, his reforms
Priestley, Danton's relations with
Procureur, definition of the office in the old regime
of Paris, during Revolution
Danton elected substitute to
Professional class, its character, numbers, constitution
Recordain, stepfather of Danton
Reform, mediæval, continuity of
action of lawyers in preventing failure of, after fifteenth century
Pitt's attempt at
impossibility on Continent
impossible to French monarchy
its rapidity helped by centralisation
Religious liberty, Danton's speech in favour of
Republic, not originated by Danton
demanded by Condorcet
declared by Convention
Revolution, French, nature of
necessity for, on Continent
its violence
questions raised by
material causes of
main causes not economic
classes it dealt with
it revives religion in villages
effect on peasantry
on artisans

    on Bourgeois
    on professionals and nobles
    theory of
    effect of Rousseau on
    place of Paris in
    summary of politics at outset of
    its task, the re-creation of France
    two periods of
    transformation of, in 1790
    summary of its results,
    Revolutionary Tribunal, created by Danton
    Marat acquitted by
    Hébert tried by
    Danton tried by
    enslaved by Robespierre
    Robespierre, a Bourgeois
    age of
    effect of education on
    joins Committee of Public Safety
    his position in winter of 1793, clash with Danton
    last interview with Danton
    speaks against Danton in Convention
    demonstration of condemned before his house
    his character
    his aims
    his misreading of Rousseau
    causes of his ascendency
    abandons Danton's diplomacy
    heads feast of Supreme Being
    proposes virtual abolition of trials
    destroys independence of Convention

attacks Mountain

abandoned by Committee

causes of his fall

his last speech

outlawed by Convention

his last rally and execution,

Roland, a professional

Danton's power over, in August 1792, interview with, in garden of ministry

calls on Santerre to stop the massacres

prosecuted

— — Madame, her hatred for Danton

she rejects his overtures to Girondins

Roman Law, its fundamental ideas of ownership and sovereignty

suited to France

not main cause of egalitarian feeling in France

Rome, transformation of her system in ninth century

the origin of French urban system

Rousseau, his effect on France

his genius and deficiencies

his faith the source of his power, essentially a reactionary

Robespierre's view of his system

Rousselin, our authority for Danton's boyhood

Saint Just, age of, compared with Danton

joins great Committee

report on Girondins

speech against Danton

second speech against Danton

proposal for bringing prisoners to Paris

with army on Sambre

fails to warn Robespierre

    on Bourgeois
    on professionals and nobles
    theory of
    effect of Rousseau on
    place of Paris in
    summary of politics at outset of
    its task, the re-creation of France
    two periods of
    transformation of, in 1790
    summary of its results,
    Revolutionary Tribunal, created by Danton
    Marat acquitted by
    Hébert tried by
    Danton tried by
    enslaved by Robespierre
    Robespierre, a Bourgeois
    age of
    effect of education on
    joins Committee of Public Safety
    his position in winter of 1793, clash with Danton
    last interview with Danton
    speaks against Danton in Convention
    demonstration of condemned before his house
    his character
    his aims
    his misreading of Rousseau
    causes of his ascendency
    abandons Danton's diplomacy
    heads feast of Supreme Being
    proposes virtual abolition of trials
    destroys independence of Convention

attacks Mountain
abandoned by Committee
causes of his fall
his last speech
outlawed by Convention
his last rally and execution,
Roland, a professional
Danton's power over, in August 1792, interview with, in garden of ministry
calls on Santerre to stop the massacres
prosecuted
— — Madame, her hatred for Danton
she rejects his overtures to Girondins
Roman Law, its fundamental ideas of ownership and sovereignty suited to France
not main cause of egalitarian feeling in France
Rome, transformation of her system in ninth century
the origin of French urban system
Rousseau, his effect on France
his genius and deficiencies
his faith the source of his power, essentially a reactionary
Robespierre's view of his system
Rousselin, our authority for Danton's boyhood
Saint Just, age of, compared with Danton
joins great Committee
report on Girondins
speech against Danton
second speech against Danton
proposal for bringing prisoners to Paris
with army on Sambre
fails to warn Robespierre

outlawed with Robespierre
joins Robespierre at Hotel de Ville
St. Priest, his dismissal demanded by Paris,
Santerre, a Bourgeois
in the attack on Tuilleries
fails to call out National Guard during massacres
Sections, replace districts of Paris, forty-eight in number
Danton demands force to be raised from
convened by Robespierrians in Thermidor
Section du Théâtre Français, replaces Cordeliers
battalion of, Danton elected commander
of Mauconseil begins agitation against ministry
begin insurrection of August 1792
September, *see* "Massacres of."
Social divisions, five principal, before Revolution
Stake, burning at, in United States, by Parliament of Strasbourg in 1789
States General (or National Assembly), term Assembly first used
elections to, in Paris
reaction against, in early 1789
success of, after fall of Bastille
night of August 4 in
queen forms party against, political attitude of Louis towards
plotted against, by court
come to Paris
appealed to, in Marat incident
action to restrain Paris
establish Civil Constitution of clergy
debate on petition of Paris
indecision of, on king's flight
Suffrage, *see* "Franchise."
Talleyrand, Danton meets, at municipality, writes letter to Louis

Danton A Study | 353

connected with Danton's diplomacy, opposes Chauvelin in London
Taxes, failure of, before Revolution
Thermidor, attempted insurrection to save Robespierre in,
Tour du Pin, La, dismissal demanded,
Towns, nuclei of France
    condition of small
Turcoing, battle of
Vergniaud, orator of Girondins, understands Danton
    present at incident in theatre
    his simile in king's trial
    explanation of his vote
    his oratory
    prosecuted by Convention
    St. Just's report against
    Danton's regret for
Versailles, Cordeliers' manifesto for march on
    king brought back to Paris from
Village community, French, decay of, loss of religion in
Vinot, solicitor in Paris, Danton apprenticed to
Wife, of Danton, *first* Charpentier married, his devotion to her
    her illness and its effect on Danton
    her death, its effect on Danton, he exhumes her body
    second (Gély) married
Young, Arthur, his comments on pre-revolutionary France